A Time To Be Born

A Time To Be Born

DAWN POWELL

ZOLAND BOOKS
an imprint of
STEERFORTH PRESS
HANOVER, NEW HAMPSHIRE

First published in 1942 by Charles Scribner's Sons and reissued in 1991 by
Yarrow Press, this edition of *A Time to Be Born* has been published in cooperation with the Estate of Dawn Powell and Yarrow Press.

All characters in this book are the invention of
the author and have no living counterparts.

For information about permission to
reproduce selections from this book, write to:
Steerforth Press L.C.
25 Lebanon Street
Hanover, New Hampshire 03755

Library of Congress Cataloging-in-Publication Data
Powell, Dawn.
A time to be born / by Dawn Powell
p.   cm.
ISBN 1–883642–41–8
1. Publishers and publishing — Fiction. 2. New York (N.Y.) — Fiction.
I. Title
PS3531.0936T5   1996
813'.54–dc20   CIP

Manufactured in the United States of America

Fifth Paperback Printing

To Coburn Gilman

1

*T*HIS WAS NO TIME to cry over one broken
heart. It was no time to worry about Vicky Haven or indeed any
other young lady crossed in love, for now the universe, nothing
less, was your problem. You woke in the morning with the
weight of doom on your head. You lay with eyes shut wondering
why you dreaded the day; was it a debt, was it a lost love?—and
then you remembered the nightmare. It was a dream, you said,
nothing but a dream, and the covers were thrown aside, the
dream was over, now for the day. Then, fully awake, you remembered that it was no dream. Paris was gone, London was
under fire, the Atlantic was now a drop of water between the
flame on one side and the waiting dynamite on the other. This
was a time of waiting, of marking time till ready, of not knowing
what to expect or what to want either for yourself or for the
world, private triumph or failure lost in the world's failure. The
longed-for letter, the telephone ringing at last, the familiar knock

at the door—very well, but there was still something to await—
something unknown, something fantastic, perhaps the stone
statue from *Don Giovanni* marching in or the gods of the mountain. Day's duties were performed to the metronome of Extras,
radio broadcasts, committee conferences on war orphans, benefits
for Britain, send a telegram to your congressman, watch your
neighbor for free speech, vote for Willkie or for Roosevelt and
banish care from the land.

This was certainly no time for Vicky Haven to engage your
thoughts, for you were concerned with great nations, with war itself. This was a time when the true signs of war were the lavish
plumage of the women; Fifth Avenue dress-shops and the finer
restaurants were filled with these vanguards of war. Look at the
jewels, the rare pelts, the gaudy birds on elaborate hairdress, and
know that the war was here; already the women had inherited the
earth. The ominous smell of gunpowder was matched by a rising
cloud of Schiaparelli's *Shocking*. The women were once more
armed, and their happy voices sang of destruction to come. Off to
the relief offices they rode in their beautiful new cars, off to knit,
to sew, to take part in the charade, anything to help Lady
Bertrand's cause; off they rode in the new car, the new mink, the
new emerald bracelet, the new electrically treated complexion,
presented by or extorted from the loving-hearted gentlemen who
make both women and wars possible. Off to the front with a new
permanent and enough specially blended night creams to last
three months dashed the intrepid girl reporters. Unable to cope
with competition on the home field, failing with the rhumbas and
screen tests of peacetime, they quiver for the easy drama of the
trenches; they can at least play lead in these amateur theatricals.

This was a time when the artists, the intellectuals, sat in cafés
and in country homes and accused each other over their brandies
or their California vintages of traitorous tendencies. This was a
time for them to band together in mutual antagonism, a time to

bury the professional hatchet, if possible in each other, a time to stare at their flower arrangements, children bathing, and privately to weep, "What good is it? Who cares now?" The poet, disgusted with the flight of skylarks in perfect sonnet form, declaimed the power of song against brutality and raised hollow voice in feeble proof. This was no time for beauty, for love, or private future; this was the time for ideals and quick profits on them before the world returned to reality and the drabber opportunities. What good for new sopranos to sing *"Vici d'arte, vice d'amore,"* what good for eager young students to make their bows? There was no future; every one waited, marked time, waited. For what? On Fifth Avenue and Fifty-fifth Street hundreds waited for a man on a hotel window ledge to jump; hundreds waited with craning necks and thirsty faces as if this single person's final gesture would solve the riddle of the world. Civilization stood on a ledge, and in the tension of waiting it was a relief to have one little man jump.

This was a time when writers dared not write of Vicky Haven or of simple young women like her. They wrote with shut eyes and deaf ears of other days, wise days they boasted, of horse-and-buggy men and covered-wagon Cinderellas; they glorified the necessities of their ancestors who had laid ground for the present confusion; they made ignorance shine as native wit, the barrenness of other years and other simpler men was made a talent, their austerity and the bold compulsions of their avarice a glorious virtue. In the Gold Rush to the past they left no record of the present. Drowning men, they remembered words their grandmothers told them, forgot today and tomorrow in the drug of memories. A curtain of stars and stripes was hung over today and tomorrow and over the awful lessons of other days. It was a sucker age, an age for any propaganda, any cause, any lie, any gadget, and scorning this susceptibility chroniclers sang the stubborn cynicism of past heroes who would not believe the earth was round. It was an age of explosions, hurricanes, wrecks, strikes, lies, corruption, and unbridled female exploitation. Unable to find reason for this madness people looked to historical figures and ancient events for the pat answers. Amanda Keeler's *Such Is the Legend* swept the bookstores as if this sword-and-lace romance could comfort a public about to be bombed. Such fabulous profits from this confection piled up for the pretty author that her random thoughts on economics and military strategy became automatically incontrovertible. Broadcasting companies read her income tax figures and at once begged her to prophesy the future of France; editors saw audiences sob over little Missy Lulu's death scene in the movie version of the romance and immediately ordered definitive articles from the gifted author on *What's Wrong with England, What's Wrong with Russia, What is the Future of America.* Ladies' clubs saw the label on her coat and the quality of her bracelet and at once begged her to instruct them in politics.

This was an age for Amanda Keelers to spring up by the dozen, level-eyed handsome young women with nothing to lose, least of all a heart, so there they were holding it aloft with spotlights playing on it from all corners of the world, a beautiful heart bleeding for war and woe at tremendous financial advantage. No international disaster was too small to receive endorsed photographs and publicity releases from Miss Keeler or her imitators, no microphone too obscure to scatter her clarion call to arms. Presented with a mind the very moment her annual income hit a hundred thousand dollars, the pretty creature was urged to pass her counterfeit perceptions at full face value, and being as grimly ambitious as the age was gullible, she made a heyday of the world's confusion.

This was the time Vicky Haven had elected to sniffle into her pillow for six months solid merely over her own unfortunate love life, in contrast to her old friend, Amanda Keeler, who rode the

world's debacle as if it was her own yacht and saved her tears for
Finland and the photographers.

This was certainly no time for a provincial young woman from
Lakeville, Ohio, a certain Ethel Carey, to venture into Amanda
Keeler's celebrated presence with pleas for Vicky Haven's salvation. Yet, the good-hearted emissary from Lakeville had the ef-
frontery to justify her call on the grounds that there were
thousands and thousands of Vickys all over the country, deserted
by their lovers, and unable to find the crash of governments as fit
a cause for tears as their own selfish little heartbreak. The good-
hearted emissary, pondering all these matters on the train to New
York, decided that even in this educated age there are little people
who cannot ride the wars or if they do are only humble coach passengers, not the leaders or the float-riders; there are the little people who can only think that they are hungry, they haven't eaten,
they have no money, they have lost their babies, their loves, their
homes, and their sons mock them from prisons and insane asy-
lums, so that rain or sun or snow or battles cannot stir their selfish
personal absorption. If their picture was to be taken with their little woe seated on their lap like Morgan's midget it would not matter to them. These little people had no news value and therein was
their crime. In their little wars there were no promotions, no pa-
rades, no dress uniforms, no regimental dances—no radio
speeches, no interviews, no splendid conferences. What unimportant people they were, certainly, in this important age! In a time of
oratory how inarticulate they were, in an age where every cause
had its own beautiful blonde figurehead, how plain these little individual women were! The good-hearted emissary, Miss Carey,
taking Vicky's unimportant sorrow to Amanda, thought about
these things hard all the way from Grand Central to her hotel,
and finally solved her indecision by having a facial at Arden's to
gird her for the fray.

2

THE HOUSE was number twenty-nine all right, and it was East not West but the young lady in the Checker Cab refused to be convinced. There was a mistake somewhere. Of course everyone knew that Amanda had done very well for herself in New York, finally landing no less a prize than Julian Evans himself, but somehow this graystone mansion off Fifth Avenue was far grander than one had imagined. The young lady in the taxi couldn't quite picture Amanda in such a fabulous setting and, what was more, she didn't *want* to picture Amanda there. As an old friend from way back she naturally wanted Amanda to get ahead but not out of sight.

"She would!" Ethel thought grimly. "Trust Amanda."

All the way to New York, Ethel had been thinking benevolently of her old school friend's success, flattering herself on her great-hearted lack of envy, but this elegant monument to Amanda's shrewdness threw her right back into her old bitterness. Still, it wasn't exactly bitterness, call it rather a normal sense of justice. Why did Amanda Keeler get everything out of life and Ethel Carey? The mood lasted but a moment, for Ethel hated to do anyone the favor of being jealous. After all, it wasn't such a palace as all that, this Evans house. And fortunately Ethel was not the sort of person to be overawed by a little material splendor, for the simple reason that the Careys were all bankers back in Lakeville and could hold their own socially or financially with anybody. Another thing, Amanda had not won all the prizes in school; Ethel had had her share. It was not Amanda who was voted "Most Likely to Succeed" but Ethel. Amanda would certainly be fair enough to admit that. Indeed, Ethel felt sure that Amanda would give respectful ear to her old friend's unfavorable reaction to The Book, regardless of the critical raves and the big sale. Amanda knew well enough that Ethel had as good a mind as she had. The book, Ethel was going to say quite frankly, is twice as long as it should have been and—you wouldn't want me to lie to you—perfectly lousy. If it hadn't been for Julian Evans' sixteen newspapers it would never have been such a sensation. And if it hadn't been for Amanda snatching Julian from under his first wife's nose—Ethel pulled herself together sternly. This was no frame of mind in which to ask favors. A few more such animadversions and she'd be ringing the bell and challenging Amanda with, "So you think you're smart, eh?"

Ethel paid the driver and got out of the cab. Facing the imposing five-story house with its gargoyles, its twin stone sphinxes guarding the iron-grilled doorway, a fresh wave of uncertainty came over her. What in heaven's name made her so sure Amanda would not snub her as she was said to snub all her old Middle Western friends? How could she ever restore her self-confidence if Amanda sent word, "Not in'? If it were not for the imperative necessity of doing something about Vicky Haven and her own brilliant plan to make Amanda the means of working Vicky's salvation, Ethel would have given up that very minute and dashed back to the St. Regis. But it was for Vicky she had come to New York, it was for Vicky's sake she was undergoing this severe test of good nature, it was for Vicky she must risk a butler's lifted eyebrow. Dear, dear Vicky, Ethel reminded herself, who had not the faintest notion of the good angels soon to bear her off to felicity and avenge her wrongs for her. Dear Vicky, the most unlucky girl in Lakeville just as Amanda had been the most lucky. Ethel braced herself with these reminders, thoroughly annoyed with herself at her fluttering heart and quaking knees. Here she was, as well dressed as any woman in New York (she was a fanatic about good clothes), money in her pocket, boat acquaintances with the best names in the traveling universe, a cosmopolitan woman in spite of the provincial roots; yet the mere sight of the mansion that Amanda Keeler's carefully milked fame and shrewd marriage had won made her stand there gawking and trembling like any World's Fair tourist. Her head swam with the doubts she tried to deny. Supposing Amanda said, "Ethel Who? Oh, but I meet so many people, and of course I haven't been back in Lakeville for years. You say you want me to do something about Vicky? Vicky Who? Oh, the little thing that had the crush on me in boarding-school? But, my dear Ethel, or is it Edna, you can't expect busy important *me* to give my time to a little sentimental duty like this Vicky what's-her-name when my days are filled with my war committees and my refugee children and my radio talks? Who would print my picture, I ask you, merely as someone who helped out an old friend? And why do you assume I would take up any suggestion of yours anyway? Really, my dear Edna, or Ella, or—"

These morbid anticipations were no whit dispelled by seeing two gentlemen emerge from Twenty-nine, one of them the celebrated liberal Senator—(the leonine, snow-white head and black loose tie were too often cartooned not to be easily recognized)— and the other a square-jawed young man whose face at the head of a political column was syndicated all over America. Yes, these were the people who were entitled to Amanda's time, these distinguished gentlemen now getting into a fine black towncar with grave faces as if they had just listened to the President himself instead of to nobody but Ethel's old friend Amanda who would never have made the best sorority if Ethel hadn't sponsored her. (The Keelers were *nobody* in Lakeville!)

The door was open, the butler stood there waiting for her to utter her business and there was no retreat now.

"Mrs. Evans," she demanded in a ringing voice, for she had just recalled that her own father had been president of the Lakeville Third National when Amanda Keeler's father was clerk in a haberdashery. Little things like that did bring reassurance, and so she was able to enter the reception hall with head high, her handsome foxes tossed proudly over her left shoulder.

The marble-floored, marble-benched foyer was as darkly reassuring as Grant's Tomb. A little appalled, Ethel's eyes, accustoming themselves to the dim light, saw grim Roman tapestries on the walls (or was that horn of plenty a Flemish trick?) and urns of enormous chrysanthemums at the foot of the broad staircase. From the hush of this place it might have been a small hospital. Perhaps, Ethel decided, if you were a public institution your home eventually came to look like one.

Of course, in all fairness, you couldn't blame Amanda for this pompous austerity since the house had been Julian Evans' home during his former marriage. Still, after two years, the new wife, if she wanted or knew how, could certainly have altered the style and set her own stamp upon it.

"She still has no taste, thank God," Ethel thought, comfortingly, but the truth was that Amanda was too successful, too arrogantly on top, to even *need* good taste. Good taste was the consolation of people who had nothing else, people like her own self, Ethel thought, inferiority feelings leaping back at her like great barn dogs trying to be pets.

The butler vanished. There she stood, alone with her doubts. She should have telephoned or written a note. It was presumptuous for anyone, worst of all an old and quite unvalued friend, to drop in on this national figure, Amanda Keeler Evans, without appointment, expecting her to fly down the banister in an old kimono, hair in curlpapers, arms outstretched in frantic welcome. It was presumptuous and worse—it was small-town. Yes, that is exactly the way Amanda would react to it, and this—as if Amanda had already made the accusation—made Ethel burn up. After all, Ethel Carey had been visiting New York from the year she was born, she had *always* been at home in New York; long before Amanda Keeler ever heard of the place, even; it was indeed she,

Ethel Carey, who had brought the New York scandals and fashions back home to Amanda and the girls at Miss Doxey's, and
now New York belonged to Amanda while Ethel was still just a
transient from Lakeville. It was not pleasant to think of all the
things about New York that Amanda knew now and Ethel had
still to learn. For instance, she had never dreamed that these private stone houses had their own private elevators like an apartment house, yet Amanda had one, and there must be many other
casual facts of New York life that Ethel had still to learn.

"Mrs. Evans is working," the butler reported, "but you may
come up with me to her living room."

Mrs. Evans' working quarters were on the fourth floor and
Ethel was soothed to find that the living room into which she
was ushered up there was refreshingly impossible. Velvet theatrical curtains, more bad tapestries, fur rugs, great ugly vases,
gold-framed expensive and enormous paintings by *Saturday
Evening Post* cover artists, huge fringed floor lamps and over-
stuffed armchairs were benignly smiled upon by a marble bust of
possibly Sappho on a corner pedestal. Mr. Evans' former wife or
even his mother (the papers said he owed everything to his
mother) must be responsible for this décor, and Ethel felt a little
fonder of Amanda for this daily cross. There was an ancestor in
a great gold frame over the fireplace, a lady ancestor with the
hooked beak and chin common to New England and the Old
Testament. Her long neck leapt hungrily out of a rather rowdy
décolletage. Ethel wondered if Amanda had finally been able to
locate an ancestor or if this was one of Evans' prides. On the
mantel were twin vases filled with varnished wheat, and a similar pastoral touch freshened a gnarled Chinese vase on an ebony-
lacquered console. In a gilded mirror above this console Ethel
saw her own face sneering. She had just been thinking that all
the place needed was a Southern Methodist pennant and a rubber plant, but she did not propose to have her expression betray

such cynical comments. She was here, after all, to get something from Amanda, to arouse old loyalties, and you couldn't stir up sentiment with your mind stained with envious mockery. The mirror, too, reminded her that her silver foxes looked glaringly new, as if she'd bought them expressly for this visit, her eyebrows were plucked too thin, her suit skirt was too skimpy over the behind, and the new white silk blouse was too white. One thing about *you*, everyone in Lakeville always said to Ethel, you always look smart, you've taken care of your figure and your complexion, you keep up, you can hold your own anywhere. Ethel, grimacing at herself with her new uneasiness, thought that what she really looked like was a woman grown pinched and desperate-eyed in the frantic effort to "keep up." She was thirty-two but she looked like a woman of forty so well-preserved she could pass for thirty-two. She had that frustrated-in-the-provinces look, that I-am-the-only-cosmopolite-in-all-Toledo-or-whatever look. It was too desperate. She tried a smile as heart warming as a dentist's. All right, she was stagestruck and likely to forget her whole mission, if she didn't pull herself together. Remember, she told herself, the visit had nothing to do with her, it was all concerned with poor darling Vicky, who was in such a mess. Yes, she said reviving her ego, she must keep in mind that she and Amanda were two securely placed women about to lift a less fortunate sister out of the morass. The thought sustained her and she was able to take out a cigarette and puff at it with an air of elegant confidence.

On the other side of the center foyer were two doors and from one of these there now emerged a stout, fat-jowled woman with bristling black brows, slick black hair, and wearing a poison-green knitted dress to set off her bulging curves. This figure helped Ethel at once to complacency by its unaffected ugliness.

"I'm Mrs. Evans' assistant," the voice was a well-placed baritone. "Mrs. Evans is working in bed today. Come in."

The rear room was a large and sunny bedroom and surprisingly enough, done in the Hollywood modern style of white rugs, glass tables, and chromium touches quite out of period with the rest of the house. A great white satin-tufted bed fitted into a white-curtained alcove with a half-moon window above it. Here lay Amanda, propped up on cushions in some sort of high-necked Chinese bed coat. Her long blond hair fell to her shoulders in a long bob and her good looks, which consisted chiefly in the contrast of dark olive skin with angel gold hair, were definitely impaired by no makeup and thick-rimmed glasses. Believe me, she needs them, too, Ethel thought with a fresh surge of friendliness, the poor darling is blind as a bat without them. Papers, notebooks, cream jars, a deck of cards and a ten-cent-store dream book were scattered over the pretty coverlet, and Amanda's bed-desk appeared to be nothing less than a ouija board with a big YES in one corner and a big NO in the other. Through her thick glasses Amanda squinted up at Ethel, then held out a left hand, her right still clutching her pen.

"My dear, why on earth didn't you phone first?" she exclaimed. "I'm up to my ears today, but if I'd known I could have canceled one interview. I had no *idea*! I thought it was that Carey woman from the Czech Relief."

"I should have wired," Ethel admitted, and sat down gingerly on the side of the bed.

The enormous green bosom that seemed to be convoying Miss Bemel's body appeared nearer to the bed, and the baritone voice croaked in interruption.

"I will make a summary of what the Senator just said for your article," said Miss Bemel. "Shall it be necessary to put it in quotes?"

Amanda squinted up at Miss Bemel.

"Certainly not," she said sharply. "After all it's my article, not his; no reason I should give him all that publicity."

"We'll need an additional paragraph to fill the column," said Miss Bemel.

"Put in some statistics about something," Amanda suggested, frowning. "Those Chamber of Commerce reports lying around there. Federal Housing figures for Savannah, maybe. You know. What time is the *Digest* interview?"

"Five," said Miss Bemel, giving Ethel a cold look. "In twenty minutes."

"Ethel, you won't mind popping off when they come, will you?" Amanda asked. Ah, how important little Amanda from Lakeville had become, Ethel inwardly mocked, all these Senators, and columns and *Digest* interviews! And above all these Miss Bemels!

The thing was to pave the way with flattery, and Ethel plunged.

"Everyone in Lakeville is so proud of you. They read about you and the *Gazette* reprints all your speeches and all of your letters from London. It must have been frightful during the air raids. I don't see how you had the guts—I mean really, just sticking it out, that way. At the school reunion the girls at Miss Doxey's simply raved about how brave you were."

"My word, I'd rather have been in a few air raids than at the school reunion," exclaimed Amanda, rather ungraciously, Ethel thought.

One thing Amanda's war experience had given her was a brand new English accent that occasionally slipped down like a tiresome shoulder strap and showed a Middle-Western pinning. This was no time to be critical, however, so Ethel went on with the soothing oils.

"Everyone talks about the book, naturally," she pursued, and then could not resist a little crack since Amanda's sudden glance at her wrist watch was a bit galling. "Personally I simply cannot read any historical novel, not even for love of you, darling."

Miss Ethel Carey's personal apathy toward Amanda Keeler's best-seller, *Such Is the Legend*, stirred the author to no reaction beyond a faintly complacent smile which made Ethel redden. All right, if Amanda liked to think all unfavorable criticism was mere jealousy, then by all means return to flattery. For a moment Ethel was tempted to insult by exaggerated praise but her instinct informed her that the most burlesque adulation was accepted as sound by some happy egos, and Amanda was one of those. She must, however, feed this appetite until she won her cause, so once more she set out.

"Everyone in Lakeville turned out for your wedding in the newsreel," she pursued. "You should have heard them buzz when the close-up came. Right along with the 'Beauty of the Yukon' and 'Pinocchio'! You'd never dream Mr. Evans is forty-eight from his picture. How in the world did you meet him, Amanda?"

Amanda shrugged and then looked at Ethel with faintly surprised curiosity as if wondering why on earth she should be expected to confide a trade secret to an humble old schoolmate when she kept it even from her own self.

"Oh, the usual way, my dear," she said.

The usual way, my eye, thought Ethel, who had heard the story last year in Miami and confirmed a dozen times since. The story was that two years ago when Amanda's novel was merely being considered by a publisher, Amanda wrangled an interview with Julian Evans, the great newspaper magnate. When the Evanses went to Miami, Amanda went, too, and hung around his hotel reminding him at every encounter with him of their previous meeting. He went to Rio alone and Amanda managed to follow and get on the same boat coming back. She struck up an intimacy with him in the bar, persuaded him to wire approval of her manuscript to her publisher, and so got it published. This feat, according to Ethel's informants, was accomplished in

Amanda's last stronghold, the bed. But you had to give Amanda credit for actually getting a prissy family man like Julian Evans to bed. After that, of course, it was easy, since he was so pious and unaccustomed to affairs that he believed divorce and remarriage automatically followed any infidelity.

"The usual way," Amanda now said, with a yawn. At that it must have given her a kick to have the people who snubbed her for years and rejected her book now start fawning over her because she was Julian Evans' literary *protégée* and eventually his bride. Then when the power of his newspapers and syndicate swept the book to sensational triumph—oh, yes, Amanda must have permitted herself a secret smile. Ethel found it in her heart to feel a sympathetic pleasure in her old chum's success—yes, they really had been chums, the three of them, Ethel and Amanda, with little Vicky as their mutual charge. At Miss Doxey's they had been inseparable. Amanda could never deny it.

"Amanda, I came to talk to you about Vicky," she said. "A terrible thing has happened to Vicky."

"Little Vicky Haven?" Amanda was roused to interest, for little Vicky had been her slave. "A man?"

Ethel nodded.

"Tom Turner."

"That old sot?" Amanda frowned. "Is he still beauing all the Lakeville virgins?"

"But Vicky took him seriously," said Ethel. "It went on for four or five years, and everyone gave up trying to talk her out of it. She did everything for him, apologized for his drinking, cleaned his flat, painted his bookshelves, made his curtains, made an absolute fool of herself. Then six months ago he eloped with her partner."

"Louse," admitted Amanda. "But how dumb of Vicky!"

"You'd feel sorry if you saw her," said Ethel. "The poor kid! All the work she did starting her little real estate business there, making a go of it, then taking that horrible widow, Mrs. Brown, in as her partner. And then having everything go to pieces at once—her lover and her partner."

Miss Bemel stuck her head in the door with a significant nod.

"It's all right, Bemel," Amanda said. "I'll receive them right here. They can wait."

"Imagine having to keep going to your little office every morning after the elopement, with everybody in town knowing you've been jilted," Ethel went on, getting excited. "Imagine having to go over your mail and your business deals with the woman who's got your man, the woman who's just been enjoying *your* bookshelves and *your* curtains in the apartment *you* fixed up. And Lakeville being so small, everybody talked and Vicky hasn't dared go anywhere because people either laugh about it or pity her, so she just cries and gets thin and has to go on with the business because she doesn't have any money but that. And you see her day after day just breaking her heart and not daring to ask Mrs. Brown to get out of the business. But that isn't the worst."

"I can't really be sorry for anybody dumb enough to fall for an old soak like Tom Turner," said Amanda.

"But now, Amanda, they're going to have a baby!" cried Ethel. "Vicky doesn't know it yet, but if she's suffered already just picture what their having a baby is going to do to her."

"Why in God's name doesn't she clear out?" Amanda asked impatiently. "Nobody *has* to stay in Lakeville."

"She's afraid to gamble on making a living anyplace else," Ethel explained. "And she doesn't want the town to think she can't take it, see. But if somebody in New York offered her a job, all secure, and sent for her—"

"Oh," said Amanda.

"I thought you'd understand," Ethel said, relieved. "You and Mr. Evans have all the contacts here. And it would be sort of a triumph for you to send for her, you being so famous now. It would help make up."

"I'll consult Julian tonight," Amanda said. She was relieved because this was less of a favor than she had expected to be asked. For a while she had feared Ethel wanted a loan. She was really quite free with Julian's money, mischievously so, knowing how sacred it was to him, almost as sacred as it had been to herself when she earned her own living writing advertising for Burdley's Department Store. But, as she often said, she did not like to be asked for loans because it made such embarrassing moments in conversation and afterward such awkward relations. A job for little Vicky was easy to manage, providing no personal contact was expected. Amanda didn't want her fine present life cluttered up with her undistinguished past.

"Julian can wangle something," said Amanda. "I'll wire her right away and then Julian can fix it up."

She looked at her watch again and Ethel obediently leaped up.

"I knew you'd be the one to fix it," she said. "She simply would never listen to any of us back there, but if you invited her on—after all you've always been her idol—"

Amanda's mouth tightened.

"I only trust I'll have time to entertain her while she's in town," she said carefully. "Anyway I'll see that she gets a job, even if I can't lead her around personally. Oh, Bemel!"

Ethel was so pleased with the happy result of her call that she did not mind being brushed out by Miss Bemel. She was shunted down the elevator and out the front door in a pleasant haze, thinking only of how clever she had been to invent this plan, and how fine it was to be able to put one's friend's successes to some good use."

"But wasn't she bitchy about the idea of Vicky visiting her," Ethel reflected, now free to be critical. "She absolutely turned livid at the mere thought of helping Vicky get the social breaks that *she* had. She probably is scared to death to introduce Vicky to old Julian Evans for fear Vicky will turn out as smart as she herself was. God, how I wish I had that vanity of hers! It's absolutely bulletproof."

She walked over to Madison to look in the shops, and at the corner paused to look at the headlines spelled out in Julian Evans' afternoon paper. Same old stuff. The Germans doing the same old thing. It would be a relief to get this war over and get back to murder and the decent privileges of peacetime. No use buying a paper any more, really. She paused before a telegraph office, tempted to wire Vicky mysterious hints of glad news to come, but that might spoil everything. No, better leave it all to Amanda and her powerful husband now. With a sigh for her relinquished responsibility, Ethel went her way.

3

AMANDA's MISS Bemel in the fourth floor chambers sent Mr. Evans' Mr. Castor in the third floor library a brief memorandum: "Place Victoria Haven, childhood friend of Mrs. Evans. Real estate experience. About $200." Mr. Evans, conferring on the day's private mail with Mr. Castor while waiting for the dinner guests to arrive, frowned over this memo, dictated a couple of telegrams and sent a memo back up to Mrs. Evans' Miss Bemel: "Have instructed Peabody Publishing Company to hire Victoria Haven in real estate news at fifty per week on her arrival in New York. Check with them on date."

This brief correspondence would have settled the little matter under ordinary conditions. Miss Bemel would have telegraphed the proposition—nay, the command—to Vicky in Lakeville, and arranged a luncheon date at a small restaurant for the two old friends (this would relieve Amanda of further intimacies), perhaps put the Haven name on the third guest list for one of the larger cocktail parties during the winter, and then friendship demands could be considered fulfilled. Julian might remember the name some evening when they were alone and might inquire whatever happened about that Peabody business and who was that girl anyway? Had she ever arrived? Had he met her? Amanda would have explained that she was the little quiet one in the corner at the Sunday party two weeks ago, that she was a school friend from Lakeville. This would have silenced Julian, for reminders of his wife's obscure past irritated him, perhaps because pasts were something even his power could not manipulate. It was not jealousy of what might have happened to Amanda's heart in those simpler days, either, at least he didn't think it was. But the contrast of his new wife's nondescript background with his former wife's august ancestry was not very gratifying, for it implied a step backward. He didn't like to have anyone refer to Lakeville for fear mention would be made of Amanda's father having run a men's clothing store, her stepmother, née Jansen, of Norway, having been a "beautician." Heaven knows Amanda never brought her family into any conversation, and it was seldom indeed that she requested favors for old Lakeville associates.

The memos having been exchanged, things were about to take their usual course, with Vicky Haven's future put through the chutes and forgotten by the Evanses. Julian fussed with some press clippings, had a tomato juice by himself, pinned up a Benson etching on the mantel to get the effect (he fancied himself an authority on wild bird pictures and made consistent purchases along that line to confound his enemies who said he was blind to art), called his wife's bedroom three times to ask if she was ready yet, was snapped at properly for his impatience, decided to drop in on her to hasten her dressing, changed his mind recalling her icy sarcasm over his occasional invasion of her privacy, had another tomato juice and then put on his glasses to read for the eighth time his own editorial in his evening paper. This being a period when no one knew which way the cat would jump, either in Europe or in home politics, Julian was reserving his ammunition for the most powerful bidder and marked time till ready with stinging criticisms of the medical profession for having no cure for the common cold, stern admonitions to childless parents (he fortunately had two children by his former marriage), and articles on Predestination, pro and con. In history's dangerous hour Julian thus offered the world an aspirin.

It was Julian's custom to spend his mornings in conferences and writing in his home, in his dark-paneled red-carpeted study, and then go downtown at noon for important lunches and an afternoon in his office. Mr. Castor, working at home, conferred by telephone with a Mr. Harnett, the office secretary and routed Julian from place to place as if he was a valuable freight car. Before dinner the master once again resorted to the home library and home affairs, usually in a disagreeable mood because he was hungry as could be at six-thirty and always had to wait for the half-past-eight dinner, one of the cruelties of the rich.

"Who's coming to dinner tonight, did you say?" he asked Mr. Castor again, and the little man—Julian could not have endured a secretary taller than himself—patiently answered that the guests would be an ex-president, an international banker, a future ambassador—possibly to St. James's—and a celebrated French titled exile. The point was, Julian fretfully wanted to know, could he get away at eleven to meet his London chief, newly arrived, and fraught with confidential information for his employer? Mr. Castor telephoned Miss Bemel on the floor above as to this point and advised his master that not only would the engagement with the London chief be feasible, but that Mrs. Evans would go with him. Mrs. Evans, according to Miss Bemel's report, believed that she could "get something" from meeting the gentleman.

"Good," said Julian, face falling at the thought of his resolute young wife's intrusion into his private kingdom. "Tell her we meet him at eleven at NBC right after his broadcast. We'll go on from there."

The first Mrs. Evans had kept in discreet shadow during Julian's life with her, and her ignorance of his business was, he sometimes thought, not such a fault after all, in spite of his initial delight at Second Wife's keen interest. At least in those days he could talk to people without interruption.

Julian Evans was five feet six, five feet seven with his built-in soles which gave him half an inch over the second Mrs. Evans (in her stocking feet), and a good four inches over the first Mrs. Evans, a stout little body who had, in her late forties, done him the favor of shrinking an extra inch, but it was too late to comfort him, for he was already in Amanda's web. He had been an earnest, ambitious young man, aided on the path to fame and fortune more by Mrs. Evans' family connections than his own sharp wits. At forty-eight he was personable enough, though bald, for he had no pot at all due to his Yogi exercises and lack of bad habits, and he was what is known as a very fine dresser. He had small hazel eyes that appeared, erroneously, to twinkle with humor and perspicacity. Very impressive, too, were his beetling iron-gray brows, firm big mouth over big white teeth, big jaw and a big commanding nose. He was positive of his importance but was beset by the fear of ridicule, and this led him to quite ridiculous extremes. If he lost his temper in the office he must, half an hour later, tiptoe down the corridor to listen for derisive accounts of the scene, and wherever laughter sounded he marked that office for future punishment, so certain was he that all laughter was insubordination and never innocent joviality. In his home he had a way of excusing himself from the guests, then standing outside the door listening for insults. The gratifying thing about this procedure was that if he did not actually hear anything he could always be sure that some crack or other had been whispered out of his hearing. He would return to the group and study one face after the other to see if a blush, a drooping glance, or a nervous gesture would not betray the mocker. One refreshing trait in Amanda was that she gave the insult direct so he had no secret misapprehensions and could fight back, fight back in his own devious way. If Amanda privately berated him he merely smiled proudly in silence, saving his retort for the dinner table where he could retell the accusation as if it were the naïve remark of a child, and here, before their celebrated guests, Amanda was obliged to accept defeat with a smiling shrug, lest a show of shrewishness give pleasure to her rivals.

Amanda could always annoy him by her laughing deprecation that "Julian, of course, has *no* humor, no humor at all," but it was she who was most enraged when important guests turned from her earnestly informed conversation to exchange nonsense with each other, nonsense which she was unable as she was unwilling to follow.

Julian was still proud of his wife's unparalleled success and had specially bound copies of her book *Such Is the Legend* to present his business friends and their house guests, and he had instructed his staff to refer to this masterpiece, either in its book or movie version, on every possible occasion. This pleased Amanda for the first year. But after a while it embarrassed her to have him boast of how he had ordered this or that "profile" of her, and how it was he who had decided she should have a weekly column or some definitive article somewhere, instead of letting it appear that these honors were the result of public demand. She could not understand, on her part, why he sulked whenever she joined him in his engagements with national figures. Julian preferred to give her these interviews secondhand, straining the story through his own vanity so that she must credit him, instead of the other person.

Julian sat scowling at his paper, pride in today's editorial spoiled by the knowledge that now his evening with old Cheever would be spoiled by Amanda taking it over. It was to his interest as editor and publisher to feature Cheever in all his papers, but after Amanda had extracted Cheever's opinions it would be his loyal duty, as husband, to feature Amanda's articles at Cheever's expense. Cheever would be sore, and as appeasement he'd probably have to raise his salary. Julian was shrewd enough to foresee the whole situation in advance and it was enough to spoil his dinner.

Amanda's dress rustled outside and she came in, looking very beautiful in gold lamé with a wristlet of fragrant Parma violets, and smiling radiantly at him as if they were on the sweetest of terms. Julian was impressionable, almost foolishly so, as many pious upright men are where beauty is concerned, and Amanda had only to exploit her blonde good looks with an arresting costume to make his blood turn to water. Almost out of perversity Amanda sometimes preferred to play the role of bohemian, and except for the benefit of special males, not her husband, affected smart tweeds, loose fur coats over flannel slacks, very Hepburn, very collegiate, and arrogantly unmade-up as to face. Tonight was a very special favor which touched him.

"My darling," gulped Julian, forgiving everything now, and Amanda permitted him a little kiss. At thirty Amanda had all the beauty, fame and wit that money could buy, and she had another advantage over her rivals, that whereas they were sometimes in doubt of their aims, she knew exactly what she wanted from life, which was, in a word, everything. She was at this period bored with two years of fidelity, but she dared not risk her marriage just yet. Julian was necessary for at least another few years, and it would be folly to risk losing him. Julian was almost pathologically jealous of her, fearing the final indignity of horns, and never able to forget that she had surrendered to him before he even asked the favor, a fact that did not reassure him of her future fidelity. He queried chauffeurs about her movements, put sly questions to her friends, but Amanda's conduct was so far impeccable. If she was restless now, it was not that she wanted an affair for lust's sake, for she had a genuine distaste for sexual intimacy and hated to sacrifice a facial appointment for a mere frolic in bed; but there were so many things to be gained by trading on sex and she thought so little of the process that she itched to use it as currency once again, trading a half-hour in bed for a flattering friendship, a royal invitation; power of whatever sort appealed to her.

Julian was suspicious of just such a state of mind as this and now speculated which one of their dinner guests had inspired Amanda to put out her glamour-girl side. He made a mental note to keep an eye on which man she played up to during the evening. Amanda, though, had no definite plan. The idea of going to a café—something Julian strongly disliked doing—had roused her interest much more than the anticipation of a distinguished dinner party. It was not enough that the international names shone at her table; she wanted to stage such triumphs in the middle of a smart restaurant for all the world to envy. It was too bad Julian disliked restaurants, though Amanda was obliged to admit their devotion to home was socially more impressive.

She could not be at her best at dinner, figuring out as she was, which restaurant to lead Cheever to, later on, some place where the people would be whom she wanted to impress. The newspaper crowd had never quite accepted her, since she had won all the rewards without the customary groundwork; Amanda could not resist temptations to further bait their envy, since their goodwill was out of the question. She wondered if her purpose would be served best by Twenty-One, the Stork, or the little French place everyone had taken up lately. The last was the best bet, for recently the columnists mentioned it every day. She was suddenly impatient to get the dinner over and get out; the game of being lady of the house, the grand hostess, seemed unbearably tedious tonight, and in her boredom Amanda forgot to ask the ambassador some of the questions Miss Bemel had instructed her to ask. Julian was didactic and told the ambassador what an ambassador's life was like, told the banker all about banking, explained the refugee problem to the famous refugee, and informed the labor leader on labor problems and their solution. It was the privilege of being a host and Julian never failed to exercise it to the full. Nor did any guests ever contradict his superior opinions, since this would have been not only rude but impractical. One never knew when this little man could be extremely helpful and the few who had dared to question his omniscience with argument had paid for their valor in one way or another. So it was Julian's evening, with no gainsaying from Amanda, who merely smiled, received compliments, autographed her book for the titled refugee who forgot to take it with him, and finally manipulated the group (minus the labor leader and ambassador but plus Mr. Cheever of London) to the little French place for a friendly nightcap.

"Is this really Jean's?" she exclaimed, puzzled, as they entered the café. "Isn't it—?"

She did not finish her question, for now she saw what a mistake she had made to suggest this place. "Jean's," the new little *boite*, was none other than her old secret meeting place with Ken Saunders. Then it was *"Chez Papa"* with red-checked tablecloths and a sixty-five cent dinner, the virtues of which they had quarreled over constantly. Ken always said it didn't matter about the low price; it was as good as the Waldorf. He would never admit, just because he was fond of old Papa, that the food was only passable. Not that she minded much, not then, anyway, but she wanted Ken to admit it was just sentiment, not quality, that made him like the place. Here was the spot she had confessed she was marrying Julian, and Ken had gotten up quietly, as if he was going to telephone, and never come back. She waited half an hour, all ready with her defenses. ("But Ken," she was going to say to him, "we always knew it would have to end sometime. We never intended to get married, you know that.") But he never gave her a chance to explain, just walked out, not even good-bye. She had not been back here since, and even though it was made over into quite an elegant little spot, it was still *Chez Papa* even to the picture of the Papa's Acrobatic Troupe over the bar. Amanda felt queer. She had never regretted giving up Ken; she had given him little thought since the parting, because she could stop thinking about a person at will, thank God, but right now he seemed all over the place. It did not even surprise her to see him actually standing at the bar, but what did surprise her was the wave of exultation that this unexpected sight of him brought. Imagine feeling this way about anyone! It must be something in the air, some secret restlessness she had not known, some craving for adventure beyond war fronts; it couldn't possibly be just seeing Ken again after three years, old Ken who had passed almost unheeded out of her life.

She knew perfectly well that he would not speak to her and even though he saw her he did not permit any gleam of recognition to shine in his eye. She half-smiled at him, as bait, but he turned away. The headwaiter was ushering the Evans party into the dining room and Amanda, chattering to Mr. Cheever about nothing, wondered how she could manage to force Ken to speak to her. She could not let him have the last insult. Besides there were all those defenses she had prepared for his accusations, and while she had no sense of guilt in the way she had broken off with him, she was baffled by his quiet acceptance of her action as if it was the cheap sort of thing he had always expected her to do. She was intrigued, too, by her thoroughly ridiculous but urgent desire to justify herself to someone of so little consequence as Ken Saunders. It had nothing to do with love, she was sure of that. It was more because of that odd hold he used to have on her because he knew her better than anyone. If he knew her so well, why hadn't he understood her marriage to Julian? What else had he expected of her? She wished he would tell her. Thinking fast, she did not sit down with the guests but went back through the bar, ostensibly to the powder room. It was an added challenge to find him no longer at the bar, as if her passing had been enough to send him away. He was in the hallway, putting on his coat—the same coat of three years ago, so he couldn't have done too well wherever he was. She caught his arm with a little cry of delight. He stiffened, then bowed.

"How do you do, Mrs. Evans?" he said calmly.

"But, Ken, what are you doing in town? I thought you were in Washington or Brazil or someplace."

"I'll have to fire my press agent, that's all," Ken answered, still not looking at her. He was with that old pal of his, Dennis Orphen, who stood waiting in the doorway, hat in hand. Amanda always disliked Ken's friends; they were always too clever and too arrogant and invariably acted as if she were poisoning Ken's life. Orphen she particularly resented, for he had once pilloried her one literary idol, Andrew Callingham, in a novel. Now Orphen had his back to them as if he was not going to see That Woman make a Fool of his Pal again. It incited Amanda to be more insistent.

"Aren't you glad to see your old friends?"

"Friends, oh sure," he said. He was going to be difficult, maybe because Orphen was there. It was mean of him to resent her success, or maybe it was her marriage that bothered him the most.

"Aren't you going to say you liked the book?" She challenged him to show his envy.

"Like it? Of course I liked it. Just mad that it isn't mine, that's all." He was being disagreeable, but Amanda was determined to be kind, this once.

"Ken, you know you're too much of a procrastinator, that's all," she reproached him. "That's why I got there first."

She kept her hand on his sleeve and she could tell he wanted to be able to shake it off but was still affected by her. She had been sure he would be, but she had not expected any fluttering of the heart on her own part. It amused her to have this faint remnant of girlish romanticism. It must be what she had been needing. Yes, this was Fate always attending to her wants at the right time.

"Let's not be enemies, Ken," she said, cajolingly. "We were such friends for so long. Let's have lunch and you tell me where you've been and everything that's happened."

He was not to be had that easy.

"Can't be having affairs with people's wives," he said, "and that's the way it would have to be."

Amanda thought rapidly. It was reckless, of course it was reckless, but she felt she simply must find out if she could win him back again, or if he still hated her. Even if she had to sacrifice a little . . . oh, she had been a bitch before, they both knew it, but she had *had* to be in order to get anywhere. She would like to explain it to him, make him see how it had worked out so much better this way. She couldn't understand why his contempt should bother her, for he was only Ken Saunders, an attractive nobody, a luxury an ambitious woman could not afford. She knew he despised her for always playing safe, never risking an inch of her advantage. But now she wanted to surprise him, make amends. It could be done somehow. This must be the mischief she had been seeking, and since here it was, offered so patly the very day she sought it, then she must make the best of it.

"Supposing we lunch at my studio on Friday?" she said.

Reluctantly he surrendered to this half promise.

"All right. I'm staying at the Wharton. Where is your studio?"

Amanda had no studio. She had, up to this moment, never had the faintest notion of having a studio. Now, she reflected that an outside working place might answer a great deal of her domestic discontent. It would have to be managed discreetly, of course, and explained so carefully to Julian that there would be no danger of tattlers ruining it.

"I'll call you tomorrow and tell you the address," she said.

She was very gay when she rejoined her table. Amanda's gayety consisted in laughing a great deal whether the conversation merited it or not. She was really excited and thinking busily under this merry front, thinking of what would be the best neighborhood, far from or near to the house, and she was thinking that this was one of the situations for which she should have prepared long ago, the way plausibly paved, protection arranged in advance. She permitted Julian to have Cheever all to himself, much to his relief. On the way home Julian had the great satisfaction of repeating and interpreting everything Cheever had reported on England's condition and he gave a flattering account of what England felt (according to Cheever) about the great Julian Evans, and how, had England such a man to control its public opinion, conditions would be far, far happier. Having been able to reconstruct Cheever's remarks in such a pleasant light without her interruption or denial, Julian felt very tender toward his wife and recalled that she had not acted her usual role tonight. He racked his brain for a moment, wondering what had occurred during the evening to change her idea of Cheever's importance to her own work. He suddenly recollected the exchange of memos.

"I'm getting a job for some girl," he said frowning. "Some old friend of yours. Who is she?"

"It's Victoria Haven," said Amanda, and took the plunge. "I'm afraid we'll have to get a place for her to live, too, darling, for she hasn't a penny."

"Hmmm, don't want her staying with us, of course," Julian agreed. "How about it, will she let us give her an apartment?"

Amanda turned a face of sweet concern toward him.

"That's just it, we'll have to be careful not to let it seem charity," she said. "I wonder if we couldn't lease a little place as an outside studio for me. After all I do sometimes want to get off by myself. Then I could tell Vicky to live there since I only use it occasionally in the daytime when she'll be at her office. It's just to save her pride, you see. We'll have to say the place is just going to waste most of the time, so it's no bother."

Julian regarded his wife with admiration. She often surprised him with some trait he had never suspected, but it was most frequently not such an agreeable surprise as this present revelation. In the light from the street lamp shining through the car window on her golden hair and frock she looked angelically appealing. It was an effort to remember from experience that if he should try to embrace her now her body would stiffen in chilly protest.

"You do have a heart," he said, and he was quite choked up about it. "Just don't let it run away with you, my dear."

"I won't," promised Amanda gently.

4

IN THE middle of the night Amanda gave up trying to sleep and slipped on robe and slippers for a smoke before her study fire, still smoldering in the grate. She drew the curtains carefully so that Julian, whose bedroom was directly beneath, would not see the light streaming out and come up for a "chat." Julian only slept in snatches, and until trained out of it by her temper, liked to tap on her door and say, "Are you awake, too, dear? Can I come in for a chat?" He would carry around his Swedish health bread, and the sight and sound of his fine big teeth crunching constantly was more than Amanda's nerves could stand. He had learned not to knock on the door, but he would be apt to tiptoe upstairs and listen outside her door for a possible call. Amanda was accustomed, on rare occasions when she could not sleep, to sit clenching her hands as she listened to the crunching outside her door, the waiting for her welcome. Lately she would get angry in the night thinking she heard the crunching through the walls, and the sound of this blameless, nonfattening, health-giving habit was as infuriating to her as the ripple of liquid in a glass is to a dipsomaniac's wife.

What made sleep impossible tonight was the unwilling surge of memories about the past brought up by Vicky Haven's coming to New York. There was the other part of her past brought up by Ken Saunders, too, but with this she was prepared to cope. Seeing Ken again was exactly what it had been before, exasperation at his insolence mingled with exasperation at herself for tolerating him, for being teased by someone she was sure she neither loved nor admired, but for some reason could not dismiss. All right, it was unbelievably stupid of her to turn the affair on once again, but that was what she was headed for. She had such good reasons for doing whatever she did, such faith in the eventual rightness of whatever she wanted, that she could not really admit taking Ken on again was a mistake. It would do *something* for her—that first hunch she had was surely right. Not being cursed with hot Latin blood, she did not mind the Caesar's wife role expected of her by the world, nor did she miss the casual passes of admirers; admirers were too conscious of Julian's power to make advances to his wife, and this was a relief to her. Still, any woman needs testimony that she *can* command the male senses, or after a while she begins asking herself, uneasily, "Is it really because they're afraid of Julian? Or is it that I'm losing my looks or that intellectual success scares men and freezes your magnetism?" Doubts like that interfered with one's general efficiency, so surely the Ken Saunders business was justifiable. But Vicky Haven, and the re-opening of those childhood chapters?

Amanda poked the fire, sitting on a little stool before it. She picked up the last Andrew Callingham book, for he was her idol, the one person she worshiped but had unaccountably never managed to meet. But even this master prose would not distract her or soothe her into sleepiness. If it weren't for Julian's wakefulness and the kind of thoughts she had, insomnia would not be so bad, for at least it was time spent alone, time stolen from Miss Bemel, from work, from conferences, time to waste, really. But when insomnia meant thinking about long-ago frustrations, about days when you had no power over your life, then insomnia was an enemy. Retrospection was a vice, Amanda felt, an unnecessary weakening of your powers, for how could you remember the past without being afraid of the future? She knew and didn't care that people from Lakeville must think she was the cruelest of snobs, dismissing all affectionate offers of hometown distinctions, and rudely ignoring friendly calls or visits from old Lakeville neighbors. But Lakeville was not hometown to Amanda, it was childhood, and childhood was something to be forgotten, like a long sentence in prison. Amanda had succeeded very well in snipping off the years that still smarted, but the name of Vicky Haven had brought them all back again. In *Who's Who* and in her other public bibliographies Amanda conceded only her birth in Lakeville, did not mention Miss Doxey's, but referred to France and Switzerland as the scenes of her early education, with a bow to Columbia for a brief course in journalism. But in the middle of the night, shivering before the dying fire, bare feet slipping out of fur mules, Lakeville was all too clear, childhood was a crime painfully remembered.

"If your father thinks *I'm* going to buy your winter coat just because he bought you your shoes, then he's very much mistaken," this was her mother's sharp voice on the train after they left her father in the station, at Cleveland. Mother was taking her to Columbus for her legal six months' responsibility. Amanda was handed to her like a suitcase in the Union Station in Cleveland by Father. "Hello, Floy," said Father. "Hello, Howard," said Mother, and then Amanda changed hands, and the heckling

began. Even at five years old Amanda had learned to let this slide
off her back, to keep a glass wall around her nerves and feelings.
If they thought they could make her cry they were very much
mistaken! She was not partial to either parent, since they ignored
her before the divorce to carry on their own quarrels over finance
and fidelity, and after the divorce Mother carried on quarrels,
taking both parts herself since Father was of course absent. At
least her father didn't talk about the demerits of his lost mate the
way Mother always did, always accusingly as if the child was
somehow to blame for this, and the child's sulky silence seemed
proof of loyalty to the other. Definitely the father was in the
wrong, any five-year-old would know that, since he did not defend himself and it was evidently true he expected Mrs. Keeler's
small income from her first husband's insurance to support
Amanda in full, his own little salary being spent on himself and
his lady friends. At that time, too, he was a big poker player, and
there were often times, during his period of parently grace, when
he was gone for forty-eight hours, involved in a game somewhere. It was perfectly possible that during these absences
Amanda would be left alone in the apartment over the store in
Lakeville with neither money nor food. This seemed to the child
Amanda not so much hardship as social stigma, and she haughtily refused sandwiches sent up by neighbors who suspected this
state of affairs, though she was quite willing to take all the candy
the Greek candy kitchen man offered her.

"No underwear, no comb and brush, no decent sweater!" her
mother would go on, unpacking her bags later. "And what's this?
Yard material? Good Lord, does he expect me to sew for you,
too? No good stockings, of course, What? A red satin kimono?
A fine thing for a six-year-old! Some sweetie of his gave you that,
I suppose."

Mother always asked questions like this, but Amanda never
told on her father. She resented her mother's incessant inquiries

quite as much as she resented her father's stinginess. She knew
that it was a toss-up between her mother's inquisition and her father's sly dipping into her birthday money when she got back to
Lakeville.

Amanda could not remember ever being hurt at this time,
merely angry at things denied her. She had considered herself
from very infancy as merely an impatient guest of her parents;
their authority was only a matter of their superior size; they were
an inferior couple whose company she would tolerate, together
or separately, only until she could make a better contact. As a
child she could not remember having any child feelings, but only
sense of outrage at the indignity of a superior person, a full-
grown princess, like herself being doomed by some mean witch
to what seemed endless imprisonment in the form of a child, suf-
fering all the humiliations of smallness, dependence, tumbles,
discipline. It disgusted her to be buttoned into leggings on someone's lap and to be afraid alone in the dark and to hurt when she
fell down when her mental inferiors, namely her parents, suffered none of these things. Obeying no discipline so far as bedtime, spinach, and manners were concerned, it was galling to
have adult hands take the liberty of administering the hair brush.
At five she perfected her own practical philosophy about corporal
punishment. It was clear that loud sobs of pain and remorse were
the required response to punishment, but little Amanda would
give her guardians no such satisfaction. Instead she shut her eyes
and pretended the victim was someone else, her cousin, or her
playmate, and that she herself was a calm onlooker. This secret
weapon of detaching her feelings from her body gave her parents
infinite discouragement and gave Amanda herself a sense of
magic power.

"You can spank her and spank her but she just won't cry," she
would hear her mother complain wearily. "How can you make
her behave if she won't be punished?"

At ten she had a perfectly adult jealousy of her mother's independence, of her mother's fur coat and pocket money and ability
to buy things she wanted. Why should Mrs. Eva Keeler be entitled to more than little Amanda? She was older and bigger, that
was all. Amanda knew she herself had more brains than any of
these grown-ups who tried to tell her things. She did not know
exactly what she knew (she hadn't *learned* it yet) but it was there,
close to her but unshaped; one thing was certain, and that was
the wrongness of whatever these outlanders said or did. You
didn't need to be grown-up to know that much.

The death of her mother meant nothing more to Amanda than
a new black outfit and a gratifying visit to the Careys in Florida. It
was the nicest thing her mother had ever done for her, though the
Southern trip necessitated playing with Ethel, at that time a fat,
bossy little girl with all her sensibility yet to be acquired.

"Why, she isn't even crying!" she heard people say at her
mother's funeral, as if it was for this moist tribute that people
died. People were always wanting children to cry and prove
again and again their helplessness, so that they might take advantage of it. She did cry a little, quite suddenly, when she remembered that now she would not get the red snow suit her mother
had promised. She certainly wouldn't get it from her father, and
she'd get as little equipment as possible, too. Her father did not
mean to be stingy, but he didn't think it mattered what children
wore. You gave them an orange or some candy once in a while,
or a dollar. He thought when Amanda insisted on shoes or underwear or textbooks for school that she had simply been spoiled
by her mother. Her tantrums, and later her chilly days of silent
accusation, were proof of it, he thought, and so did his lady love,
Miss Jansen, at the beauty shop, though she stolidly provided out
of her own savings.

Besides the gift of detaching herself from bodily pain, Amanda
had another magic secret. This was the secret of looking confident,

and she'd learned this so long ago it seemed her own invention. It had begun by discovering that if you took long deep breaths you didn't get rattled in games or examinations. In piano recitals it always seemed that the persons who walked leisurely across the stage, adjusted the seat calmly, idled a moment to glance at the audience or adjust a sleeve, were the ones who played the best, even before they touched the piano. Success was in the takeoff, in the initial appearance of complete confidence in one's adequacy. Amanda carefully studied the external manners of all experts, in dancing, talking, playing, and if she had insufficient cause for external poise, she believed the careful aping of the external effect would eventually stir the inner fire. It worked out in many cases. She studied the casual manner of the trained horseman, so her first ride did not betray her ignorance. Body straight, but not too straight, heels at proper angle, knees exactly flexed, reins between proper fingers, face nonchalant, Amanda was credited with good horsemanship before she's even started.

With these private secrets at her command Amanda had finally broken through the cage of childhood into independence and the privileges of maturity. One of these privileges was to drop your childhood into a wastebasket, forget it, burn it, destroy all evidence of past weakness. Another privilege—and this, she arrogantly felt, was her special right—was unlimited power. To deny the first was to forego the latter.

Amanda suddenly flung her cigarette in the fireplace, thinking of how Lakeville was creeping in on her in the shape of Vicky Haven. It had to be, of course, if her plans for Ken Saunders were to be plausibly covered. But it fretted her, as if, even this long after her escape, there was chance of Fate shrinking her into helpless childhood again and denying her everything she wanted once again, just because she was too little to get it. The shame of dependence, of weakness, of not knowing things! It came over her in a great surge of anger. The time she had hidden under the table and bumped her head on it when she stood up, an indignity, she raged at the time, that would never have been visited on an adult! At least she had sufficiently awed her betters to discourage pet names. She had always been Amanda, never Baby, never Mandy, never Tootsie. She rather suspected that Julian had always been Editor Evans, too, judging from his grave infant portraits. This did not endear him to her. The thin, precocious little face in those early pictures seemed ridiculously naïve to her. It was all very well for your Amandas to have been born grown-up, but a man, to be a great man, should have once been a boy.

This reflection gratified Amanda so much that when she heard the inevitable crunching of Swedish toast outside her door she flattered Julian by asking him in for a smoke, though it was actually for the sole purpose of twitting him with this observation.

"I was always precocious, yes, my dear," Julian said, frowning over the effort to be fair, "but I don't think your conclusions could really be proved in a census."

But it nagged at him all night, as Amanda's little pinpricks always did, for here, like ancestry or race, was something neither money nor power could correct.

2

$\mathcal{V}$ICTORIA HAVEN, AT TWENTY-six, was considered one of Lakeville's brighter young women. She had a nice little growing business of her own (real estate), an office in the newest and tallest building on Main Street, two bank accounts, one with $462.83 in it (the office account), and one with $44.67 (personal), an annual full-page ad in the Chamber of Commerce booklet and an annual interview, sometimes even a speech at her college Alumnae Day. Vicky, like everybody, was sure she was far smarter than the average and it sometimes surprised her that she was so dumb about the simplest things, such as understanding politics, treaties, who was who, the use of oyster forks, service plates, back garters on girdles, the difference between Republicans and Democrats, and the management of a lover.

"There's no doubt about it, the female mind can't hold anything very long," she reflected sometimes, blaming her own shortcomings on the entire sex. There she was, an honor student at Miss Doxey's and for two years at the nearest college, yet knowledge had scampered through her brain as if it had been warned to get out within twenty-four hours. Yes, Vicky decided, the female mind, in its eagerness to shine afresh every day, had to have a very rapid turnover. There was no attic treasure chest or ice box where the good education was stored, mothproof, mouse-proof, and shrinkproof. There was only a top dresser drawer where names, dates, fragments of facts were flung without mates as the information hurtled through. Vicky sometimes examined her own top drawer, horrified at these things she once knew but now only recognized the face; names like Bunsen burners, re-torts, grids, Wagner Act, Robinson-Patman Act, Seabury Investigation, Diet of Worms, *pons asinorum*, Catiline, Hatshepsut, Munich, Chapman's Homer—or was it Homer's Chapman—egg-and-dart, Smoot-Hawley, Bill, Muscle Shoals, Boulder Dam, plum ciculio, Brook Farm, Kerensky, Glazounov, geometric progression, Javanese scale, pituitary, and five hun-dred rags and tags that must have belonged to a whole fact at one time but in their present futile tangle were nothing more than cues in a quiz program. Vicky, embarrassed by her own confused background, wondered if that wizard of the ages, her good friend Amanda Keeler, really assimilated the stiff facts of her own articles. Since Amanda, in the old days, had been concerned largely with wangling smart vacation invitations and devices for getting faculty favors without too much work, it was only rea-sonable to wonder if ten years had actually transformed the op-portunist into the scholar.

As for love, Vicky had bungled that from the very first grade right up to the present time. She had one boyfriend from the age of ten till nineteen, the basis of their attraction being that they were next-door neighbors. As soon as he was twenty-one he was dazzled by the mystery of a girl who lived seven blocks away and had impetuously placed her under a long engagement contract till he finished college, medical school, and hospital training. Vicky realized at the time that her ten years of spirited disagreement with everything he said, and articulate impatience with his plodding nature, may have had something to do with his final departure. She was inconvenienced by this break more than she was crushed. And then she did fall desperately in love with Tom Turner, fifteen years older than she was, an architectural engineer, when his drinking permitted, and exciting enough to the young women of the town.

"I shouldn't have tried to reform him," she lamented, wisely enough, in the aching months after he ran off with her more sophisticated partner, Mrs. Brown. She should have tried to be at least as sympathetic as his favorite bartender if she was to compete with the latter. Mrs. Brown had been. When Tom went on a bender to celebrate his appointment to a most eminent advisory staff, he called up Vicky to join the spree.

"Darling," Vicky had said, getting maternal at the hint of what this advancement might mean to their relationship, "don't you think you'd better go home and sleep, so as to be ready for your conference tomorrow?"

Mr. Turner, in turn, gave her a piece of advice which she forgave, being certain he would be sorry for it tomorrow, but this turned out not to be the case. Eager for feminine companionship and remembering a few pleasant nights with the sharp-faced Eudora Brown, Vicky's business partner, Tom had no difficulty in getting her merry assistance in painting the town. They showed up at the conference, married for no reason at all, and it was a gala occasion. It was a good lesson, Vicky tearfully admitted to herself, that reform was something to attempt after the ceremony, never before.

But if she was so smart, and if an education was any good at all, why didn't it teach a jilted lady how to recover her poise, how to wind back the will to live, to dance, to love? Her top dresser drawer information was as useless here as in any other crisis. All Vicky could do was to read the women's magazines and discover how other heroines had solved this problem. The favorite solution, according to these experts, was to take your little savings out of the bank, buy a bathing suit, some smart luggage, put on a little lipstick, throw away your ugly glasses and go to Palm Beach or Miami for two weeks. There you lay on the beach doggedly in rain or shine, your glasses hidden in a secret compartment of the hotel cellar, and not-at-all-dangerous hair tint bringing out the highlights in your new permanent and the smart but inexpensive bathing suit bringing out other highlights in your figure. On the fourteenth day, if not before, a tall bronzed Texas oil man would appear and be bowled over by your unaffected passion for peppermint sticks, unlike the snobbish society women he knew, and if you turned to page 114 you would find yourself, as heroine, bumbling down the church aisles without your glasses led by the Texas oil king and possibly a Seeing Eye dog.

Vicky was not convinced by this remedy, nor even certain she wanted to live in Texas, or that the sight of her rather thin figure in a smart but inexpensive bathing suit would knock a millionaire off his feet. In fact she was pretty sure that the bathing suit would have to be pretty expensive and very carefully cut indeed to "do things for her." Furthermore, the stories of How to Get Over a Broken Heart by Getting Another Man were invariably followed by other stories on what to do after you lost him again, after, say, ten years' marriage. The expert storytellers appeared to be as certain you would lose him as they were that you would get him. You usually lost him on your tenth wedding anniversary to some girl in a bathing suit lying on a Miami beach with a lipstick and no glasses. The way you gained him back was to take your savings, put them into a new hair-dye do and permanent, take a figure-reducing course and erase that middle-aged spread which is the only thing that's holding you back, call up an old beau who is always waiting for you at the nearest hotel and who sends you orchids at this faint beckon from you, and by getting a little flushed with champagne (instead of disagreeable over gin) and learning the newer dance steps, your husband is refascinated and comes whizzing back for a second honeymoon. Vicky deduced that it was just as well for you to start saving again, however, since there was no permanent way of keeping your man outside of nailing him to the floor. The lesson of all the stories boiled down to saving your money, since all the secret solutions devolved on dipping into this ever-present savings account. And that was the trouble with Vicky's comeback after Tom had run out. The profits of her six years in business had been steadily put back into the business, new office equipment, printing, one thing and another, so that the personal savings account that was to see her to Palm Beach and Prince Charming was scarcely enough for the train fare, let alone two weeks of glamorous idleness. The thing was to make money, and in Lakeville money was made by a slow fairly honest process that might, after ten years, enable you to turn in your car every two years for a new one and have a little house just around the corner from next-to-the-smartest neighborhood. If she could only get to New York—if she could only find some excuse for dumping the business on her partner, now the wife of her lover, instead of this perpetual chin-upping about their wretched triangle.

"I suppose you wish I'd get out," Mrs. Brown had candidly said the day after the wedding. "I know that would be the decent thing to do, but the truth is I need the money coming in till Tommy gets his bills paid."

"No need to leave," Vicky stonily answered. "I couldn't afford to buy you out right now, anyway, and I'd have to train somebody else. We can manage. Providing you don't let your husband hang around the office."

"Oh, goodness, he wouldn't dream of it," Mrs. Brown's laughter pealed out richly. "He's simply scared to death of you."

So day by day they kept up the illusion of an amiable business partnership and the sight of Mrs. Brown's disposition slowly souring under the effects of marriage to the man Vicky loved did not keep Vicky from wishing to God she was in the other woman's shoes.

"I'll get over it," she said to herself grimly. "It may take a couple hundred years but I'll get over it."

And then Ethel Carey got back from New York with exciting stories of plays, nightclubs, brilliant parties, gossip about Amanda, and sly hints that there were Texas oil men in New York as well as Florida, just waiting to heal broken hearts. Vicky was obliged to wearily declare that she did *not* want any man, none at all, all she wanted was to get out of this hateful town of Lakeville and make some money. Almost at once Amanda's wire came, and then a letter about the idle studio waiting for her to move in, and next, as Amanda was an impatient woman, a letter with a ticket for the following Tuesday.

"Never mind about the office," Ethel insisted. "I'll get Papa to manage the whole thing, talk to Eudora and make all the arrangements. Your job begins and you have to leave. It's an emergency."

Having warned Vicky not to expect any friendly or personal gestures from Amanda, who, don't forget, was a very busy and a very important person nowadays, Ethel was dumfounded at the offer of hospitality in Amanda's own studio, hints of a welcoming dinner the first night in town, and all Ethel could conclude was that it was her own description of Vicky's plight that had won these favors. She only hoped both of them would remember this and not sit around the fire in the long New York nights ganging up on her the way old friends generally did.

"I know how you feel about our friendship now, Vicky," she said wistfully. "But what if you turn out as successful as Amanda? Then you'll forget all about poor old Ethel."

Vicky warmly denied this. Ethel had been her only friend, her only confidant in these trying months and she would never, never forget it in the almost certain glory of her future New York success.

"I only hope you'll stay the same," said Ethel, "only not such a fool next time, dear, I hope."

At home Vicky met with more difficulty than she had anticipated. She rented a room from her brother's family in a pretty little house on the lake and had lived here at his suggestion ever since she left college. It had often occurred to her that for the same money she could get a little place in town, but her brother's family had gotten to count on her little contribution with their three children growing up. Brother Ted, who was ten years older than Vicky, liked to act smug about "giving Vicky a home now that Mother was gone," and the exchange of money for this kindness was never mentioned. Vicky had expected, from veiled remarks overheard in the last two years, that her room could be put to good use with the children growing, and even as it was she shared her bed with Joan, the oldest. So she imparted the good news of her departure with every expectation of hearty rejoicing. Instead the news met with shocked silence, brother and wife looking at each other significantly, the baby's burst into sobs quite ignored. Little Joan, age thirteen, scrawny, freckled, but happy in a "permanent" caught the cue of disapproval from her parents and looked from one face to the other, eager for Aunt Vicky to get scolded.

"I didn't think you'd do a thing like that, Vicky," her brother said, ladling out the veal potpie with careful justice. "You got a nice little business started and then you drop it and run wild."

"But I'm not running wild," Vicky protested. "I have a job and Amanda's giving me her studio to live in—it's the chance of a lifetime."

"You give a person a home and what thanks do you get?" observed the brother's wife.

Brother was more fair.

"I wouldn't say that, honey, I wouldn't put it just that way," he said, "Vicky's always paid a nominal rent and I know she would have raised it when she got to making more, of her own accord."

Vicky, who had been secretly contemplating moving and had no intention of paying more for the privilege of sharing her brother's expenses, stared in astonishment from one face to the other. The three little faces on the other side of the table, from Joan to Junior to Baby, frowned back in harmony with their parents.

"Can I call up Gertrude and tell her about Aunt Vicky going?" Joan asked.

"Hush, children! The point is, what do you want to go bumming around New York for," Bother continued judicially, "that's no kind of life for a nice girl, a girl as well thought of in Lakeville as you are."

"Aunt Vicky's afraid of being an old maid," bitterly offered Brother's wife, and the children tittered.

"Now, honey," appeased Brother again, "you can't blame Vicky for wanting to marry some day. But that's just the point, Maybe she did lose a beau or two here, true enough, but that don't mean there aren't other fellows here in Lakeville. Good solid boys she went to school with, know the family. That's what Vicky wants. You can't blame her for that, honey, and wanting some kids of her own like ours."

"Well, I'm not so sure that's what I want," Vicky flared back, looking with sudden dislike at the three smug little faces. "What do I want with kids when I'm trying to earn a living?"

"Vicky wants to have all that salary to spend on herself," again Brother's wife was accusing. "Every penny to put on her own back, I suppose."

"I've stayed with them too long," Vicky thought with immense perspicacity. "They want to own me as if I was a government bond that paid a nice little dividend all the time. In another year or so they'd be suing me for breach of promise if I left."

"I can have a room to myself if Aunt Vicky goes," said Joan. "I can have Gertrude come and stay all night whenever I like."

"If Vicky feels that she wants to let a good business slide and go fool around with strangers, I won't stop her," Brother went on gravely. "She knows all she owes to us, and she'll find out what it means to pay strangers for all the little comforts she gets here without thinking. Piano, radio, use of the car—"

"The car's half mine, after all," Vicky said in a small voice.

"All right then, go," said Brother's wife, losing her temper. "I suppose it means nothing to you that we'll have to let Bobby go to public school next year, then, instead of to the Academy, and Joanie will have to put off boarding school another year ("But Mama!" wailed Joanie, "Gertrude and all my bunch are going!") Oh, no, you'll be putting your good money on a fur coat, something for yourself, maybe a diamond wrist watch. Take a cruise, why don't you? We won't be even able to go to Canada for August like we planned. And a lot you care."

Vicky sat very still. She had not really given much thought to her fifty dollars a month contribution. It was no bargain as Lakeville prices went, but it was all in the family. Brother earned a fair enough salary at the printing company, but it was plain that that little extra fifty was what Belle counted on as gravy. It was Belle's little private windfall and she never thought that it would cease or that its donor had first rights to it. Brother, even trying to be fair, could not help a look of somber disapproval.

"We're thinking of your own good, Vicky," he said.

"Fun's all she's thinking of," cried Belle. "Fun and fur coats."

Junior, aged nine, brightened.

"Can I have Aunt Vicky's typewriter when she goes?" he asked.

"I want it," said Joan. "I'm the oldest. You can have her radio."

"The radio's broke," howled Junior. "I don't want an old broke radio, I want a typewriter to make writing on. Mama says I can have it."

"Hush!" cried their mother, and this set the baby to screaming convulsively. "It would be just like your Aunt Vicky to take them along to New York with her."

Vicky pushed aside her plate.

"Oh, Mama, look, I've broken off my fingernail!" exclaimed Joan dolefully. "And I've been growing them all winter so they'd be longer than Gertrude's. Just look."

"Well, you'll just have to cut them all off," snapped her mother.

"But, Mama, they'll look perfectly awful!" wailed Joan, holding out the maimed hand with its long red talons. "I'll just have to paste it back on or *something*! It's just a whole winter's work ruined, that's all it is."

"Shut up, we're talking about Aunt Vicky," barked her father.

"But look!" sobbed Joanie. "How can I wear my *formal* and have nasty old sawed-off fingernails like Aunt Vicky? You've got to do something about it, Mama, honestly, you just got to!"

"I think I'll start packing," said Vicky.

As she left the room to the tune of Joan's quiet sobbing, she was not consoled by hearing her brother say, "Now, honey, we mustn't be too hard on Vicky, even if we do need that little extra help she gives. Don't forget Vicky's been through a lot having Tom throw her over and then everybody in town kidding about it behind her back. That takes a lot out of a girl, and Vicky's getting on, so she's got to get somebody quick. After all, Vicky's twenty-six!"

"But Mama, just look," Joanie's voice rose in despair. "You won't even look at that nail! You don't care how I look, that's all. You want me to grow up and be an old maid like Aunt Vicky, that's what!"

2

THE TUESDAY she was leaving Lakeville, Vicky drove into town after breakfast with her brother Ted and little Joan. Usually she dropped Ted at the station to take a train into Cleveland, where most of his business was transacted, and she continued by the lake road, dropping Joan at school and then driving on to her office. But today Ted's business was right in Lakeville, besides it was his brotherly duty to take care of Vicky's trunk and ticket. Vicky would rather have driven in all by herself this morning, for she loved the car, and she loved the lake road, having thrashed out most of her problems in the last few years while driving along the blue water to work. Ted was not the natural driver that she was, either, so you could not relax and dream with him at the wheel, but must be constantly jarred by his nervous exclamations at every red light and every other car. "Look at that turn, will you? License ought to be taken away from him. Ah, of course. A *woman* driver. Might have known."

Vicky kept her eyes out the window, thinking, "This is the last time. Good-bye, Lake Erie, good-bye lake road, good-bye all the morning thoughts I used to have driving along this road to work, wondering if I'd be able to pick up Tom at the car tracks, wondering if we'd dare get married with all his debts and his drinking. Then after a while wondering how I could manage to *duck* seeing him at the tracks, and how I could get through the day with *her*. When we get up to the crossroads up here I'll look the other way so I don't see our special secret beach with the old burnt pavilion where we used to have our Saturday night suppers. Anyhow Eudora doesn't like that kind of thing, so they don't go there together. That's something."

Ted would never put the top down when he drove, and he resented having the windows open, too, for fear the dust would spoil the new upholstering, so that even on the hottest days the car was filled with his after-breakfast-cigar smoke, while a mere pane's width away lay the crisp azure lake air, as tantalizing as the crown jewels behind the jewelers' invisible glass window. Vicky opened her window this morning, defying Ted's customary argument about economy.

"It's the last time I'll smell Lake Erie," she said, and drew a long breath of the tingling freshness of lake winds, steamer-smoke, fish, and automobile gas—all the things that made up a Lakeville autumn morning. This is what she would miss, she thought.

"Last time for a month or so, maybe," chuckled Ted.

They were so sure the great city would throw her back here. They were fond of her, certainly, but part of the family fondness was in knowing that nobody else would ever like you or excuse your faults as they did. It would have been the same, had her mother lived, because Mother had been devoted to her son and her best wish for Vicky was that there would always be Ted on hand to protect her from her own folly. "Don't let Amanda Keeler's leaving town put ideas in your head, Vicky, my girl," Mother had warned her when Vicky had wanted to leave Miss Doxey's and go to New York just because Amanda had done so. "Our family has never liked big cities. We're country people and don't like to show off. Our women aren't show-offs like Amanda Keeler. We're just simple folks, marry the boys we grow up with, raise our families in the same town. No use your talking about being a newspaper writer, because none of our family has ever been writers. You can talk about times changing, blood don't change. When you get out of Miss Doxey's, you'll find something to do right here in Lakeville or maybe Cleveland, doing something quiet the way we like to do. Any of our family in New York City would be like fish out of water. You stay here where Ted can help you out when you need help."

Families could give you a fine inferiority, out of their affection for you, all right. Very likely if Mother was still alive, Vicky would never dare take off, at all.

They came to the old Haven house just outside the town limits. It was in good shape, but the lawn around it was overgrown, and the porch covered with brown autumn leaves, fluttering around the boarded-up windows. Vicky remembered her mother and Aunt Tessie sitting on the porch watching the buildings going up all around them, as the town extended. The city's extension program beat the depression by a few months and left the Haven house, relic of 1900, wedged in between rows of two-story, tax-paying business buildings. In twelve years the town hadn't gotten enough money together to continue its project so the Haven house, owned by the city, stood idle and the new buildings flanking it remained half-untenanted. Mother died, and Aunt Tessie lived in Cleveland. There was her childhood home, Vicky told herself. Take another look and say good-bye.

"Belle's going to get Aunt Tessie to take your room," Ted said.

So they had sat up last night making their plans.

"She can help with the kids," he pursued. "She lives alone there at the Willerton, so Belle thinks it would do her good to have a little home life. You want a family around you when you're getting on like she is. Somebody handy in case you get sick."

Her income will come in handy, too, Vicky thought.

"But you promised I could have Aunt Vicky's room!" Joan's eyes were wide with hurt surprise.

"I guess you won't mind sleeping with your Aunt Tessie," her father said.

"I *do* mind!" cried Joan. "Sleeping with an older person takes away your strength. Mrs. Murphy said so. It's hygiene."

"Course, when Vicky comes back we'll just have to throw Aunt Tessie out," Ted said, with a hearty laugh. "Can't have an old maids' home."

"You could do worse," Vicky said.

She cast a backward glance at the lake, twinkling blue and clear in the morning sun, and there, in spite of all her care not to see it, was the end of the car-line where she used to pick up Tom. There was a man standing there, now, and she was so sure it was Tom that she turned around hastily and looked straight ahead. It couldn't be, of course, but it was enough to remind her that she must get away as fast as possible.

"Will you sent me autographs of any movie actors you meet?" Joan asked urgently.

Again Ted laughed.

"I guess your Aunt Vicky won't be meeting anymore movie stars than you will, toots," he said.

"You'd better send me *your* autographs," Vicky said.

She must have looked unusually serious, for Ted patted her shoulder.

"Don't worry about Aunt Tessie taking up your room," he comforted her. "The little bit she'll bring in doesn't count that much. We'll put you up, anytime, broke or not."

Of course Ted was fond of her and wanted to be kind. But in her present supersensitive state she hated his clumsy references to losing her rent money rather than her company. Families were so damnably commercial. At your very christening they were already quarreling over who would get your locket if you died.

They dropped Joan at her school. Joan leaned out of the car and saw that the schoolyard was almost deserted and this brought from her a wail of disappointment.

"Gertrude and the bunch have already gone in!" she cried. "And I wanted to tell them about my aunt going to live in New York City! Oh, dear!"

Vicky laughingly kissed her, and in the embrace noticed that Joan was not only wearing her best perfume but had "borrowed" the chiffon scarf Vicky had tried to find that morning. It would be a trial for the child to have Aunt Vicky's nice things supplanted by Aunt Tessie's ancient scrap box. Evidently thinking about this or about Aunt Tessie taking away her strength in the night like some poison flower, Joan's pretty eyes filled with tears. Vicky was touched.

"Stay in New York City till I get through school, Aunt Vicky," Joan begged, waving her handkerchief after the car. "Then I'll get married and come live with you."

Ted took her trunk to the station and then brought Vicky back to her office in the Bank Building. They stood by the elevator, neither knowing what to say. He was her big brother, all the family she had left, but now he was his wife's family, and not a big brother anymore. It was high time she broke off from this symbol of the old nest, but Vicky had a feeling of panic, that even if this nest became more and more thorny, it would still be better than the great bare world into which she was going. Here was the bulletin board of the City Bank Building, with her name on it—"Victoria Haven, Room 652–653," and there it was again, "Haven and Brown, Real Estate, Room 652–653." The second mention was what straightened out her wobbling sentiments and stiffened her chin. The "Brown" stood for Mrs. Eudora Brown who had married Tom Turner that cruel day, and whose presence everyday in 652–653 was eternal reminder that Tom was gone, love was gone, four years of adoration mocked away.

"I guess you'll miss having your own business, Vicky," Ted said, looking at the bulletin board. "Not many kids your age ever got that far in Lakeville. It was too bad—"

He would say something about Tom Turner, now, and she couldn't bear it, so Vicky threw her arms around him and kissed him, feeling, as she ran into the elevator, as if she was Little Eva floating off to a land far-off and bleak.

Her own name on the door was a fact more immediate than the chilly Paradise waiting a bare seven hundred miles away. Vicky braced herself, as she did these days, to say "good morning" to her partner and to hear whatever stabbing anecdotes of the Turner honeymoon Eudora cared to reveal. Fortunately Vicky had begun to smile, even though wryly, at the silver-framed portrait of Tom over Eudora's desk, since for four years this very picture had hung three feet to the left over the Haven desk. That the man should have traveled so slowly in four years did begin to seem funny.

Eudora looked pinched and red-eyed, as if she and Tom had been quarreling. A bender with somebody else's boyfriend was usually a gay, reckless occasion, but a bender with your own husband, if he was a man like Tom, was likely to end up in a fight, especially if the bender money was provided by the bride. It was easy to read the Turners' career.

"I don't know whether I can swing this office by myself or not," Eudora said, plaintively. "It takes two, really. I doubt if Caroline is going to work out."

Vicky sat with her hat on at her desk, emptying drawers, looking over memorandum pads, little reminders of how much this office had meant to her.

"Of course Tom thinks I'm so silly to worry," Eudora said. "After all, I did a good job of selling bonds before I ever came in with you."

"Sure," said Vicky.

She was trying to keep her mind on the necessity to be fair. After all, it wasn't exactly Eudora's fault that she liked a party with other girls' men, and if the men liked her best and one of them did marry her, that wasn't her fault, either. The person at fault was, obviously, the man. Having cleared this matter up once and for all, Vicky was assailed by a fresh wave of dislike for Eudora and a passionate desire to be in her shoes as Mrs. Turner, red-eyed, unrespected, and all.

"Is that what you're going to wear to New York?" Eudora inquired, critically.

"It's the only suit I've got," Vicky said curtly.

What did Eudora think a woman should wear on a train—that black satin, low-bosomed, picture-hat outfit that she got herself up in for city street wear?

"I saw Howard Keeler standing in front of the store," Eudora said, after a moment, still watching Vicky as if she expected her to give up these departing arrangements at the last moment, and say the whole thing was a joke. Eudora did feel that Vicky's leaving was an open reproach to her for taking her man, and probably the town would feel the same way. Impossible as the present cozy situation was, it would be worse with Vicky flown.

"Did you tell him I'd be seeing Amanda?" Vicky asked.

"I did, but he didn't say anything. Didn't send any message or anything." Eudora meditated on this, her sharp eyes still following Vicky. "I think he's still so glad to have Amanda out of his hair that he doesn't care whether she's on top or on relief. Tom says he thinks Keeler doesn't have any feeling about Amanda at all, except that she always nagged him when she was a kid for things he couldn't give her."

So Tom didn't think Keeler had any feelings! A fine one to talk about feelings!

Vicky began dawdling, because she wanted to put off the words of farewell to Eudora, words that must sound natural and calm, and even friendly. She had to wait, though, because if she was taken off-guard she might say, "Good-bye, Eudora, good-bye because I can't stand being in the same office with you anymore. And good luck, Eudora, because women like you always have good luck anyway, because you aren't afraid to hurt anybody. Yes, good-bye, Eudora, and if you'd had any decency you would have been the one to go instead of sending me to a big lonely city where I'll very likely die of loneliness."

Eudora stopped looking over the mail and began fiddling with her fingernails.

It was time to go. There were a million and one things to be attended to around town before she went to the train, and she would not be back in the office at all. It would be silly to say good-bye to Tom, Vicky thought, or would it be sillier to *avoid* saying it?

"I suppose you think you've left me a pretty good thing here," Eudora said, trying to keep the bitterness out of her voice. "You march off to New York, and it's my luck to be left with *this*. Oh, never mind, I know it's better than what I was doing when you met me, and there's money to be made in it. But why should it always be *you* that gets everything?"

Vicky was dumfounded, particularly since Eudora then put her head down on the desk and started sobbing. You would have thought it was Vicky who had won the husband, and not Eudora. Vicky had wept too often herself over Eudora's piracy, not to be steeled against her now. She took a firm grip on the doorknob to make sure of a quick exit if emotions got too high.

"You've got your husband, Eudora," Vicky said weakly.

Eudora lifted her face, shaking her wavy red hair impatiently.

"I don't need a husband!" she exclaimed. "It's too much responsibility! I want to go places, and lead my own life, and have a little pleasure out of life!"

She blew her nose, choked back further sobs, and said, in a restrained voice, "Good-bye, Vicky. Hope you have a good time."

Vicky hurried out and down the elevator once more, confused and unhappy over this mixing up of cards. She wished the train left at once instead of hours later, for the longer the delay the greater chance there was of seeing Tom Turner and breaking down. Later, when she actually got to the station she saw his battered Buick parked by the depot, and her heart failed her. She managed to get on the train without turning around, even when she heard his familiar voice calling, "Vicky! Hi, Vicky, good-bye!"

3

No sooner had Amanda started the strings working for Vicky than the idea seemed a brilliant life-saving inspiration. This younger protégée from the Middle West would be a springboard to freedom for her, Amanda thought, a perpetual alibi, a private cause that Julian could not touch. She had not dreamed, until she saw Ken Saunders again, how restricted her life as a public figure and public wife was becoming. She had been complacently certain that she was a person to be envied by thousands, men and women alike, and this knowledge had sustained her to such an extent she had given little thought to whether she enjoyed her position herself or not. But then the meeting with Ken Saunders opened a whole cage of gagged, imprisoned thoughts, the desire to be loved for herself alone—what nonsense, but there it was!—the wish to gratify perfectly idle, time-wasting whims. From this long-concealed cage was also released an astonishing reserve of resentment at being denied simpler rights of an average woman; she did not dare flirt, have little adventures that the most ordinary pretty waitress might have, yield to a first impulse, overeat, make a fool of herself, play with the wrong people, in short she was actually underprivileged as a female. Amanda wanted to conquer the established world rather than rebel against it, so she was not prepared to kick over her crown for a peasant frolic. She wanted both. And she was obsessed with the idea that Vicky could be manipulated to provide her with these lost rights. It wasn't really as if she was preferring the careless pleasures of the average woman to the prerogatives of her lofty position; it was simply, so Amanda told herself, that in order to be a really great person you must have all the experiences of the *simple* person! This was very much what Julian had told himself when he divorced his first wife for Amanda; he had assuaged his genuinely painful remorse by telling himself that a man, to give the full power of his genius to the public, must be sexually well adjusted. So Amanda, planning secret consolations, assured herself that it all came under the heading of "the full life making the full human being."

Amanda kept Miss Bemel so busy with little memoranda about her arriving friend from Lakeville, that the secretary took an active dislike to the newcomer. Miss Bemel admired more than anything else the ruthlessness of her employer, and in the case of this Miss Haven, Amanda appeared to be acting like an almost normal, if not sentimental, person. Why should Mrs. Evans, having made a point of silence regarding her Ohio background, implying usually that this had been a mere taking-off place for foreign travel and a most sheltered convent life abroad, suddenly risk this desirable picture by sponsoring a schoolmate who was certain to be no credit in any way to the household? Miss Bemel hoped this was not the beginning of philanthropic symptoms on her employer's part, for that she scorned. As a woman who from birth had been ridiculed for bulk, hairiness,

varicosities and greed, Miss Bemel had always been forced to
humble herself, not merely to win friends, but to keep people
from loathing her on sight. Thirty sordid years had been spent in
placating those richer, prettier, kinder, wittier, older, younger,
than she. Therefore her position with Amanda Keeler offered
heavenly release to Carrie Bemel, sweet vengeance for all those
years. As the great lady's personal, private secret-keeper and
buffer, Miss Bemel was allowed to insult at least a dozen people a
day, and to enjoy immeasurably the spectacle of her superiors
fawning over her as representative of a great name. Boys having
left her strictly alone during the formative years, she had been
permitted leisure to acquire an excellent education and to de-
velop her brain to a point where its outcome was well worthy of
Amanda Keeler Evans' signature. She even enjoyed the arrogance with which Amanda mentioned "*my* articles," "*my* opinion." To have confessed to being more than Amanda's patient
secretary would have lowered Amanda's prestige, and would
have done herself no good. So Miss Bemel gloried in Amanda's
insolence and multiplied it, herself, by a hundred.

Every morning Miss Bemel turned in a complete digest of the
dinner conversations or chance comments of important officials
who had visited the house. Miss Bemel had taken all these words
down in shorthand in her unseen chamber outside the dining
room or from invisible vantage grounds elsewhere in the house,
and these were then checked with other information, and eventually woven into the printed words as the brilliant findings of
Amanda Keeler Evans. Miss Bemel saw nothing the matter with
this arrangement, since her own rise to power accompanied her
mistress' ascension.

To tell the truth, Amanda would have been genuinely surprised to learn that any writer of consequence had any other
method of creation. There were a number of minor scribes on
liberal weeklies who were unable to afford a secretary, that she

knew, but she had no idea that this was anything more than the necessary handicap of poverty. The tragedy of the attic poets, Keats, Shelley, Burns, was not that they died young but that they were obliged by poverty to do all their own writing. Amanda was reasonably confident that in a day of stress she would be quite able to do her own writing, but until that day she saw no need, and in fact should a day of stress arrive she would not be stupid enough to keep to a writing career at all, but would set about finding some more convenient means of getting money.

Even if the public had discovered, through malicious enemies, that Amanda's first knowledge of what she thought about Britain's labor problem, Spanish Rehabilitation, South American Co-operation, America First, War with the Far East, was the moment she read Miss Bemel's "report" above her own signature, no one would have thought the less of her intelligence, for the system was blessed by pragmatic success. The most successful playwrights, the most powerful columnists, the most popular magazine writers, seldom had any idea of how to throw a paragraph together, let alone a story, and hired various little unknown scribblers to attend to the "technical details." The technical details usually consisted of providing characters, dialogue and construction, if the plot was outlined for them, as well as the labor of writing. Sometimes the plot itself was assembled by this technical staff, for individuals were far too busy in this day and age to waste time on the petty groundwork of a work of genius; it was enough that they signed their full name to it and discharged the social obligations attendant upon its success. The public, querulous as it was with the impractical gyrations of the unknown artist, made up for this by being magnanimously understanding of the problems of the successful man, so it all evened up in the long run. Amanda was just as entitled to her "genius" as any of the other boys on Broadway or in the public prints.

Miss Bemel was going over the dinner list with a frown.

"It won't be necessary to include this Haven woman in the Wednesday dinner, will it?" Miss Bemel asked.

Amanda was in a devilish temper today, and Miss Bemel had noted the temper seemed to have sprung itself simultaneously with the wave of big-sister sentimentality for her friend from Lakeville. It was another mark against the coming visitor.

"Certainly, Miss Haven will be invited," snapped Amanda. "Her name's there, isn't it? Does that usually mean the person is to be omitted? Am I in the habit of giving you a list of people NOT to ask, Bemel? For God's sake, Bemel!"

"But she is only arriving that day," said Miss Bemel. "Perhaps she will be tired."

Amanda flung a cigarette into the ashtray at Miss Bemel's elbow, clearly hoping that the still burning ash might set the too assiduous creature on fire. Part of Amanda's nervousness was due to the unexpected effort of doing considerable arranging on her own hook, for she had selected and made all the plans for the "studio" she was presenting Vicky. She had done this because she intended to keep this secret from Miss Bemel—from Julian, too—who merely knew such a place existed and that Amanda had no interest in it beyond a gracious means of helping her protégée.

"Never mind your private thoughts, Bemel. Who's next?"

"I don't recognize the name of Saunders," pursued Miss Bemel, gnawing the end of her pencil thoughtfully. "Refugee?"

Refugees had been perfectly acceptable on Amanda's invitation list for some time, inasmuch as they were in her line of public work and those on dinner lists were in no unpleasant *need* of dinner. But Miss Bemel suspected the name "Saunders" was merely another Mid-Western refugee, and consequent cause for alarm.

"Mr. Saunders is for Miss Haven," Amanda said with forced patience. "You can't expect a girl that doesn't know a soul in town to have any fun with those old bores we're having. The least I can do is furnish her someone young enough to beau her around."

Miss Bemel's eyebrows lifted in silent sarcasm. Fun? Who expected fun at an Evans dinner? Bores? Ambassadors, princes, congressmen, movie stars—bores? Not when their informal chitchat kept Amanda's name before the public. Miss Bemel shrugged pointedly and returned to her memorandum book.

"You're to be at the Welcome Home at twelve for two hours' auctioning," said she. "The child evacuees from the London slums will be there and the proceeds will go to their Jersey farm project."

Bemel was getting on her nerves.

"Telephone them that I can't possibly," Amanda said. "I'm worn to the bone with that thing. Tell Mr. Castor to tell Mr. Evans to send them a check."

"You might drop in for a minute," said Miss Bemel. "The photographers will be there promptly at twelve and you could leave right after."

"All right," granted Amanda more calmly. "I suppose I could spare a few minutes. I ought to do that."

"Where can I reach you if Washington calls?" inquired Bemel.

"My God, can't I have ten minutes to walk around the park?" cried Amanda.

"It's raining," answered Miss Bemel practically.

"For God's sake, stop carping," said Amanda. "Where's that damned elevator? Who's using it all this time? All right, all right, I'll walk down. Let the servants ride up and down all day, I don't care."

Miss Bemel shrugged and returned to her duties as Amanda, by way of punishing everyone, including herself, started tearing down the four flights of stairs.

This did not prove a wise move, for she collided with her husband on the library floor and he led her inside. He was wearing the black Chinese robe in which he fancied himself, as it gave a dignified Oriental effect to his bald head. He had a telegram in his hand, and Amanda, bursting with impatience to get out, saw that he was in one of his Personal Discussion moods.

"I was about to send Castor up with this," he said, seating himself pontifically behind the great desk so that she sat, like a respectful employee, in the less majestic chair on the other side. "Then I decided to bring it up myself. We can get Florello."

"Florello?" Amanda made no effort to disguise her complete lack of interest in her husband's portentous news.

"Florello, my dear child," he said, smiling, "is the greatest fencing master of the present day. Does that mean nothing to you?"

"No," said Amanda.

Her husband took off his glasses and wraggled them back and forth as he beamed fondly at her. He was always fondest of her when she confessed ignorance to something, and this was seldom enough, so he made the most of his advantage.

"Your publishers, I believe, are waiting for the sequel to *Such Is the Legend*," he said, and Amanda realized he was going to be a bore about it, but she could not stop him since it was, after all, being a bore about her own work, which excused the fault. "They suggested, if you recall it, my dear, and of course you do, that you take the further fortunes of your leading character, Raoul Le Maz, carry him through his Virginia adventures and through the Revolutionary War. As the story would naturally require research, I have had the advice of a number of experts on what facts should be checked, *et cetera.*"

"I wish you wouldn't say that," Amanda said.

Julian looked mystified and a little hurt.

"I mean *et cetera*," said Amanda, a little ashamed. "I mean it sounds like a salesman's pep talk."

"I'm sorry if my language offends your ears," Julian said, still smiling but with a little aloofness now. "As an editor and publisher of thirty years' standing—(Editor, publisher and office boy first, Amanda thought)—I am glad to receive any suggestions on language from a young author."

"Now, Julie," Amanda said, giving him a conciliatory pat on the knee. "Go on."

"Very well. Since Le Maz was a great duelist, I have hired Florello to supply you with information on that subject for two hours a week." Julian ticked off his words on his short, pudgy fingers. "For a historical survey of the period, I have engaged Doctor Pudkin, of Columbia University, to talk to you one hour a week and provide you with suitable inside stuff. For sketching out the plot I suggest Hervey Allen, say, or, if his price is too steep, possibly this fellow, Stark Young, since I understand their work is something along your line."

"Oh, Julian," Amanda exclaimed, "you can't get people like that to work for other writers. You simply can't."

"Who can't and why not?" Julian demanded. "We are not poor, my dear, and where the matter of your creative work is concerned I will gladly pay anything. Anything."

"You just can't even suggest it to well-known people," Amanda went on. "You just can't."

"But you don't want Mr. Thirer again," Julian reminded her. "He needs the money and would be glad to do it but after the last book you said you couldn't stand him."

"Oh, he's all right," Amanda said, reluctantly, "it's just that he acts so possessive about the thing. Not anything he *says*—just the way he acts."

"We'll discuss that part later, then, my dear," said Julian. "I only wanted you to know that in the press of all these foreign affairs I don't forget my wife has a career to forge. Do you want Castor to send a note out to the press, that you are engaged on the new book?"

If Julian would only stop acting as if her career was a project of his own and she was only a departmental head in charge of its execution! It was woeful the way he could take the fun out of everything. It was fine having his power behind her, but if he only had a faint touch of humor about it! On the other hand, whoever heard of humor as an asset to power?

"Please, Julian, don't heckle me about that book," she pleaded. "I'll do it—oh, of course I'll do it sometime—but what's the hurry? Margaret Mitchell hasn't written a thing since *Gone With the Wind* and that's been years. And it isn't as if I wasn't busy all the time. For that matter people are still talking about the old one. Look."

She opened her bag and drew out a clipping, from some Johannesburg paper. Julian adjusted his glasses and read it, with a quiet smile.

"Greatest novel of this or perhaps any other generation," he read aloud, and then handed it back with a nod. "Sounds all right, doesn't it, for a man that says *et cetera*?"

Amanda's face fell.

"Oh, Julian, you didn't! It wasn't you again!"

"Couldn't trust Boggs out there to do it right so I wrote it myself and cabled it to him direct," Julian said, pleased even yet at the idea.

Spoiled. Everything spoiled by having it bought or bribed. Tears sprang to Amanda's eyes. If he were only not so brutal about it! But he acted as if the only possible way her work could get applause was by buying it. And he couldn't understand, since the results were just the same either bought or freely given, why she should make any fuss about it. All right, let him spoil everything.

"I suppose you arranged that article about me in *Letters* this quarter," she said sarcastically. "I suppose you take a bow on that, too."

Julian looked at her in silent reproach.

"My dear child, I would have given a fortune to have known about that article in advance," he said tenderly. "I would have bought the magazine outright just to stop it. By God, I'll do it yet. Castor!"

The idea was too pleasing to Amanda to resist. A literary magazine has the nerve to ridicule her work with highbrow arrogance, and now it would be bought by Julian and brought to its knees. She could see next month's issue devoted to praising words about her by Julian's own private brain trust, while the former editors ground their teeth. Yes, in a way she could forgive this fault of Julian's in leading her career by a leash. It had its points.

Somber, little Mr. Castor materialized from the shadows of the cubbyhole adjoining the dark library and Amanda rose to go.

"By the way, this list for Wednesday's dinner," Julian fumbled through the papers on his desk till he found the pink memorandum from Miss Bemel. "Who is this Saunders? Is he Saunders steel?"

"No, darling, he's just a newspaper man like yourself," said Amanda. "Young, presentable, quite dull, but we have to have an extra man around for my little girlfriend. After all, you can't expect her to be as interested in ideas as we are. Let's try to get her a beau while she's here."

"Hmm, yes," agreed Julian, still examining the list. "Better brush up on our dancing young men friends—if we have any."

"We'll just have to shop around for some," said Amanda.

"Another name here," said Julian, "Victoria Haven. Who's she?"

"She's the girl we're talking about, for God's sake!" Julian really could get you down by that stupid way he had, but the sharpness in her voice caused him now to look up. He saw the new hat, the orchids on her sable jacket.

"A rendezvous?" he inquired. "My, my we do look fancy."

Amanda drew on her gloves carefully.

"Photographers," she said. "The Welcome Home with me holding London slum kiddies on one knee and my American flag on the other."

"Ought to be at least a paragraph in it for Sunday," approved Julian.

"Stingy," teased Amanda and patted his hand. It was Julian's afterthought that she never caressed him anymore except in the safe company of a third person or on her way somewhere. As he was by nature a faithful husband, no matter who the wife might be, this apathy of Amanda's was often very inconvenient for him. He would never for the world have thought that perhaps this second marriage was not a complete success, because of course it was a success, or at least had been right up to the wedding day.

2

"AREN'T YOU TAKING on a little more than you should with this schoolmate of yours?" Julian gently inquired of Amanda, the day of Vicky's arrival. "People don't appreciate it, you know. They expect all the more. Very likely the poor girl thinks you'll be at the train to meet her."

"Naturally I'm meeting her," Amanda said coldly, though she had had no idea of doing so until Julian spoke. "After all, I am the one who suggested she come to New York."

"But time—time—time!" exclaimed Julian, for they both hoarded time, respecting it as if it was the stockholders' money, not to be spent on anything but the highest-paying, most reliable securities. In their reports to these mythical stockholders they were honor bound to account for every split second, classifying their expenditures something like this: SLEEP (for efficiency purposes) 7 hrs. 18 min.; CONVERSATION WITH STAFF (for goodwill and *esprit de corps* purposes) 12 min.; TALK WITH BARBER OR MANICURSUT (for purpose of man-in-the-street comments on affairs) 15 min.; JOKE with storekeeper (for aid to digestion) 3 min., *et cetera*. So Julian expected to remind Amanda that although he did not question her money expenditures, the time account was in both their names and it was not quite cricket for her to overdraw on a mere whim. Anything in the way of a human outlay excited his jealousy, for the one consolation in his wife's lack of warmth toward him was that nothing else drew fire from her, either. Already he was a little jealous about a past that was being rewarded in the person of this Miss Haven. Quite aware of this, Amanda now instructed Miss Bemel to have the car ready to meet Miss Haven's train, and to cancel the luncheon engagement with her new research man. Julian was getting far too possessive about her career, Amanda thought, restlessly; it made it rather a lark to annoy him by this little waste of time.

Halfway to Grand Central Amanda began to regret her decision. To annoy Julian was one thing, but to plant future annoyance for herself was something else. It would mean very little to Vicky that an extremely busy woman troubled herself to meet a train. Probably the child would take it for granted and assume that further personal gestures were quite in order. It would have been much wiser to start out on a different basis, let the first meeting be at dinner tonight when Vicky would see the sort of life Amanda now led and have the consequent tact to keep her distance. Amanda hated to doubt her own decisions, and she frowned now over the two sides to this question. If she was too remote with Vicky, then her new friendliness with Ken Saunders would stand out too conspicuously, because God knows there was no legitimate reason for taking him up—no reason that would bear weight with Julian or Miss Bemel. All right, here she was, great lady being welcome committee to visiting Cinderella. Amanda left the car impatiently and entered the station.

She did not know whether it was because she traveled so seldom by train these days that a railroad station was strange to her, or whether it was because it was unusual for so many people to look at her without recognition. At any rate she had an odd feeling of being stripped of herself, of being either lost or dead. She could hear her heels clack on the stone floor of the great mausoleum, but people hurrying by seemed strangely noiseless and ghostly, whatever cries they gave melted into one dull, muted motor noise. Daylight, dingy, diluted, sunless daylight coming through the skylight far up caught the moving figures in its pale web, permitting them to circle around until dark passageways opened up and offered escape. In this vault where seconds and minutes were treasured, Amanda had a sense of loneliness and fear she had never experienced. All these unseeing faces were testimony to a world still unconquered by her. Fear suddenly gave way to impatience at the stupidity of crowds who reacted only to accidents, freaks, movie stars, kings. There was so much she had yet to do, Amanda thought almost with self-pity, so many worlds yet to be subjugated; it was Julian's failure, not her own, she thought, that he was not able to buy *all* of them.

She resented being jostled, and though she was used to her good looks attracting attention she resented the approving eyes of strange men, as if she was a dish not only to their taste but well within their reach; above all she resented Vicky's train being half an hour late which made Julian right. Oh, definitely. She should never fritter away her time with these unnecessary little gestures. She used to rebel against Julian's counsel on her career; nowadays she rebelled against his *making* her rebel merely suggesting something she knew was wise.

"Ken," she suddenly thought, for Ken's hotel was just a block away. At least he would give her back her identity, raise her from crowd level to her proper eminence.

She telephoned him from a booth, and asked him to meet her in the Commodore Bar, a concession to his habits that brought an unexpected laugh from him. As soon as she hung up she was cross at the feeling of guilt, which she thought was in some obscure fashion the fault of Julian or Ken or of Vicky Haven, these people who cluttered her path and made her do things not in her plan. Why should she add mistake to mistake by calling up Ken? A gaunt black-eyed girl with Garbo as her model and a big red patent-leather purse caught Amanda's arm.

"Could you give me two nickels for a dime? I gotta 'phone," she said. This sort of familiarity irritated Amanda, always, not for snobbish reasons but because it obliged her to give priceless time to the trivial uses of worthless people. Frowning, she drew two nickels from her bag and handed them over in silence.

"My boyfriend's waiting to hear if I got here," the girl explained, as if this linked her with all other women calling boyfriends, and entitled her to the courtesies of the club. Amanda nodded silently and went on to the Commodore entrance across the aisle. A man coming out looked at her twice and tipped his hat. The square Irish face under the derby hat, and the natty Chesterfield coat, paisley-patterned scarf, seemed familiar enough but Amanda did not place him.

"Haven't seen you for a long time," he said to her, looking her over with pleasure. "A mink coat, too! Burdley's must be paying better than when I was there."

Burdley's. That was the department store where Amanda had worked for two years as advertising copywriter. Searching her memory not too willingly, she remembered this man was in Burdley's lamp department just outside the executive offices. He had never seemed to know there was anything special about her beyond her looks, anything any different from the cash girls, for he asked them all for dates with complete lack of discrimination.

"How do you do," she murmured, with her usual dismissing smile.

The old friend was not so easily dismissed.

"It's been six, seven years, hasn't it?" he said genially. "Where you going? Commute? I'm married now. Live in Pelham. That wouldn't prevent my buying you lunch someday if you say when. Where do I get you—still at Burdley's?"

What triumph was there in her work if the people from her past whom she wanted to "show" simply would not be shown? This man thought she was still punching a time clock at Burdley's, taking orders from a dozen departmental heads, arguing over raises and bonuses, fending off dates with buyers and bosses. In the station, mixing with this nondescript crowd, there was nothing to mark her as different from the black-eyed girl with the red purse; there were still hundreds of people, probably, who thought she was still working in Burdley's, people who read Amanda Keeler Evans and thought, "I knew a girl by that name once. In fact the girl I knew looked just like this woman's picture." But they were positive it was not the same person. The person they remembered could not *possibly* have written this great book or married this great man. With a faint thought of revenge, Amanda said, "Yes, do call me at Burdley's," but it was the man who had the last word, for he said, "Let's see—what's that name again? Mary—Mary—Mary–don't tell me, it'll come to me."

"Smith," said Amanda icily, and went through the door.

Already Julian had proved how necessary he was to her, a reminder that Amanda did not at all relish. She sat down at a table and waited for Ken, angry at herself for increasing her nonentity by waiting for another nonentity. It did not improve her temper to have him tweak her hair as he came up behind her. She wanted to have the privileges of any other woman, but she didn't want to be *treated* like any other woman.

"All right, you've proved it. I'm still on a leash," he said, sitting down. "Wasn't that all you wanted to know?"

"Stop saying things like that," she said curtly. "You spoil everything."

"Double whiskey sour," he said to the waiter.

"Coffee," said Amanda. It took her aback that the waiter showed no sign of recognizing her, nor did the couple at the next table whisper her name. She was so accustomed to go only to those places where she was known that this anonymity was a new experience. She didn't like it. She had resented it for all the years before she married Julian, the years she wrote perfume copy in Paris, unsigned, bitterly envying every name that brought nods of respect, envying the Hemingways, Hepburns, Windsors, and Edens equally, without regard for the nature of their achievements, merely envying the applause.

Ken used to be her applause, assuring her she could do anything she set her mind to. He hated it, though, when she proved he was right. He still hated her, even though they were lovers again. Maybe he was just being clever. Maybe he sensed that once he gave in completely to her again she would be through with the game.

"I can't stand you drinking in the morning," she said suddenly, looking at his drink. "It's so weak of you."

"Another whiskey sour," Ken said to the waiter. "Double."

He looked at her with cold hostility.

"Why am I honored by your summons today?" he asked. "You proved I would come back running when you whistled. You proved that yesterday. Twenty-four minutes of glorious abandonment, by the clock—"

"Hush!"

"—not that I didn't appreciate the favor. Not that I don't want you in the same bed this very minute—"

"Ken—please!" She was really angry. "I might have known you'd be like this. I want to be nice, and you hate me for it."

He looked stonily at his drink.

"Why not, for Christ's sake? You kick me around for three years, you kick me out, then you want to see if I'm damn fool enough to come back. Just for the fun of it. You never had anybody love you the way I did, knowing all about you, knowing what a five letter woman you are and always will be, and still being fool enough to love you."

Amanda did not hush him now, for this soothed her, brought back her power, reminded her that she was Amanda, the Amanda that nothing could hurt except anonymity. She was soothed, but she was curious, too, that anyone should care so much about anyone, and be so affected physically by any other human being. She looked at his face surprised and gratified that it should show pain, because this was a tribute to her of a sort she could not understand.

"So you call me up and say you have sixteen minutes and two seconds with no one to walk over, and I'm fool enough to come." He tossed his drink down, and beckoned for the check. In the silence she glanced at her watch and he caught it.

"Have you found out what you want? Is my time up, now?" he mocked.

Amanda had found out what she wanted and his time was up, true enough, if truth was what he wanted. She felt warmed and satisfied, the little bruises of a few moments before quite forgotten. Now she was ready for Vicky, at least as soon as Ken would humble himself to ask for the next meeting. He would. He might try to be stubborn but she knew he would have to ask before they got to the door, and she was not going to make it easy for him. He surprised her by keeping grimly silent to the very moment of their parting at the train gates. He was doing it on purpose, she thought, because he knew she was too sure. It was clever of him, she admitted, for now she wondered about him and wondered if she really dared be sure again.

"Good-bye," he said resolutely.

"Dinner tonight, you remember," she said.

He nodded, still refusing to ask for another secret date, and now she was put out because she had taken the studio for no other reason than that. He was holding off to make her presumption seem silly, and a pleasurable sense of panic came over her. How stimulating it was to be uncertain of him! How clever, how terribly clever of him to tease her this way—unless he did mean a little bit of it. . . .

"Tuesday—between three and four," she murmured, plunging.

He gave no indication of agreeing. She wouldn't know until she had made all sorts of complicated arrangements with Bemel to cover her movements for that day. But of course he would be there. Of course she was right to be sure of him. Disappointed at the game losing its charm Amanda watched the crowd pouring through the gate. She hadn't seen Vicky for ten years but she recognized the slight figure in the brown suit, the eager, restless walk, and the shining eyes. She was glad to see her, she was surprised to find, but even before Vicky had caught her eye Amanda was beginning to wonder how much would be expected of her. So her greeting was a shade less warm than Vicky's, managing subtly to hint that the old intimacy was not to be counted upon.

"Why, it looks like any other city," Vicky exclaimed, looking around the station. "It might be anywhere."

Someone behind them laughed, and Amanda colored. She had never found provincialism refreshing and was impatient already with her protégée. She did not like it any better when Vicky gave an audible gasp at sight of the limousine.

"Oh, Amanda! How wonderful!"

"I'll drop you at the studio and see you tonight at dinner," Amanda cut in brusquely, and Vicky, accustomed to taking any uncomplimentary hint as specially made for her, did not find much more to say during the drive, nor did there seem any way of crossing the gulf of their long separation. Amanda clearly was not at all interested in any Lakeville news, and by a detached polite manner conveyed the idea that the Amanda of the old days was no more. Vicky was more subdued by this politeness than by any snub, and changed her manner immediately to the tactful taciturnity evidently required.

"Dinner tonight, as I said," Amanda said in parting. "I'll send for you."

Vicky was too awed, this time, to even thank her friend. Thanks were probably highly provincial, she gathered.

Amanda drove on home in a state of rising irritation. Now she had started something, she thought, but no one need think her time or friendship would be commanded. No matter to what use she might put others, they would soon find Amanda Keeler was not to be used.

4

THE EVANSES KNEW EVERYONE, and by "everyone" I certainly do not mean you or me or any one *we* know. This meant that they had no time for friendships or personalities, since "everyone" shifted and "everybody" became "nobody" so often that it was silly even to remember first names. Neither Amanda nor Julian liked society, except as they could manipulate it in their own home. They knew whom they had there and what they expected to get out of them. At other people's dinners half the time you were wasting your time just because the host wasn't clear in his explanation of who his guests were.

"So that Craver chap was Southern Textiles," Julian would bitterly complain to Amanda, reading the paper next day. "And I wasted the whole evening talking diamonds to that Hindu. Damn the Thorps, anyway, I'm too busy to waste time at their dinners!

"I spent half an hour being nice to that Corrigan," Amanda indignantly responded. "I thought he was Pictures, and all the time he was just Little Theatre."

This wanton waste of their time by other people was the cross Mr. and Mrs. Julian Evans shared in common, and they felt so completely justified in their complaining that they admitted it freely to would-be hostesses. It was as if they had to make up for the first twenty years of their existence which had been wasted in marbles, dolls, hoop rolling, and scooter racing. They might have spent those years building a social trust fund of Contacts and Culture instead of dawdling away at the maternal breast. No more idle fudge making or agate swapping; every smile, every "hello" must pay. At last, confining their social life to their own home as much as possible, the Evanses still regretted that they missed so much by lack of proper cooperation from their friends.

"Mr. Evans, Mr. Harris," hostesses said, and when Julian impatiently whispered his inquiry, "Who is Harris?" he only received the bright reply that Mr. Harris was from the Middle West, and had a very handsome wife. Who in heaven's name wanted to know that Mr. Harris was Zeke Harris, a bright Lutheran boy from Indianapolis who ran away from home to be a brakeman on the B. & O. Railway, became dispatcher, married a million, had a tough time all around before he reached the top, but always idolized his mother? Mr. Harris was, in the Evanses' labor-saving shorthand, "Wall Street." Elva Macroy was not just a stunning blonde who never got the man she wanted so ran through four marriages to forget him. No. Elva Macroy was not that unhappy individual, she was "Washington"! The insignificant little man with the careful English was not Mama Felder's little boy Izzy, but "Pictures, Inc." and here and there, annoyingly disguised as human beings, were The Theatre, Bethlehem Steel, Education, Palm Beach, Southern Pine, Racquet Club, The Ballet, and of course Russia. Naturally the persons symbolizing these matters changed from time to time and for that reason it always seemed a waste to Julian to learn their names. A few names, if sufficiently in the public prints, naturally did stick but no one felt more cheated than Julian, if after remembering for years that Hawkins was Public Utilities, and Public Utilities was Hawkins, suddenly Hawkins became Cotton, and Public Utilities was Purvis.

In their own home, however, the problem resolved itself easily, with Miss Bemel and Mr. Castor providing guest lists with their social value in parentheses. In the case of Vicky Haven, the parentheses enclosed the terse apology "(school friend)" and in the case of Ken Saunders, Miss Bemel had not even considered his name in journalism of sufficient importance to mention but merely said "(escort)," adequate excuse for any male guest.

Having been instructed by Amanda, before Wednesday's dinner party, that he was to take a paternal interest in her young friend. Julian remembered to direct a look of keen concern in Vicky's direction during the cocktails, occasionally stepping to her side and asking, "Well, Betty, are you having a good time?" but being set straight on the name remembered to call her "Verna" the rest of the time. Since this was the only personal attention Vicky received during the cocktail period she was grateful to him, and tried to act very much at ease by taking a martini every time it was offered and refusing the canapés. This was because what she really wanted was the canapés, having had nothing but coffee since she got off the train, but she had learned long ago that whatever she wanted was certain to be bad form or in some way wrong. So, when she wanted a highball, she took a martini, and when she didn't want to smoke she took a cigarette. She was not helped in poise by her inner astonishment at actually being in New York, actually being here at a fabulous dinner party at the Julian Evanses', hobnobbing with all these great names, for she knew they must be great names even if she couldn't quite catch them.

At Amanda's dinners the gentlemen were never permitted to have their brandy alone because Amanda had a pathological horror of being left alone with women, particularly wives. Life was too short, she felt, to waste on these creatures of her own sex who had nothing to add to either her glory or her information. For the same reason neither Amanda nor Julian dared injure their acquisitive faculties by drinking. While guests had martinis, the Evanses had tomato juice; at table they permitted themselves only a solitary glass of champagne during the wine course, this as a concession only to the dignity of the vintage, and during the liqueurs they sipped at ice water. For some reason this temperate example made the guests go to extremes of thirst, and it was rumored around town that although the Evanses' dinners usually ended before midnight the sedate worthwhileness of the event sent the guests afterward to dens of ripest vulgarity. Taxi drivers hung about the corner watchfully when the Evanses entertained, well aware that at least one elegant group, emerging from the mansion, would demand Harlem, even Coney Island, while others, restrained for hours in intellectual converse, would demand a tough waterfront dive or Third Avenue beerhall.

Vicky, without knowing the legend, felt the same way and found herself getting slightly fuzzy during the dinner, which made the affair seem even more wonderful than before. It was true she had as yet found no way of cracking the conversation, and so far as the party went she was positive she was a great dud, but it was a fine thing to sit between a genuine lord and a millionaire banker, having them talk monumental matters across your face for six courses. It made her realize how insignificant a small-town nobody like Tom Turner was, and she could look back and marvel that she had ever wept over such a trivial person. Of course dinner with a trivial person like Tom used to be fun, no element of which ever intruded into the Evanses' dinner. But fun and glamor, perhaps, didn't mix, and at least this was something to write Ethel Carey about for home-town gossip. Vicky felt very pleased anticipating how this would sound in a letter and how it would chagrin the Tom Turners. For some reason women, flouted in love, invariably find an incomprehensibly satisfying revenge in soaring socially. "I will give a white-tie dinner for eighteen," they promise themselves. "How he will burn up when he hears about it." Or else they will be the guest at such functions. The idea that the defaulting lover will be hopelessly chagrined by this social soaring (no matter how he may abhor such a formal life) is as fixed in the female mind as is the child's dream of avenging itself on Teacher by slowly flying around the room with smiling ease. The net effect on both teacher and lover is more apt to be merely a mild astonishment tinctured with irritation rather than remorse. But Vicky treasured the thought that Tom would realize what a superior person he had thoughtlessly tossed away when he heard that she was being sponsored by the great Julian Evans and the famous Amanda. It might make him a little discontented with the ordinariness of his present wife, who could never possibly achieve such distinction.

Vicky watched her old school friend with awe and admiration. There was Amanda conducting the dinner as a symposium, herself the leader, extracting facts, data, opinions, and then repeating the routine in the after-dinner coffee hour, during which Amanda and Julian refreshed their minds on what they had learned at dinner with further discussion, Julian giving out a good deal of it as his own original thought and Amanda repeating the best she had heard without quotes. It was as if anything that went in her ear forthwith belonged to her by the laws of nature, and the lives or opinions of her guests belonged to her in the same say. Amanda's very lips seemed to move simultaneously with the lofty statements of her experts; she signed the words the second they left the other speaker's lips. Vicky saw no harm in this but only cause for despair that she herself had nothing to contribute to Amanda's store. While the Lord Somebody on her right told one on Churchill, Vicky combed her mind desperately for some comparable tidbit, but what Uncle Charlie said to the new farmhand back in Lakeville did not seem appropriate, or what Amanda's daddy said when he sold the Howard suit to the candy store man next door.

It was not, Vicky thought, that she was embarrassed by being present in such distinguished company; it was worse than that— it was that she wasn't even present. She was surprised when one of the master minds spoke to her, so certain was she that she must be invisible. It was like having actors in a film suddenly talk back to you. She saw herself in a mirror and said, "Well, I am here all right, that dowdy little thing must be me." The new dinner dress had seemed a treasure till she set foot in the Evanses' house and then Amanda's trailing cloth of gold made everything else seem the dullest of rags. Vicky had, in her first uneasy effort to establish the old girlish intimacy with Amanda, asked if she looked all right—should she wear the little gray capelet in back like a cowl or in front over her bare bosom?

"Either way you like, dear," Amanda had graciously advised with an appreciative glance at herself in the mirror. "You look sweet just as it is."

Then with a final fond stroke of her hip line and a tender pat to her blonde hair Amanda turned from the mirror and led the way to her other guests, leaving Vicky with the conviction that Amanda's eyes saw so little but Amanda that she wouldn't have known if other women's dresses were wrongside out or upside down.

Thinking of how to describe to Ethel Carey this thrilling debut into New York life, Vicky looked carefully at the men. There must be someone among them on whom she could fasten as a possible suitor, mentally if not in reality. She hadn't really expected, after the weeping, worry and fatigue of packing of the last few weeks, to look her best, but she had expected to get at least a polite flicker of interest. Up to the second round of liqueurs no one had fallen at her feet, and Vicky was obliged to console herself with the thought that they were mostly so old that such a fall might prove fatal anyway, and no girl's charm is enhanced by a flock of elderly corpses around her hem. The one young man who looked possibly human sat in a corner staring stonily into space and addressing no one. This was the Mr. Saunders Amanda had explained she had invited for Vicky's exclusive delight. Vicky, casting a hopeful glance at him from time to time, saw nothing to encourage her, but for the sake of her letter to Ethel made private notes on his appearance, and the manner in which he divided his looks between Amanda, Julian, and the opposite wall, with gloomy intensity.

"He must be *somebody*," Vicky thought. "He couldn't be here without being *somebody*."

He was dressed correctly—or at least like the other men—his shoes gleamed, his white tie was in place, his large squarish hands manicured, but this made his unshaven blond face more baffling. His thick fair hair was very pretty, Vicky thought, but his large quarrelsome nose was certainly no beauty. The heavy brows over his blue eyes were very dark and his lashes, considering the square masculine lines of his face, were ridiculously long, curling up like any glamour girl's, and giving a look of bright innocence to his face. His mouth was large and his chin was thrust out sulkily, adding to the pugnacious effect of his thick shoulders. His silence and immobility seemed to disturb his hostess not one whit, but Vicky caught Julian occasionally studying this silent guest with a thoughtful look. After a while, Vicky noticed, he took to repeating whatever he had said to the others in a louder voice in the direction of the silent Mr. Saunders, who continued to reward this graciousness with a glazed, hopeless eye.

"I was just telling Mr. Shebus, " Julian bent toward the backward guest and raised his voice, "that I have Andy Callingham covering Finland for me."

"Andy Callingham, think of it!" Amanda turned brightly to Saunders. "Isn't that wonderful for Julian to get Callingham himself?"

Mr. Saunders rose at this and walked gravely across the room and grasped Mr. Evans' hand in congratulation. He proceeded then to Amanda and grasped her hand. Without speaking he resumed his seat in the corner and looked at the wall. The guests looked at him uneasily.

Vicky ventured to show interest.

"I thought Andrew Callingham *had* to go to all the wars," she said in a voice she had never heard herself have before, though it may have become a little rusty from disuse this evening. "I mean—what I mean is—I thought he had to be seen at all the wars." As the guests turned courteous uncomprehending faces toward her she floundered on, "I mean the way Peggy Joyce has to be seen at all the—er—the night clubs."

In the silence following this inadvertent reflection on a public hero Vicky seized her drink wildly and gulped it, and Mr. Saunders rose, walked over and shook her limp hand. Why, he's tight, of course, thought Vicky in surprise, he's as tight as a mink. This time he carefully parted his tails and took the seat beside her on the sofa. It was embarrassing because now it was quite clear to every one that here were two interlopers in the club. Mr. Saunders, Vicky thought, is nobody, but nobody. It made her feel a little better, even though Amanda, she was sure, was not actively displeased with her, and Julian had dismissed both of the nobodies by showing the book of his collected editorials to the banker Shebus and the visiting baronet.

"The foreword, you see, is by Callingham himself," he explained. "See here—'the greatest editor of our time, Julian Evans'—I care more about that little remark from Callingham than I do about any compliment I've ever had. A great man himself, Callingham."

"I missed him in London," Amanda said. "Of course we saw all the same things, the same people—Churchill, Beaverbrook, de Gaulle."

Julian laughed patronizingly. There were few advantages that Amanda would grant him, but Callingham was his own, not hers.

"I doubt very much, my dear, if even you could command the interviews Andrew Callingham could," he said tenderly. "After all, he's been an international idol for years—he could wangle contacts that even I couldn't possibly arrange for you."

Amanda's frown of irritation deepened.

"I believe my last book sold about twice as much as the last Callingham book," she said quietly.

Mr. Saunders again rose and was about to congratulate her but Vicky hastily pulled him back by the coattails. As this gesture was even more strange than Mr. Saunders' motion, Vicky blushed and shrank back.

Amanda laughed, without amusement.

"I'm afraid we all frighten Miss Haven," she said. "Victoria is from Ohio, you know."

Mr. Saunders leaned forward with intense interest.

"Then of course you knew Churchill," he said.

Vicky shook her head, inarticulate.

"De Gaulle? Is de Gaulle the darling he seems really, Miss Haven?" pursued Mr. Saunders eagerly. "And you must have some firsthand stories about Eden."

"Ken, please," Amanda cried out, definitely angry.

Mr. Saunders sank back.

"Confidential, I suppose," he murmured. Vicky moved away from him a few inches. That would be her luck, to be snuggling in a sofa corner with the man who was insulting the rest of the party. That was the way Tom Turner used to be. That was the way she always ended up—with the outcasts, apologizing for them the next day, explaining that they were really too intelligent for their own good. At least she hadn't brought him there. Amanda couldn't hold that against her anyway. And when she left it would be clear enough that they did not come boxed together like Amos and Andy, or the Dead End Kids. Mr. Saunders' brief exhibition had brought about a lull in the conversation, and while Julian was rather awkwardly holding his book, waiting to revive interest in it, the banker and his Mexican wife rose to go. The alacrity with which host and hostess leaped to the adieux was indication that eleven o'clock was departure time at the Evanses, and others straggled to the door.

"Too bad we had no chance to hear the Signora sing," said Julian. "We do so much talk here we forget we have musical guests."

"Her gaucho song would have interested you, I think," said the banker, quite as anxious to exhibit his exotic wife's talents as Evans was to set off his own.

"I hope it's as interesting as her moustache," Mr. Saunders said pleasantly to Vicky in an alarmingly loud whisper. Vicky looked beseechingly toward Amanda but that young woman was at the door with her other guests, an example to all in how to handle a difficult situation. Vicky got up to go, since that seemed to be expected. She had had chance for no more than a few words with Amanda, and after tonight's demonstration of her inadequacy she was certain there would be little chance of reviving the old friendship. Amanda was loaning her her studio and securing her a job, but there seemed no warmth in the kindness, rather just a sense of duty. Well, sighed Vicky, she would have to find her circle elsewhere, wondrous as it would have been to bask in this golden light. Amanda had not even asked her how she liked her place, and outside of a note explaining the place and her further appointment with a Mr. Peabody, Vicky was afraid she was to be left quite on her own.

"Everything all right at your place, Vicky?" Amanda now remembered to ask lightly, as the wraps were brought. "Call the superintendent if anything's wrong."

"Will Mr. Saunders see that she gets home?" Julian asked.

Mr. Saunders was at the moment frankly helping himself to a Scotch and soda from the table.

"Oh, I'll get there all right," Vicky said quickly.

"Of course she can," Amanda said. "Why don't you take her to the street, Julian, and get a cab?"

"I thought—" hesitated Julian with a puzzled look toward the one remaining guest, Saunders, who was now dreamily gazing at the lady ancestor above the fireplace. The look seemed to rouse him for he said, "You know in my family we have mooseheads over the fireplace. Real ones, I mean, not just the picture."

No one said anything. Julian rang for the elevator and Amanda looked at her beautiful hands. Saunders turned and looked at her, put his glass down, and came out to them.

"I'll tell you all about it on the way home, Miss Haven," he said. "Good night, Amanda. Good night, Evans, old snort."

Vicky was still murmuring confused thank-yous and good-byes as the door closed on Julian and Amanda standing there in silence. She could not understand why Saunders had fastened on her as a fellow rebel, and she could not understand why, if Amanda had asked him on her account, she seemed so displeased when they left together. She could not understand, too, why she was so glad to have his protection, especially since she had to hold his arm going down the street to keep him from swaying, if that's what you call protection. In the cab he lapsed into silent gloom once again.

"You shouldn't have called him snort," Vicky finally ventured. "You really shouldn't have done that."

Mr. Saunders looked pained.

"I rather thought it would please him," he said. "Do you think I should go back and explain?"

"No, no, no," Vicky said. In front of the florist shop on Lexington the cab stopped and Vicky said, "Good night." Saunders suddenly leaped out of the car and stared at the shop and the twin windows just above where Vicky was to live.

"So this is it," he said slowly, still staring upward. "So this is it."

He was still staring up at her windows when she went inside.

2

THERE WAS A Mr. Peabody in the Peabody Company and this was only one of many things to distinguish it from other Peabody Companies. The Mr. Peabody in this case—Otto Erasmus Peabody— even had a small, a very small percentage in the business, but otherwise was the patient moderator and representative of a temperamental board of directors whose success in other fields led them to consider themselves experts in managing a smart monthly magazine. As Mr. Peabody, in addition to his tiny percentage, drew a good salary from the company, he was tolerant with his board's eccentricities, faithfully carrying out whim after whim and refraining from comment when this week's loss exceeded last week's loss. When the magazine gained subscribers it lost the most money, according to a rule of publishing economics too complex to discuss here, yet it was constantly launching expensive campaigns for this very purpose. Mr. Peabody had grown not only gray but absolutely yellow (this was as to face) in the work of cooking up such circulation ideas. After fifteen years of listening to his directors shout and scream at each other his own voice had dropped permanently to a weary whisper, which, in its own way, was quite effective in calming the shredded nerves.

He was a tired fat man with a motherly face and a rather mother hubbard figure, that is, it was unmarked by waistline, and neck and knees had conspired to merge in a loose bundle that was shapeless without being actually gross. Other men— take his contemporary and friend Julian Evans, for instance, contrived to retain their masculine charm through their forties, even fifties and sixties, but it was difficult to believe that Mr. Peabody had ever, even twenty years ago, appealed to any woman as anything but a sympathetic uncle. Yet he had a family which lived quite fashionably somewhere in Greenwich and in his cups, which was rare, he was as able as anybody else to lure some pretty thing to his anonymous lap. He had a way of combing his long black hair over his pate to conceal his baldness, which was the only thing that worried him about his appearance. The loose jowls, and anxious furrows in his yellow brow and cheek, the weary eye pouches, the uncomfortable upper dental plates, even the surprisingly red hair that sprouted gaily from his ears, were no concern at all. On the whole it was a round friendly face, the gray eye as kind as it was shrewd, and if there was any bitterness in his soul after all these years of preserving his inner honesty in a wicked world, such a thing had left no record in his appearance.

Mr. Peabody was the first person, and for some time was the only person, with whom Vicky Haven felt at home in New York. The outer reception room where she had waited for him had been terrifyingly impressive, and the young women employees who dashed in and out, a few with their dogs on leash, all exchanging elegant remarks in a diction so full of mystifying gargles and squeals that Vicky knew it must come from the best finishing schools. She began to wonder uneasily what would be expected of her and how she could ever compete with these poised beautiful young creatures, none of whom, she was sure, had ever had a moment's doubt of her place in the world. You wouldn't catch any of these competent young things permitting another woman to take away their Tom Turner or any other man. Vicky couldn't picture them permitting even desk space to a stranger. She was sure Mr. Peabody would be an exquisitely groomed man of fashion, a cross between Cary Grant and Roland Young, and with neither type had she ever been a pet.

Mr. Peabody therefore, smiling at her from his unpretentious personal office, was a great relief, and to Mr. Peabody, used to demands from his directors for distribution of favors in unworthy directions, Vicky was a relief. They sat beaming at each other across the desk without saying anything for a full minute and then Mr. Peabody remembered to welcome her, so he reached across to shake her warmly by the hand, repeating, "That's fine, that's fine, yes, that's just fine," until Vicky felt quite happy, without knowing what he meant at all.

"Not from New York?" he asked.

"Ohio," she said.

Mr. Peabody nodded as if he had know at once that brown eyes, sandy hair, and a tan sport suit could only come from Ohio, or that particular state's borderlines with Kentucky or Indiana. To be recognized at once as provincial was not her dream of dreams but Vicky was pleased now because Mr. Peabody seemed pleased. It might be, she reflected, that he too came from Ohio. This turned out not to be the case, and she was to discover later on that this was all the better, for there is something more annoying than pleasant in finding neighbors from back home chiseling in on your own exclusive New York. It mitigates your triumph in having conquered the great city and brings home the ungratifying truth that anybody can do it. Mr. Peabody was from Maine and the Peabody place near Bangor had been a showplace for three generations, housing Peabody senators, cabinet officials, university heads, and being an eternal inspiration to younger Peabodys that a penny saved is a penny earned, save the pennies and the dollars will take care of themselves. This bone-deep tradition was why our Mr. Peabody at fifty thousand a year, bought only one newspaper a day, no matter how curious he was to see what another paper had to say about a subject, and why he could not bring himself to spend more than a dollar for a tie, though the cost of sending a few of his office boys to business school or college never seemed to cause him a second's hesitation.

"What is my job?" Vicky asked, knowing now that of course she could do it, because Mr. Peabody looked at her as if she could.

"The magazine has started a real estate service," said Mr. Peabody, "and that's your work here. Julian tells me you did that before. You will visit country places and apartments that we advertise and have a shopper's guide sort of page."

It sounded simple enough. The only thing that worried Vicky was the thought of those other girls brushing past her in the reception room.

"Do I bring my dog to work?" she asked.

Mr. Peabody chuckled.

"That's our Social Register front," he explained. "We try to staff the fringe of the magazine with Junior League girls—the better names in society from a publicity point of view. Pretty, too, because we use them in photograph releases. Jockeys up our advertising value for luxury stuff."

Across the glass-paned wall to the next office Vicky saw two flawless coiffures of the "up-do" type, nothing that could be contrived in one's own bathroom mirror on the way to work. The two girls were gesturing—Mr. Peabody was happily sound protected in his office—over what seemed at first a rose on a ribbon as they passed it back and forth, but then as they each tried it on over the two wonderful heads became a hat. Peabody's eye followed Vicky's.

"That's what I'm scared of," Vicky confessed. "Girls like that. They make me feel as if I had hay in my hair."

"I've worked in this business for twenty years," said Mr. Peabody. "And I still have hay in my hair. It's a business asset, Miss Haven."

"I'd still rather have false eyelashes," said Vicky.

"You will," sighed Mr. Peabody. He had been doodling with a red crayon on the pile of papers on his desk, and now saw that he had defaced a newly typed report with the same hourglass ladies' figures that had marked margins of his Third Reader. He hastily threw down the pencil and looked sternly into the next room.

"That's one of the Elroy girls, the tall one," he said. "She does something on the fashion end. The other is one of the Trays, the Newport Trays."

"I suppose business experience never can quite make up for your picture in the Sunday rotogravure," Vicky said ruefully.

"Now, now," soothed Mr. Peabody. "It wasn't your experience, it was Julian Evans, that got you this job. Just as bad as social background, you know. Same thing."

He telephoned for a Miss Myers to show her to her office. More girls appeared in the glass office next door, laughing, trying on the silly bonnet, all of them testifying to three hours a day spent on their hair, unless the blue-haired one took another hour on hers. Like some girls' school, Vicky thought, some snobbish up-the-Hudson school, instead of like a business office. The walnut paneling cut them off below the shoulders and the sound-proofing cut off their voices, so she had a curious impression of being in a Buck Rogers strip, invisible herself, and gazing into another planet.

"Don't worry about those girls," Mr. Peabody admonished. "They are our front, but then we have a basic staff of professionals. The only thing is that they all get so they talk and act like this. It's hard to tell the difference unless you know the names."

"Another thing," he added as he padded down the narrow hall—why, Vicky thought, he wears high laced black shoes like some old lady with varicosities—"the professionals get paid, to make up for the lack of family. They won't bother you much, really, those girls. I hope you don't try to be like them, though," he gave a long sigh, "but I suppose you will. It won't be long."

They came to the main hall and here were the two signs Vicky was to remember, one with the arrow pointing left was marked

EDITORIAL: FASHIONS: EXECUTIVE: and the one to the right was marked "Business." Even in the brief moment necessary for Mr. Peabody to greet a man coming out of the elevator Vicky could see that one was the front door and Business was the Delivery entrance. Her office was the Delivery Entrance. Glamour belonged in the other end.

Nevertheless the young woman seated in the little two-desk office when they reached it was gotten up very much like the girls Vicky had seen next to the Peabody office. She was, if anything, even more lacquered. Her black glossy hair was brushed up to an impeccable topknot of curls, her eyebrows were thin penciled arcs of perpetual surprise, her mouth was wide and not too noticeably rebuilt, while her skin was a masterpiece of beige wax that looked more like a glossy magazine cover than human skin. She wore a severe, elegant green tweed dress with a row of wooden charms around the neck, and all that could be said of her legs, stretched out in sandaled "wedgies," was that at least they were freely exposed.

She acknowledged Mr. Peabody's introduction with a cool measuring eye. Miss Haven and Miss Finkelstein were to work together on real estate. Miss Finkelstein had been with the company twelve years. Miss Finkelstein knew the ropes. Miss Finkelstein could show the ropes to Miss Haven, who was an expert real estate woman previously employed by Julian Evans in an out-of-town advisory capacity. It was Miss Finkelstein's steely reception of her new coworker that must have prompted Mr. Peabody to throw out the magic Evans name, for she visibly softened at it and, except for a patronizingly cultivated accent, cultivated, like the other girls to the point of intranslatableness, was quite pleasant in explaining the files, and the general system. She clearly enjoyed pressing buttons for typists, file clerks, and other underlings, by way of impressing the newcomer with the importance of her office. Vicky watched her busy activities quite humbly, hoping that Miss Finkelstein would not be too severe a chief.

"I adore Amanda Keeler Evans' work," said Miss Finkelstein, pausing from her exhibition of efficiency to do a little work on her amazingly long red nails. "Do you know her personally?"

"Oh, yes," said Vicky and explained the relationship. It was as if she had said she knew Windsor himself, for Miss F. leaned on her desk with her long enameled face cupped in her two hands, charm bracelets silenced for a moment, in enthralled attention.

"She must be an absolute Movvel," said Miss F. "Absolutely too heavenly. How does she wear her hair now? Up?"

"Up," said Vicky. "No, down."

"I can weah mine down, you know," said Miss Finkelstein. "I must say I'm rahthah surprised that Amanda Keeler does. Oh deah, I mustn't forget that beastly dinnah at the Plaza! These frightful press agents. As if anyone wanted to meet Bette Davis."

Vicky was uncomfortably aware of Miss Finkelstein's eagle eyes putting price tags on her suit, her hair, her shoes, and was relieved when a dolorous, undersized office boy appeared with a batch of mail.

"We use George at this end mostly," Miss Finkelstein said, "I don't know why they're giving us Irving today. Please, Irving, tell Mr. Fiske we must have George back. Really. I mean. Really."

Irving stood gaping at Vicky.

"She taking Miss Moiphy's place?" he inquired.

"Yes, she is," snapped Miss Finkelstein.

"I thought you was gonna be permoted to Miss Moiphy's place," said Irving. "I didn't know you was gettin' a new boss. You said next you was gonna be boss."

It was the first Vicky had heard that Miss Finkelstein, far from being her chief, was to be her secretary. It was frightening news for her.

"Nevah mind what I said, boy," said Miss Finkelstein. "Please."

"I'm your brudder, ain't I?" inquired Irving. "I should tink if you stay here all dis time you'd get a break instead of always getting somebody shoved in over you."

"Irving, please!" remonstrated Miss Finkelstein, only she gave it a very agreeable "Uvving" sound. "Oh, yes, tell Mummy I won't be home for dinnah. I'm dashing up to the Plaza for some horrible affaiah."

"Mama'll be sore," said Irving. "She's made meatloaf. When'll you get in?"

"Latish," said Miss Finkelstein, patting her perfect mouth with her flawless hand.

"How late?"

"Elevenish," yawned Miss Finkelstein. "Twelvish. Maybe oneish."

"Don't forget ya gotta three-dollar taxi bill all the way home from the Plaza," Irving said severely. "Mama's waitin' for ya to give her last week's dough anyway."

"Don't be vomitish, Irving!" Miss Finkelstein said coldly. "IF you don't mind."

"AHH!" Irving cried out in helpless irritation. "Ahhh!"

He ran out of the office tearing his hair. Vicky, somewhat baffled by the little scene, stole a look at Miss Finkelstein to see if she was at all perturbed, but her secretary was calmly dialing the telephone.

"I must call Mummy," she murmured. "I hope you don't mind my having this desk. It was Miss Murphy's but really, I think the other is quite as good. If you don't mind sitting by the door."

Vicky didn't mind. She was too astonished by her new work to mind anything. She realized now that Miss Finkelstein, in her efforts to model herself after the debutante members of the office, had gone a little overboard on some things but it might all even up someday.

"Imagine Amanda Keeler still wearing her hair down," mused Miss Finkelstein, gracefully hanging over the telephone, awaiting her number. "I must tell Mummy. Irving is horrible, but Mummy is rather an old deah, you know. A complete peasant, you know. You wouldn't believe!"

Vicky found her head nodding dumbly. She rather wished she had Ethel Carey here now to tell her what to do next.

5

*A*MANDA'S FURNISHED "STUDIO" in which Vicky was free to live from 5 P.M. to 11 A.M., so Amanda stated, was in the Murray Hill section just off Park. Vicky was delighted with it and pried out of the janitor the discouraging news that it was $135 a month. This meant that she must dismiss the idea of having anything of the same sort on her own salary. It was as full of balconies, staircases, and doors as a regular house, so that it was surprising to find it technically a one-room apartment. There was the foyer with its four doors that might lead to four other chambers but in reality led only to a vast closet, service entrance, kitchen, and bath-dressing room. An iron railing separated the foyer from the studio which was four steps down and in this "dropped living room" were more doors leading to cedar closets, linen closets, wood closets, and here were French doors leading to a small balcony of no earthly good except to keep the happy tenant from falling out of her room. The furniture was simple, the original owner having left only the barest living necessities, and there was little to indicate Amanda's creative work here beyond typewriter supplies, a few reference books and a few toilet trifles in the dressing room. Vicky was careful to conceal as much of her own personal effects as possible, since evidence of a foreign presence might disturb Amanda's working moods. It was really Amanda's after all, and she must try not to feel too much at home.

"The place is too heavenly for words," she wrote Ethel Carey. "New York is wonderful, the Peabody Company is marvelous, Amanda has been good to me, and I am so *happy* to be away from Lakeville."

She found it wise to include in her glowing report a sly insinuation that there was a Mr. Kenneth Saunders who seemed frightfully interested in her, so that Ethel would let it be known in Lakeville that Vicky had a New York beau already. Having posted the good news Vicky then cried some more over Lakeville and Tom Turner, sniffled some over her mistakes at the Peabody office and the misfortune of having a telephone that evidently had no bell. It is one thing to forget the old love in the triumph of new fortunes, but it is another matter indeed to try forgetting him wandering by yourself around a great strange city, neglected by the new world so that the happy lost past is inevitably thrust on your thoughts. At least in Lakeville people said hello.

On her solitary evening ventures to the Newsreel or to Radio City to see Melvyn Douglas or Cary Grant, her favorites, or bus-riding to the Cloisters on a Sunday, window shopping at twilight up and down Lexington or Madison, Vicky puzzled constantly over what she had done at Amanda's dinner party to annoy her sponsor. She must have done something wrong, since Amanda never called her. The fact that Amanda had left theatre tickets twice with a brief note was no comfort, for there was an implication in the gift that Vicky could expect no personal contact with the donor. Once Vicky had taken Miss Finkelstein to see "The

Male Animal" but the overbearing airs of that competent young woman luxuriating in an orchestra seat had ruined the evening for Vicky. With Amanda's next tickets Vicky had gone alone, certain that in New York going alone to a theatre was next thing to going on the streets. Her agonized Alice Adams efforts to act as if she were reserving the other seat for a most distinguished but delayed escort, spoiled that evening too for her.

She saw Ken Saunders in the Peabody building one rainy noon, but she was wearing rubbers and a fearful raincoat and hat that looked as if she anticipated a tidal wave, an ensemble in fact that had been suitable enough for a Lakeville storm but was a drab contrast to the smart, filmy inadequacies worn by the Peabody glamour girls as they dashed from taxi to marquee and marquee to taxi. Vicky had been conscious of her error as soon as she saw Miss Finkelstein's eye on her that morning and prayed for the clouds to burst and torrents to come just so her hurricane precautions might be justified. But noon had reduced the shower to the merest drizzle and Vicky was trying to scuttle, invisibly, out of the building when Ken Saunders yelled at her, "Hiya, neighbor, going fishing?"

"No," said Vicky sourly, "I'm off for the Embassy Ball."

He was coming out of the drugstore on the street floor and in his battered hat and trench coat did not look elegant enough to be so sarcastic, Vicky thought, but then with men appearances don't matter. Vicky saw he was about to catch up with her and in a wave of wounded pride ran out the door with a furtive farewell nod to him. Then she dashed madly back to her apartment to change into something that would look pretty, at least until the first drop of rain should ruin it. But once prepared, naturally, she did not encounter Saunders again, though she looked in the drugstore hopefully on her return. Opportunity, clearly, never knocks at the right moment.

It was the same thing with Amanda. Twice she got up courage to call Amanda to thank her for tickets but both times Miss

Bemel took the message because the brilliant girl was in conference. Expecting rebuffs as she did, Vicky was not at all surprised.
"In conference," "at dinner," "in her bath," oh certainly, that was
what the great always said to the mob.

Losing a lover does to a woman what losing a job does to a man;
all confidence in self vanishes. There is the overwhelming conviction that you alone are singled out as unfit for the simplest privileges of life, and the days are filled with tiny testimony to this—the
salesgirl's rudeness, the invitation denied, the luncheon Special
crossed out when you arrive. Everything happens to you. So it was
that Vicky was in no frame of mind to storm past her friend's ne-
glect with sunny insouciance. Two "in conferences" from Amanda
and she gave up all hope of ever seeing her friend again. When she
ran into Amanda by accident one day in Saks Fifth Avenue she
was half-impelled to slink into a corner, thus saving herself the
embarrassment of being cut. But Amanda did rescue her this time
so that once again Vicky became her admiring slave.

It was a Red Letter day for Vicky in many ways. For one thing
it was the day she had decided to Do Something about
Everything. Instead of squirming under Miss Finkelstein's critical eye every day and creeping along back halls to avoid contrast
with the glamorous editorial staff, she would Do Something. She
would plunge into glamour herself, and so rebuild her faltering
ego. She would get a hat as much like Miss Elroy's as was decent,
a coat like Miss Gray's with large pearl buttons and accessories
similar to the dashing items affected by the Peabody "front" staff.
There was no use in seeking an original style for herself because
what she wanted right now was to look exactly like everybody
else, so that no one would look at her twice. That was what a
crippled vanity did to you—a man following you made you certain he merely wanted to say, "Pardon me, lady, your slip is showing," and his glance at your legs only convinced you that your
new stocking had sprung a run. Yes, Vicky intended to use her

first month's paycheck to begin the new Vicky, the New York Vicky Haven. She was going to do something perfectly wonderful about her hair, too. It was sandy and she had been for many years perfectly pleased with it, until she saw what breathtaking things the "front" girls did to their hair—bars of dyed gold in brown hair, blue-gray tuft over the left temple, scrolls of curls as carefully designed as a permanent work of art . . . yes, she too would have her hair made to look suitably artificial. When Ethel Carey arrived next month from Lakeville Vicky was determined to show her how marvelously New York had changed her. She would like to have some new friends to show off, too, but in New York that appeared to take time.

In the elevator at Saks, when Vicky caught a glimpse of her benefactor, Amanda Evans did not really look so superior to any other shopper. She wore no diadem and the valuable body appeared to be quite unguarded. Here was a simple everyday young woman going about her simple errand of buying a few dozen boxes of hose or matching a lost glove. Her black felt tailored hat was pulled over her blonde hair in rather collegiate style, and her simple sport suit was unadorned by any of her furs. In fact, Amanda's costume was so startlingly simple as to seem almost gaudy, and the other ladies in the elevator, furred and feathered as they were, shrank back from this lesson in elegance. Vicky, too, shrank back, but Amanda caught sight of her and snatched her arm with unexpected warmth.

"I'm having a hair trim," stated Amanda, "but let's have some tea afterward. I want to hear all about you. Where will you be?"

"Millinery," said Vicky, beaming under Amanda's sudden friendliness.

"Do get something nice," said Amanda. "Wait, I'll go along."

Flattered as she was at Amanda's interest, Vicky was uncertain whether she wanted this witness to her intended economies. She foresaw what would happen and what did happen—with

Amanda nearby she dared not ask prices but must consider only preferences. Amanda was as fussy and absorbed in the proper selection of Vicky's hat as even Ethel Carey would have been, and this sudden interest so flattered and confused Vicky that she forgot all about Miss Elroy's hat and decided on the only one that the saleslady and Amanda agreed was a "must." It was a tall black business with a snood effect and demanded an entirely new wardrobe to go with it. Dazed, Vicky began counting out the necessary twenty-seven dollars until she felt Amanda's hand closing over hers.

"My dear, you're not paying cash!" The incredulity in Amanda's voice had such a touch of horror in it that Vicky hastily pushed her money back in the bag.

"You never get any service paying cash, darling," Amanda, now amused at Vicky's consternation, explained. "I'll have Bemel arrange for your charge accounts around town and meantime charge things to me. Cash is simply money thrown away, so do put it back. I'll meet you in Suits when I get through. Tell Miss Blandet to fix you up."

Miss Blandet "fixed" Vicky up with a hundred-dollar suit and a twenty-dollar blouse but these were quite free as they were charged to Amanda, subject to changing to Vicky's account later. A feeling of helplessness handicapped Vicky's choice of purchases and she feared that between Amanda and Miss Blandet she would be mesmerized into buying out the whole store. When Amanda came back Vicky was sitting down trying to figure out how much she had spent and how long it would take her to pay it. She hadn't gotten one thing she wanted, just the things Amanda and Miss Blandet wanted. It was probably much better for her but it rather spoiled the fun. She was a little silent as she and Amanda waited for the elevator. Then she felt someone's hand on her arm and saw none other than Miss Elroy from the front office in the very hat she had coveted, smiling happily at her.

"My dear, how wonderful running into you here!" cried Miss Elroy radiantly, who had up to this time never spoken to Vicky beyond the exigencies of office demands. "I do want you to meet Mother. Mother—"

An elderly well-groomed woman was thrust between Miss Elroy and Vicky, whose name, in spite of her interest in her, Miss Elroy had obviously forgotten. They shook hands, murmuring.

"Mother and I are quarreling over every stitch of my trousseau," laughed Miss Elroy gaily, and then Vicky saw that both Miss Elroy and her mother were staring fixedly at Amanda. She hurriedly introduced them and was disconcerted to find both Elroys fairly pouncing on Amanda's reluctant hand. Clearly, it had been for the sake of this introduction the young Miss Elroy had been so happy to see Vicky.

"You know the Carsons, the Beverly Carsons," Miss Elroy cried to Amanda. "They're simply mad, but mad, about you!"

"Oh, do you know Bev and Madge?" Amanda said.

Vicky, at first pleased at having been able to introduce anyone, especially someone from the "front" office, to Amanda, realized that in New York introductions were like cash, and were not to be thrown about but used only when absolutely necessary. Amanda was cool and the cooler she became the more pressing the Elroys became. Wouldn't Amanda and Vicky join them for a spot of tea this minute—shopping was so exhausting? Or perhaps they would drop around the corner to the Elroys' apartment a little later. Vicky dumbly accepted. Amanda said it would be terribly nice but made no promises.

"We don't know Bev and Madge so well," said Miss Elroy, "but we know cousins of theirs very, *very* intimately. The Crosley Carsons."

"We've know the Crosley Carsons for years," Mrs. Elroy said benignly to Vicky who murmured that they were fortunate indeed.

By the time they had reached the street floor Vicky was aware that the prized nod from Miss Elroy was due completely to the Elroys' desire to meet Amanda Keeler Evans, either for her own or her husband's sake. It was astonishing to see what lengths these well-bred ladies were willing to go in order to clinch some future contact. Vicky found their anxiety contagious and tried to ease their feelings by babbling away to Amanda how effective was the full page color ad of Miss Nancy Elroy smoking a Felicity cigarette before the portrait of her old grandmother. Both Elroys brushed this faltering support aside, for to tell the truth they loved the feeling that they were meeting and conquering wonderfully superior people. It gave them a feeling of accomplishment and progress to wear down snubbing, and they felt there was something secretly the matter with anyone who did not make use of his or her position to be arrogant. The merest Astor had only to step on them firmly to utterly enslave them, challenging them to further humble gestures. As this type of social masochism was unknown to Vicky, she thought Amanda's coolness was wounding the Elroys instead of tantalizing them.

"If Mrs. Evans can't come this afternoon, at least you will, won't you, Vicky?" begged Miss Elroy, having apparently caught at least the first name from Amanda. "Do come over around five, Vicky. We have so little chance to get acquainted at our sweatshop."

The friendly gesture touched Vicky enormously, for she fully expected Amanda's refusal to cancel her own invitation. Of course she would come. This would be something to tell Ethel Carey, she thought happily, and she would certainly illustrate the letter with one of the printed pictures of Nancy Elroy to further impress Lakeville. She had a little matter to attend to on her job first, but she would surely be there at five. Having beamingly parted with the Elroys, Vicky waited with a defensive air for Amanda's comment on them. She was prepared for Amanda to make some subtly sardonic reference to the Elroys' eager play for her, but Amanda said nothing. They paused at the glove counter for some purchases and still Amanda kept a discreet silence about the Elroys.

"Isn't she attractive?" Vicky finally murmured.

"Very," said Amanda, and it was another lesson for Vicky in how certain women preserve their own importance. Amanda's silence was more damning than a contemptuous remark, for it implied that the people were of so little importance that they were unworthy of discussion. Vicky, in this case, knew that the Elroys were at least socially, if not financially, better placed than Amanda, but she was affected by Amanda's dismissal of them anyway. Amanda believed in honoring no rival by her envy, nor decorating any other woman by a witty jibe. She determinedly fought off any instinctive outbursts of malice, being aware that they often gave the object unexpected importance, for persons may build into public monuments merely by the stones hurled at them.

Vicky, at first prepared to defend the Elroys from Amanda's scorn, missed it when it was not forthcoming as a simple gesture of feminine equality. She was increasingly confused by Amanda; further there was Amanda's unexpected friendliness today, her warm interest in her younger friend's clothes, and the next moment she was making it clear that their worlds were far apart. No further words at all about meeting again. Not even an inquiry about the apartment which never bore any trace of Amanda's work, though cigarette butts, a small cellar of sherry and Scotch, and a smart housecoat, testified that she dropped in occasionally at least.

"Four-ten!" Amanda now exclaimed, glancing at her watch. "I should have been home at four. Bemel will be on her ear!"

Vicky thanked her for her help in shopping.

Amanda shrugged.

"After all, darling, somebody has to help you, you must know that," she observed unflatteringly. "Remember me to Ethel when you write."

She nipped into a taxicab, leaving Vicky in her usual state of wondering what wrong thing she had done to change the mood from warm friendship to the chilly stay-in-your-place parting atmosphere. The Elroys had helped destroy that first fine rapport, that was plain enough, but there must have been something else.

"I probably acted too friendly with the Elroys," Vicky decided. "I shouldn't burble over people that she is trying to snub. That's it."

Nevertheless she was excited at the thought of seeing the home and background of one of the "front" office girls, even if her obvious pleasure did annoy Amanda. She spent the next three-quarters of an hour in hastening through the work she had sacrificed for shopping. This was the investigation of a house for sale on East Forty-ninth Street for her page in Peabody's. She made her notes briskly and jotted down her opening paragraph. "The death last month of Mrs. Humphry Zoom iv, in Palm Beach, has resulted in the dismantling of the fine old Zoom mansion on East Forty-ninth Street. Except for the drawing room walls, the furnace, and the upstairs floors, the house is in excellent shape for a future owner. Either for residential purposes in its present form or remodeled into smaller apartments for modern demands, the Zoom property offers a fair opportunity, etc., etc., etc."

This brilliant item would be illustrated by a picture of the house itself, and with the connivance of the advertising and glamour departments, there would probably be a photograph of one of the elegant older girls examining the house's garden and wearing a costume and holding a pedigreed pup, both advertised elsewhere in the magazine. Having disposed of this little duty, Vicky powdered her nose and hastened with great anticipation over to the Elroys' address.

At last, she thought complacently, she was getting a toehold on the city.

2

THE ELROYS lived at the Marguery in a spacious suite that was yet not spacious enough to keep the little family from getting frightfully on each other's nerves. Papa—Beaver Chauncey Elroy that was—had been dead some time, so it was a household of women. Mrs. Elroy always allowed people to believe it was the crash of '29 that broke her husband down, but it had really been his liver, an organ the late Mr. Elroy had kept dancing from the very moment he had disgraced himself at his own wedding reception. The Elroys were all famed as gourmets and Beaver was said to have the most fastidious palate in the family, taste buds so exquisitely developed as to recognize the most mysterious of herbs in the most complicated of sauces. There was a legend that once Beaver had confounded the very Sabatini himself, in London, when he leapt to his feet in the middle of the Savoy's most brilliant banquet and cried out the proportions of basil over dill—("basted with a Swiss *fendant*," he had declared)—in a certain roast of veal. There were less reverent tales, too, concerning the time he had gone into Cavanagh's kitchen and selected with lordly arrogance the steaks for his party. "How will you have them, Mr. Elroy?" respectfully asked the chef. "Raw," declared the epicure imperiously, and at once astounded the kitchen by proceeding to devour all the cuts then and there. The fact was that on his expeditions into gourmetism Mr. Elroy basted his stomach with such a solid coating of any old whiskey that a thoughtfully ordered dinner with cautiously plotted wines, might just as well have been pork chops and Doctor Pepper, since the diner was already stupefied. Furthermore the career of gourmet cost a fortune and Beaver was one Elroy who had started piling up debts almost the instant his voice had started changing. It was this snarling pack of debts which speeded

Beaver into the first World War and unquestionably caused him to become quite a military hero. He distinguished himself at Belleau Wood, and in Château-Thierry he went over the top as if he were chased by six process servers.

Mrs. Elroy had spent a good part of their married days voicing just such crass derogation of his character that it must have been quite a relief to escape her cultivated voice by rolling into a soundproof grave. Mrs. Elroy had been a Chivers from Columbus and felt that Park Avenue offered nothing that could not be bettered by the exclusive social life of her native city. Nancy and her young sister Tuffy had had the Chivers' superiority so drilled into them from infancy that they had actually come to believe in it, and in the Social Register put down their homes as New York, Palm Beach, and Columbus. They were convinced that although the Elroys were regarded as top-drawer in New York they would never have made the Chivers' set in Columbus, a little conceit that the Elroys politely ignored. When Mrs. Elroy heard of her daughters being in Harlem or going about with dubious persons she would gasp, "It's not that I mind myself, but supposing someone from Columbus had seen you!" It was a source of regret to the gentlewoman that both her daughters merely came out at an Assembly dance instead of in the old Chivers' home near Columbus. She only forgave Nancy's connection with Peabody's because nowadays all the League girls were doing odd things, and competed with each other by nightclub singing, screen tests, and gown shops instead of keeping within the honorable limits of social functions. They even did this in Columbus nowadays, so it must be all right, and certainly it gave Nancy a great deal of pleasant publicity, without the expense of lavish entertaining. The pity was that this publicity had gone so much to Nancy's head that she had allowed several promising young men to go their way and was finally obliged to settle on something less than top drawer. He was not bad considering the times. He worked in an architect's office, there was money and a polo tradition somewhere in the family, and he was second cousin of somebody who was somebody in Canada. Harry Jones wasn't much of a name in itself, but when you put Cosgrove in the middle and a Roman IV at the end you had something that would look presentable enough on a wedding invitation. Nancy didn't mind him very much; he was taller than she was for dancing, which was nice, and his ears were laid neatly to his head, a point on which Mrs. Elroy was extremely insistent. As Nancy had been out ten seasons and had expected too much of her good looks, the Harry Jones offer seemed almost a last chance, especially since Tuffy was about to come out and was going to be a problem. At least with her plainness and ill health it was going to take a lot of money to put Tuffy over, both Nancy and her mother felt. Uncle Rockman Elroy, who was paying for the launching of Tuffy, was of the opinion that Tuffy would sweep the younger set off its feet by differing so conspicuously from the type. So far he was wrong but fond of Tuffy, so he paid willingly.

Uncle Rockman, a bachelor of fifty, a scholar of some note and a thoroughly unworldly man to all appearance, had offered his home to his brother's widow and daughters, and then had had the admirable taste to move out himself, maintaining only a nominal residence in the apartment, a maid's room in fact. He lived at the Gotham Hotel with the privacy and comfort that his habits required and popped in to his "home" with his brother's family as little as was required. He paid their expenses and unless some designing woman got her clutches on him first, was expected to leave his money to his sister-in-law and nieces, a prospect that added to his happiness since it gained him their love and respect. Mrs. Elroy was constantly calling him up to augment her authority with the girls, or writing him messages which he ignored as often as possible. ("Dear Rockman: I do wish you'd give Tuffy a talk. She insists on using her birthday money to take flying lessons instead of making herself look decent with a mink jacket Nancy and I ordered for her—")

Mrs. Elroy was still a handsome woman with a girlish figure and a well-chiseled face, features arranged in an expression of indefatigable sweetness and gentility. Nancy looked like her mother, only of course with a youthful sheen and radiance. She had her mother's beautiful clear blue eyes, widely spaced, the composed brow, the lovely mouth and corner dimples, all belying the nasty temper and selfishness that Mrs. Elroy felt were the rightful prerogatives of pretty young women. The breakfast table was a bedlam of feminine snarlings, rages, taunts with Tuffy, Nancy and their mother going at each other furiously, wrangling over their mentions in the newspaper columns or over abuses of charge accounts. Yet their public manners were charming, even to each other, and probably kept in all the finer condition by not being wasted in private.

The Elroys, mother and daughters, knew cousins of practically everybody ever mentioned in Cholly Knickerbocker's column. They had the curious conviction that *cousins* of somebodies sounded much more impressive than the somebodies themselves, just as vice president or brigadier general sounds finer than mere "president" or "general."

"No, we don't know the Smith-Gareys, but we know their cousins very well indeed," they would cry proudly as if this was much better. This crowing over cousins was so imbedded in the Elroy conversational routine that if they had a duke in their drawing room they must add to the triumph by boasting that he was more than that, he was a second cousin of a very dear friend of Mrs. Elroy's sister in Columbus. There must have been some secret logic in this preference for the inferior connection; perhaps the intimate life and soul secrets of the great person were more clearly revealed by the gossip than by actual presence. It was certainly true that Mrs. Elroy had a perfect storehouse of libelous material on most prominent figures, all the information coming from cousins or assistants to cousins. Mrs. Elroy was not a gossip herself and not even malicious, but she read so few books that she found innocent substitute in seeing the lives of the somebodies put together by little tidbits from out-of-the-way sources.

So it was that Vicky Haven was genuinely welcomed to the Elroy family bosom since the unexpected discovery that she was a minor connection of Mrs. Julian Evans.

"I had no idea she was anybody," Nancy exclaimed to her mother, "until I saw her shopping with Amanda Evans! She looks very nice of course, but I never *dreamed*!"

"She probably knows all there is to know about Amanda," meditated Mrs. Elroy, taking out the old knitting bag and assuming the fixed benevolent smile she wore for charity knitting. "Poor Margaret Evans! But then the first wife always has to pay! You remember what her sister told us at the British Relief the other day—she hasn't gone to a single function since the divorce!"

"Oh, Mama, she never did!" Nancy exclaimed impatiently. "The first Mrs. Evans was an old Boston fud from the beginning. The Peabodys knew her. They were utter fuds, Mr. Peabody said. What would she do if she did go out—she's fifty if she's a day."

"She could do the Lambeth Walk," suggested Tuffy.

"Shut up, Tuffy," said her mother pleasantly, "and when Nancy's friend comes take your beau in Uncle Rockman's study."

"Beau!" mocked Nancy. "Beau, my foot. He's only coming here to borrow Tuffy's banjo. Tuffy couldn't get a boy here unless she promised him a reward or something."

Tuffy lay on the love seat in a torn dirty white sweater and paint-smattered slacks, with her legs thrown over the end. Her scant mousy hair had already lost the reasonably neat if not glamorous swirl which Robert of the Plaza had put into it for her dinner dance two nights ago. Her complexion was sallow and bad and, what was worse, Tuffy didn't care. It kept her mother and sister conversationally occupied which permitted Tuffy to think about other matters such as boys, for she was definitely boystruck. She waggled her small dirty feet in their incredibly battered little brown sandals in complete comfort and thought dreamily of having a terrific love affair with some fiendishly sophisticated older man. This was a perfectly practicable dream since her one charm—and that was completely deniable—was that she was fifteen, and often that in itself is enough to entice an elderly beau.

"I can't take my callers into Uncle Rockman's study," Tuffy said calmly, "because Uncle Rockman is in there taking a nap. As for whether I can get a beau or not, Miss Nancy, I could get yours away if I cared to sleep with them."

"Tuffy!" gasped her mother. "Please!"

"Now you know what I mean, Mother," said Nancy. "We simply can't have her around when we have guests. She's simply impossible."

"I must have Rockman speak to her," said Mrs. Elroy.

Tuffy languidly collected her arms and legs and stood up, yawning.

"Okay, I'll go wake up Uncle Rockman," she said obligingly. "He can clap a sermon round me if he likes."

She wandered away, head high, happily conscious that she was a constant source of irritation to her mother and sister.

"Is anyone else coming besides Mrs. Evans' friend?" asked Mrs. Elroy, needles now flying piously for Britain.

"Probably Harry," Nancy answered with a slight frown. She could hardly wait to marry Harry so she could be rude to him legally and prevent him intruding on her social life.

"I didn't realize Rockman had come in today," pensively remarked Mrs. Elroy. "He can pay cook."

Uncle Rockman gave his sister-in-law a large allowance sufficient to cover all expenses, but Mrs. Elroy found it more convenient to use the money as ready cash and send all bills to him. In spite of this caution she was sometimes trapped into paying a servant herself so she tried to prepare against such a mischance. With Nancy's wedding coming on she was certain to be caught with all sorts of unforeseen little expenses so she closed in on Rockman on every occasion now. She met little resistance from him because for many years the wary man had suspected she would like to marry him and he was glad to placate her with money instead of his freedom, having observed her disciplinary measures with his late brother.

The news of Uncle Rockman's rare presence in the apartment caused Nancy to be thoughtfully silent for a few moments, too, for she had a few favors to ask herself. She frowned impatiently when banjo thumpings were heard from the direction of Uncle Rockman's "study."

"Uncle Rockman isn't scolding Tuffy at all," she exclaimed angrily. "What's happening is that Tuffy has tapped him for a car of her own. Honestly, Mama, nobody can get anything out of Uncle if you let Tuffy always get at him first! You make me furious, Mama, honestly."

"Oh, shut up, Nancy," her good mother answered, for she knew what Nancy said was true, and that Tuffy had once again taken unfair advantage of her uncle's preference for her and made other demands unseasonable. Never mind, she had guided herself through Rockman's pockets before with perfect grace—she could do it again.

3

It was unkind of Amanda, Vicky kept thinking, to deprive the Elroys of the simple favor of her company. No matter how grand she herself might become she was certain that she would always be grateful of her admirers; if they found her presence inspiring, then she would be present; on no account would she dismiss their fond regard with a haughty shrug.

"But probably Amanda is quite right," she reflected after this noble resolution. "The public really doesn't like its idols to be folksy. Probably you get knocked off your pedestal soon enough without jumping down of your own accord."

The Elroy apartment had just been done over by an interior decorator, in preparation for Nancy's wedding, and it seemed to Vicky far more impressive than the Julian Evans' home. The drawing room had an air of blithe informality with flowered taffeta drapes, white wool rugs, glass tables, bowls of flowers and ferns everywhere, and an array of modern paintings that were gay and expert. Mrs. Elroy had arranged herself and her tea table with the care she always took for strangers or cousins of strangers, and looked regal in her flowing pink teagown. The first chill of November was in the air so that in spite of the fire her aristocratic nose was tinted lavender with her seasonal sinus trouble, a disorder that kept her dabbing daintily at her nose from time to time, until the gesture took on interesting punctuation value.

"My dear! How darling of you to come!" Nancy cried on greeting Vicky and much to the confusion of both of them started to kiss her warmly, but as Vicky was unprepared for such a welcome it merely knocked her hat off, leaving both girls breathless with apologetic murmurs.

"Mother! Vicky Haven's here!" Nancy cried out as if this was the happiest news the house had ever had and Mrs. Elroy looked up with a benevolent smile, her slender jeweled hand outstretched.

It simply showed that your real New Yorkers were as friendly as anybody else, Vicky thought, taking the low chair beside Mrs. Elroy. Nancy, radiant in a green corduroy dinner suit, seated herself gracefully on the footstool, hands clasped girlishly about her knees.

"Don't let Mama force tea on you if you really want a cock-tail," she advised. "Or how about a sherry?"

Vicky looked uncertainly from the sherry in Nancy's hand to the teacup in Mrs. Elroy's and was about to solve this problem by having neither, but Nancy answered for her.

"We'll warm up on tea," she decided, "and then we'll clap our tongues around a martini."

"Does Amanda Keeler Evans drink martinis?" queried Mrs. Elroy. "I believe we read someplace that she drank nothing but a single pony of armagnac a day, and that before breakfast."

"The first Mrs. Evans never drank," Nancy said. "Unless of course she was a dipsomaniac and did it in secret the way so many women used to do. Didn't they, Mama?"

"Even so, I doubt if they were any worse than the young girls nowadays drinking like sailors almost before they're out," Mrs. Elroy sighed, her pretty hands fluttering over lemon, cinnamon sticks, and blackberry jam, a bit in each cup. "I sometimes wonder what sort of mothers they have to bring them up that way."

"Were her people—well—top-drawer?" Nancy asked, and Vicky saw that her visit was to be spent in giving guarded answers to this quiz on her friend's private habits. Even if she told all she knew she was certain it would in no way throw light on Amanda or damage her, either. It would please these people mightily to be told a few little stories about Amanda's prefamous life, and as there was nothing derogatory in them Vicky decided to earn her welcome by being as garrulous as she knew how. She told about Amanda's brave gesture in taking over the Keeler Haberdashery for a summer when her father was too sick to work, and she told about Amanda's amusing habit of always getting engaged every semester at Miss Doxey's to somebody new and she told about Amanda going to Cleveland to study pastry cooking for six weeks when she was sixteen because she was going to run a tea room.

"How do the people in Lakeville feel about their famous representative now?" Mrs. Elroy said.

"Oh, they're very proud of her," Vicky loyally exclaimed. "And they respect her for paying off every cent of her father's debts because so often children don't feel responsible, you know."

"Yes," said Mrs. Elroy thoughtfully. "That's quite true."

Something must have sounded a little wrong about the little anecdotes, for Vicky saw mother and daughter exchanging quiet glances that must have meant something. It was plain that what the home town found as virtues in Amanda were regarded by the metropolitan minded as mere proof of inferior background. Vicky grew suddenly silent, her face very red.

Voices from the back of the apartment announced the coming of Tuffy and Uncle Rockman, and once again Nancy and Mrs. Elroy exchanged a look of meaning.

"That Tuffy!" bitterly muttered Nancy. "Mama, I wish you'd talk Uncle into sending her someplace. College or New Mexico or anyplace. I'll bet she's talked Uncle out of a car and that means we won't dare ask him for anything else for months!"

Tuffy appeared carrying a bottle of Scotch under her arm and two glasses in her hand. Uncle Rockman followed her, chuckling, in bright red lounging coat and pipe.

"I knew there'd be nothing but those foul martinis," Tuffy said. "Uncle and I can't stand anything but Scotch. Who's that?"

"Tuffy, please!" her mother implored. "This is Miss Haven, a friend of Amanda Evans. And Vicky, this is Rockman, my husband's brother. Soda, Rockman?"

"How do you do," said Rockman, sitting down. "Water."

"Ah, don't let Mama mix it, she puts it in with an eyedropper," said Tuffy, seizing the water carafe and at some danger to her mother's tea table mixing her uncle's highball. "I'm the only one that can make a decent drink around this house. Clap your face around this, Uncle Rockman."

"Uncle Rockman writes for the scientific magazines," Nancy said to Vicky. "Are you home for a few days, Uncle?"

"Does that question sound ominous or inviting to you, young lady?" Uncle Rockman inquired, turning to Vicky. "My family here gets along so mighty well without my presence that I'm afraid Nancy only means to warn me off."

"Now, Uncle!" said Nancy. "You know Julian Evans, Uncle. Vicky is a great friend of the family. She says that Amanda Evans' father runs a haberdashery store back in the Middle West and owed so much money Amanda had to pay it off herself."

"She studied to be a pastry cook, it seems," Mrs. Elroy added. "What could have gotten into Julian after being married to poor Margaret—one of the best families in Boston, really!"

"Dozens of lovers before she met Julian, so Vicky says," brightly added Nancy.

"She didn't nail him till she was nearly thirty," Tuffy exclaimed. "God, Nancy, you wouldn't expect her to stay a virgin that long."

"Don't use the name of the Lord, Tuffy—how many times must I tell you?" Mrs. Elroy protested gently.

"You merely told me not to say 'Jesus,'" Tuffy defended herself. "What else did you find out about the lady?"

Vicky, during these lurid interpretations of what had seemed to her merely friendly gossip, had a hideous sensation of sinking through the floor. She couldn't imagine how her hostesses had been able to find so many dark meanings to her remarks and she wondered fearsomely how soon all this would be spread through the town, all carefully attributed to Vicky Haven. She gripped her teacup grimly as if it were her sole support and wondered how she could clear herself of having so unwittingly smirched her friend's name. If she talked about Peabody's office, she would appear to have no interest except business and that would not do. Casting her eyes about uneasily she encountered Uncle Rockman's kindly bright blue eyes.

"Amanda has really been awfully good to me," she said apologetically.

"Who is she?" politely inquired Uncle Rockman.

"Julian Evans' new wife—you know," impatiently explained his sister-in-law. "Amanda Keeler Evans."

Uncle Rockman sipped a highball in silent thought, then shook his head.

"Never heard of her," he said. "Any relation of Doctor Vestry Keeler at Leland Stanford?"

"Oh, *uncle*!" Nancy cried, with an apologetic smile at Vicky. "Of course you've heard of Amanda Keeler!"

"Oh, leave Uncle be," said Tuffy. "If you want to work on somebody's education, you got your future husband. They don't come any dumber."

"Mama!" Nancy exclaimed, flushing helplessly. "Uncle, please!"

"Harry is the all-time low in the male animal," Tuffy turned graciously to explain to Vicky. "If he can even braid a basket, I'll eat it."

Uncle Rockman was chuckling in fond appreciation of his ugly duckling's remarks so that Nancy proudly shook the tears from her eyes and set out to stir a martini. Vicky tried to keep a fixed happy look on her face though she had not been so embarrassed by a family gathering since she left her brother's roof. Mrs. Elroy frowned sternly at her younger daughter. She had always considered it a pretty woman's right to be a fiend in private, but to balance this state of society it was up to the plain girls to rigorously uphold the banner of breeding and constant good nature. Unfortunately Tuffy had never seen eye to eye with her on this and had the audacity to have all the selfishness and ill-temper of a belle. The awkward silence while Nancy sulkily poured martinis, Mrs. Elroy silently frowned, and Vicky squirmed, was broken by the maid's announcement that Mr. Plung had arrived to see Miss Tuffy.

"Don't let him in here," said Nancy. "Take him straight to the nursery."

This remark was sufficient to slay Miss Tuffy, who turned an angry red.

"It's not the nursery anymore, damn you," she exclaimed. "Mama, she's got to stop calling it the nursery now!"

"It's always been the nursery, Tuffy," Mrs. Elroy said calmly. "I agree with Nancy. Take your caller to the nursery."

Tuffy stood up, her fists clenched, eyes flashing.

"I can't take a man with a beard to the nursery!" she wailed. "I can't, can I, Uncle Rockman?"

Uncle Rockman was sputtering over his highball in a fit of silent mirth and only shook his head at Vicky helplessly. The caller announced as Mr. Plung marched into the living room without further warning, and it was quite true that by some extraordinary miracle his pasty young face had managed to accumulate enough red fuzz on the chin to pass as a beard. This feat appeared to have exhausted the young man to the point of being unable to speak or bow, for he stood in the doorway in soiled tan raincoat and most elaborately mottled sport shoes, quite as if he were frozen there.

"Run along, you two," Mrs. Elroy said imperiously.

"And don't start murdering that banjo again," added Nancy.

This humiliation in front of her bearded friend crushed Tuffy sufficiently for her to stalk out of the room very near tears.

"Come on, Plung," she said in a stifled voice. "We're to go to the nursery. With Nancy getting married, God knows it may be our last chance to see it."

"Mama!" Nancy said tensely. "Uncle Rockman!"

Uncle Rockman, by this time, had adjusted his expression to one of innocent vagueness. He shook his ice around in his glass thoughtfully until his older niece, in some irritation, took his glass and refilled it.

"Doctor Vestry Keeler was a very fine scholar," he observed. "Perhaps you read his book on 'Light.' Most illuminating—ha, ha—excuse the pun. Yes, I worked with Doctor Keeler at the University of Chicago a few years ago."

"I didn't know that," Vicky said quite truly, adding, with less conviction, "that must have been very interesting."

Uncle Rockman's round plump face glowed rosily out of his frame of curly gray hair. He had bright childish blue eyes, not too honest, the innocent eyes of a man who lied to himself in all the realities of human behavior, but was radiantly fearless in the face of Cosmic Theories. He considered Vicky now with interest, as if she had just made a rather profound remark.

"No, I can't say it was interesting," he reflected. "Nothing to the fun of working with Shapley. I suppose you recall his delightfully audacious statement that not only could the Finite be measured but that he personally could give the exact number of atoms. Ha, ha."

"Ha, ha," said Vicky, and she was so relieved at the switch from personalities to the abstract that she laughed as heartily as if Uncle Rockman had been quoting Jack Benny. She was hushed by the look of astonishment exchanged by the Elroy mother and daughter, but Uncle Rockman's further conversation, encouraged as he was by his unheralded success, obliged her to continue in her new role of the merry savant. Mrs. Elroy took up her knitting, Nancy sipped a martini and Uncle Rockman described many a pedantic roguery, gasping with merriment over Sir William Bragg's delightful *mot* on light theories. (On Monday, Wednesday, Friday one must teach the corpuscle theory, and on Tuesday, Thursday, Saturday the wave theory.") How brilliant of Edison, he added, to name the unit a "wavicle."

"A wavicle," repeated Vicky with a burst of laughter.

"Rockman, are you quite sure you want another highball?" gently reproached Mrs. Elroy as her brother-in-law's plump fingers encircled the pinch bottle again, tenderly.

"Quite," answered Rockman firmly and poured a rather mighty blast into his glass. In this pause Nancy sprang into action with a long discussion of Amanda Keeler's wedding, which she had only heard described, and Mrs. Elroy probed Vicky on the matter of whether Amanda's Lakeville family had been represented at the function, and whether it would look too imitative if Nancy were to follow Amanda's custom of having the Calypso singers at the wedding reception. Vicky answered very guardedly on both these points, and Mrs. Elroy then discoursed favorably on the beauty of her own Columbus wedding. During this talk Uncle Rockman appeared to be listening attentively but betrayed himself in the high point of Mrs. Elroy's anecdote by absently humming a snatch of Gilbert and Sullivan. This was a baffling habit in such a courtly gentleman, a habit so revealing of his utter lack of interest in any conversation but his own that he would have been horrified to learn of it. It would have been far better had he interrupted, but he was too polite to do this; he merely fixed his attention on the speaker and presently his light preoccupied hum would rise louder and louder till the speaker would be practically drowned out.

"I'm afraid," said Mrs. Elroy, drily, "that Rockman has heard all this before."

"No, no—no, no, go on, my dear," Rockman blandly replied, quite above sarcasm.

Sounds of a banjo came from the other end of the hall.

"I suppose that's going to go on all during the wedding," Nancy said in a stifled voice, pacing proudly up and down the room. "I suppose Maury Paul will have quite a nice item about it in the paper. I imagine the photographers will have a perfect riot getting *that* in the picture."

"Oh, Nancy, do shut up," said Mrs. Elroy patiently. "I don't know why my children should both turn out so nasty natured. It probably comes from my letting them spend their summers with their father's family."

"Of course it does, my dear," agreed Uncle Rockman amiably. He drank his third highball at a gulp and rose. "Well, I must be off. Dinner with Doctor Falman at the Faculty Club."

"Another martini, Miss Haven?" Mrs. Elroy graciously inquired. "Nancy, do look after your guests. I don't know how in the world you're going to manage in your own home."

"I must go," Vicky said.

"What do you mean, how will I manage?" Nancy laughed. "I daresay I'll manage all right until you decide to come and live with us, Mama."

Vicky, seeing Uncle Rockman rise, was afraid to spend any more time with her two new friends, and hastily made for the door.

"Since you're all alone in the city, you must let us share our home with you, my dear," benevolently urged Mrs. Elroy, dabbing at her patrician nostrils with a delicate handkerchief. "We can't let a friend of Amanda Evans get homesick, you know."

"Thank you," said Vicky. "It *is* a lot like home, Mrs. Elroy."

"Let's have lunch tomorrow," begged Nancy, following her to the door. "I have loads of things I want to ask you. And everybody else in the office is so horrible, don't you think?"

"Oh, yes," Vicky agreed, anxious only to get away from the charming fireside and get back to her harmonious solitude.

Waiting in the little vestibule for the elevator she was surprised to see Mr. Rockman Elroy suddenly emerge from the apartment door. He was tugging at his topcoat, a somewhat sportive tan checked affair, and panting a great deal as if his haste to escape from the home was quite equal to Vicky's

In the elevator he said nothing although his kindly regard indicated approval of her. In the lobby the doorman rushed to get them a cab.

"Can I drop you anywhere going up?" inquired Uncle Rockman.

"No, thank you," Vicky said.

Mr. Elroy appeared to have something else on his mind, for he stood with one foot on the cab step and a finger thoughtfully placed beside his nose. Vicky, looking about her, would have liked to ask him something too, for she saw they were in a huge square courtyard with no apparent exit, and she fully expected to be beating around the palm-fringed colonnade all night hunting for an escape.

"Miss Haven," Mr. Elroy finally found courage to inquire, "are you interested at all in the atom smasher?"

"I am, indeed," she answered with enthusiasm. "Is that how you get out of here, Mr. Elroy?"

"Hop in, and I'll drive you where you're going," said Uncle Rockman. "I can't tell you how much I've enjoyed our conversation, Miss Haven."

Vicky was afraid to ruin this fine impression by a spoken word and her silence spoke so well for her that after a ten-minute monologue on the atom Uncle Rockman left her, repeating the compliment again and again.

6

THE CHIEF PROBLEM IN Ken Saunders'
life for the past three years had been the putting off of tomorrow.
Ever since Amanda's desertion he had devoted himself to not
thinking, to taking whatever trains or boats were leaving at
whatever station he happened to be. It struck him with some bitterness that at no point in his career had he ever arrived at any
station in time for the Grand Orient Express; his voyages were
never first class, his destinations never glamorous, his duties
never poetic. He was no goodwill spreader in South America, no
brace digger for secrets of the Aztec in Mexico;—no, he was
merely compiling fruit statistics for an export journal. In Brazil
he had no secret mission from the government to investigate the
spy rings and unmask the Nazi agents—he was pamphleteer for
a commercial hotel. In China he saw the war but nary a Soong
sister, for his undistinguished duties there were in connection
with a secondhand typewriting concern, and his social contacts

more bibulous than political. This definite marking time in the career of such a promising journalist as Mr. Saunders had its penalties, for the Tomorrow he had postponed was bigger and blacker for the postponement. Saunders had usually pictured Tomorrow armed with a large club crouching behind night's corner ready to pounce, and the greedy ogre was all the more bloodthirsty for the delay. There was Tomorrow waiting at the boat for him the instant he landed back in New York. Serious work to be taken up again, and a benumbed heart brought properly back to the pain of living. You would have thought, since travel is educational, that three years of it would have brought the young man to a better understanding of life's burdens, but the truth was he had even less heart for them than before. The ambition to write novels seemed the silliest work in the world for a grown man, with war on every side; and the postures necessary for the new type of journalist were quite out of his nature. The fact that Amanda had made such a success of both these careers did not make them any more appealing to him, so that he ended up as Assistant Home Editor for no less a periodical than Peabody's. Peabody's had only recently taken an interest in the Home, but since the world of fashion seemed cracking up, smart editors were frantically trying to substitute interest in the hearth for interest in the pencil silhouette. Mr. Saunders, having been raised in an Oklahoma boarding house and being singularly uninformed on the mechanical and decorative equipment of any home, had at least a novel approach to his task and the recommendation of his friend Dennis Orphen. It was well paying and left his mind free for the friendly discussions of the tavern and resulting erudite arguments on international affairs. To tell the truth, drink seemed the only protection against the lacerations of his mind, now that he was back in New York, his foot rocking away once more on the much touted ladder of success. At this time the famous ladder was propped against nothing and led

nowhere, and anyone foolish enough to make the world his oyster was courting ptomaine; yet the ladder tradition was still observed, and until the flames reached them young people were still
found going through the motions of climbing.

Saunders was thirty-three, old enough to have been disappointed a thousand times, but still young enough to be surprised.
He knew the world was filled with lies but he was always expecting the truth to pop up triumphant; its delay angered but did not
disillusion him. In his hotel rooms he had the rejected manuscripts of the books he had written after his first eager, rather bad
little novel. He and Amanda used to talk about how bad it was
and how astonishing its success. Then they talked about how
good the rejected books were and how astonishing their rejection. They talked, went to bed, argued, took each other for
granted, then out of a blue sky Amanda married Julian Evans.
Then Ken lost his job on a morning paper. Then he tried in vain
to sell his old stories. Then he wrote a play that did not sell. Then
he wrote a series of articles for a magazine that promptly went
bankrupt. Then he looked out his hotel window and saw, as the
final blow, that there was no use jumping, because a bare ten feet
below was a roof for sunbathers from MacKinney's Turkish Bath
House. Suicide there was impossible and murder—for he would
have flattened a few toasting fat men—was not to his fancy. So
his wanderings began, and the not thinking. Back in New York,
every ache was back with compound interest.

Seeing Amanda was worse than not seeing her. Everything in
his nature recoiled from what she now represented. He resented
the years he had mistaken her cool indifference for restraint.
Her life seemed monstrous to him, and the fact that he was still
in love with her was as frightening to him as if he found himself
in bed with General Motors. Failure frightened him, looming
up all the sharper by Amanda's success. He seldom slept. He
wondered if he was through. He was thirty-three. Sometimes

people were through at thirty-three. Thirty even. They became old drunks. The world was full of old drunken failures. Has-beens. Warnings. Men who didn't realize they were never any good anyway—just lucky enough to hold a job a few years and then—zoom! He, at least, had been wise enough to take whatever job had come up, a thought that was at least a comfort on payday no matter how unpleasant such compromises were the rest of the week. But, unless he went to bed tight, he stared at the ceiling all night, smoking cigarettes, waiting for Tomorrow to spring.

What did other men do whose lives suddenly came apart like a cheap ukulele? What did they do when they realized that perhaps there would be no second chance, no reconsidering, no retrieving? What did they do when the hopes that push the wheel stopped, when magic failed, and fear alone remained, rusting the soul; when the days rattled off like dried beans with no native juice, no hope of flavor; when fears, batted out the door like flies, left only to return by window? What did other men do, suspecting that what was for them had been served—no further helping, no more love, no more triumph; for them labor without joy or profit, for them a passport to nowhere, free ticket to the grim consolations of Age? Was it true, then, that this world was filled with men and women merely marking time before their cemetery? When did courage's lease expire, was there no renewal possible? What specialist in mediocrity determined the prizewinners and ruled what measure of banality was required for success? These were the thoughts that brightened Ken's nights, and since they were very similar to the dark queries that clustered around Vicky Haven's pillow, it was the most natural thing in the world for them, these two frightened people, to have the merriest lunches together in the Peabody Building. Since neither Ken nor Vicky was the sort to reveal private problems, each found the other most comforting, and almost disgustingly carefree.

"You're even beginning to look like a Peabody front girl," Ken accused her, one noon at Chez Jean. "Have you done something to yourself or is it just that propinquity has opened my eyes?"

Vicky pretended this question was merely academic and shrugged her shoulders.

"I mean it," Ken insisted, frowning at her. "I ask you out because Miss Finkelstein tells me you're the type girl who's very deep. I try to talk to you about life in the large and all you do is waggle your little peepers and look seductive."

"I wasn't trying to look seductive," Vicky maintained. "I was only trying to look interested. I'm the type girl that tries to give everything to what the gentleman is saying. Later I mull it over in my mind and can't make head nor tail of it."

Ken continued to study her in some perplexity.

"What have you done? Either you're fatter or thinner or you've had your hair dyed. It's always something like that when women change."

"Not dyed. Highlighted is the new word," said Vicky. "Can't I have any secrets? It's this hat, too. And new clothes. Now I spend every cent on my back."

"A fine thing in times like these," rebuked Ken.

"It gives me all the more to donate to Bundles for Britain," said Vicky stoutly. "Nancy Elroy told me so. And then I charge everything because, with inflation, money won't be worth anything anyway. So that leaves me cash for massages and rhumba lessons and perfume that drives men mad."

Ken looked at her with unmistakable pleasure.

"If you were twenty years younger I'd make a play for you, no fooling," he admitted.

"I wasn't always the girl that I am now," Vicky warned him. "I was fat and freckled and bald. Typhoid. I was crazy about the boys and I let them cheat off my quiz papers. I giggled all the time, too."

"Youth is all I demand of a woman," said Ken. "Too bad you're too late to get me. I would have been your man. Have dinner with me."

It was one thing to go out to lunch with someone from your office, man or woman, and it was quite another to have anyone desire these contacts prolonged into the private hours after five. Vicky was as delighted as she had been when Nancy Elroy had promoted her to the lofty level of personal and family friend. Mr. Saunders had never made any overtures toward her outside the office, beyond escorting her home from the occasional parties to which Amanda invited them. Vicky alone got a secret kick out of Julian's taking for granted that Ken was her beau, but Mr. Saunders did not seem to realize this attitude of Julian's. The couple was plainly enough linked together by being the two nobodies in a drawing room of notables, all uttering notable remarks. Taking her home, Saunders usually made caustic comments on the group or else was moodily silent; in either case left her at her door most impersonally. Vicky might have thought it odd she was never asked to the Evanses' without Ken, except for the fact that she liked that part about the evening the best, counting on him for support.

Today, after his offer, she was suddenly emboldened to make an advance herself. She had secretly thought of doing so, ever since she first met him, but his manner, genial but impersonal, had discouraged her, heretofore. Ethel Carey had wired that she was coming to New York that day. What fun it would be to exhibit apartment and new man to friend from home all in same blow!

"Why don't you come to my apartment?" she now invited him. "I'll make a curry. Besides I have a friend from home coming."

Mr. Saunders did not seem at all appalled at the brazenness of the suggestion. He even declared that he personally would make the rice. He was such a superb ricemaker, he stated, that he could, if necessary, make rice for fifty to a hundred guests at the drop of a hat. This offer decided Vicky to make a real party of it.

She would invite Nancy Elroy and her fiancé. She was so puffed up at the prospect of her first social undertaking, that it was all she could do to keep from inviting the entire Peabody staff, from Mr. Peabody right down to Irving Finkelstein. She was even more set up when Ken walked down the corridor to visit her office, on the way back from lunch.

There Miss Finkelstein, in a brand new sleek Dorothy Lamour hairdo and a great deal of clanking jewelry to which she referred as "Spanish Barbaric," gave Mr. Saunders a gracious nod. Vicky saw that her own stock had risen with her secretary because of being lunched by a young male member of the staff. Even the front office girls and models seldom had Big Dates at noon; they clustered around the drugstore lunch counter downstairs in the building, feasting on tuna fish sandwiches and malties.

"Someone has been trying to get you on this telephone, Mr. Saunders," Miss Finkelstein informed him, and handed him the receiver.

Vicky hung up her hat and combed her hair. She would send Irving out for supplies, she decided, and then carry them home herself in a taxi. She would order some wine—but before that she must send Miss Finkelstein up to Nancy's desk with the invitation to dinner. This would be a big night, maybe the real beginning. And then Vicky saw that Kenneth was stammering over the telephone looking embarrassed.

"It's Amanda," he said to Vicky. "She wants you."

Very well, she would invite Amanda, too. Julian, Miss Bemel—anybody.

"Darling," Amanda rushed to speak before Vicky could begin. "Ken tells me he had some sort of tentative engagement with you tonight. The thing is, I want you both here, Julian has to fly to Washington and there will just be three or four of us."

"But I can't," Vicky said. "Ethel Carey's coming for dinner, and perhaps some other people."

There was a shocked pause.

"You can get out of that," Amanda said curtly. "Simply leave a note for Ethel."

If she'd said to bring Ethel, too, it would have been easier, Vicky afterward reflected, but Amanda was taking no chances on old friends outside of Vicky.

"I'm sure Ken would rather come here," Amanda said, with a short laugh. "Your cooking may be better than my Pedro's, but I swear your liquor isn't, and that's what counts with Mr. Saunders. So, just leave a note for Ethel and I'll see you around eight."

"But I haven't seen Ethel for months," Vicky protested. "No, Amanda, I'm sorry.

"We might as well go," Ken murmured.

This decided Vicky. Whatever she had to offer was nothing in the face of a royal command from Amanda, in Mr. Saunders' eyes. Very well, let him go there. But that was no reason for letting Ethel down.

"I'm sure I'd like to, Amanda," Vicky continued carefully. "Ken will probably come up, but I couldn't possibly."

"Oh, the hell with Ethel Carey!" Amanda's voice was impatient, almost shrill. "There isn't a reason in the world you can't do me this little favor. You don't need to go through life being kind to Lakeville!"

Vicky was puzzled by being wanted so much, but she was adamant. If Amanda let down old friends, she, Vicky, didn't have to. Amanda was genuinely angry with her for being so stubborn, and after she hung up Vicky saw that Ken Saunders was looking silently at the floor with an expression she didn't understand, but which must mean disappointment. He must have thought she would actually hold him to their engagement, so she quickly set him right.

"I'll ask you another night," she said, trying to sound very cheerful. "You go up to Amanda's."

He stood there, lighting a cigarette, looking as if he was about to say something. Then he shrugged his shoulders and smiled. "All right," he said. "We'll make ours some other time."

Miss Finkelstein, gliding back in, looked sharply from one to the other. Silent partings always looked like romance, but whatever romance there was in this scene must have ended unsatisfactorily, for Miss Finkelstein's keen eyes did not miss the fact that Vicky was dabbing at her nose with a handkerchief and trying to hide her face by picking up invisible matters from the floor.

"Miss Haven!" Miss Finkelstein exclaimed, in awe. "Did something happen? Did he—Miss Haven, you're not *crying*!"

Vicky took a firm grip on herself.

"Hay fever," she explained. "I always get it this time of year. I think it's the martinis."

With the baffling remark she blew her nose so many times you would have thought she had to test the instrument thoroughly before permitting it to leave the factory.

2

No sooner had Ken Saunders disappointed her and Amanda gotten mad than Vicky knew that there would be more grief to come. Some people's nerves react to approaching evil or approaching beneficence as to temperature changes. They have a sense at night of danger rolling up like rain clouds, a sense, too, when the danger has passed. Something clutches the heart, a cold wind blows by, the thing is about to strike. This faculty is not connected with the intellect nor is it a supernatural power, but a gift as simple as a good sense of smell.

"There will be a letter," Vicky prophesied gloomily as she walked home that night. "Or maybe it will be a telephone call, somebody at the door."

Passing a gypsy tearoom she was almost tempted to go in and try to draw mysterious information from the fortune-teller, but she remembered that the last time she had done this, the gypsy had foretold an unpleasantness that had immediately come true. No use running out to meet trouble. A gypsy should be required to be wrong, or else she became an affront to science.

If she was to lose her job such news would surely have reached her at the office before she left, so it could scarcely be that. At the newsstand on her corner, Vicky surrendered to an Astrology magazine, and rather guiltily looked up Virgo's chances for today and tomorrow. Today, advised the journal, Virgo was under Saturn. Up till 1:30 P.M. she should have traveled, concluded arrangements to stabilize finances, collected outstanding debts, sold property, settled domestic issues, challenged life, increased earning power, made personal contacts; 1:30 to midnight should be devoted to getting at basic facts, postponing journeys, forming ideas, making personal adjustments and saving money. Tomorrow, under Neptune, she was to travel, write, speak her mind freely, take a long walk, and avoid gambling. After 1:30 journeys should again be avoided, investments made, old debts collected, responsibilities accepted and temper held in check.

Reeling at the generosity of the advice given, Vicky hastily replaced the magazine on the rack. Evidently, to please the stars, millions of Virgos, if that was their plural term, were racing around on journeys all A.M. and trying to get back to base in time to postpone any P.M. journeys. Her own muddled hunches were far more reliable, she decided, and since whatever was to be was bound to be bad from the chilly feeling down her spine, she might as well go straight home and get it over.

No mail in the mailbox, however. The janitor denied that any telegram had been delivered. But no sooner had she gotten in her apartment than the telephone rang and there was mischief itself on the other end of the wire. It was Ethel Carey, just arrived in New York.

"Come right up, dear." Vicky managed to sound convincingly happy over the telephone. "I can't wait to see you."

There was a pregnant pause and then the blow fell.

"Vicky, I can't." A sigh. "Darling, can you stand some bad news?"

So this was where it was coming from.

"That's what I live for," Vicky encouraged her.

Ethel plunged into the worst.

"Tom Turner and Eudora were on the same train with me. They insisted on coming to my hotel—we're at the Barclay—and now I'm tied up for dinner with them."

Vicky opened her mouth to speak but words did not come. The very thought that Tom was within a dozen blocks of her this minute made her head start swimming exactly the way it used to do, and every drop of common sense in her system seemed to evaporate that very second. Vicky reached for a chair with trembling fingers and sat down. What were Tom and Eudora doing in New York? He'd never made enough money to come here before.

"The awful thing is the Eudora suggested you come along to dinner with us," Ethel wailed. "Can you imagine the nerve of her? She's here buying an outfit for the baby—it's due in three months—and she actually thinks you'll shop with her. She thinks that working on Peabody's, you'd get a discount."

For some reason this did not seem as outrageous to Vicky as it did to Ethel. At least the Turners seemed to be certain Vicky was no longer sensitive about them, and that was an advantage. She couldn't have stood having them consider her feelings.

"I'd come down and see you all," she lied with fine calm, "but I have friends coming in so perhaps we can meet tomorrow."

Ethel seemed relieved at Vicky's matter-of-fact attitude.

"You're over it, aren't you, Vicky? That's wonderful. . . . Maybe we might even drop in tonight and see you. It would serve them right to see you with your New York friends. It would just serve them right."

Hanging up, Vicky thought, yes and it served herself right for lying about friends coming in. She couldn't bear to have them see her the way they were going to—all alone, depressed, quite date-less. She thought desperately of calling Amanda, but then Amanda was having a dinner, a dinner that required Ken Saunders. She thought again of Nancy Elroy, but Nancy had said she had another engagement.

Vicky's head buzzed so busily with the necessity for doing something devilishly shrewd and effective that movement was practically paralyzed, suggestions popping up so fast they can-celed each other. A dozen courses of action flashed through her mind and she set about following them all at once, painting two fingernails a victorious red, then drawing a bath but forgetting the stopper; ordering chrysanthemums from the florist, then re-membering there was no vase big enough unless you counted the umbrella stand; shaping one eyebrow then deciding to eat dinner first. She ordered a reckless dinner for one sent over from the nearest Longchamps as the solution to her confusion, then re-membered her tub and sat in it while the dinner got cold. The one thought that completely numbed all normal processes was the thought of Tom Turner. It is possible that a gentleman who leaves one love to run off with another feels wretchedly at the mercy of both the rest of his life, and is not at all complacent at the implication two women have found him irresistible. It is pos-sible that whatever disgraceful situation his lack of chivalry has induced, is as painful to him as it is to his jilted love and even to his favored new one. But the general conviction has always been that here is a man gloating over his double triumph—one lady left sobbing with heartbreak over him, another reveling in the magic of his touch. That was the way Vicky thought of Tom Turner and it made her furious with him, first that he should be so conceited, and second that he should be so nearly right. After all she *had* cried a good deal over him. For all she knew she would burst into tears at sight of him again. Supposing he sat and held Eudora Brown's hand. Very likely he would. Married people were always doing that in front of their unmarried friends. Alone they might spit and snarl at each other, but there was some law, apparently, which required a public exhibition of satisfaction with the married state.

How should she act before them? Hysterically happy—that was the usual pose for the jilted one—or proudly reticent? All she could decide offhand was to be glamorous, and she set to work studiously on the routine approved by the Peabody beauties. Her new dress, when shaken out of the box and slipped on, astonished her by fitting, at least in most places; and her hair done up in its new way looked encouragingly Peabodyish except for a few wisps at the back of her neck that no polite person would notice unless they were snooping around behind her. She was particularly pleased with the new earrings she had copied from Nancy. These were in the shape of javelins and, though only clipped on, were cunningly devised to give an impression of stabbing through the upper to the lower lobes of the ear, a picture of self-torture that magnetized every eye and was very smart that month.

Vicky sat down to the coffee table where her dinner was spread, still undecided which facade she should present to the Turners. One thing was certain, whether she was haughty or whether she was effusively friendly, she must show that Manhattan was her natural background, and if anything had gone wrong in her Lakeville career it was merely because she was too big a person for the place.

The doorbell rang and Vicky, with a deep breath, prepared to face it. But instead of Ethel Carey and the Turners there stood Ken Saunders, looking rather sheepish.

"I took a walk around the Evanses' diggings," he said. "I decided I couldn't make it. I like this place better anyway."

Vicky was beaming, though she tried to look reproachful at the man who dared to defy her friend Amanda.

"But you've never been here before," she reminded him.

Ken reflected on this.

"That's so," he agreed. "Put your coat on, we're going out to dinner."

Vicky pointed to her dinner, just begun. Ken eyed it with a revulsion.

"Smelts! Fried oysters! Shrimp salad!" he exclaimed incredulously. "What did you do—go straight down the fish list?"

"I suppose so," Vicky said. "I thought it saved time."

"You can't eat that horrible stuff. Come on, get your hat, we'll go and get a real dinner."

He jerked his thumb toward the door and Vicky very happily ran to powder and get her things. If the Turners came they would see that in New York, Vicky Haven was too popular to be kept waiting. Too many men were eager to take her out. When she returned, she was astonished to find her guest seated on the coffee table busily finishing the last crumb of her dinner.

"I'm ready," she said. "I see you've already had your dinner."

Ken looked at the table.

"So I have," he said. "I was thinking of something else. I'm such a busy man."

"It's all right," said Vicky. "I wasn't awfully hungry. I'll bet Amanda's mad at you for not coming there."

"I wouldn't go there alone," said Ken. "Amanda would hate that."

Vicky was puzzled by this remark. Why couldn't he go to the Evanses alone? Other men did. Important gentlemen, of course. Ken kicked at the fire with his shoe and appeared to forget that Vicky was waiting to be taken out. When he turned to speak to her she was sure he was going to explain his curious insinuation that he was only welcome at the Evanses when properly escorted by a lady—in this case, Vicky.

"Smelts," he stated, "are a nasty little fish. I'm surprised at you. I would have said 'now there is a girl who orders venison with the best of them.' But no. Smelts. Smelts. Fried oysters. Shrimps."

"You can't judge by a girl's face, after all," Vicky said humbly.

Mr. Saunders suddenly reached in the wood cupboard where Amanda kept her cellar and extracted a bottle of rum. He appeared to have a rather uncanny sense of direction, for Vicky herself had not discovered this supply till a few weeks ago. Not knowing exactly what to do with a man who had first made a date, then canceled it, then honored her by retrieving it, then eaten her dinner, Vicky sat down humbly on the ottoman to wait his lead. He opened the bottle and poured two drinks, one of which she obediently took and sipped. He drank his swiftly without speaking. He drank another, and then the bell rang.

This time it was not the Turners but none other than Mr. Rockman Elroy, who stood on the threshold. Her amazement made Mr. Elroy back away in embarrassment.

"Nancy told me you had invited her to dine tonight," he said, as if this would at once explain his unprecedented visit. "Inasmuch as she could not come I thought I myself would pay a call. Here."

With the "Here" he thrust a large coffinlike box in her arms.

More chrysanthemums, of course, and no place to put them. Mr. Elroy stood uncomfortably watching his flowers being carried tentatively from cocktail glass to double boiler and finally stuffed into a tall wastebasket with an ash tray of water at its feet.

"Thank you, Mr. Elroy," said Vicky, flushed from these clumsy maneuvers. "And this is Mr. Saunders."

"Of course," said Mr. Elroy, bowing stiffly.

Ken looked cross at the intrusion.

"When I bring violets, they *have* violets," Mr. Elroy ruefully observed. "When I bring these big things they have no place to put them but in an eye cup."

"It's the same with me," Vicky admitted. "When they bring me violets I don't know where to pin them and when they bring me these I end up parking them in the bathtub, for days. I've taken more baths with chrysanthemums."

"White tie!" observed Saunders, looking coldly at Mr. Elroy. "I'm afraid I'm not dressed for this call, Miss Haven."

"My goodness, I *am* flattered," Vicky exclaimed.

Uncle Rockman looked at his evening splendor with the puzzled expression of a man looking at one of nature's wonders for the first time. Then a light dawned.

"I'm giving a speech tonight," he said. "The associated paper men."

"So paper is your subject," said Saunders with a certain belligerence, Vicky felt.

"Not at all," Mr. Elroy said, "I am going to talk about the concern felt by Earth over the receding of the stars. That is closer to people's lives than mere paper."

"Of course," said Vicky. "I'm Virgo myself. September 3rd. So far the stars haven't done me much good."

"Give them another million years," advised Uncle Rockman. "By that time they will have receded indefinitely to Red and the universe will or will not be blown up."

"Two gets you five that it won't," said Ken.

He was being unnecessarily aggressive. And Uncle Rockman was being unnecessarily pompous. They couldn't have disliked each other more if they had been brothers. Vicky was very distressed because she was enormously touched by Uncle Rockman's visit. What could be handsomer, too, than a man of fifty with a fine glowing nose, crown of silver curls, and a body sufficiently weighted to keep him squarely on his feet in the stiffest of winds!

She was disappointed that Ken did not appreciate Uncle Rockman's fine points.

"This paper banquet must be an elegant affair," she said, admiring his snowy shirtfront and glittering studs.

Uncle Rockman stroked his chin doubtfully.

"As a matter of fact the dinner is right in the factory and I recall being warned against dressing," he said. "But I always wear tails when I speak. It gives me something to wave about when I get stuck. I forget a point so I walk up and down the platform flapping my coattails till the thought comes back."

"Isn't that brilliant?" Vicky appealed to Ken.

Mr. Saunders merely gave Mr. Elroy a bleak nod, the hostility of which was not lost on Uncle Rockman. He sat down resolutely, however, and Vicky poured him a drink. The slight difficulty he had in coordinating the quivering of his fingers with his excitement over the drink hinted at his already high alcoholic content. That, of course, explained the boldness of his visit. Inasmuch as Saunders' visit was equally unprecedented Vicky began thinking that he too had been propelled there by over stimulation. Her sudden popularity seemed less and less flattering. And the way the two men disliked each other was a problem for any hostess to handle, especially one with no dinner. In vain Vicky sought to find them a common ground but Mr. Saunders was sarcastic and curt, Mr. Elroy was courteous but silent. Vicky talked busily about the office, about her friends from Lakeville, about anything, but her two guests refused to use her words as a springboard to general talk.

Somewhat desperately Vicky plied them with rum and on the moment she was opening the second bottle a slight thaw began to take place. By the time the bell rang to admit Ethel and the Turners, Uncle Rockman was nestling back half-asleep on the sofa laughing fondly at everything Ken Saunders said. Ken had taken off his coat and necktie and was deeply engrossed in the task of proving that extrasensory perception, as explained by Uncle Rockman, was nothing more nor less than a poor man's version of the match game. Both gentlemen were too absorbed in their new friendship to pay any heed to the entrance of Vicky's guests, or to be aware of the startling impression they created.

3

So HERE was Tom Turner, who had broken Vicky's heart to run away with her business partner, Eudora Brown. Here was Eudora, once a bosom friend, now holding her hands over her convex lap, looking enviously around Vicky's living room. Desire makes its object worthy of desire, and for four years Tom Turner had been the worthy object of Vicky's affection. Now he belonged to somebody else and desire had been shocked by frustration into a numb despair, which Vicky discovered was modulating into a hostile disparagement of the man. All right, it was sour grapes to sit there silently criticizing everything about him—what was the matter with sour grapes? Sour grapes was as comforting a philosophy as any other, and a lot better than tearing your heart out with undying passion. He was as handsome as ever, in his dissipated ham actor way, and his voice was as richly effective as ever, but both of these hollow charms irritated the new Vicky. And how did he dare talk about Labor problems in the Middle West, having spent most of his time dodging hard work (unless there was no connection between these two fields)! She saw that she was by way of curing herself the moment she found herself being more tolerant of Eudora than she had dreamed possible. Even when Eudora shocked everyone by her sarcastic cracks at her husband, "That's what *you* think! . . . Oh, listen to the expert! . . . Isn't it wonderful to know everything. . . ." and so on. Vicky merely laughed as if this was good-natured fun that needed no apology.

She could tell, too, that Tom was impressed as was Eudora over the new background, new friends, and apparent happy recovery of their victim. That was why he wanted to argue about every subject that came up.

"You're quite wrong there, old man," he stated disagreeably at every remark made by the other two men. He was one of those men who betray their secret frustration in this way: taken into a handsome mansion they fall silent, coming slowly to an indignant mental boiling point of "This should be mine!" until out of a clear sky they start to shower insults on the innocent host. Married to a plain wife they take it as a personal grievance when they meet a single beauty, and cannot forbear pecking at the beauty with criticisms of her left thumb, her necklace, her accent, as if destruction by bits will ease the outrage of not being able to have her. Unemployed, they jeer at the stupidity of an envied friend working so hard for so little pay. In the unexpected presence of an admired or celebrated person they are reminded gallingly of their own inferior qualities and humiliate themselves by inadequate sarcasm, showing clearly how impressed they are and how irrevocably inferior they know themselves to be.

Vicky found herself seeing her late adored with such a clear unsympathetic eye that she brought herself up sharply. It was no truer that he was terrible now than that he was wonderful before. And if she had any stability at all she would not be disloyal to her old feelings. It would be much more to her credit, she admonished herself, to have her senses thrown in disorder by his presence in the room. This callous hostility brought on by being jilted merely proved she was a girl incapable of a deathless love—a scatterbrained emotional butterfly. Seeing through old lost lovers was not a gracious talent.

"Let me make the drinks," he said to her. "Unless of course your New York men friends have a special knack for mixing that us backwoodsmen don't get."

"Vicky looks like a new person, doesn't she, Tom?" Eudora asked urgently.

Tom would not compliment anything that was out of his reach so he merely smiled and shrugged.

"I don't see any difference. Hair looks a little funny, maybe. No, New York hasn't done much to Vicky."

This was naturally a remark intended to discipline any young woman who thought she was transformed into a beauty by loss of a lover.

Vicky finally decided that her nervous irritation was pure hunger, and ordered an immense supply of sandwiches from the delicatessen. She nibbled away while Ethel Carey and Eudora endeavored to supply her with the latest reports on Lakeville life. Her brother Ted had informed everyone he expected her back for good by spring. The children had been kept home for a few days during the infantile paralysis scare and had set fire to the house in their boredom, involving Ted in some legalities about collecting insurance. The Haven-Brown Real Estate office was affected by the imminence of war and it was Ethel's whispered suspicion that Eudora might have to give up the office and come down to mere desk space in the bank.

"You were the brains of that office, anyway," Ethel whispered in the privacy of the bathroom, to Vicky. "Eudora as good as admits it. She flies off the handle too fast and antagonizes people. Especially now, of course."

Tom was considering building a government base somewhere in the Pacific islands, but again Ethel whispered to Vicky that this was all big talk and Mr. Turner had no intention of leaving Lakeville unless it got bombed. Other news was that Howard Keeler and wife had left haberdashery and beauty parlor to gypsy down the Florida coast in a secondhand trailer, with a pack of grocers, plumbers and other Lakeville creditors about to gypsy down after them. Ethel's own papa had been summoned to an important advisory post in Washington and had promised Ethel a lunch at the White House one of these days, though everyone in Lakeville was still Republican and called F.D. "that man in the White House." Every girl in town had Amanda Keeler Evans scrapbooks (except for a rebel group called the Joan Crawford Fan Club, of which Vicky's niece was the president), and items about Amanda or her husband were in great demand. Eudora Brown had been assured by her physician that a glass of wine could not possibly injure her coming heir, and on the strength of this medical support was drinking straight Bacardi whenever she could get the bottle out of Mr. Elroy's or Ken Saunders' hands. After her initial hearty but shamefaced greeting of Vicky, she allowed her conversation to lapse into one chief word, which was "stinks."

Even if Tom Turner had not been there the little group would have been a difficult one for any hostess to organize. Ethel carried on a constant flow of gossip about characters Uncle Rockman and Ken did not know, Vicky ate sandwiches and tried to avoid Tom Turner's urgent, curious gaze, Eudora drank and made sardonic exclamations, and Uncle Rockman and Ken talked feverishly of the atom. In occasional efforts at general conversation Tom Turner described the Lakeville Country club inner politics to Uncle Rockman, who vanquished him with learned commentary on the splendid work on the Soul being done at the Yale Institute of Human Relations by somebody named Burr. Swinging lightly out of this, Uncle Rockman dealt with the Inverse Square Law, and finding his audience quite crushed he was able to take up the atom again, of which he spoke fondly as if it was a dear little Cupid flying through space making statistics for every good child. Ken Saunders eagerly encouraged this monologue as a means of freezing out Tom Turner, and Uncle had somehow gotten into quantum this and quantum that when a final sip at his drink made him slide farther down into the corner of the cushioned sofa and fall asleep.

Ethel Carey nudged Vicky.

"Is he keeping you?" she whispered. "I mean I don't see how anybody would let him go on like that unless he paid the rent."

Marriage had not improved Eudora Brown nor had pregnancy given a dewy light to her eyes. There was little that pleased her in the world or in the present evening. Her bridegroom, inheriting the floor on Uncle Rockman's fade-out, talked so instructively of current events, the war, and secret white papers, that Vicky concluded he must have no job; such vastly informed men usually had their time to themselves. This turned out to be something like the case, for Eudora cornered Vicky in the course of the evening.

"Could you loan us five hundred bucks?" she whispered. "You see this war is ruining Tom's business—and I'm going to have to let the office go after next month. Ethel says you've been doing so well—"

Vicky was too bewildered to answer at first and Eudora took this confusion as a criticism.

"After all, the way I look at it is this," she said. "If it hadn't been for me, it would be you in this spot right now, so I feel you owe me a *little* something!"

Vicky was so embarrassed that if she had had any money at all she would have poured it at once in Eudora's hat. Instead she gulped out something about "maybe later on," which angered Eudora.

"You're just like Amanda," she declared. "I wrote Amanda and she high-hatted me, too. said she was doing all she could for refugees. Hell, I could have been a refugee if I'd gone abroad when everyone else went."

Eudora's last remark was overheard by Ethel Carey, who was so shocked at the idea of asking Amanda for money that the two women were soon snapping at each other.

"Amanda stinks," Eudora repeated several times. "Amanda stinks on ice."

Mr. Saunders took offense at this.

"Say what you will about Amanda," he stated. "Let us not forget that she is the lawfully wedded wife of that great leader, Julian Evans."

Eudora observed that Mr. Evans also stank on ice.

"Possibly," admitted Ken. "At least he will bear watching."

"Sixteen papers and not one of them first-rate," stated Tom Turner. "A joint circulation of over—well roughly, let's say ten million readers—"

Suddenly Mr. Elroy struggled to his feet from the depths of the sofa.

"Did someone mention paper?" he inquired, blue eyes wide with anxiety. "I must talk to the paper men. Excuse me, please."

He waddled hastily to the door, Vicky running after him with coat and hat. Ken Saunders hurried ahead to get a cab and assist his new chum, but Uncle Rockman would have no assistance. He was in his own car and his own chauffeur knew exactly what was to be done. He was gone as swiftly as any fairy godmother, leaving Vicky's friends with the impression that he was something more than an elderly adviser, particularly since she could give little information about him or his reasons for calling on her. Even Ken Saunders seemed baffled.

Eudora Brown declared that any man that age who ran after a girl Vicky's age really did stink on ice. She said that was why she and Tom had gotten on so well, they were the right age for each other. Her husband caustically suggested that she stop being a damned fool but added that he really did not expect any such luck.

"Go ahead, say what you're going to say," said Eudora shrilly. "Tell everybody right in front of me that you're still crazy about Vicky. I don't care. Go ahead. Go on."

Ethel Carey grew white at this and suggested that they all leave. They could see Vicky tomorrow, maybe, unless she was as busy as she should be.

"Certainly I'm crazy about Vicky," said Tom Turner coldly, without looking at Vicky. "I always have been—always will be."

"There—that's all you wanted to hear, isn't it?" Eudora sobbed. "God knows I hear it often enough—*you* might as well."

Tom Turner planted himself in front of his wife.

"All right, let her hear!" he shouted. "I couldn't get Vicky to sleep with me—that was the only reason I walked out on her. No trouble like that with you. So what are you kicking about?"

"Tom! Eudora!" pleaded Ethel, holding their wraps in her arms. "Mr. Saunders, do get us a cab. We can't have this go on."

Vicky sat stonily in a chair, too numb to say good-bye. Ethel, with mixed feelings of horror and shocked delight, herded her two friends out, Eudora still weeping angrily and Tom haughtily removed from the lot of them. It was the worst evening she'd ever spent, Vicky thought. It was as if her onetime love for Tom must spoil even the tiniest hours of pleasure in her life forever. Anyway Uncle Rockman had missed the worst of it. And Nancy Elroy hadn't been there, that was something. But Ken Saunders had. He might tell Amanda and Julian. Or worse yet, he would just look at her and be scornful of anyone involved in such a sordid mess.

Ken Saunders came back, rumpling his fair hair in utter perplexity.

"Do I gather what I just gathered?" he asked. "You don't need to tell me if you don't want to."

Vicky nodded.

"And the guy is still crazy about you?" he wanted to know.

Vicky wanted to say yes, for that was after all what Eudora had insisted and what Tom had said, too. But the instant they began torturing each other before her she had sensed that the truth was much less flattering—they only used her as the whip for their relationship. Eudora and Tom understood each other, counted on no nobility in each other, relied affectionately on each other's vulgarity, lashed at each other's weaknesses and bound themselves together by these. They belonged together. She had always been left out. They hadn't even looked at her when they were shouting about Tom's continued love for her. They didn't think of her as a person, hardly, but merely a name they used to excite themselves with. If Tom had really still been in love with her, Vicky thought, he would never have said so. But she couldn't explain this to Ken Saunders. She did tell him most of the story, though she did not like him to know how stubbornly she had held out against an affair with Tom, nor even how glad she was now that she had refused. Men always seemed to think this showed a serious flaw in a girl's character, a willfulness that might prove further acquaintance most unprofitable. It was best to keep this willfulness a secret.

"We do know how to pick out trouble for ourselves," Ken said. "Here we are, both of us in the prime of life, all messed up because we picked the wrong people. If we had any sense we'd have picked people like each other. But oh, no."

"Oh, no," said Vicky. So he had been in love with the wrong person, too!

They sat up in her kitchen till four o'clock comparing mistakes in their lives, holding hands and bewailing the thought that they could not fall in love with each other. Later he scrambled eggs with anchovies sprinkled over them and made coffee most competently. He had a knack for knowing where everything was—cigarettes, liquor, salt, coffee. In fact, Vicky wondered about it after he left. She decided that either his lost love's place must be very much like hers, or else there were a lot of apartments around New York fitted exactly like this one.

7

*J*ULIAN EVANS FELT THAT he was big enough to carry the world's problems with almost godlike dignity. He did not lose his temper over Russia as many men his junior did; he saw both sides of Chamberlain, found a calm word for Lindbergh, was thoughtful—not shrill—in his devotion to Roosevelt. In conferences with the nation's leaders, he did not permit himself to go "off the deep end" over politics, but preserved—at least publicly—a tolerance that would have done honor to the Supreme Court bench. This, at least, was his own secret conviction. But with the problem of Amanda he was in a state bordering on hysteria. Scarcely an hour in the day passed now that something she said, did, or indirectly caused, did not pop up to vex him. Fundamentally, there was the matter of sex; the manner in which she stiffened at his touch, as if he were some monster, as if, indeed, he was attempting something that was outside his lawful rights and even outside his ability. And

then there was her open ingratitude at his management of her career, a career which God knows was becoming increasingly embarrassing to him. It was on this he was pondering as he sat in his
study scowling at a carafe of orange juice. Mr. Cheever, his
London man, stood at the window smoking his pipe and con-
tributing not a little to Julian's vexation.

"Understand, Evans, I am not reflecting in the least on your
wife's talents," Cheever said in measured tones. "Amanda Keeler
Evans is unquestionably one of the finest minds of our times, a
real force. I'm not denying that. I merely ask to be given first
crack at my own territory, and if the stuff is printable at all, let it
be under my byline. I don't see the logic of scrapping my stuff
and then letting Amanda spill it as hers. I feel there's a certain
amount of injustice in that."

His superior moodily sipped his orange juice. He had known
this was coming for some time. He had seen the signs months
ago when Amanda flew to London and Cheever had gallantly
placed his material at her disposal, to her credit and implicitly to
his loss. A beautiful young woman spends two weeks in London
and is magically able to give an accurate and complete survey of
the whole situation, when the regular correspondent had spent
twenty years there apparently unable to grasp things. It would
never be understood by the public that Mr. Evans had permitted
Amanda a freedom of opinion that was denied Cheever. More of
this sort of thing was happening constantly since Cheever's stay
in New York. Amanda took the cream, still. Julian had wanted
to give it to her, but there should have been a little more discretion in it, so as not to lose Cheever. Being a pretty egotistical man
in his own right, once his gallantry had worn off, Mr. Cheever
was unquestionably in a mood to make trouble over his rights.
He would be a hard man to replace. Certainly no newcomer
would be able to supply Amanda with the historical and social
documentation that Cheever had done. It was a moment for the

utmost tact, Julian knew, just as he knew Cheever was in the right. But a consciousness of being in the wrong seldom puts a man in good humor, so he flew into a childish rage.

"Damn it, Cheever, the war isn't copyrighted!" he shouted, banging the desk, but not too hard, as it was easily marred. "The stuff is there—anybody with eyes can get it, and anybody with brains can sum it up! I can't be bothered with personal feelings in a public crisis like this! I've got my responsibilities to my papers, and the American public! By God, Cheever, if you want to be picayune about this when millions of men are being killed—"

He drank down a glass of orange juice and then mopped his brow. There were moments when he wished for some heart ailment which would oblige people to take care of crossing him. As it was, he managed, by clutching at his heart and then wiping his brow, to convey the effect of a strong man about to crack up. Cheever looked at him dispassionately over his pipe and said nothing, which irritated Julian even more. He would have liked Cheever to be in a temper and he, the chief, to be patronizingly calm. All this trouble was Amanda's fault. He had created this public figure and it was getting to be a bigger responsibility than anything he had hitherto taken on, and he was a man who had bought railroads and even mountains. The angrier he was at Amanda the angrier he was at Cheever, since rage with Amanda was a confession of her superiority.

"This is no time for personal vanity," Julian sputtered. "By-line! A fine thing to be worrying about, with children being bombed, homes wrecked. By God, Cheever, I'm too big a man to be subjected to this sort of thing! You can't expect me to waste time worrying over whose name is signed to what paragraph, with Europe burning!"

"If it's so trivial as all that, why do you insist, then, that full credit on my material be given to Amanda Evans?" Mr. Cheever inquired in an insultingly calm tone. "If the paper ever made a slipup on *that* byline there'd be hell to pay and you know it, damn you!"

In the twenty years Amos Cheever had worked for Julian he had never been guilty of such open insubordination. Julian was shocked almost out of his anger, and his first instinct was that Cheever would never have dared take this stand unless he had some bigger job around the corner. All the rumors he had been hearing lately of a great Western syndicate combining with his nearest Eastern rival now catapulted through Julian's mind. The rumor must be true, and Cheever must have been offered more money there. The increased power of a rival did not alarm Julian very much for he would bide his time to outstrip that move. A little shrewd planning, a few conferences with bankers, lawyers, gamblers—a little discreet hijacking possibly—and Evans would be on top again as usual. What did disturb him was the damage Cheever could do him by leaving him. A man who had worked for him for twenty years, knew all about his family, Margaret and the children, had been cited for international dignities because of his journalistic work, knew England as well as he knew America—a man with such professional prestige Julian naturally felt was completely an Evans creation—and his moving to another employer would not fail to create inquiry. And Cheever, being angry, would talk. He would make a fool out of his only employer. He would say Julian Evans ran his business as a convenience to his wife's career. He might even say Amanda Keeler was the power behind the throne, edging out any employee who challenged her authority. How would that make Julian Evans look? Everyone would whisper when they saw him, everyone would laugh at him. The king lets his old prime minister be executed because the new queen is really king.

Such thoughts scampered through Julian's brain, scattering fear, and Julian's face was even pale when he turned again to Cheever.

"Let's not quarrel, Cheever," he said, with such a change of manner that Cheever looked at him in utter bewilderment. "We've been together too long, old man. As a matter of fact, the thing that bothers you is going to be cleared up in no time, anyway. Amanda is getting far too busy with her new book and of course, her work with the refugee children, to have time for editorial comment, either on the air or in our pages. We'll have to depend pretty much on you, old man."

The "old man" overture did not relax the grimness of Cheever's expression. He tapped his pipe on the huge Abalone shell Mr. Evans used as an ash tray.

"Hasn't she got all the publicity out of that child adoption committee that she needs?" he asked. Again this insolence was so unprecedented as to convince Julian that Cheever was as good as laughing at him over the rival office this very minute. He would not permit himself to be annoyed, though he knew that he would be in a private fury about all this all night long.

"My dear Cheever, do you realize Amanda has—with my help—placed over two hundred children from England, France, even Czechoslovakia? Good homes, mind you, homes of friends of ours, often. Homes that never had a child and didn't want one, but by God, Amanda got them in and she deserves credit."

It was a nice point and Julian sat back, continuing to nod his head convincingly.

"I notice you have never inconvenienced your own home with any of these little visitors," Mr. Cheever answered thoughtfully.

Julian's cigar dropped from his fingers at this final bombshell. Here again were implications that were far more disturbing than the mere impudence of the remark. Cheever was saying something other people must be saying, and what other people were saying could roll into a tremendous scandal. Being a clever man, Julian saw at once how fatal was this discrepancy between Amanda's public good works and her private selfishness. He was

perfectly aware of the important connection between preaching
and practice, and in his publicized campaigns tried to exhibit
proper regard for this. But Amanda was different. Amanda was
a phenomenon. Julian blamed himself now for being too lax with
her. He should have put her on guard against this sort of criticism. It was still not too late.

"As I told you, Cheever, Amanda's time is taken up more and
more with her book. With her relief work and other public activities, she has scarcely a minute even for me." Julian was feeling
his ground carefully and dared not allow Cheever's cool gaze to
dismay him. "If we were to take the responsibility for any of
these children Amanda would insist on giving them her entire
time and, of course, she serves our cause far better by giving us
her talents. So—"

"So her time is her own," Mr. Cheever observed with an unpleasant smile. "No matter what else is going on in the world, at
least the Evanses are at peace. They sleep under a roof, they eat
four meals a day, they count their money, they collect. Whatever
happens the Evanses collect, and never pay. God's pets."

Julian's secretary, Castor, had crept in and out during this discussion, with letters, memoranda, and at one point with a pair of
glowing Northern Spy apples—a four o'clock habit of Julian's
which he was always willing to share with a guest. The tenor of
the talk had plainly given the little secretary tremendous concern,
for he was accustomed to see Julian in a rage and the visitor in the
proper state of dignified but servile silence. Here was Julian
Evans trying to propitiate an indignant employee and the employee refusing to be smoothed. The saffron face of Mr. Castor
was flushed with excitement, even terror, over this unexpected
turn. Even if Cheever had not been mad, Castor would have been
alarmed to see Mr. Evans anything but majestically patronizing to
an employee. The secretary could not help feeling that in a moment perhaps the caller would whip out a revolver, as God knows

many enemies had threatened to do, and there would Julian Evans be, making news in his own home, body stretched across the floor, while Ernest Castor took charge of the investigators.

"I was typing Mr. Evans' editorial on 'Eyes Front, not Backward,' for the Sunday magazine, officer," Castor heard himself already explaining with quiet authority, "when I heard voices. I came in to the library and found Cheever, our London man, cursing Mr. Evans and waving a revolver. As it is up to me to protect not only Mr. Evans's private interests but his own person, I sprang at Cheever, a much larger man than I. I had the advantage of him by a certain elementary knowledge of *jiu jitsu* as well as a cool head. However, he had a gun. In a flash, I saw Mr. Evans on the floor, and the smoking revolver lay beside him. I saw at once that he was beyond hope. Blood was streaming—"

It was something of a disappointment for the imaginative little man to see that there was no gun, and that Cheever's anger was so far confined to cold statements which Mr. Evans found himself obliged to defend. Castor's secret passion for the theatrical was frustrated by Julian's namby-pamby handling of the rebellious employee. Like Miss Bemel, his great compensation for the indignities of his position was to see his employer inflict worse indignities on better men. But here was Julian almost apologizing to Cheever for the Evanses' not taking on the responsibilities Amanda's propaganda inflicted on other people. Castor stood just outside Julian's door in his own little cubbyhole and gnawed his fingernails desperately. He had a sudden daring inspiration when he heard Julian speak.

"That's quite an accusation you are trying to make there, Cheever," Julian was saying in a grave, shocked voice. "I gather you are trying to say that my wife and I do not live by the things we preach."

"*Trying* to say? I *did* say, for God's sake!" Mr. Cheever cried out in exasperation, and then Castor tiptoed into the room with a sheet of paper which he laid before Julian with a preoccupied air, as if he had no inkling of the argument he was interrupting.

"It's rather important, sir," Castor said meekly. "Mrs. Evans wants to know whether you wish the new boy brought here directly from the train or whether he is to go to your country place with the other refugees. He's in Montreal, waiting further instructions."

For a moment Julian looked blankly at his secretary, and then, as was his custom, took as his own work this gift from Providence.

"We'll keep him here as long as he's happy," he commanded briskly, and then said to Cheever with an air of grieved patience, "Do you really mean, Cheever, that you think Amanda should keep her personal charges here in the city with her just for the publicity value, when the country air is what their health demands?"

Cheever shrugged. However it had been done, Julian had as usual turned the tables in his own favor. He had made it appear that Amanda's personal sacrifices were never mentioned, and that such crass critics as Cheever objected not so much to her failure to inconvenience herself, as to her failure to advertise her private goodness. Julian himself believed this as soon as Castor had given him the opportunity. He would make it true. He would, if necessary, put his foot down with Amanda as he did with his staff. She must see it as he did. They must take on the burden of a refugee child in the home.

Castor tiptoed out of the room, his elation at his diplomacy not for an instant showing in his yellow sharp little face.

Cheever put his pipe in his pocket. It was turning out like all of his other interviews with Julian Evans, as long as he had known him. There was no defeating such a man. You raised an issue over a major point and Julian cleverly sidetracked you to some trivial complaint which he then settled in a noble way. He had come to settle with Evans over the matter of Amanda stealing his stuff, and the discussion ended with Julian triumphantly declaring that

Amanda was nobly and modestly adopting a war refugee. You couldn't beat Julian because he refused to meet you with your own weapons on your own field.

Through the half-opened door little Castor watched Cheever leave and could see that the man was resigned momentarily, though he might still be hostile. For a moment Castor felt a little pity for the vanquished Cheever and a secret antagonism to Julian Evans, who signed this little minor triumph as if it had been his own instead of his secretary's. Julian had a hundred people to sing his virtues, but Castor had only Castor to admire Castor's astuteness. He admired himself now, silently, for that hunch about Mr. Evans's letter. The Mrs. Evans mentioned, of course, was Julian's former wife, Margaret. Poor, stolid Margaret still followed her husband's advice on good works faithfully, shifting from longshoremen to sharecroppers, opening her home to the underhoused or the undersexed, whichever campaign Julian was fomenting at the moment. Now her big home on the Hudson was filled with dozens of leftovers from Julian's various public causes. Even her bitterness toward Julian's new wife did not prevent her from earnestly doing her Christian duty in the Amanda Keeler Evans adoption plan. Few people knew of this, however, so Castor was justly proud of saving the second Mrs. Evans at the expense of the first. He stood for a moment in the doorway to Julian's study, half-expecting his employer to commend his quick thinking. But as soon as Cheever had left, Julian was on the telephone sending for Miss Bemel, since his wife was not to be found. The next moment he was telephoning his downtown secretary, Harnett, to start working on a *New York Times* man, now in Geneva, as a potential successor to Cheever.

"Promise him anything he likes," Julian was saying. "Don't commit me to anything. Act on your own. If he won't play ball, then he can't go around saying he turned down Evans. Feel him out. I want to be protected just in case. Cheever's getting too damn troublesome."

Even Castor marveled at the efficiency of his master. He had saved Cheever whom he needed, but the danger of losing him was already insulting Mr. Evans. Men didn't leave him. He fired them. Cheever wasn't going to be able to say he walked out on Evans because his wife ran the paper and took all the gravy. Evans was going to be able to say, on the contrary, that he let Cheever go because he was a troublemaker. His flash of mild pity for Cheever as he saw the bearded distinguished figure go down the hall immediately vanished. All Castor thought was, "The poor fool! If he is sap enough to let this happen, then he deserves it!"

2

AMANDA HAD this in common with Julian—the belief that any calamity befalling someone else was simply in the course of nature, whereas the merest hitch in their own arrangements was the fault of someone in their service. The rain of complaints suddenly falling on Amanda for her refugee work was clearly due to Miss Bemel's inefficiency, or, to be fair, the joint inefficiency of Miss Bemel and the relief headquarters' secretary. Castor's memo from Julian urging immediate if temporary adoption of one or more refugee children was distinctly traceable to the stupidity of Amos Cheever. No matter whose fault, however, it was Amanda who must suffer this injustice, and what with these and many other matters she was in a state of high nervous tension. Ken Saunders, instead of proving a solace to her feminine vanity, was undermining her perpetually by breaking dates, quite as if his time were as important as hers, and that therefore he had the same justification that she had for such behavior. In spite of their new restless relationship, he obliged her to think about him, to wonder what he meant by this and that; no sooner had he convinced her he was again infatuated with her than he upset her as-

surance by ignoring her for days. Assurance of her sexual fascination was increasingly important to her other work, and
Amanda was furious with Ken for interfering with her career by
his capriciousness. As if, she thought in astonishment, she was
just a woman, just *any* woman. She would call him to say that if
she could finish an appointment with a congressman and dispose
of a delegation of admirers from Argentina *and* shorten her luncheon engagement with a Burmese correspondent, she would
meet him at the usual place sometime between two and three-
thirty. It was incredible that, on arriving at the spot promptly at
three-fifteen, Ken should not be there, yet this happened many
times. It was the sort of minor annoyance that was most disturbing to Amanda's larger work. It was equally disturbing to find
herself more anxious than ever to see him, to find out again if
there were power in her caress, to wonder if indeed it was not she
herself who was intrigued this time instead of vice versa.

Ethel Carey, visiting New York once again, contributed to
Amanda's bad temper.

"I just want to be sure that man is all right for Vicky," Ethel
said over the phone when Miss Bemel finally allowed the connection to be made.

Amanda, busy with all her other matters, was not in the least
interested in Vicky's beaux. She resented being regarded by
Lakeville as responsible for Vicky's progress in the city, so she
was curt with Ethel.

"I'm sure Vicky can pick out her own boyfriends, my dear,"
she said. "She's a big girl now, Ethel."

"The *old* one, that Rockman Elroy, she says is just a friend,"
Ethel said confidentially. "I finally believed her on that. But the
young one—the Saunders one—certainly knows his way around
her apartment."

"Saunders? Did you say Saunders?" Amanda repeated blankly.

Ethel was pleased to finally capture her friend's attention.

"He's been there two or three times when I've been there," she went on eagerly. "I don't know how far things have gone but I can tell that Vicky's sort of crazy about him. So I thought I'd find out what sort of person he was. Is he married?"

The idea of Saunders seeing Vicky except under her command or in the necessary routine of their office, was beyond Amanda's comprehension. It was scarcely worth considering. But it was not agreeable to have Vicky's friends taking it seriously.

"I don't really know whether Saunders is married or not," she told Ethel. "I'm sure he's not the sort of person to be interested in Vicky, so she's foolish to get it into her head. Heavens, that girl deliberately makes trouble for herself, I'm afraid. I'm beginning to wonder how she can get on at all, if she stays so naïve."

"Oh, dear!" Ethel sighed. "I suppose it's going to be another one of those things. I hope she isn't having an affair with him! Rebound, you know."

Amanda was chilled at the mere idea.

"Vicky doesn't appeal to men that way, my dear," she said. "Do stop worrying about her. I'm sure Saunders isn't interested in her, so the best thing you can do is to straighten her out about him. She's such an idiot about those things, really, now."

Even to herself Amanda sounded unconvincing, which made her even more annoyed with Ethel Carey, and with Vicky Haven, too. These simple-minded females who thought the important thing in life—even in such times as these—was to make a suitable marriage, find a new beau, prove their femaleness. It was not the first time Amanda had been contemptuous of her entire sex with their insistent devotion to the trivia of life. She brushed off Ethel's hint of an invitation to lunch or tea, and sailed into her refugee correspondence with savage briskness.

"Mrs. Corpen thinks she has the nicest refugees of all the women in her organization," Miss Bemel reported, reading off the stack of mail with her new harlequin glasses, green-rimmed, giving her thick, dark face a somewhat hippo effect. "The children are dears, so she says, but now that their mother has arrived she is having trouble. The mother is a very charming young woman only she's been having affairs with all the husbands in the neighborhood. Mrs. Corpen says here she is rather suspicious of her own husband and she knows about the gardener and the chauffeur for certain. So she wants the committee to do something."

"What does she think I am—Dorothy Dix?" Amanda cried, exasperated. "The woman's just a jealous old thing, that's all. I can't be bothered."

Miss Bemel continued to look at Mrs. Corpen's plaintive letter with a speculative expression, no doubt thinking that the young refugee mother must be having a far better and gayer time than Miss Bemel was having, and being protected at it, too. A furtive seed of rebellion was sown in Miss Bemel's soul that very moment, and she was not content to drop the matter.

"After all, Mrs. Corpen is in a spot, Mrs. Evans," she said doggedly. "She can't send the woman away, can she, without people saying she's a Fascist or something. She's got to go on and let her take her husband or everyone will say she's unfair to England."

"I'm sick of women being so trivial," Amanda said sharply.

Miss Bemel laid the letter reluctantly aside, half deciding to solve Mrs. Corpen's problem on her own hook. She wouldn't quite dare but it was a temptation, for these ruthless refugee women were a constant burn-up to the loveless Miss Bemel.

"Here's another request from that woman's magazine asking for an article on how you personally handle your little war charges," pursued Miss Bemel. "That makes the tenth such request."

Amanda's pretty brows met in a frown.

"I don't understand why everyone is jumping on me right now," she said plaintively. "What's a person expected to do—outside of working on one novel and a dozen speeches and articles? Next they'll be at me for not doing my own cooking! You can send a memo to Mr. Evans that he can do anything he likes about this matter, I'm far too busy."

Miss Bemel bowed over her typewriter, happily. It was always a pleasure to send the ball back to Mr. Castor. While she typed, Amanda drummed on the desk, frowning. In half an hour the young man who was assisting her in writing her new book would arrive for two hours' conference. After that came a vital interview with an international banker. A roundtable discussion with six foreign correspondents was booked for a six o'clock broadcast. It was a very full day for even Amanda, a day that required her to be on her toes even more than usual. It was unfair in every way that her mind should be unable to throw off the matter of Ken Saunders. It was outrageous that she should, in this busy hour, be speculating how she could manage to see him during the day in order to scold him for allowing girls like Vicky Haven to fall in love with him.

"It's all Ethel Carey's fault," Amanda murmured to herself. But as soon as she had delegated the blame for her own confusion on someone, she felt a little better, and was fairly civil to Miss Bemel for quite a while. This civility enabled Miss Bemel to snub the morning's callers with double vengeance, for it took only a kind word to give her her head. The entire household gathered, by Miss Bemel's high-handedness, that at last her mistress must be in a calmer mood, and proceeded accordingly.

3

ETHEL CAREY was able to assume a friendly detachment about Amanda's success while she remained in Lakeville, but no sooner did she set foot in New York than she was thrown into a stew of exasperation. Everything that used to stimulate her about New York now seemed to gently remind her that this was Amanda's own kingdom, and nobodies from Lakeville, no matter how well dressed, would be regarded as interlopers, here. To shop in Jay Thorpe's or Bergdorf's—once Ethel's greatest joy—was to yearn desperately for a never-to-be-won invitation to Amanda's elegant soirées. To buy a newspaper here was to see that even the war belonged to Amanda and her husband. Annoying above all was the sacred manner in which Amanda's staff protected her from contact with mere old friends. It was Ethel's firm resolve to batter down this reverence if she had to telephone the Evanses' house a dozen times a day.

"Good heavens, she's bound to have a few human traits like anybody else!" Ethel exclaimed to Vicky over their lunch at Chez Jean. "The way everybody acts about her you'd think she was above even going to the bathroom! Why shouldn't I drop in on her if I feel like it? Why is she any different than you or me except for being richer? When I asked her to lunch you would have thought I'd touched for actual money."

Vicky looked uneasily around the restaurant, fearful that by some chance Amanda might be in the next booth. She felt guilt that Amanda should have favored her with more personal attention than she granted to Ethel, especially after Ethel had confessed to first stirring up Amanda's interest in Vicky. It was true, too, that Vicky was quite as horrified as Miss Bemel herself at Ethel's debonair proposal to "drop in" on Amanda, and when Ethel was inspired to telephone Amanda to "come on down for a hen session" Vicky could have died of shame, just as if it was everyone's duty to keep out of the royal path, cower in the background as much as possible lest the goddess be sullied by some ordinary human touch. It was disgusting to be a toady, Vicky thought, but that was what Amanda made of everyone, except of course Ethel Carey.

"I know of course why she doesn't ask me to her parties," Ethel said, attacking her dainty squab with a savagery that might indicate the bird had pulled a knife on her first. "It's because I might say something about her stepmother's beauty shop back home, or about her father being a good-for-nothing. After all those little allusions she makes to her sheltered childhood, never exactly saying so, but just short of implying that Daddy was a Southern colonel, and mummy was a lady, and the Keelers in England were all dukes. I'd let fly with something, you can be sure of that."

Vicky honestly couldn't see why Amanda would want to risk having Ethel Carey reveal her lowly past, or why Ethel thought of that privilege as her lawful right, but she dared not say so for Ethel would certainly accuse her of toadyism. It would be a fine thing to be like Ethel, to look everyone from king to Garbo, straight in the eye and say, "Move over, there, I'm on this street, too."

"You know of course who paid for her tuition at Miss Doxey's," Ethel said and whipped out her lipstick for the purpose of readjusting her mouth after the scuffle with the squab. The manner in which she leveled this crimson trifle was so resolute, so ominous, that it foreboded a reloading of her guns, and Vicky resigned herself to further bombing of the Amanda legend.

"Wasn't it her father?" murmured Vicky.

Ethel twisted her newly made lips to an unpretty pucker which involved a sardonic wrinkling of the nostrils, as well.

"Where would Howard Keeler get a thousand dollars? she gently mocked. "Not that it's such a sum. Goodness knows Miss Doxey's is the cheapest school in the territory, and I wish to goodness I had followed Daddy's advice and gone East, but I was always so homesick. But at least I *could* have gone to Dobbs Ferry or Spence and none of the rest of you could."

"That's quite true, Ethel," Vicky was glad to agree on anything that might calm Ethel's ruffled vanity. "I know I could never have gone if my brother hadn't loaned me the money, and even he had to borrow it, so—"

"Howard Keeler's girlfriend, the beautician, paid it, believe it or not!" Ethel whispered dramatically. "I know on account of Daddy's bank. All the time he was running around with her,

Howard was deviled to death by Amanda. She didn't want to live over the store, naturally, even as a kid. And you know how snooty she was, not with you, maybe, because you were so much younger, but with all the rest of us. It burned her up to be just nobody that way. So she just raised perpetual Cain with her father. His girlfriend hated her and thought it was worth her while to send her away."

"Amanda didn't want her father to marry again, I know," Vicky cautiously admitted.

"Well, after all the woman did for his child, the poor man had to!" Ethel exclaimed. "She knew what she was doing, all right. She got Amanda out of the picture and then she marched her man straight down to City Hall and nailed him. It cost her all her savings, but at least she got him."

"Amanda couldn't stand her," Vicky recalled. "Remember how she used to hide when they came to school for visits?"

"That was because the second Mrs. Keeler said 'ain't'," said Ethel with some satisfaction. "So did the first, for that matter. They said 'ain't' from morning till night like mad. It killed Amanda."

The spectacle of the buxom blonde stepmother sending this naughty elision echoing over Miss Doxey's formal gardens, baying it from the chapel steps, writing it a hundred times a minute on the heavens, made Vicky break into hysterical laughter.

"What gets me," said Ethel, with vast bitterness, "is the way all the fuss about Amanda has made even Lakeville take her say-so about her family. They *know* Mrs. Keeler still had the beauty shop, they *know* Howard Keeler still has a dinky haberdashery store. They know Amanda was brought up over the store and went to Miss Doxey's lousy little school. But they think they must all be mistaken because it says in all the papers that Amanda had convent training abroad and her folks were 'land poor.' I can't tell them any different. 'Look,' they say, 'it says all this right here in black and white.'"

Vicky wanted to be sympathetic to Ethel, who after all had not been received by her old friend as warmly as she should have been, no doubt about that; however, in all fairness she did not see how Amanda could be blamed for not wishing to be reminded of the humble past Ethel was only too eager to recall. She saw Ethel picking up her salad fork with the air of marshaling new forces, and sought to sidetrack her.

"Lakeville is such a stupid town, anyway," she said. "I don't blame you for getting mad at it."

This was not a wise thought, it appeared, for Ethel held her fork poised in air a moment to give Vicky a level, haughty look.

"My dear Vicky, don't *you* go New York on me!" she exclaimed. "After all, if I wished to, I could live here, too. Personally I prefer Lakeville. My home, you must admit, is one of the prettier homes in the state. It's Frank Lloyd Wright! They don't come any better, you know. I travel. I hear all the best concerts in Cleveland. I go to hunting parties in Virginia. And Lakeville is *not* a slum."

"I know," Vicky nodded.

"We do quite as much for war relief as Amanda does, I assure you," Ethel went on proudly. "We have our adopted refugees just the same as anybody. We have our Bundles. You're not fair to Lakeville because you had an unfortunate experience there—"

Ether could not forgive Vicky for appearing to recover from her "unfortunate experience" so easily. It seemed a personal affront to one who had devoted herself to ameliorating the "experience." The least Vicky could do was to need more sympathy.

"And now she was to write a sequel!" Ethel recalled her special grievance with access of fresh spleen. "Now she's announcing a trilogy, just because that's the one thing she's never tried! She *must* have everything!" With this thought she made an innocent-looking watercress salad the victim of her avenging fork. "Of course that will be a hit. How can it fail? Actually they tell me Julian has the reviews made up already and in type, all ready to spring on his readers. Almost before it's written, mind you, it's a hit."

Vicky squirmed under Ethel's rising voice. It was a pity, she thought, that anyone who admired outspokenness and candor the way she did, was always so terrified when she actually heard it, and must always suffer this anguish that it was being overheard. It must be, she gloomily reflected, that she came of a long line of downstairs ancestors, governesses, chimney-sweeps, stablehands, housekeepers. Obviously Ethel, on the other hand, acquired her fine arrogance from forefathers who were squires landed gentry. You wouldn't catch Ethel looking around apologetically at possible eavesdroppers, putting out an extra coin hastily when the waiter frowned at the tip, trying to smile at the policeman scolding you for crossing the street. Even while she admired Ethel's high-handedness, Vicky was plotting to distract Ethel from her subject by some wily femi-nine confidence.

"I was really glad to see Tom Turner and Eudora the other night," she said artlessly the moment she could break in. "I knew the minute that he stepped in the door it was all over, and I really in a way didn't want it to be. I just didn't want to find out I was that superficial. I was disgusted with myself for not having the guts to go on having a broken heart, honestly I was."

Ethel was only momentarily put off the trail.

"Honey, you're young yet. Besides, it would have been differ-ent, believe me, if it had been a real affair. I always thought, *of course*, that it was. I had no idea of anything else."

Again Vicky felt guilty. She should never have confided the sordid fact of her chastity to Ethel. Nowadays you didn't dare tell a thing like that to your own mother, or she'd have you analyzed to see what made you so backward. Certainly, it was proof of ar-rested development in anyone over twenty, and Vicky blushed to think of it. Ever since she'd told Ethel, the latter kept pondering over the strange fact, acting a little resentful about it, as if her sympathy had been extracted under false circumstances. At least Vicky knew enough now to try in the future to give an impression of a proper background of adult love affairs.

"I think Amanda doesn't like the idea of your seeing that Saunders man," Ethel said. "Thinks he's too good for you, I suppose. I told her I thought you were falling for him in a big way."

"Oh, Ethel!" protested Vicky. "I told you not to tell!"

"What of it? I can read you like a book. You think every word he says is the most brilliant thing you ever heard. You sit there gawping at him like some little goon. Even Tom Turner talked about it. Said he didn't see much in that fellow. Of course that brought Eudora down on him in a big way. 'What's it to you, if she's got somebody else?' she said. 'All right, go back to her. You got me in this condition, now you want to leave me and go back to Vicky. All right, all right, I can stand it.' You know. The usual."

Never, never would she tell Ethel another secret, Vicky vowed, it was worse than telling all Lakeville and her own family.

"Don't act so snooty, honey," Ethel laughed, in great amusement over Vicky's suddenly stern countenance. "You are crazy about Ken Saunders, and that's all there is to it."

"Supposing I am," Vicky burst out in a flash of anger. "You don't have to tell the world! Amanda, Eudora—everybody in this restaurant!"

With this Vicky looked boldly around, fully expecting to see the entire staff of her office as well as Amanda Evans bending courteous ears to this broadcast of her weaknesses. When she actually did catch a horrifying glimpse of a bushy blond male head in the booth behind her, her heart failed her. It would have to be Ken Saunders, of course, And he must have heard every word.

"Oh, Ethel, how could you?" groaned Vicky. "Now I daren't even leave this place, I'm so embarrassed."

Ethel's teasing smile changed suddenly to a look of blank consternation. She peered gingerly around the wall of the booth, and had the grace to cover her eyes with a cry of remorse.

"Oh, Vicky, I didn't mean—oh, how awful! It just couldn't happen!"

At this point Ken Saunders rose and stood beside their table.

"If you think it isn't just as bad for me!" he said, very red-faced. "Of course I missed the first part and that was probably the best. But now I suppose you're going to hate me for hearing that last. It's not my fault." He had a sudden idea and looked from Vicky's downcast fact to Ethel's. "Say, you saw me there and were doing it on purpose, weren't you. Of all the dirty tricks! And I fell for it!"

"We just wondered how much more we had to feed you before you'd get on to it," Ethel laughed, with a triumphant look at Vicky. "You didn't actually think it was on the level, did you?"

Ken looked doubtfully at them.

"I do have a normal supply of vanity, I suppose," he said. "It never has seemed a screaming joke that any lady should be 'falling for me' as you put it. I won't forgive this for a long time."

Vicky managed to draw a breath of relief.

"It was the only way we could get you to talk to us," she said.

They walked back to the office together, and Ken reproached her again for playing such a shameful trick on his vanity. Vicky was so relieved at this happy misunderstanding that she did not think, until late that night, that perhaps Ken was only tactfully trying to save the situation. He didn't *want* her to be falling in love with him, and he refused to let it be said. He was deliberately pretending it had been a joke so he wouldn't have to cope with a love he didn't want. Having destroyed her sleep with this unpleasant thought Vicky got up and lit a cigarette.

"I wish there was some way to keep from seeing through things," she thought savagely. "I wish there was some pill like an aspirin that could stop your common sense. Common sense never did anybody any good."

8

*E*VEN AS ASTUTE A publisher as Mr. Peabody
had difficulty keeping his magazine a nose ahead of the public
taste in these confused days. A "farseeing" editor can only live up
to his name when the future looks pretty much like the past, and
the public is reacting as it has before. Now surprises lay waiting in
every corner, and *Peabody's* was obliged to be guided not by an editor and a board of advisors, but by a committee of circumstance.
It could be reasonably assumed that so long as there were women
there would be safety in Fashions, but this department, old as it
was, had the most desperate of scrambles to keep up. In the early
days of the war the Paris correspondents sent back helpful
sketches of what milady should wear to a bombing, what combi-
nations of color and fabric were advisable for the matron, the
dowager, the debutante, for the arousing of patriotism, bravery
undying love, or respect. Forward-thinking readers at once sent
in angry letters, canceling subscriptions, berating Mr. Peabody

personally for assuming that the fair sex were interested in anything in war times except target practice and tank driving. Compromising with these objections, the magazine showed pictures of the smarter *abris* in Paris, and made suggestions for uplifting military morale by a show of orchids, costume jewelry and lace stockings. This, too, was roundly criticized as too frivolous for the hour. Indignant women's organizations sent letters of protest at this insult to the gravity of the feminine mind; committees approached and even picketed Mr. Peabody's home, declaring that his publication was an affront to American womanhood, now massing its strength for war and not for fun. It was hard to steer a profitable course between these groups and the actual facts, which continued to prove soaring sales in furs, nail polish, lipsticks, perfumes, wrinkle creams, and other peacetime consolations. Mr. Peabody and his associates finally solved the problem by throwing their weight almost entirely on the Home and America, two blameless subjects for editorial reflection. If it was wrong to admit interest in bodily adornment, then *Peabody's* would instruct its readers how to make their little homes into inexpensive castles of great beauty; if it was unpatriotic to praise Capri skies or to photograph Mediterranean resort activities, then *Peabody's* would loyally devote themselves to the hidden charms of Route 21, the bouquet of western vintages, the decorative possibilities of gilding horse chestnuts.

Peabody's "Home in America" department became an instant success. Past frivolities were forgiven. Other fashion magazines and women's periodicals tried vainly to keep up with this noble lead. The real estate advertising department took on fresh life, and a somewhat woolen note crept into the hitherto shimmering copy. Economy was a word fraught with imaginative nuances. Many of the Peabody League girls and their illustrious mothers were absolutely refusing to wear their jewels or sables for the duration, and mere working girls were easily detected now by their fur coats, having no alternative of well-cut cloth wraps as their richer sisters did.

Vicky Haven, with her real estate page, profited by the new homespun policy of the magazine and found commissions and bonuses added to her fifty dollar salary. Ken Saunders, in charge of the actual research into the American Home, was the gratified recipient of all manner of bribes, from electric razors to vacuum cleaners. He moved from his hotel to an apartment which he was able to furnish almost completely with "gravy"—sofas, mattresses, gadgets pressed on him by earnest manufacturers in hopes of public mention of their product.

"Here is the charming home of the Bumbys in Plymouth, Ohio," the Home in America section would begin. "If the Bumbys can live this well in our great country on only $30 a week, surely you too can."

"Taxes are higher, wages are less, jobs are fewer," another issue would declare. "But see how pleasantly the Carmichaels live in a rented house in Bayonne, New Jersey, on the fruits of Father Carmichael's endowment insurance."

Photographs of the happy family would be included, menus of their simple but tasty fare, lists of books read by Sonny in the Knights of Columbus clubrooms, pattern for sweaters knitted by Mama after she had deftly put the wash to soak and the pot roast in the oven and was waiting for her Red Cross homework to arrive. It was a splendid means of building the American morale in time of fear and waiting, and it was even more profitable than the magazine's former luxury propaganda. True, the idea was not without its financial complications. Families on $30 a week had a tendency not to make the most of their native opportunities, so that in order to make them photographically appealing, *Peabody's* frequently had to send advance men to the locale to furnish and decorate the house themselves into which they popped the surprised and delighted typical Americans. Sonny and Sister had to be outfitted by the magazine, Daddy had to be calmed with a cash down payment, Junior had to be allowed to keep the bicycle which he, for photographic purposes, was supposed to have bought by saving money from lawn-mowing jobs. Sometimes, after the Peabody photographers and reporters had left the scene, the typical family found it impossible to take up their typical lives as they had lived them before being singled out for the honor of publicity. There were even suits brought against the magazine for loss of wives, husbands, jobs, when the publicity and unprecedented domestic conveniences were gone. However, *Peabody's* increased its legal staff and took care of these cases as they came up, insisting fairly enough that each was a typical American family only as long as the particular issue was on the stands, and it was now someone else's turn to be typical.

The "Home in America" research men made monthly expeditions into darkest America, under the instructions of Kenneth Saunders, departmental editor. The findings were even used, with proper payment, by the government and by educational and advertising agencies, and inasmuch as such august patrons could not be denied, there was oftentimes need for witchery. That is, if a typical home in Florida was promised for a certain issue, but Florida was under rains, then the camera staff and research writers must fly to southern California or even Alabama to capture the typical Florida home. These hazards were all in the game and very likely the less said about them, the better. Ken Saunders grew horrified as he saw his little brainchild blossom into this smiling Frankenstein, and begged to be let off. Mr. Peabody reasoned with him.

"It will rattle down to something worthwhile eventually," Mr. Peabody prophesied, solemnly doodling away with a red pencil on the outgoing mail his secretary had just brought him. "What worries you about it, Saunders!"

Ken stamped out a cigarette butt on the office floor, and lit another. He felt, under Peabody's kindly paternal gaze, like some little Lord Fauntleroy who had just found out there were rotters in the world. ("Peabody," he might as well have cried, "we chaps just don't *do* those things at Greyfriars!") It was a squirmy feeling and reminded Ken again that at thirty-three the carapace should be a little thicker.

"I think we should go overboard and make it complete fiction," he floundered, quite disgusted to find himself in the role of Decent Chap with Certain Standards. "Or else we ought to print the straight facts."

Mr. Peabody sighed and without looking up began carefully to erase his doodling. This involved moistening a large India rubber eraser and make a deal of a mess on his vest front and tie, a matter which brought his clean kerchief into play as dustmop.

"Print the straight facts!" he repeated with another deep sigh. "I've been in this business twenty-five years, Saunders, and one thing I can assure you from experience. A fact changes into a lie the instant it hits print. I can't explain it, but there it is. No, it isn't the time lag. It's words. Printed words. You're lucky to siphon off ten percent of the truth from any printed word. The most documented statements in the world. *World Almanac*. The printed word, speaking as an old editor, is *ipso facto*, a lie."

Saunders laughed. Mr. Peabody, however, was not only serious but deeply moved by his own words. He was so accustomed to listening to other people, his employees, his trustees, and his family, and keeping his opinions pretty much to himself, that in his rare moments of garrulity he was as fascinated as anyone else to hear what he had to say. The words he now heard himself saying were news to himself, and he could not keep a look of pleased surprise from his face as he spoke.

"It's the print that does it," Saunders suggested. "Maybe truth lies only in the fountain pen."

Mr. Peabody shook his head.

"It's not print, it's the word," he declared. "The spoken word, too. The lie forms as soon as the breath of thought hits air. You hear your own words and you say—'*That's* not what I mean.' And you go on and on, qualifying, groping, remembering a case that already cancels what you're saying."

Ken was impressed.

"That's absolutely true," he said thoughtfully.

Mr. Peabody's momentary elation vanished. He scratched his head, frowning.

"I doubt it," he said. "Every word is a lie, probably. However, I'm as good a word eater as anyone else. I daresay I have enough to nibble on the rest of the week. Anyway, don't take this job so hard, Saunders. If it makes you feel any better, call your department another name."

"The 'American Fantasy,' maybe," Ken said.

"All right, all right," Mr. Peabody shrugged his shoulders. "This is wartime. National fantasy is necessary."

Mr. Peabody stroked the long lock that covered his bald head very carefully. He saw by Ken's expression that the young man was impressed by his argument and this seemed to disturb him. For years he had thought of himself as an honest man in the midst of shrewd traders and well protected scoundrels. It shocked him now, listening to his counsel to Saunders, to find he was very likely as discreet a trader as the next one. He was buying the young man's confidence with a few seemingly honest confessions. That was just one more method of corruption. Finding cause to scold himself was one of Peabody's favorite occupations. It was a means, as he very well knew, of maintaining his high opinion of the rest of the human race. Whenever he stumbled on something evil in an associate, something that could not be denied or overlooked, he examined himself and usually was able to find some faint trace of a similar vice, so that he was in all honor forced to condone it in someone else. Since he knew himself to be a decent, kindly man, it followed that these suspect associates must also be. He found himself wavering between "All men are scoundrels" and "All men are saints," finally arriving at "All men are men." He thought of himself as an almost too complacent optimist, but the proof of his cynicism was that although he was never shocked by the depths of human sin, he was constantly staggered by the slightest evidence of human civility. He was even astonished that the necessary evasiveness of the magazine should worry anyone.

"This Saunders must be a remarkable fellow," he could not help thinking, and at once berated himself for being surprised at a simple show of candor from an employee. Good God, what had happened in his life that he was surprised when a servant didn't steal and when a child didn't lie? Mr. Peabody, who rarely wrestled with his soul, continued to stare at Ken Saunders, whose simple complaint about his department had brought about this psychic dredging. The latter was no dewy-eyed choirboy, certainly, and he bore no evidence of having been tenderly nurtured in a cellophane vacuum.

"Where were you before you came here?" Peabody inquired.

"Traveling. Odd jobs in China, Mexico, and Chile. Before that I was on the *Express* here."

"Let's see," Mr. Peabody tried to recall the letter he associated with the name of Saunders. "Oh, yes, you were sent here by Julian Evans."

Ken whirled around.

"I beg pardon, I came here on my own, sir."

Mr. Peabody was certain now of his data.

"Evans asked me to take you on. That's right." He pushed a bell. "I'll get the letter right now, if you like."

Ken stared at him, knowing at once it was all too true.

"All right, but I didn't know he had done it," he said. "I have been boasting to my friends that I just walked in here and made a niche for myself. All on my own."

His face was scarlet with suppressed anger. He might have known that Amanda would find some way of deflating him. He couldn't have the tiny triumph of getting a job on his own. Amanda had to wangle it by waving her husband's name. Ken knew that if he had the support of just one drink he would throw up the job that minute. But there were debts, and above that, the old fears that kept you tied to what miserable security you had. He wished with all his heart that he really *was* drunk, and dared shout his hatred for his so-called sponsor, Julian Evans, and deny him the honor of being able to get any man a job by the mere use of his magic name. After all, was the reckless honesty of the inebriated so much worse than the sly caution of the sober-headed? The answer depended, of course, on which you were.

"Miss Haven is here on Evans's account, too," reflected Mr. Peabody. "I shouldn't be at all surprised if Julian thinks he's the genius behind our Home campaign since he placed you two people."

He chuckled silently, but since Julian Evans's opportunism was no laughing matter to Ken, he scowled into space. He thought of how arrogantly he had boasted to Amanda that he could always get a job by just walking into a place, and he thought of his secret, shamefaced pride that the thing was going so much better than he even wanted it to go. All the time she knew exactly how he had gotten the chance. If she'd only told him, flaunted in his face! Anything was better than this secret use of her damned power, smiling silently at the little starved buds of a masculine ego shooting up.

'He's one of the stockholders, so I suppose he might as well think he guides our policy," Mr. Peabody went on, highly amused. "Well, carry on, Saunders. It won't be for long, anyway. We're staving off our bombproof home department as long as we can."

Saunders managed a smile and said good night. His head was still burning with contempt for himself. He might as well be a sleek-haired gigolo and give up working altogether. Amanda was getting jobs for him through her illustrious husband and saying nothing about it as if it was the most natural thing in the world. Especially for a man as incompetent as Kenneth Saunders. Oh, certainly, some woman had to look out for such a failure, or at least she must ask her husband to do so.

"Damn her hide!" Ken muttered with clenched fists, as he went down the corridor to his office. "Oh, damn, damn her hide!"

There must be some way to put an end to loving someone you hated. There must be some drug, some herb slipped under your pillow, some incantation, that immediately stopped another's power to destroy you. Another love, of course, but that was not so easy. The gestures of love were easy enough to simulate, but the counteragent had to be as strong as the poison itself. Who could ever match the poison of loving Amanda? He hadn't really tried before to love anyone else, Ken told himself, but now he must, if there was to be anything left of himself.

"Damn her, damn her," he was still softly muttering, so concentrated on this futile prayer that he passed Vicky Haven without even seeing her, a circumstance that brought a surprisingly similar remark to that lady's lips.

"What have I done that he doesn't speak?" she murmured, resentfully. "Now he knows I like him. Now he knows, so he's brushing me off. Oh, *damn* Ethel Carey!"

2

THE MANEUVERING required for a meeting with Ken Saunders was a course of gnawing irritation to Amanda. She refused to go to his new apartment since certain ladies from her Bundles' committee lived in the building. She was afraid to telephone him at his office for fear someone might recognize her voice, so that arrangements were dependent on his telephoning her or upon telegraph communication. Once agreed on the time, she must take some circuitous route to Vicky's apartment, faking a profound interest in a honey and maple syrup shop across the street, so that her excuses would be ready if anyone chanced to see her. There was, in addition to other difficulties, the possibility that he would not or could not come, after all these precautions had been taken. It was the first time in many years that Amanda had permitted herself the luxury of indiscretion, and she did not like it at all, but was perversely unable to put a stop to it.

Picking her way across the slushy street one day, her feet in toeless, heelless sandals disagreeably wet, and a raw February wind blowing her newly done hair into disarray, Amanda felt a burst of indignation that at this peak in her career she should still be victim of the same little torments that troubled any shopgirl. Here she was, supposedly in her right mind, making a fool of herself over an old lover, just because his contempt made her doggedly determined to win him in some other way, and because she could not give him up until she had revived completely his former infatuation. What did it matter, she demanded of herself in extreme exasperation, whether a merely average young man saw in her nothing but a merely average young woman? You would have thought, from this insistent sting to her vanity, that her whole career was planned in hope of pleasing Ken Saunders. It was exactly like the horrid little literary monthly (a journal surely no one ever saw, so why should it matter), that made her stay awake raging at night over its patronizing dismissal of her writing. That one miserable, utterly unimportant, minority voice became the one voice she must have sing her praise. So she must have Ken Saunders forced to admit she was important, something special.

As she was about to enter the building, she saw the Romanian count who was due for dinner that very night, coming out of the adjoining house. Amanda walked hurriedly on, head bent, until the man was whisked off in a taxicab.

"Stupid!" she scolded herself, and for a minute had half a notion to give up the whole thing, take a cab and dash home where she belonged. "Why in heaven's name do I let myself in for this?"

But then Ken would mock at her for being so cowardly. Afraid she might make a social error, afraid she might lose her reputation or her husband by one little false move. She could not understand for the life of her just how Ken had won this terrible advantage over her, obliging her to apologize to him for her success, keeping her in this silly, footling state of trying to placate him, trying to make him yield completely once again. If he ever did—she would not admit this openly to herself but she knew it was true—she could be through with him, and go on about her life happily relieved of this maddening thorn. She was certainly not fool enough to be in love with him, she despised his arrogance toward money and power, the things that mattered, and what seemed to her his adolescent rebelliousness at Things as They Are. She disagreed with his point of view on everything, she always felt ruffled and humiliated when she left him, and why did she keep up this dangerous, unsatisfactory, but somehow compelling game?

"This is the last time, the very last," Amanda vowed, and let herself into her "studio."

Ken was already there, with a drink. Amanda braced herself. They always began by quarreling.

"I see you have to dull the pain of our meetings with alcohol," she said, drawing off her gloves. She had beautiful hands, long and slender, but she no longer expected him to praise them. She saw by the mirror that the cold rain had really damaged her coiffure, and she bit her lip, annoyed that she had been foolish enough to have had it done especially for Ken, and doubly annoyed that it should be hanging now in damp blonde wisps against her cheek.

"You hair looks charming," Ken perversely remarked. "You appeal to me most when something has gone wrong with your perfection."

Amanda looked around the apartment, frowning.

"Who do you suppose Vicky entertains?" she speculated with mild curiosity. "Every time I come here now I see new dishes, cocktail mixers, flowers."

Ken had something on his mind, she saw.

"You're worrying about her coming in, again," Amanda guessed.

"I would rather we were at my place," Ken admitted.

"I've told you a dozen times our arrangement. The place is mine—except weekends—till five. Vicky wouldn't dream of breaking the rule unless I'm out of town."

Ken poured her a drink. Amanda shook her head, then saw Ken lift his eyebrow in that exasperating way he had.

"That cautious regard for the liver is such an endearing trait!" he remarked. "Imagine what might happen if you took a drink and said or did something quite unrehearsed!"

Amanda picked up the glass and drank it down. She rarely drank whiskey, certainly never except when it was socially necessary, but here was Ken, as usual, making a fault of a harmless virtue. The sharp tingling produced by the drink was unexpectedly agreeable. When she reached for another, Ken laughed, pleased with the collapse of this minor fortress. That was what he wanted of her, Amanda thought bitterly, he wanted her to lose everything she had ever gained, he wanted her to be poor and degraded and ugly, so that he could have the whip hand. The only way to really make him happy would be to forget a speech, break down and cry, fumble an article, make a public show of her feelings. Then he would step in and be the hero and protect her. Or would he then walk off and leave her?

"I have to be home to work with Emerson on my book," she said. This also was part of the game, pretending that today was to make an end of all intimacies, no time for that sort of thing today. Amanda was particularly savage in her tone this time, to show that whatever effect he thought the liquor might have on her, he was going to be badly fooled.

"Ralph Waldo?" Ken asked. She hated him when he joked. She was quite aware he thought she had no sense of humor, for he liked to make little jokes just to prove this lack. What of it? What was so wonderful about a sense of humor? You didn't see any of the big people going around giggling, did you?

"I'm very interested in this new book of yours, my dear," Ken said. "From what you tell me, you have managed to combine the characters from *The Three Sisters*, with the plot of the *Three Musketeers*. I like that little variation of *Anna Karenina* too. That will read very well. This man Emerson seems a very good little collaborator, indeed."

"Just because only one of your books was ever printed," Amanda said smiling at him steadily. "Darling, don't you think your jealousy of my work is just the least bit cheap?"

"It's all I can afford," Ken answered. He looked away from her, afraid she might be right. Maybe he was jealous, not just scornful of mediocrity too lavishly rewarded. Even now, he could not stop baiting her, as if this was the only relief from the endless torment of his chains.

"I wonder what field you will tackle next," he said. "After all you haven't been the first white woman in Lhasa—you haven't invented a new death ray, you haven't designed a new type of bomber—you haven't done a mural, God forbid. Doesn't that burn you up to think of all those things you have left undone? Maybe things that even *you* can't do. Fancy!"

Amanda's smooth olive face did not change expression. She saw him pouring her another drink, challenging her to say she must conserve herself for her work. Stonily, she picked up the drink and drank it. She was seething with anger, but when words came, they were the plaintive apologetic phrases that he somehow managed to drag out of her.

"Of course I realize the millions of things I can't do, Ken, dear." Really, she could not understand herself with this man. "I've had more than my share of luck in some things. I do know you're much more brilliant than I am. You know I always said you had ten times the talent of a man like Andrew Callingham, You know I did, Ken."

"I know," said Ken. "That's because you want to minimize Callingham. He's the only person you can't even compete with yourself, so you're willing to let me have the bulge on him. Thanks."

Amanda stood up quickly, eyes flashing. She picked up her hat, and gloves. She would not stand it. It was fantastic she should go to all this trouble twice a week to be beaten down by this man who was nothing, literally nothing to her.

"Good-bye," Ken said calmly.

She went and put arms around him.

"Ken, we mustn't go on doing these horrible things to each other!" she gasped, looking imploringly into his face. "As if we hated each other!"

"We do," Ken muttered. "I hate you for everything you've done and you hate me for all the things I haven't done. It's no go. Why do you come here? Why do you want me? You ruined everything once. What in God's name do you want of me now?"

Amanda looked at him, almost frightened. He was pale and beads of perspiration stood on his forehead. His clenched hands were trembling. It astonished her that anyone should have such violent feelings, and she felt a surge of excitement to think she had caused it. She even felt her own body trembling, as if by contagion. It was a strange experience for her. Why, your body really can act quite separately from your mind or your intention, she thought, interested in this new discovery, quite as if she had suddenly found a talent for magic.

"But you love me, Ken!" she said. "You know you love me!"

"No," said Ken.

He stood up, trying to push her aside.

"You'd better go," he said.

"You can't treat me this way, Ken!" Now she was even saying things that surprised herself, pulling at his folded arms, trying to press her face to his. "You've no right to make me meet you this way and then send me away—you know you haven't! I can't stand it!"

Why, I'm actually crying, she thought, feeling a warm tear on her cheek.

"You're the only person, Ken, you know that—"There were even more of these unexpected words tumbling from her. "I am the only person you've ever loved, you know that, Ken, you've got to say it. I can't bear anyone else to touch me—I—"

He forced himself free of her and stood gripping the table.

"You don't want me or anyone else to touch you," he said bitterly. "You've only kept me on all this time because you got a kick out of seeing how much it meant to me. If you can keep me under your feet just by letting me make love to you once in a while, you're willing to endure it. That's all. And it's not good enough for me, my dear. Do you hear me? It's not damn good enough for me!"

Amanda again felt the curious wave of excitement at seeing this show of feeling. She wanted to fling herself in his arms, surrender desperately to love, somehow capture for herself this luxury of feeling. It was oddly agreeable to have these little sympathetic tremors going down her spine, and it was a new sensation not to be repelled by seeing a man lose control of himself, in fact to be curiously captivated by it, wanting more and more of it, wanting—yet not daring to be wanting—tears, surrender, collapse complete. In her elation Amanda grew flushed and breathless. She stood on tiptoe, head thrown back, eyes closed, waiting to be kissed, demanding to be kissed.

"No go," Ken said. "It's no go, old dear. I can't bear it anymore. I can't I tell you."

Amanda stepped back, drawing a long breath. Ken would not look at her. Awkwardly he picked up his hat, and walked toward the door, still not looking or else not daring to look at her.

"I'd better go first," he mumbled.

The door closed behind him.

Amanda stared incredulously at the door as if this object was somehow to blame, as if the door must be lying, it had not closed, it had not shut out this person she wanted. It could not be. If anyone was to do any denying, surely it should have been she. She sat down, holding her hot temples tightly, wondering what had happened to her, how this tumult had unloosed itself in her brain, so that she couldn't remember what it was she had planned for the next hour. It was unthinkable that there was anything she wanted as much as she wanted Ken Saunders, that she could not have. It was wicked that she should be denied, denied in the very way she denied Julian. She began combing her hair very carefully, as if this external tidying up would serve some inner purpose as well. She thought if Ken had gone home to his apartment she would go there, too, wait in the hall till he got there. It didn't matter who saw her. Nothing mattered but getting him back, forcing him to give in to her. She would promise anything, she thought. If he wanted promises, he could have them. Why, she thought, I'm talking out loud. Which was true. She must be going crazy. She went on combing her hair, carefully. Her lipstick was still a smooth rich cherry line. He hadn't kissed her once. Not once. That ought to bring back her senses, she told herself. She put on her hat and then her gloves. She went out, closing the door quietly behind her, and in the street she did not allow herself to look westward to see if he might be still in sight, but climbed into a taxicab very calmly. It occurred to her that she might run into Julian when she got home, and he might notice that she was nervous.

"As if he would notice anything but himself!" Amanda answered herself sarcastically. She wondered what it would be like if she got home and found that Julian had dropped dead. Things like that happened in books. It was only fair that they should happen in real life, too. By the time she reached her door Amanda was fully composed, having occupied herself pleasantly with the definitely attractive possibilities of Julian being dead.

"It's not as if I made it a wish," she told herself, a little shocked at how far the idea had carried her. "It's just that I can't get the idea out of my head!"

9

$\mathcal{I}$T WAS SHEER LUCK that Amos Cheever's lady friend from London was unexpectedly granted entry into the United States, a matter which kept the rebellious man in a state of dazed calm while Julian Evans pulled his forces together. As Mr. Cheever had a wife in America, there were complications to be ironed out, all very much to the advantage of the foreign visitor inasmuch as she was much stronger, younger and newer than Mrs. Cheever. She had, furthermore, the whip hand of a surprise attack, and the good sense to know that it was now or never with Cheever. Mrs. Cheever, whose domestic nagging had made Cheever what he was, a fine foreign correspondent, was stunned into a divorce agreement and Cheever catapulted into a permanent arrangement with his Dody, something he had never really craved. Dody's firm intention was to stay in the States for good, and so Cheever found himself in the embarrassing position of backing down in his demands on

Julian Evans, as gracefully as he dared, and hinting at a permanent New York post.

Evans's staff was well aware of Cheever's personal predicament and kept the master informed on its nice points, and presently Julian came to feel that it was his own brilliant strategy that had adjusted his difficulties with Cheever. As long as Cheever had London, there would be complications with Amanda, complications that would expose Julian to ridicule as an editor and as a tame husband. It worked out much better for him to shift his former Geneva man to London. The latter was happy to have the new post and for a while would not know just how his material was being plucked by Amanda. It was, perhaps, rather a pity that his work was greatly inferior to his predecessors, so that Amanda's weekly articles were forced to suffer. But this circumstance was not really remarked on for some time, and meanwhile Amanda was distracted by other matters. This period was the beginning of the faintest possible cleavage between Julian's interests and his wife's career. Amanda was still obsessed by the Wagnerian spectacle of the world in flames and herself leading the warriors into Valhalla. Julian's shrewd eye was turning homeward more and more. Exploiting American problems for circulation purposes was a publishing gamble that did not interest Amanda since there was no star role in it for her, so Julian, with his new game all to himself, was all the more engrossed.

Julian had two New York papers, one for the Big Man, and one for the Little Man. The paper for the Big Man had been slowly in retreat since its unattractive stand during the Spanish War, but the paper for the Little Man had been snowballing to what seemed unlimited success. Julian himself was astonished one day to look over the figures of its meteoric rise, and at once decided to make a big change in the management of it, since its appointed editor had had the bad grace to take credit to himself for the achievement. Obviously Cheever was the man for this work. Cheever was not sure of himself on home ground and would therefore permit Julian's dictation, and besides, Cheever was in a spot. It was all most fortunate, or as Julian believed, most clever of himself to have manipulated Destiny in this fashion.

The Little Man now became Julian's obsession. You would have thought the Little Man was a wonderful new boy doll to hear Julian's fond talk of him. No toy steamboat, no pet pony, no firstborn child, even, was ever as cherished by Julian as was his dear entrancing Little Man, a wistful little chap about two feet high looking appealingly like Paul Dombey, perhaps, a little on the tubercular side, very underprivileged, very underhoused, very dependent on Big Man Julian for spiritual guidance. The Little Man's newspaper cost two cents more than the Big Man's newspaper, but this was because there was so many of him, and it was true that the reporters on the Little Man's paper received higher wages than the Big Man's reporters. For a slightly less wage Amos Cheever was glad to help Julian lead the Little Man out of darkness and to pamper him with platitudes, vague fight talk, and somewhat defeatist exhortations to be proud of being a Little Man or a Little Man's wife or a Little Man's family.

There was one trouble Julian found in his *Little American*. That was the irritating habit some little men had of not admitting they were little men, of acting and even proclaiming that they were big men, on their way up out of Julian's jurisdiction. This did not happen often, but it made Julian's blood boil to have a taxi driver speak with lofty complacency of his independent business and his patronizing pity for the underdog, the little fellow.

"You're a little fellow, yourself!" Julian wanted to shout angrily, because there's no reasoning with a man who doesn't know he's an underprivileged, underhoused, underdog, but then Julian would think the taxi driver might look over his five-foot-six of fare and make some insulting comeback. So he confined his wisdom to the printed page and glowed over his clippings as tenderly as if they were a set of Dolly Dimple paper dolls.

These setbacks were minor, however, and *Little American* was lauded by the President himself for its fair play and foursquare talk, and many intellectual weeklies began referring to Julian as an intellectual equal because of his pity interviews with the Little People. The Little People were not, of course, the folks that poured down the mountain in pointed shoes at the stroke of midnight, but Julian's conception of them was quite as extravagant.

Julian had, in fact, fallen in love with the superstition that any nontechnical worker or any uneducated human being was automatically endowed with a rare and incontrovertible well of wisdom. Everyday he ran interviews with truck drivers, cops, waiters, dock hands, busboys, janitors, and street cleaners, and their explanations of the government problems was God's own word, unless they spoiled the effect by mentioning a book or some source of documentation. Julian did not like it at all if it developed that the simple sage had been corrupted by an average education, or if he betrayed a normal interest in reading. The subjects of his research must be one-syllable little men, not articulate literates, as if lying, confusion, bigotry and corruption never came in one syllables, and in book learning alone was there sin and woe. This reverence for ignorance was apparently so deep-seated in the public, as vouched for by *Little American* circulation, that it seems astonishing citizens continued to support colleges and schools. It would have been logical to assume that the serious parents would raise their children to be oracles of ignorance, uncorrupted by the nuances of language, able to couch their primitive impressions in as simple a form as "Ug."

Mr. Cheever, uncertainly happy with his new Dody, tried to forget the more dignified privileges of a London correspondent in wartime, in delving with Julian into the world of Little People. Being more of an adventurer than Julian, he was able, to his own surprise, to work up considerable enthusiasm for the new world. The collaboration brought Julian and Cheever closer together than they had ever been, for in one way it was a conspiracy against Amanda. It was the first step Julian had taken since his marriage with Amanda's profit in view. Each day that found Amanda still preoccupied with her own chosen fields gave Julian a sense of guilty elation. The Little Man was all his. Cheever had a little corner of him, maybe, but in name only. It was as exciting as a secret, which, in some ways it was, for Amanda did not quite realize the quiet rocketing to success of Julian's venture. While it was not theatrical or international enough to appeal to her, she would very likely have found some means to spoil Julian's pleasure. As it was, he spent less and less time at home, leaving Castor to fuss with the home correspondence, while the master hurried downtown, sometimes even by subway, to play with his new darling.

There was a change in Julian, too, observed even by his most indifferent associates. He now said good morning occasionally to the elevator man, and when he upbraided a waiter for bad service he spoke to the headwaiter, too, so that there was no discrimination.

"The test of a publishing genius, Cheever," he said to his newly reconciled friend, "is the ability to keep ahead of the times, to change your whole set of standards, overnight, if need be."

As he seemed pleased with this thought, it could only be deduced that Mr. Evans had passed his own test satisfactorily.

2

JULIAN HAD a secret from Amanda. He felt very guilty about this secret, but on the other hand it enabled him to shrug off Amanda's little thrusts which had formerly kept him in a constant state of hopeless wrath. Amanda had noticed with relief that he was not so inquisitive about her every minute spent away from the house, nor did he insist on his usual long lectures on the conduct of her future. It must be his increasing devotion to his *Little American*, she thought, and was grateful.

Miss Bemel finally got on to the secret quite by accident, if you could call Miss Bemel's methods ever accidental. Devoted as she was to Amanda's interests, there were many times when she was jealous of Mr. Castor's opportunities. He heard more gossip around the house, for one thing, and the servants were far too distrustful of Miss Bemel to share their little tidbits. In the three years she had worked for Amanda, she had taken great care not to let the staff think she was on their level; no, she was an official in the establishment, not a servant. In spite of her satisfaction in her position, it irked her that she was denied the duty of hiring and firing chauffeurs, cooks, and other dictatorial privileges enjoyed by little Mr. Castor for no reason except that he had done it for years before Amanda was on the scene. No one liked him, downstairs, but at least they were used to him and he was quiet.

Yes, there were times when Miss Bemel regretted the pedestal on which she had planted herself, some feet below her mistress's pedestal. Times when she went down to the kitchen with some instructions from Amanda and found the chef, the maids, chauffeur, and sometimes even Castor, laughing together over something, and then shutting up as soon as she entered. And then there were the times she asked for a cup of tea, knowing the others were having it around the kitchen stove in friendly fashion, and the butler would say, "You want it sent upstairs, of course, Miss Bemel." If she wanted it upstairs it would have been simple enough to make it in her samovar, and drink it by herself. But even a Bemel had her moments of yearning for conviviality, exchanging a complaint or two, maybe, letting out a little steam. No one was going to be foolish enough to make complaints around Miss Bemel, however, for she was certain to carry them straight to Amanda. It was a matter of chagrin to the staff when the cat got out of the bag, the day Miss Bemel came down to discuss the evening's dinner with the chef's wife. The chef was Swiss and pretended not to understand, though Miss Bemel had reason to believe this was only to protect himself from the lectures she liked to administer, since he looked equally blank when she tried them in French or German. Mrs. Pons was her husband's assistant and interpreter, her interpreting consisting of leveling a cool eye at Miss Bemel during her speech and keeping silent until the very end when she summed it up in one pithy word for her husband, the word invariably accompanied a disdainful shrug. Today Miss Bemel was a tiny bit lonesome; she would have liked to unbend just a little, to make a joking offer of opening some sherry for the kitchen, because she had scolded one day about their tippling. So she stood at the pantry doorway, slowly sipping a glass of water, wondering what the chauffeur had been telling them that talk must stop while she was there.

"When you come back from taking Mr. Evans to the station, will you drive me up to the Bronx to see my sister?" Miss Bemel asked of the chauffeur, cocking her head coyly at him, to show her request was woman to man rather than Private Secretary to Menial.

The chauffeur, a young Irishman, looked at her sulkily, and then bit into a thick sandwich he held in one gloved hand.

"Goodness, didn't you have any lunch?" Miss Bemel laughed, pointing to his sandwich, a bit of joviality that brought only scowls to the others' faces.

As the chauffeur, Robert, continued to be silent, and Miss Bemel's face was slowly reddening, a sign of either embarrassment or future revenge, Mrs. Pons took it on herself to answer, with a minimum of grace.

"How can Robert drive to Hudson and back in time to take you uptown?"

"That's right," said Robert.

"Oh, I didn't know Mr. Evans was driving to Hudson," Miss Bemel murmured, confused for a moment, since she hated to have the staff think she was not informed on every little movement of the family. She recovered her poise by advising Mrs. Pons to change the dining-table centerpiece, and chided her, smilingly, not to let Robert have any beer before his long drive, and so was able to make a respectable exit. She heard a muffled titter as she left, but refused to be disconcerted.

Hudson, she thought! Why was Mr. Evans going to Hudson when he had indicated, through Mr. Castor, that he was taking the train to Albany on business? And then the answer came to her. Far Off Hills, the first Mrs. Evans's estate, was somewhere around the town of Hudson, this side of Albany. Neither Mrs. Margaret Evans nor her two grown children were on friendly terms with Julian since he married Amanda. It was understood that their affairs were conducted completely through their lawyer, and that the two children harbored undying resentment toward their father. Miss Bemel pondered this matter on the way upstairs, and seeing Castor in the hallway decided to take the bull by the horns.

"Since when had he been visiting Number One?" she inquired, eyebrows beetling as if this ugly look would terrify the little man into a proper state of subordination. Mr. Castor, having for once the inside trace, was not to be conquered so easily, but threw back his little head and pursed up his lips proudly.

"Since when has our department been any concern of yours?" he nipped back, and could not resist adding as he took his important little tin letter file into the door of his own little cubbyhole, keeping it well behind his back as if the Bemel eye could bore through any metal. "Must Mr. Evans have written permission from you to visit his own family? Perhaps you want him to report to you when he gets back."

Amanda's bell ringing prevented Miss Bemel from putting the little man in his place, which she could not have done very well being so astonished at this news. Why should Julian Evans be visiting his first wife, and what if there should be a reconciliation? Some mischief must be going on or it would not be kept secret.

"Does Mr. Evans ever see his family?" Miss Bemel could not help but ask Amanda when she got back to the study. She wanted to see if Amanda knew of this infidelity, but it was perfectly plain that Amanda was only bored by such a question.

"What a question, Bemel!" Amanda exclaimed. "You know how nervous that whole outfit makes him! Certainly not."

So Miss Bemel knew that her apprehensions were right. If Amanda was in the dark, and the whole household knew it, then there was mischief. Once on the scent Miss Bemel did not spare herself. There were many things you could find out by pretending you knew them already, so she was able to extract a little bit here and a little there, from the parlor maid, the garage, and a fortunate bit of eavesdropping on Mr. Castor's telephone extension. Mr. Julian Evans was going up to Hudson at least once a week. Stores were calling up to ask if Mr. Evans had not made a slip in ordering certain purchases sent to his old address, Far Off Hills. (So he was sending gifts up there!) The mail contained two notes from Hudson, showing that the family had taken up writing to its former head once again. Miss Bemel could only figure out that something was going on which she could not yet get at. Perhaps Amanda's increasing bursts of temper were evidence of new friction, and Mr. Evans was returning to his peaceful, if drabber former ways. Miss Bemel began to worry about the security of her own position if the present marriage should break up. She made little efforts to put Amanda on guard.

"Is Mr. Evans going up to Albany again this week?" she inquired craftily, but Amanda merely exclaimed, "I'm sure I don't know, Bemel, but it's too late to cancel that dinner party, anyway."

So Amanda refused to be warned, and Miss Bemel continued to puzzle, until a maid from the Far Off Hills told Miss Bemel's cousin, who was a dressmaker in Troy, that poor Julian Evans had taken to visiting his ex-wife in order to pour out his troubles to her. He was a lonely man these days, he was reported to have said, and while he had not exactly said that Amanda did not understand him, his behavior indicated just that. It was his custom for the past three for four weeks to drop in on his first wife after conferences in the State Capitol, and recite in a loud voice the entire business while Mrs. Margaret Evans, stout little gray-haired woman of fifty, sat and nodded over her knitting, and agreed with him that he was indeed a wonder. The children, aged twenty and twenty-four, were not completely won over but were beginning to be tolerant of their father. Having delivered himself of his troubles the great man then looked over his kennels, talked to the various refugees, reformed convicts and war orphans that his preaching had caused Mrs. Evans to take on, and then leaped in his car and rode back to town, a freer, happier man. If Mrs. Evans seemed troubled about these visits, finding this demand on her sympathy a painful reminder of other days, it was too bad, but then someone is bound to suffer for the good of others, and Mrs. Evans had already proved that she could suffer nicely.

If Miss Bemel could not fathom the wherefore of this new routine of Mr. Evans, she could at least act as if she knew. "If anything comes up tonight about the White House appointment, can we reach Mr. Evans at Far Off Hills?" she would ask Castor calmly over the phone, knowing this would take the wind out of his sails, since Castor enjoyed his secrets as much as she did prying into them.

3

ONE THING Amanda would not permit in Vicky, was any expression of gratitude. Vicky knew the studio which she shared with

Amanda was a hideaway from publicity so she must not mention
Amanda's sponsoring it, in public. But that was no reason it
should be brushed curtly aside when the two of them were alone.
Besides Vicky could perfectly well afford her own place now, and
she was wondering how to break this to Amanda. If Amanda
would not be thanked for the place, then it was even harder to
tell her that her generosity was no longer necessary. In her own
home Amanda's talk was on such a lofty political plane, that
there was little chance of breaking into the mood with "Speaking
of housing, Amanda, I appreciate you letting me use your studio,
but if you don't mind I'd like to have my own place now, and not
have to feel gratitude to you. For that matter, I'd like to be able to
run in and out all day without being afraid of interrupting one of
your creative moods there, and I'd like to be able to break things,
and be a hostess, not a permanent guest. I do appreciate it, but I
want my freedom now."

Having been dismissed whenever she started to say something
along these lines, Vicky had finally settled the matter by leasing
an apartment on West Thirteenth Street, and with the lease in
her pocket was prepared to make short work of her news. "I've
moved," she would say, and Amanda might even be relieved to
know her responsibility was over.

The evening seemed propitious for introducing a personal
note, for the guests were merely a minor Eastern college president, Mr. Cheever and his Dody, and Mr. Peabody, as near a family group as the Evans dining room ever achieved. Ken Saunders
was not present, but he had not been present at the office, either,
recently, so Vicky concluded he must be away on one of his routine research trips. She was sorry because she had wanted to ask
his advice about this problem of gracefully returning a present
such as an apartment. When he was around she did not feel so
much like an Extra Woman in a city full of extra women. Mr.
Peabody would do, of course, but Mr. Peabody was still Boss, and

no matter how friendly your relations with him were, Boss was still Boss. Vicky bided her time during the dinner for an opportune moment to catch Amanda's eye and ear. Meantime her head swiveled back and forth from the college president to Editor Cheever and Editor Peabody as they sounded forth their worthier thoughts for Amanda's approval. Even the lightest conversations at Amanda's seemed to Vicky like baccalaureate speeches, and she had learned to keep a bright glazed look while pursuing her own trivial thoughts. Sometimes, of course, as tonight, people kept popping their faces in front of yours, and demanding, "Don't you agree, Miss Haven?" and then you were obliged to tie up your wandering fancies and attend to other people's facts.

The college president was the loudest tonight, crowding Amos Cheever and even Amanda into silent corners with his resonant chapel voice, and his "Ah-ah-aha—ah—er-e-er—" hemming by which he kept his place in the conversation when other words failed him. He was a vigorous, ruddy, massive man with iron-gray hair, an iron-gray moustache, and hard, black eyes that must have seriously dented all the objects at which they aimed. The outside world was protected from these dangerous rays by unrimmed bifocal glasses, doubtless crash-proof, since he leveled his glance straight at people as if he neither knew nor cared that it was loaded. Vicky kept leaning as far away from him as she could when he singled her out for target, though when his eyes missed you his booming voice could always find you.

"I'm theoretically anti-Nazi, of course," he roared, "but still I can't help feeling grateful to the régime. Look at the faculty board I got together last year! Carler of Vienna, Chasen of Munich, Lieber of the Sorbonne, Steinbrock of Berlin! Our little college could never afford such men in a hundred years! But Hitler shakes the tree and I get the plums! So I say Heil Hitler! He's done more for our college in ten years than all the trustees and alumni have been able to do in a hundred years!"

Julian Evans did not like such opportunistic talk, especially if it was true. He believed that inner chicanery should be balanced if not completely excused by lofty utterances from the tongue. A little reproof was in order.

"You actually feel, Doctor Swick, that it's civilized procedure to ravish three fourths of the world for the enrichment of one nation? You say every time Hitler has a pogrom and five thousand people are killed or expelled from their homes, we win one first-rate teacher?"

"We're the Byzantium of the future," boomed Doctor Swick. "The Byzantium of the twentieth and twenty-first century. You agree, Miss Haven?"

"I—" answered Vicky.

"What kind of a teacher could I get for the salary I pay Chasen?" Doctor Swick pounded on the table, making a surf in his wine glass, which Vicky watched apprehensively for fear it would add to the other dangers of his proximity. "I have to run my college on very little money. I want the best. I'm in the market for bargains. What do you say, Miss Haven?"

"I—" said Vicky, and was saved by a small baptism of wine from Doctor Swick's glass.

"That's nothing," apologized the doctor, brusquely. "Just put salt on it. What do you say, Miss Keeler, or rather Mrs. Evans?"

Amanda pensively drew her hand over her shining golden locks and leaned her chin on her hand. As this gesture brought the curve of her slim breasts into focus, Doctor Swick bent forward and waited with renewed voracity for her answer. Cheever and lady exchanged a frown, Mr. Evans coughed, and Vicky gazed raptly at her lap, which was now mottled with a mixture of claret and salt which the doctor had impulsively dumped there.

"Naturally Amanda feels as I do," Julian said in a strident tone of rebuke. "What you're saying is that American colleges can make money on Hitler's triumphs. Really, Doctor Swick!"

Amanda now lifted her dark, gold-framed face from her wrist, thus releasing Doctor Swick from an ocular spell, and permitted her pansy blue eyes to travel over the bowl of floating gardenias to her husband.

"'Really, Doctor Swick!'" she mocked Julian with a musical laugh. "Really, Mr. Evans, you might say! Haven't your newspapers made a lot of money out of the war, Julian? Millions, of course—not just a few hundred dollars saved the way Doctor Swick means!"

Julian looked at his wife, jaw dropping, wounded surprise radiating from every fiber of his being.

"Exactly, exactly!" shouted Doctor Swick. "And exactly the way you have, too, Miss Keeler, I'm sure you were about to say."

As Amanda had had no intention of saying or thinking any such thing, she drew up rather frostily. Julian was relieved at this qualification from the doctor and relaxed, very slightly. Mr. Peabody dropped a fork and hid under the table gratefully for an alarmingly long time trying to recapture it, knocking heads with the butler who was down there for the same purpose. Mr. Cheever, at a nudge from his Dody, a silent square-jawed Scotch girl, leapt into the service of his master. His heart was not in it wholly, for as long as the master had known Cheever, he had known of Cheever's chronic indigestion, but made no concessions to this disability when he invited him to dinner, so that Cheever must either eat oysters Rockefeller and Roquefort salad dressing or starve. Tonight he had chosen to starve, permitting himself only a nibble of Swedish health bread, and he longed to end the dinner so that he might go to a Childs restaurant and stuff himself on his approved diet. He dabbed his napkin daintily over his handsome brown beard, which he doubtless wore to conceal not a weak mouth but a weak stomach, for he'd had both the indigestion and beard the same length of time.

"Whatever profit any of us here make of the war is accidental," he said soothingly. "If Amanda Keeler's public work makes her a profit, it also profits the right cause. That goes for the Evans's newspapers, and for Mr. Peabody's magazine, I'm sure. After all, Doctor Swick couldn't accuse us of warmongering. That I'm sure."

Doctor Swick machine-gunned the circle with his glittering eyes, his final ocular bullet piercing Vicky's quivering form.

"Ha! I don't know what your All-Out for Britain is if it isn't warmongering! And if there was prestige as well as more money in isolationism, I'll bet you'd all be on that side." He roared at this friendly joke and was quite undaunted by the silent response. "Come on now, I speak frankly, why can't we all do the same? We're among friends," he added, though never was this statement less supported. He took this silence as encouragement to continue, and Vicky found herself wishing guiltily for Ken since he would have reveled in this catastrophic attack on the castle, and in the doctor's innocent belief that he was making a splendid impression.

"No, no, I'm not moron public," chuckled Doctor Swick, nudging Vicky quite brutally in the ribs, and appalling host and Cheever by this insult to their Little Man. "I see the whole picture. You war ladies, for instance, who lunch with Ciano and Goering and Pétain, Daladier—all the rest, dance with them, have a good time with them. You write or talk about them with an anti-fascist flavor, but you played up enough to them personally so that you could make a graceful pirouette backward if the ball goes their way. They know it, too. They don't care about your little pieces, because they know it's all a matter of who's in fashion. You ladies weren't radical until it was chic, ha, ha—isn't that right, Cheever?"

"I—" choked Cheever, who unfortunately believed exactly as Doctor Swick did on this one point, but disliked the man, and moreover was duty-bound to stand by the two Evanses.

"Right, eh, Miss Haven?" nudged the doctor, and Vicky murmured, "Oh, I—I mean—"

"Vicky's not doing anything about the war, Doctor Swick, so she can't very well speak for or against you," Amanda said coolly, and rose. "Shall we go?"

In the drawing room with coffee and brandy, Doctor Swick was rather thoughtful, though he still had no sensation of walking around with a cut throat, something Cheever could have warned him about if they were better friends. Any favors Doctor Swick had hoped to wangle from the Evans syndicate were as good as scrapped already, but he would never know why.

"Well, Vicky," Amanda said, turning her back deliberately to Doctor Swick, who saw in the gesture merely an invitation to admire the satiny olive texture of her skin, "what's new in your life?"

"I'm moving," Vicky blurted out, knowing this was her only chance to break the news. "I want to thank you for the studio, of course, I do thank you for being so good to me, but now there's no reason why you should, so I've taken another place—"

Amanda's face glowed a dull red, and to Vicky's surprise she looked as if she had received an uncalled-for slap in the face.

"What? You're moving?" cried Amanda, unheeding the expressions of mild wonder about her. "You know perfectly well I got that place expressly for you, and you daren't walk out of it like that."

"I thought it might be more convenient for you—for me—I mean—" Vicky was so disturbed by Amanda's strange indignation that she found her throat choking up ominously.

"It's absolutely ridiculous for you to move anyplace else," Amanda rushed on warmly. "The place is there, why should you leave it? You can't just take a person's apartment when you find it convenient and then jump out when it suits you, without even consulting—without—it's perfectly nasty of you! Vicky, I'm disappointed in you!"

Not knowing what she had done that was so horrible Vicky was unable to know how to justify herself. She sat twisting her hands, opening her mouth to protest, then closing it helplessly.

"Is it so necessary to give up your present place, Victoria?" Julian intervened in his judicial manner. "Let's talk this over first. After all, you are more or less our charge, you know, and it may be the wiser thing to stay just where you are."

"I won't have it!" cried Amanda, seizing Vicky's wrist. "You're just doing this to hurt me, I know. Ken Saunders put you up to it. Didn't he? Didn't he, now?"

Vicky was startled by the violence of Amanda's manner, her flashing eyes and her far too firm grip on her wrist, and could think of no answer to excuse her little declaration of independence. Doctor Swick and Mr. Peabody were busily pretending to look over Julian's latest etchings in a big folder in the corner of the room, while Mr. Cheever and Dody, being on the same davenport with Vicky, were forced to tone down their expressions of utter amazement to polite interest.

"Why should anyone put her up to it, as you say, Amanda?" Julian inquired sharply. "If Vicky wants to move, she doesn't need putting up to it. I don't understand you, Amanda—I—are you sure you're feeling all right, my dear?"

Amanda rose precipitately and flung her cigarette into the fireplace.

"All right, then, move. I don't give a damn, you little stupid! But why do you have to make a public scene about it?" And bursting into tears which she refused to brush aside, Amanda rushed out of the room, leaving a silence that must have reverberated around the block. Vicky had been afraid when Amanda first attacked her that she would burst into tears herself, but Amanda's unexpected breakdown steadied her. She felt calm in a numb sort of way, as if there was something final in this scene and something she would never understand. Amanda must hate her, she thought, yet she could think of no reason for this, or why, hating her, Amanda felt duty bound to invite her there. There was nothing to do but to get out of the house as quickly as possible, and when she started to go, murmuring something to the Cheevers, Julian made no effort to stop her but sat gripping a glass of ice water without moving, staring straight ahead.

"I'll drop you, Vicky," Mr. Peabody said. "I'm going on down to the station, anyway, for my train."

Vicky heard Julian's voice behind her as she got into her wrap.

"Sorry Amanda's in such a nervous state tonight. This war is affecting all of us, you know—don't know when it will strike here—and Amanda has put her whole heart into it. Then she's working very hard on her new book—ah, must you go too, Amos? Doctor Swick has to catch his train, I realize that . . ."

And the house was emptied as if Amanda's outburst had been a raid alarm, guests tumbling over each other to get into the safety of a taxi, leaving Julian staring at an Audubon painting of the booby gannet, his latest purchase, pinned up on the wall. After a while he tiptoed back to Amanda's quarters and rapped gently on the door. There was no answer and he went thoughtfully back to the drawing room. His eye fell on a cigar, half smoked, smoldering in the saucer by Doctor Swick's chair. For some reason this seemed the last straw. "Damned pedants!" he growled through clenched teeth. "Ought to be in jail, every one of them!" For the whole unpleasantness was, of course, the fault of no one but Doctor Swick.

4

MR. PEABODY and Vicky rode down Park Avenue in stunned silence. Maybe Mr. Peabody thought she was in some way guilty, Vicky reflected uneasily, for no one would believe Amanda's outburst was completely uncalled for. It was a wild night with the wind whipping raindrops across the taxi cab windows and rattling ash barrels along the areaways till it sounded like a bombardment. A fine night for Cinderella to be sent home from the ball in rags and disgrace.

"I suppose when people give you something they feel outraged that you shouldn't keep it forever," she ventured, presently. "I don't see what difference it makes to Amanda whether I stay in her studio or not."

"Evidently it does make a difference," said Mr. Peabody, guardedly. "Frightful night, isn't it?"

"I couldn't stay after what she said tonight, anyway. You can see that, Mr. Peabody, can't you?" Vicky went on. "I couldn't keep the place another minute."

Mr. Peabody rubbed a clearing on the windowpane to see the street signs before answering.

"When I was a boy in New England I used to run to my grandfather who was blind and deaf, always sitting by the stove in a shawl, and I'd tell him everything that was going on. "Grandpa, it's raining," I'd shout at him, and I remember he's always shout back, 'Let 'er rain! We're in the dry!'"

Vicky managed a weak laugh, but refused to be distracted from her problem.

"Why should she call me a little stupid?" she murmured, puzzled and hurt. "Why should she say Ken Saunders put me up to it?"

Mr. Peabody peered out the window again.

"Would you like to dash in here for a nightcap? There's a canopy."

"No," said Vicky. "Why should he put me up to anything?"

Mr. Peabody gave up his efforts to change the subject reluctantly.

"Maybe she doesn't like Saunders. Or maybe she does. Or maybe Saunders doesn't like her anymore. He seemed pretty upset about finding out she got him his job. That's why he resigned."

Vicky was startled at these tidings.

"So he's gone for good! Oh, dear!"

Mr. Peabody sighed.

"It was pretty sudden." He pondered a moment. "I wonder where he went. He threw up the job the day after I told him Amanda had recommended him. Haven't you heard from him?"

"No," said Vicky in a low voice, for it would be a calamity to lose Ken. Thinking of the possibility of never hearing from him again, her heart slid to her boots. It was a possibility, too, for she was certain she liked him better than he did her. She had tried not to fall in love again, but here she was, liking him much too much, thinking about him all day, dreaming about him all night, trying to meet him in the office hallways, running like mad to make the elevator he was strolling toward, in short, making a fool of herself all over again. So now he had vanished. And while she was wondering about everything else, why had he been so upset at learning it was Amanda who had sponsored his job? And did Amanda know he had quit?

"Why should Amanda care whether he put me up to this or not?" Vicky's thoughts went around in a circle, and she kept appealing to Mr. Peabody as if this motherly soul must know everything. "After all he's nothing in her life."

"They're old friends," Mr. Peabody said absently. "I used to see them around together before her marriage."

For some reason this surprised Vicky enormously. It was odd Ken never had mentioned knowing Amanda before, all the time he had asked questions about the old Amanda whom Vicky knew. You would have thought he might have contributed a few anecdotes himself.

"Doctor Swick was a curious specimen, wasn't he?" Mr. Peabody said cheerfully. "no wonder he's not able to wangle money for his college. Wonder what he wanted of Julian."

Mr. Peabody was determined to be of no help; it was almost as if he knew exactly how Vicky had offended Amanda and was too much of a gentleman to tell, if she was so stupid as not to guess of her own accord. Vicky was irritated with his attitude and was glad when he left her, though she'd forgotten her keys and had to wake up the janitor to get in the house, scampering in the rain to the basement entrance and adding water spots to the claret stains on her best dinner dress.

In the studio she looked around, hating it now that it had made this trouble for her with Amanda. If it hadn't been raining, she thought, she would get out that very night, bag and baggage. Leaving here was as bad as when she had left her brother's house and had been reproached for it. Neither time did they want her to stay because they were fond of her, it was something else in both cases. For that matter nobody seemed to care enough about her to help her when she was in trouble like this. Except Ethel Carey, of course, but Ethel couldn't cope with this sort of mysterious trouble. Vicky sat on the couch and wrung her hands. If Ken Saunders only liked her a little better. . . . Suddenly she decided to call him up. It was eleven o'clock and she knew perfectly well it was an Eudora Brown sort of gesture, but you had to have somebody to whom you could turn.

Mr. Saunders was in. Mr. Saunders said further that he had just begun a fresh bottle of crystal clear gin freshened up with the merest sprig of tonic. He would like nothing better than to share this dainty refreshment with a lady, since he had been confined to his room with a hangover for the past forty-eight hours and had no contact with the outside world.

"I only wanted to tell you I want to move out of this place tonight," said Vicky, confused by his intimate manner, his "darlings" and "Vicky, dears," even though she knew it meant only that he was drinking. "And when I told Amanda she got furious."

There was a pause and then Ken said, "I'm glad you moved, Vicky. I didn't like you there."

"I'm glad," Vicky said with relief. "I mean I'm glad somebody's glad. Thank you."

There was another pause and then Ken said, "Look here, Vicky, why don't you try and fall in love with me?"

"Why," stammered Vicky, "I suppose it's the difference in our religion. Your being a Moslem and me an Eastern Star."

"I'm not kidding," said Ken. "Don't you hear that tremolo in my voice? That's strong-man-choked with feeling."

"Spiritual or animal?" Vicky said wildly.

"Animal. I can even name it. It's an anteater. Look, I've made my offer. Put on that sou'wester of yours and come over and fall in love with me. I know you've got it in you. Why aren't you over here pitching?"

"I'd only break your heart," said Vicky, "and then go round laughing about it behind your back. Why did you quit your job?"

"Never mind about that. What I'm saying is that you've led me on long enough. Honestly, Vicky, you're a sweet girl and I'm going to fall in love with you if it takes ten years. Why don't you do the same? Just set your teeth and start going. Come on. I'll give you advice and l'amour and gin and tonic and all my loose change and a copy of *Shropshire Lad* with marginal doodlings by my own hand."

"I'll be over," Vicky heard her own voice saying, to her utmost astonishment and even terror, for it's a terrifying thing to hear you voice saying things before you've even had the thought. "It's too rainy to stay at home, isn't it?"

"You *are* a darling."

At daybreak Vicky woke up with her head nuzzling somehow in Ken Saunders's neck and their arms twined around each other. She looked at his beautiful long baby lashes and his tousled blond hair and she listened to him breathe, smiling a little to herself, as if breathing was a very special talent. She was happier than she had ever been in her life. She wanted to wake him and tell him so.

"Ken," she whispered in his ear.

He murmured something without waking, and Vicky decided to let him sleep on. She was almost asleep again herself when the word he had murmured clicked in her mind. Amanda. He had said "Amanda" in his sleep. Vicky was suddenly as wide awake as if he had shouted the name. So that was it. He had been in love and wished he wasn't, he had said to her once. Amanda. Mr. Peabody used to see them together. Ken knew all the things about her apartment the first time he came there. He came there to see Amanda. That was it. That was why Amanda was angry tonight to have no more cover-up for the affair. That was why he was glad she was moving. "I didn't like you in there, Vicky," he had said. Slowly the pattern fitted together.

"This is awful," Vicky thought numbly. "This is awful. What will Amanda do to me now?

She got up and dressed very softly, but hoping he would wake up and stop her, and say nothing was true but last night. But he didn't. She tiptoed down the stairs and into the gray daybreak. Buildings, trees, sky and street were ghost-gray and rain still hung in the air waiting for the wind to shake it out. An alley cat stalked up the basement stairs, and it, too, was gray. No cabs were in sight on Fifty-sixth Street, so she had to walk to Sixth Avenue to find one. Then she kept it waiting for half an hour in front of her apartment while she packed her things, flinging them into the trunk pell mell, panting a little, and whispering under her breath over and over, "Oh, dear, oh, dear, oh, dear!"

10

"YOU'RE SURE YOU FEEL all right, Miss Haven?" Miss Finkelstein asked for the tenth time, staring fixedly at her office chief.

"I must look awful to have you keep asking that," Vicky answered.

Miss Finkelstein cocked her head critically.

"We-ell—" she admitted.

She ruffled through the card index box with glittering red talons, and after a moment's thought decided on the proper way to couch her criticism.

"You look like you did when you first came here, sort of," she observed enigmatically. "I don't mean your hair, because of course you've done wonders with that. Why don't you try it in a pompadour like Miss Elroy's and mine?"

True enough, Miss Finkelstein, following the Front Office lead, had swept her sleek black locks into a Gibson girl pompadour, though hers was, as usual, at least two inches higher than the others'. Vicky looked wanly at this example of the latest hair-dressing and had a fleeting vision of her own small face haloed by a terrific tire, amber-colored instead of black like Miss Finkelstein's, but just as formidable. Maybe the starch in such a coiffure would favorably affect her whole being. Maybe it was little things like these that gave you the stamina to face the world.

"I like Miss Tray's Defense Hairdo," pursued Miss Finkelstein, favoring Vicky with a more intensive examination of her possibilities. "It's more off the face. Maybe that would suit you better. Or that Foreign Correspondents' Coiffure that they say Antoine invented for girls on assignments in India and China and those places where they can't get a wave-set. The picture looked frightfully attractive."

"I like mine this way," Vicky was goaded into reply. "Spectator style."

It seemed to Vicky that everything had happened to her in the last two weeks, and that furthermore it showed. She'd broken with Amanda, or Amanda, rather, had broken with her, she'd spent the night accidentally with Amanda's lover and fallen fatally in love with him, Ethel Carey had wired her that the Tom Turner heir had arrived, and lastly she'd moved for no reason at all, had no telephone so she didn't know whether Ken wanted to see her again or not. These fourteen cataclysmic days had resulted in a feeling of numb impotence. It didn't matter whether her stockings, or even her shoes, were properly matched, whether she found the belt to her dress or not, whether the hat she idly clapped on her head was straw or felt, what she ate or when. Discrepancies, as indicated by Miss Finkelstein's eagle eye, were beyond her power to correct, just as it required more mental effort than she possessed to read her own proofs for next issue of *Peabody's*.

"I suppose moving takes it out of you," Miss Finkelstein said, understandingly. She opened her right-hand desk drawer and took out a beauty kit. Opening her mouth wide as for a dental examination she applied a lipstick brush tenderly, mapping out first a rich curve considerably outside her natural lip line, then filling it in as reverently as if she were restoring an old master. Vicky watched this process with gloomy fascination, wondering why it was Miss Finkelstein abandoned herself completely and wholeheartedly to only one thing, the trail of glamour. Maybe she, too, had made mistakes in love, and maybe this absorption was quite as satisfying as any other escape. For a second Vicky considered going to the beauty shop across the street and getting a shampoo, a facial, a manicure, or all of them at once. This was how girls like Miss Finkelstein and Amanda kept in trim for their separate battles.

"Mr. Chatham is taking Mr. Saunders's place on Home Research," observed Miss Finkelstein. "They say Mr. Saunders is that sort. Never stays long in one job. Why do you suppose he never married? I think it's so *funny*."

What was so funny, Vicky wondered, though she knew Miss Finkelstein's use of the word "funny" covered many situations but never anything humorous.

"Probably in love with some married woman," mused Miss Finkelstein, now applying a minute brush to her eyelashes, sweeping them with a vigorous upstroke as if they were the glory of the Seven Sutherland Sisters. "That's always the way. Mr. Chatham is really more for us, really, I mean. He's in the Register, of course. Mr. Saunders—well, I know he's a friend of yours, but honestly, didn't you have the feeling he was not—well—not quite top drawah?"

"I don't see why," Vicky answered perversely. "The top drawer seems awfully big. So does the Social Register."

"I see what you mean," politely disagreed Miss Finkelstein.

Vicky wondered what Miss Finkelstein would think of a person who went to bed with a man who wasn't in the Register. Miss Finkelstein, though, gave no evidence of ever regarding men as anything but means of social advancement. There was a Sam who called up every day or two and received frowning discouragement from Miss Finkelstein. ("Oh, Sam, don't be a *sil*! How could I get to your mother's birthday party when I had to go on with the crowd? . . . Oh, you know. The usual. Well, you know what Saturday night at the Stork is . . . Frightfully sorry, Samuel, but it was just one of those things . . ." She called him "Samuel" with a special, teasing inflection, as if using the full name was both witty and coquettish.) There were also "this man from out of town," which signified something rather swell to a girl born and brought up in New York, and various press agents and advertising men in close contact with the socially favored, who took out Miss Finkelstein, but only roused her emotions by letting her meet wonderful other people from the Front Office set. Evidently poor Samuel had nothing to offer but his secondhand roadster and School of Dentistry dances, but Miss Finkelstein did not quite want to lose him since most of the fun in "getting around" is in the boasting to your old, less fortunate friends.

Very likely Miss Finkelstein was right about Ken. Very likely his ineligibility was the whole secret of Vicky's present wretchedness. You wouldn't catch a Social Register man making love to a girl and then not calling her up, no matter where she was, to see if she was sorry or glad or what. You wouldn't find Racquet Club men getting a girl crazy about them and then dropping her. Ah no, these *faux pas* were made only by the commoners.

The telephone rang and Vicky snatched it with a leap of her heart. If it really should be Ken, what should she say, how should she act? If she acted casual, he would think what happened was the usual thing with her. If she acted all choked up, as she was afraid she might be, then he would be afraid she was going to claim him for a husband. She said "hello" before she had made up her mind.

"Mr. Evans?" she repeated, stupidly. "Mr. Evans Who?"

"Mr. Evans!" exclaimed Miss Finkelstein, eyes wide. "My *dear!*"

"Oh. Oh, Julian, of course," Vicky finally grasped the name and pulled herself together. Julian had never called her. Neither had President Roosevelt for that matter. It seemed ominous.

"Victoria, you spoke of moving the other evening," said Julian, in the patient, fatherly, but pressed-for-time voice he assumed for the Little People. "Have you taken steps yet?"

"Steps? Oh . . . Yes, I've already moved, Julian."

"Good, then I'll have Harnett go over and make arrangements to close the place. Amanda, of course, doesn't use it."

"Well . . ." Vicky answered for there was an inquiry in his inflection. "I wouldn't know about that, you see, because I didn't realize she'd gotten it just for me until the other night."

She was saying too much, probably, but what was she supposed to say?

"Just a minute while I write down that address, Victoria."

She waited, puzzled, until she heard his impatient, "Yes?"

"What?" she asked stupidly.

"The address, my dear, the address."

She gave it to him, feeling dimly that there was something odd about all this, but nothing she could do about it.

"Thank you. I'll have Harnett go right over. Amanda's too rushed right now to attend to these details and apparently Miss Bemel knows nothing about it. How's your new quarters? Good neighborhood, I trust. See you soon, child. Good-bye."

It seemed odd that he should not have gone directly to Amanda for the address. Odd, too, that he made no mention of Amanda's rude behavior the other evening. Vicky pressed her hands to her head, dizzy with the whirl of events and conduct that she could not understand. She tried to concentrate on the proofsheets before her. House in Sutton Place for sale or rent, former home of Whatsis Whosis, now active in Washington. Photograph of Miss Nancy Elroy, soon to marry Harry Cosgrove Jones, IV, cousin of Sir Henry Cosgrove Jones of Toronto, examining the attractive view from the terrace of the new Cattleby Towers, rents beginning at $2200, ready July 1st. The letters in Cosgrove *montaged* into Cattleby and Nancy's satiny five-color face smiled, frowned, smiled, frowned, like the spectacle advertisements in opticians' windows. Vicky was conscious of Miss Finkelstein's steady scrutiny.

"You really do look sick, Miss Haven," said the young woman earnestly. "You didn't go out to lunch, either. Why don't you dash along?"

Miss Finkelstein was always "dashing," though her movements were better described as "springing," for she modeled her carriage on Nancy Elroy's, a lithe springing from the toes, head balancing imaginary book, shoulders pulling up torso. Vicky, far from a desire to dash along, thought she would be lucky to merely crawl along, so low were her spirits.

"I'd rather not get to my place before I have to," she said gloomily. "There's only a studio couch and a percolator and a lot of things to unpack. I can't bear the idea. I expect it will stay that way, too."

Miss Finkelstein pursed up her new lips speculatively.

"You poor angel!" she finally exclaimed. "I know what I'll do. I'll run you home myself and fix you up. I *love* fixing up apartments."

Vicky was too beaten to protest, although Miss Finkelstein terrified her as much as Amanda did. But first Miss Finkelstein must call up Mummy and explain the situation.

"Angel, I won't be home for perfect hours," Miss Finkelstein gurgled into the telephone. "Miss Haven isn't well and I'm looking after her."

Vicky watched Miss Finkelstein's preparations to take charge of her and felt herself growing smaller and weaker in comparison, for no matter how modest Miss Finkelstein's contribution to *Peabody's* was from nine to five, from five on till her bedtime she was *Peabody's*. Vicky saw the five o'clock metamorphosis coming over her, a drawing of arrogance held in check during the day, a summoning of all the Front Office airs and the complacency of all the de luxe subscribers. Looking at herself intently in the office mirror Miss Finkelstein tenderly okayed her pompadour, checked on her Chinese yellow foundation makeup which left a rim of pollen on her suit collar. Then she adjusted her smart little toasted straw sailor with floating pink veil on the top of her pompadour, a fitting crown for this monument to glamour. With a finger gloved in dusty pink suede Miss Finkelstein pressed a button.

"I'll tell the boy"—she always called the office boy the boy even though it was usually her brother Irving,—"that I'm taking you home because you're ill. By the by, you want Mrs. Evans to know, don't you?"

Vicky realized by the eager glint in her eye that Miss Finkelstein's gesture was more a means of contacting Amanda Evans personally than helping Miss Haven.

"No, no," she answered hastily.

"Come on," urged Miss Finkelstein gayly. "You need looking after, and I'm going to do it."

Vicky smiled wan gratitude mingled with feeble alarm. Amanda used to look after her. Now Miss Finkelstein was taking over. Maybe that was progress.

2

"West Thirteenth?" Miss Finkelstein frowned, on their way downtown. "Are you sure that's a good neighborhood?"

Good neighborhood again. She sounded so exactly like Amanda and Julian that Vicky felt it was the voice of the whole world.

"I don't know why anyone in New York worries about good neighborhoods," she said. "They never see their neighbors anyway so it might as well be a bad neighborhood.

She had signed up for the apartment one lunch hour, visiting it and leasing it very fast for fear her resolution would change. She had chosen the neighborhood because Ken Saunders spent a great deal of time down there with his friends the Orphens, and she was reduced to these shameless bids for his attention. She had figured so craftily on how far her apartment was from the Orphens' on Fifth Avenue and Eleventh, that she had paid very little attention to the apartment she had leased. She now saw that, of all the blocks in the district, the one she had selected was least savory, since it was filled with department store trucks backing and snorting into their slips on one side and a vast publishing house spewed out arithmetics and *Gone With the Wind*s on the other, so the progress of their taxi was as cautious as if on some Alpine footpath. Miss Finkelstein's face betrayed her disappointment as they threaded their way through these dangers to the new address.

"I like the trees downtown," Vicky feebly apologized.

"Trees?" queried Miss Finkelstein, quite rightly, since Thirteenth in this block was largely warehouse, and instead of the charming trees that graced neighboring blocks its sidewalks and curbs grew three piece tapestry living room sets, floor lamps, and porch swings all in brown paper waiting for surly men to shunt them onto vans and out to the hungry bare rooms of Astoria and points west.

"I should have brought my *Cue*," mused Miss Finkelstein further, as if that little magazine guidebook to the pleasures of Manhattan would solve all their problems.

The cab driver kept thrusting his head out of the side window like an inquisitive turtle, finally pausing at a small brick house before which jingled a tin sign card bearing on a white background the cheerful picture of a black puppy having its ears boxed by a black kitten.

"A bar!" Miss Finkelstein exclaimed, in a low, wounded voice.

"No," Vicky, reassuringly. "It's just a pet shop."

"A pet shop on the first floor? But Miss Haven! Really!" gasped Miss Finkelstein. "How *icky*!"

The pet shop explained the group standing transfixed on the sidewalk as Vicky and her friend got out of the cab, for the enlarged first-floor window permitted a half dozen newborn Scotties to exhibit their vivacity on one side, while on the other side of the wire a Siamese cat regarded the passerby with impartial scorn. On either side of the little brick house were three-story houses of similar vintage but evidently given up years ago as anything but wrecking material, for the dingy windows were broken, and the paint trim of windows and doors scaled to what might have been solid soot. On these Miss Finkelstein's eye rested, even while Vicky was admiring the tiny geranium beds on either side of the steps of her own residence, and the other evidences of special care in the polished brass knocker and freshly painted white door.

"I hope you're going to like this district," said Miss Finkelstein, shaking her head doubtfully.

Miss Finkelstein's hostility gave Vicky perverse satisfaction, convincing her that here was at last her very own niche, a place unrecommended by any one of her more aggressive friends. The steps and indeed the whole house listed with antiquity. Inside, the walls burst through their flowered wallpaper with plaster secrets; the tiny hallway downstairs had barely enough room for a marble-topped reception table without crowding the visitors to the pet shop, and if the place bore ever so faintly the fragrance of the caravan it was due to little runaways from the pet shop, who staggered with little mews and squeals up and down the staircase, poking their heads through every aperture and between every rail at greatly enjoyed risk to their lives. From the ceiling hung tipsy chandeliers, the cockeyed doorways had doors swinging on them at odd angles, pulling at the upper hinges like little boys at Mother's apron. All it needed to make Vicky love it with a warm joy of recognition—"This, now *this* is really *me*!"—was Miss Finkelstein's puzzled frown and delicate twitch of the nostrils.

"I'm on the top floor," Vicky said, running ahead with her key.

"A walk-up!" said Miss Finkelstein. "How quaint!

The stairs were as crooked as the rest of the house, and the bends looked like an accordion, one end caving in and the other stretching out to full width. At each landing was the conventional old-time niche designed for easing the passage of coffins up and down stairs, though this grim function was camouflaged by little pots of trailing vines, their blossoms and leaves largely chewed off by visitations from the little pets below. The handrailing was to all intents and purposes made of taffy, certainly nothing to be relied upon, for it swung out at the slightest touch. On the third floor a square skylight lit up a square hallway which managed as many changes of level as the sea bottom, and was further complicated by large bundles of bedding in brown paper from Macy's for Miss Haven and a small radio in a carton. There was a Western Union envelope slipped under the door, and Vicky opened it.

PLEASE INFORM JULIAN IMMEDIATELY THAT YOU ARE RETAINING STUDIO ON RECONSIDERATION. AMANDA.

Too late now, Amanda, Vicky thought, not without satisfaction. Whatever purpose she had served Amanda by using her studio was lost now, and the good thing about Amanda's attack on her was that it left her free to do as she liked, no need for eternal gratitude now that Amanda had revealed her cards. Vicky saw Miss Finkelstein's inky eyes fastened on the yellow slip.

"It's from Amanda," Vicky was about to say, knowing this would please her, but suddenly she didn't want to please Miss Finkelstein, or to excuse herself to her. She only wanted to be alone with her new house so definitely hers, because nobody, Amanda, Ethel, brother Ted, Eudora Brown, Ethel Carey, nobody would ever have selected it for her, and so it was the beginning of her own life. The doubting look in her companion's eye only reassured her that she was on the right path.

"I really should be at my Red Cross tonight," Miss Finkelstein said when she saw the little apartment with the swaying floor, the dinky bathroom, and the clothesline across the back window. "You could have gotten modern conveniences for the same money."

"I know," said Vicky. She saw the studio couch, her sole piece of furniture, neatly shoved in a corner by the fireplace.

"I think I'll lie down till I feel better, so why don't you run?" she said, and apparently Miss Finkelstein was almost ready to be persuaded, for she stood looking about the two rooms, so definitely shabby, so definitely Greenwich Village and shaking her head. She had pulled off her pink gloves and picked up a broom with a conscientious determination to "fix up" the apartment as she had threatened, but there seemed no place to start. Vicky lay back on the uncovered green mattress, her felt hat and shoes tossed to one side, her arms clasped behind her head. Through the two little back windows she could see the budding tops of trees in the afternoon sunlight and she thought of how pleasant it would be to wake up in the morning to the sight of green leaves and birds. The roar of trucks on Thirteenth Street made the little house shake and hum, but this too was something Amanda would never have permitted and therefore it had a special charm. There was a fireplace in each of the two rooms, their marble mantels sinking into the walls at an angle, their little black grates heaped with cannel coal and bulging out of the narrow little arched fireplace. She would have charcoal steaks, Vicky thought dreamily, but that reminded her of those Saturday night shore picnics with Tom Turner, and she shivered.

"I really don't know where to begin, Miss Haven," Miss Finkelstein admitted, and after another moment's thought removed the jacket of her brown covertcloth suit, hanging it carefully in the closet, then adjusting her pink sweater so that it clung properly to the seductive curves of her Gay Deceivers. As if I gave a damn, marveled Vicky, as if there was anyone around to admire a fine bosom, however false, but its owner. (Then she was ashamed of herself for not appreciating the girl's kind intentions!)

"In a way, maybe I should have taken you over to Mummy," reflected Miss Finkelstein, gingerly sweeping. She gave a merry lilting laugh. "I was just thinking how surprised Mummy would be to see me fixing up someplace when I'm so *awful*, really, about my own room. But I couldn't help thinking when Mr. Evans called you, that *they* might come down to see you and you looked too absolutely shot to do anything yourself. Do you think they might come? Oh, *shucks*! I meant to bring my *Such Is the Legend* along for her to autograph!"

It struck Vicky quite unfairly that she might well be at death's door, but Miss Finkelstein would play Florence Nightingale only long enough to get Amanda's autograph.

"She won't come," she said. Wasn't she anything at all, she wondered, without Amanda's protective name? Mice, that's what she was, she thought, chased around by her brother's family and Eudora and Ethel Carey and then Amanda. It would be almost better to be a nuisance, a bad girl, anything but this mousy nonentity colored only by Amanda Evans's sponsorship. Even Ken Saunders had been presented to her by Amanda, true, not for love, but as a suitable companion. All these months in New York and she wasn't even as free as she had been in

Lakeville. She was Amanda's little pawn, a Miss Nobody-but-Friend-of-Amanda Keeler Evans to even Miss Finkelstein. She ought to leave *Peabody's* at once, cut the whole tie, even if she starved.

"She might come, of course," Miss Finkelstein said slowly, and put the broom carefully in the kitchen cabinet. "I should think she would, really, when she finds out you're sick."

Vicky lay still, her face slowing reddening.

"You didn't—" she began in a low voice.

"Oh, yes, I called her," Miss Finkelstein said brightly, holding out her brilliant fingernails for a last fond examination. "You said not to, but after all, she is your best friend. I left word with her secretary."

Vicky felt a growing sense of defeat.

"What did you tell her?

"I said you'd had an attack in the office," obliged Miss Finkelstein, now getting into her jacket, and carefully dusting off the British War Relief pin so that Amanda, if she came, might recognize a fellow worker at once. "My dear, if she sees this place! I wish now I'd worn my fox scarf."

"That telegram was from her, saying she wasn't able to come," Vicky said, after a little thought.

Miss Finkelstein's face fell.

"It would have been *grand* meeting her at last," she sighed.

"Thanks ever so much for bringing me home, because I did feel faint," Vicky went on, resolutely determined to dispose of her eager assistant. "There really isn't anything to do, though, and I'll just go to sleep."

"You're sure I can't get you anything to eat?"

"Oh, no. The superintendent will bring up something," impatiently lied Vicky.

"Well," hesitated Miss Finkelstein, drawing on her gloves once more. "If you're sure there isn't anything—"

In another minute Vicky was sure she would have to scream, "For God's sake, leave me alone," but Miss Finkelstein made her exit just in time.

Vicky sat on the bed quietly, torn between such bitterness as she had seldom known and a desire to cry her eyes out. She wished she'd never come to New York. She wished she'd never known Amanda. She wished she'd never been born. Or if she must be born, why couldn't she have been Amanda Keeler, or Eudora Brown, or Miss Finkelstein, or Nancy Elroy, or any of the other women who knew what they wanted and knew how to go after it? Anger prevailed finally over self-pity and she had a sudden inspiration. She had backed out precipitately when Eudora took Tom Turner away. She had backed out again when she found she was falling in love with Amanda's lover. Of course, there were other factors in the latter situation—her shock at discovering how shrewdly she had been used by Amanda, for one thing. but the truth was she really *was* mice, never fighting for anything she wanted, always bowing out with a weak little apology, giving way to these stronger women. That's the way she might do all her life, and what would it get her?

"It must be this place is taking the hex off me," Vicky thought, amazed at the surge of energy and resolution coming over her. "It's the first time since I've been in New York that I feel myself. I know what I want. I want Ken Saunders. Maybe he's still in love with Amanda. Maybe she still wants him. It looks as if she does. But I don't care. I have a right to fight for what I want. It's more respectable than scramming all the time to keep out of people's way."

She put her shoes back on and made up her face as elaborately as Miss Finkelstein herself, though some of the freckles over her nose were still visible, on one side, and her beautifully carmined lips had the same cockeyed lilt to the left as the doors of her new apartment. She examined herself in the gilt mirror between her front windows, and except for her usual chagrin that no matter what she wore or did to herself she always looked like nobody but Vicky Haven, she decided she was presentable enough for the plan she had just formed, which was to track down Ken Saunders and try to win him completely from Amanda. She was quite aware that one word would send her flying back to cover, but still it was something to have even a teaspoonful of courage.

In the hallway she stumbled over a small black kitten which was investigating her radio battery with an inquisitive yellow paw. Black cats were unlucky but nobody said anything about a very small black one with yellow paws to take the curse off, did they? In fact, Vicky thought, she would ask the janitor tomorrow if she couldn't keep it.

She thought of the neighborhood bars Ken had mentioned, as she went downstairs. He was spending his days, after leaving *Peabody's*, in steady drinking and in the company mostly of his friend Dennis Orphen. There was a bar near the Orphens' which he talked about. Martin's. That was it. Vicky set her face boldly toward Fifth Avenue. This was the way Amanda had gone after Julian. This was the way Eudora had gone after Tom. She began swinging along in a lithe, springy manner very like Miss Finkelstein's, a sense of power and immense resourcefulness surging through her veins like the very spirit of spring. This was the way, all right.

3

WASHINGTON SQUARE Arch loomed up at the foot of Fifth Avenue like a gate to freedom. Vicky was not familiar with this end of Manhattan, but there was a spaciousness and tranquility about it that charmed her, just as the cozy antiquity of her new apartment had done. Ambitious, frantic New York faded into soft leisurely twilight here, student lovers from the University strolled along,

hatless, arms around each other; stately old churches embroi-
dered the sky with Gothic ramparts and steeples, their arched
open doorways revealed hushed candle-lit altars glittering
through the plush darkness like ornaments in a jewel box. A
flock of planes whirred far overhead in the dusky blue, guardians
of this peace, and the rim of a new moon hung over the Jefferson
Market spire. High up a penthouse roof was fringed with an architectural moustache of budding hedge. That must be where
Ken's friend, Dennis Orphen, lived. Vicky hesitated in front of
the apartment house, half minded to go in and ask for Ken. It
would be easier to look for him in the cafe, though, and easier to
explain. Walking briskly toward Martin's Café, Vicky thought of
how startled Miss Finkelstein would be to see her sprinting along
without the slightest sign of illness. She was counting so blindly
on finding Ken that she stopped short outside the bar, realizing
how foolish was this confidence. People were never where you
wanted them to be at the time you wanted them there, at the
time you had found the courage to be your real self with them.

In the bright daylight, Martin's dark interior looked almost
sinister, though no more so than the score of other dim-lit cafés
in this area. Indeed there was no more reason why Ken Saunders
and his downtown friends should have thrown Martin's their
special favor rather than Tony's, or Marta's, or Tom's, or Bill's, or
Frank's. But drinking men have peculiar fancies, and they swear
that the fragrance of Martin's front room is entirely superior to
and different from the conditions of an exactly similar room
across the street called Bill's. It is impossible for them to savor a
martini in this rival spot, it is quite out of the question for them
to have any pleasure whatever outside the glamorous confines of
their particular little haven. Drinking, to the devoted habitués of
Martin's, was a homey, laudable occupation around the little pine
bar of the front room, and even intoxication here had the stamp
of respectability for it was Martin's martinis, under Martin's roof,

and an agreeable, friendly manner of helping Martin support his family. You would have thought, from the loyalty the patrons bore whatever host they favored, that the man had particular qualities of sympathy and generosity that made special appeal. But this was seldom the case, and Martin was as sharp-faced, shrewd and cold a fish as any of his rivals, despite the tenderness with which his customers asked for Martin, Martin's health, Martin's wife, family, and future. On the credit side, Martin's endearing qualities must have been that he seldom if ever bought anybody any drinks, he freshened up his liquor stock each night with a little more neutral spirits than the law allowed, he charged ten cents more for old-fashioneds than Bill's did, and although he permitted old customers to charge food and drinks, he sent them duns at such frequent intervals that they were harassed with guilt over the burden they were putting on good old Martin's generosity, and either showed their remorse by increasing their bill lavishly or by creeping around the corner to hang their heads and bills in less desirable taverns.

Inasmuch as Dennis Orphen spent a large part of his life in Martin's, it was quite reasonable to expect to find him there, and since he was Ken Saunders' bosom pal, it was logical to assume Ken too might be found here, and such was the case this afternoon. Mr. Orphen, his lady friend, Corinne Barrows, and Mr. Saunders had dropped into Martin's at noon for medicinal treatment of sorts, and by a fortunate chance had found themselves conveniently at the bar when the cocktail hour came on, a circumstance they were making the best of. They had profited by the afternoon in striking up conversation with a couple of soldiers on leave from Fort Dix, so that they felt quite rightly that their time could not have been spent more patriotically. The two uniformed strangers further served a good purpose of stopping a budding argument between Dennis and Corinne which would have in time flowered into a threesome, with Ken taking

Corinne's part, then Dennis', and eventually being kicked out by the two as a troublemaker. At least that was the pattern these intimate little parties usually took.

"I think this time I will have a daiquiri," stated Corinne, a plump, honey-colored little creature doing her best to look tweedy in a dark green suit and hat, but somehow betrayed by ruffled blouse, red fox furs and a bracelet of tiny topaz hearts. She had considered leaving her husband for Dennis Orphen for two or three years, and during her delay her grave, business-minded husband had unexpectedly been taken with an affair of his own, which resulted in divorce all around, with Corinne still confused by this turn of events. She loved Dennis as wildly as ever, she kept assuring him, but somehow it didn't seem like real love without a husband in the offing. She wanted a little more time to consider marrying Dennis, she felt, and since she was at heart an extremely affectionate, friendly little creature, thought it would be less lonely living with Dennis while she made up her mind. Whenever she drank she remembered that she was a deserted wife and grew very sad and abused, sorrowfully accusing Dennis of future infidelities.

"You can't change to daiquiris," said Dennis firmly. "You had martinis and scotch and you can't change to daiquiris."

"I always change," Corinne declared. "It makes me feel that I'm just beginning, so of course then I don't get tight. I pretend I'm just coming in."

"That's all right, what the hell?" agreed Martin, with a shrug, wiping off the bar where the soldiers had just spilled their beer.

"Have I got to stick to beer when I join up?" Ken asked.

"We shouldn't let Ken join up," Corinne protested to Dennis. "Darling, tell him there might be a war and then think how he'd feel!"

"She doesn't know there's already a war," Dennis informed Ken. "She thinks you could get a little soldier suit up at

Schwartz's Toy Shop and have just as much fun playing here at Martin's"

"Are they all c.c.c. boys at Fort Dix?" Ken asked the soldiers.

"Sure. And they're all named Moe, Bo, and Maxie," said one.

"That's a big lie," said the other.

"Nothing like getting information," Ken said.

He had been drinking so steadily ever since he left *Peabody's* that his system had reached a stage of amiable saturation that transcended drunkenness and offered a facade of exaggerated sobriety. His decision to enlist had come about three o'clock and had been supported by earnest telephone calls to a lawyer friend, an army doctor friend, and a fireman buddy from the firehouse near his hotel. By four-thirty, Dennis and Corinne were addressing him as Corporal, and at six he had been promoted to Colonel. He was already upbraiding his friend Dennis as a slacker, in spite of Corinne's protests that Dennis simply did not have Ken's warlike nature but was a sweet-natured, lovable little fellow who might well bring about peace between nations merely by his sunny smile. She wanted to go home, but was afraid to leave the two men for fear Dennis would be persuaded to march out of Martin's straight into the United States Marines, or worse yet, the two of them would find feminine admiration for their military natures elsewhere. When Vicky Haven came into Martin's, Corinne was very glad she had stayed, not being quite sure whether this new face belonged to Ken or to her own Dennis, always a problem. Taking the realistic approach she acknowledged Ken's introduction very warily. You never knew when a new woman was going to snatch away your lover, so it was wisest to start right off being enemies.

"Can you beat this for coincidence?" Ken asked the world. "The very person in all the world I wanted to walk in here, and by God she does."

"Maybe she heard your regiment was on the march," Corinne suggested. She put her hand in Dennis' pocket very tenderly so that the new girl would know who was whose. She was not to be fooled by Vicky's radiant absorption in Ken, and besides Dennis did keep looking at the girl.

"Bastard never mentioned this one," he muttered in an undertone to Corinne. "Must be serious for her to track him down here."

Vicky was delighted with the stained glass illuminated portraits above the bar of a saintly faced Beatrice demurely holding her robe up above the knee while a lecherous-looking Dante leered. She was charmed by bald, fish-faced Martin himself, by the beauty of the yellow pine bar, and the extraordinary bouquet of her old-fashioneds. She found the conversation of the two soldiers and of Ken's two friends brilliant beyond words, and she remembered the titles of Dennis Orphen's novels, and after a third drink could almost swear she had read them and found them surpassingly good. This generous frame of mind was due, unquestionably to her new purpose in life, and her delight over actually having found Ken at the very moment she wanted him most. She didn't care a bit that his flattering devotion to her was due to drink, just as it must have been the other night. So long as he was glad to see her and called her darling, she was not going to inquire into the reasons.

Dennis Orphen, on the strength of selling his last novel to Hollywood, was buying highballs for the soldiers, but this did not promote the good feeling anticipated. Moe and Bo were deciding that the army was a rather exclusive affair which had no room for amateurs like Ken and Dennis. Even if we got into the war, they were certain that the two stinkers now buying them drinks would never be wanted.

Corinne put a quarter in the jukebox to play "Let's Be Buddies" five times, and having provided this treat for the others, beckoned Vicky to the Powder Room, otherwise ladies' confession chamber.

"I don't like politics, do you?" she began. She took her green hat off and began combing her long brown gold hair before the little vanity mirror. "Personally I wouldn't advise Ken to join up just because he's at loose ends. Supposing this country gets in the war and he's actually have to *fight*?"

"I suppose you people have known him a long time," Vicky said. Corinne nodded.

"Years. All the time he was crazy about Amanda Keeler, or maybe I shouldn't have said that."

"Oh, no," Vicky said. "I know all about it."

"I can tell when he's started it up again, because he's ashamed to see Dennis and me then because we don't like her. Then when it's all off again he comes down all the time. Did you know Amanda?"

"Yes, but—" Vicky felt the name choking her, for it seemed to her that her whole happiness lay in cutting Amanda out of her life.

"Dennis thinks she ruined Ken for anybody else," Corinne confided. "You know. She put him through so much. Everyone says she's so beautiful. Pooh. If you call a stick of wood beautiful!"

Vicky was afraid of a reply that might be too unfair to her old friend Amanda, so she became reserved in her answers and as haughty as being slightly sick over her old-fashioneds would permit. When they got back to the bar the soldiers had gone off to Trenton, quarreling with each other, and Dennis and Ken were wrangling over mighty world problems with which they now felt in perfect condition to deal. Ken was spilling his drinks and now Vicky could tell by his eyes that he didn't know whether she was there or not; he felt sociable enough, but he wasn't Ken anymore.

"I want to go home," Corinne said plaintively. "I don't want to have to stay here all night just to keep Dennis from going home with somebody else."

"Have another daiquiri," invited Dennis. "Or change to a stinger and pretend you're just coming in."

"I don't want anything more to drink," Corinne said resolutely. "I'm the home type. Let's go home and I'll cook some old-fashioneds for supper, sort of a buffet."

"We could go to my new apartment," Vicky said. "There isn't any furniture, of course, but it's homey."

"I never look at people's furniture when I'm invited into a private home," stated Dennis. "I just look at their books."

"He wants to see if his are there," Corinne said.

"I turned down plenty of women just because they didn't have a book in the house," pursued Dennis confidentially. "Not even the Holy Writ."

"I turned down plenty because they didn't have a drink in the house," Ken Saunders said. "Not even a small pocket rye."

"I like a house with no furniture," Corinne said. "Let's go to her house and furnish it up with something. If we go to our house the maid will bark at us. Have you got a maid?"

"No," Vicky assured her. "I think I've got a cat, though."

"Six-thirty-five," said Dennis, consulting his watch. "This is the hour my animal love comes out. Let's go to this place."

"What the hell?" Martin cried, genially. "Joining up right now? I was just buying a drink."

As this was such a rare occurrence, they were bound to take advantage of the miracle and have the same all around except for Corinne, who decided to try a side-car because she'd had them on a Bermuda boat once and had a very gay time. The effect was not the same this time, however, for she suddenly began to weep, dabbing at her eyes with her yellow suede gloves in a most pitiful manner.

"I can't bear Dennis going off to war," she said tremulously. "You know you ought not to go 'way and leave me in this condition, darling."

"Are you in a condition?" Dennis asked, startled.

Corinne dried her eyes.

"It's just luck that I'm not," she murmured, sadly.

"It's Ken that's going," Vicky reminded her. "Don't you remember Dennis has to finish a novel first?"

"First we have to furnish your apartment," Ken said, with a burst of efficiency and after a few struggles with his legs and wallet and hat and the law of gravity, managed to lead the way to the great outdoors. This accomplished, he decided he must go back in and telephone.

"No, you don't," said Dennis. "He thinks he's going to call Amanda and it's over my dead body."

"Please stop him," Corinne begged Vicky. "He gets this way every time he's tight."

Vicky remembered to keep smiling.

"I have a message for her," said Ken, patiently. "I wanted to remind her to go to hell."

"I thought she told *you* that," said Dennis. He looked at Corinne and shrugged his shoulders. "Ah, what can you do? Maybe he'd better join up, by God. He couldn't make any worse fool of himself. By the time this country gets in he might be a general."

"What are we going to do with him?" Corinne wailed. "He gets started on Amanda and it's like a cat fit—!"

"I'll look after him," Vicky said brightly. "I won't let him telephone anybody."

They started up Sixth Avenue in the gathering darkness, Dennis and Vicky keeping a firm grasp on Ken's arms, and Corinne, mysterious grief forgotten, giggling behind Ken, pushing him along smartly. At the liquor store Dennis stopped and got a bottle of rye, at Corinne's inspiration, and at the delicatessen Vicky stopped and bought sandwiches.

Ken was now being marched around the corner by his three friends in the manner of a victim just rescued from death by freezing.

"What'll we do if he passes out in your place?" Corinne asked.

Maybe she would come to her senses next day, next week, next year, and realize she was being a fool to go after a man who was still in love with somebody else, and who only made love to her when he was tight. But she didn't care. You had to take leavings, if you didn't get served the first time. You had to fight for even those.

They marched up the cockeyed stairs of the little house and into the bare, jolly little room. Mr. Saunders was deposited at once on the bed, and Corinne made a housewifely search for bitters and glasses, both of which were missing.

"I can see why you don't need chairs," she said reproachfully, "but your folks should have told you about glasses and bitters."

"No ice," Dennis observed, after an inspection of his own. He looked at the sandwiches, spread out neatly on the mattress beside Ken's sleeping frame. He shuddered.

"Sandwiches without mustard," he exclaimed, incredulously. "Oh, no, Vicky. No, no. Drinks without ice, maybe, or without bitters, but sandwiches without mustard! Come on, let's go back to Martin's"

"Martin's, of course!" echoed Corinne.

"We can park the general here, can't we?" Dennis asked.

Vicky looked at Ken, who was resting with what seemed an air of finality, with his hat as pillow. If she went he might wake up and call Amanda.

"You two go ahead," she advised. "I'll stay here and guard the body."

Ken stirred as the door banged behind them, and he reached for Vicky's hand. "Don't you go, Vicky," he begged. "Don't you ever go."

4

INVITATION TO the Elroys for Sunday night supper again left Vicky with mixed feelings. First she was comforted to think that at least somebody liked her and was kind to her, and then came

the crushing reminder that the Elroys liked her only for her contact with Amanda. Maybe she should tell them, "Thank you for
asking me, but Amanda is mad at me now so naturally you will
want to withdraw the invitation." But she was unhappy and
lonesome in her new bare little apartment, feeling guilty because
Amanda had treated her as if she *was* guilty, and she was sick and
stunned over her discovery of Ken and Amanda. She was entitled to a little pleasure, even it is was under false pretenses.

"Do come early," Nancy begged. "We're having cocktails for a
raft of people first, but just family for supper."

The cocktail party was in no sense a reassuring occasion to
Vicky, for Mrs. Elroy insisted on introducing Vicky to everyone as
the friend of Amanda Keeler Evans, who, Mrs. Elroy intimated,
had also been invited and might drop in at any moment. After a
while Vicky cowered in a corner talking feverishly to Tuffy's inarticulate young man named Plung who was equally overpowered
by the Elroys and anxious only for oblivion. New faces were a
menace, for Mrs. Elroy must present them at once to her special
prize. She would send a smiling glance around the room, spot
Vicky crouching behind little Mr. Plung, and would swoop down
upon her gracefully, drawing the new guest.

"You don't know Nancy's friend, Vicky Haven, do you?
Vicky is one of our pets. Well, Vicky, have you seen Amanda re-
cently?" Then, to the other guest, "Vicky and Amanda Keeler
Evans are devoted friends. Grew up together."

"Really?" the guest was bound to exclaim. "Oh, do tell us
about her! What a woman!"

There was nothing to do but to smile desperate assent or else
to make a fool of her hostess by saying this great friendship was
no more.

Once Vicky thought wildly of saving Mrs. Elroy the trouble of
introduction by pouncing on each guest as they entered and saying, "How do you do? I'm a personal friend of Amanda Evans.

Isn't that perfectly wonderful of me?" Then let Mrs. Elroy face the embarrassment! Well, she must either stay away from the Elroys from now on, or else accept the character they gave her. Not such a flattering character, at that. Mrs. Elroy was saying, in essence, "Here is a young woman of no consequence as you can readily see. But she has justified her existence and her presence in our home by the virtue of personal acquaintance with the great lady of our time, Amanda Evans. If there is any other charm to be found in Miss Haven greater than this one we mention, we have failed to perceive it."

Miss Finkelstein all over, Vicky thought savagely. She began to yearn for Uncle Rockman's kindly red face, but Uncle plainly would have none of the younger set collected by Nancy and Tuffy.

"He'll come in for supper, though," Tuffy answered Vicky's inquiry. "He won't come to any of these prewedding parties and besides he can't stand Nancy's beau. God, who can?"

"I'll betcha he gives Nancy a whacking good check for a wedding present," mused young Plung, thoughtfully fondling his fragile beard.

Tuffy laughed raucously.

"Don't be an idiot, Plung. It if wasn't for that wedding check Nancy would call the whole thing off in a minute. The man's a complete drip! But Nancy's passed up too many chances already, and besides she can't hold anybody very long."

It was a fact that although Nancy had had many men fall for her violently at first sight, she had no holdovers, either among beaux or women friends. She took up with people quickly and was immediately dissatisfied, feeling vaguely cheated. She brushed them off with such callous rudeness there could be little fondness left for her, then snatched hungrily at some new casual acquaintance and repeated the whole process. She was like a child taking one greedy bite from every bonbon in the box, restlessly searching for some unpredictable sensation, spoiling the lot for herself and for others.

"Old Nancy's pretty fickle all right," agreed Plung wisely.

Vicky felt called upon to make some defense of her friend.

"I think you're unfair to Nancy," she began, but Tuffy brushed aside this protestation.

"Oh, she and Mama hang on to you because you've started Uncle Rockman coming to the house again. He always asks first if you're coming, so Nancy and Mama ask you to keep him in good humor."

"You sure need Uncle Rockman," chuckled young Plung.

At that moment Nancy spied the little group in the corner and hurried over.

"Vicky, don't run away right after supper, because Harry and I are going out for a little nightcap. You'll come along, won't you, angel?"

Chaperoning an engaged couple was not the most fun in the world, or being an extra woman, but Vicky was touched by this evidence of Nancy's affection.

"Don't do it," Tuffy nudged her. "Why should you be stuck with him just because Nancy has to be?"

This remark irritated Nancy so much that she rushed to her mother immediately, imploring her to make Tuffy behave at parties, for she ruined everything by her talk and bad manners and insinuations about Harry.

"It's not that I don't like Harry, Mother," Nancy said plaintively. "It's just that we don't have the same interests, Mother. He's a terrible bore, but Tuffy has no right saying so."

Mrs. Elroy looked alarmed, and glanced hastily around to see if such naughty words had been heard in the clamor of the party.

"Nancy, you mustn't say such things about your fiancé!" she exclaimed in a hushed voice. "Not until you're married!"

"At least Vicky will come along with us tonight," Nancy sighed, for the only possible way to get through the evenings with Harry was to have an affair with him or have a sweet, harmless person like Vicky along to share the burden of boredom. An affair was out of the question, for no matter how free a girl might be with other men she had certain moral scruples about sleeping with the man she intended to marry. She had managed to get through the courtship period by dragging Harry to Twenty-One or the Stork Club or the many other places Manhattan provides for couples who hate to be alone together. In such noisy surroundings it was possible to sit for hours with no more conversational expenditure than a word to the waiter or the little grunts necessary to a game of gin rummy. Occasionally they would see another bride-and-groom-to-be showing open affection for each other and this was a cue for Harry and Nancy, too, to hold hands. Neither one had close friends to join them, and it made Nancy cross to find that people left an engaged couple alone as if the condition was dangerously contagious.

There was really nothing wrong with Harry's manners or looks, and that was against him from the start, for having nothing offensive about him was an offense in itself. He had a clean, round face with neat little features and neat little ears and brows. He took care that his hands were nicely kept with lotions and immaculate manicures, since hands were so important in card playing. No over-fragrant fumes rose from his sleek brown hair, and his toilet water had only a tang of blameless pine about it. Ears and nose were free of vagabond hirsutae, and his teeth were as faultless as if they were false. As for his clothes they were purchased at the proper places and unobtrusive, for Harry was convinced that everything conspicuous was bad taste and everything inconspicuous good taste. His voice was pitched to a soothing monotone, and his language suspiciously genteel. You would have thought from his careful diction and proper grammar that he had never been to college at all, but had been brought up by some menial with a vulgar reverence for the dictionary. He said "Agreed!" and "Surely!" and "in that regard," and "aren't I?" If he witnessed some restaurant brawl he was pained. "You just don't do those things, you know!" he would say. "You just don't!" and Nancy sighed with annoyance, because Fate had sent her a would-be gentleman in the season all the girls were marrying roughnecks!

"After the wedding it won't be so bad around here, maybe," Tuffy said hopefully. "Mama and Nancy are trying to make Harry join the Canadian Air Force so he can have his uniform in time for the wedding. He won't look so sappy, then. And it will give Nancy a chance to fly back and forth to Canada to visit him the way the other girls are doing. Plungy, why don't you do that? Nancy'll burn up if I get a chance like that too."

Mr. Plung seemed extremely infantile to be of any value as a warrior, but for that matter so did all the other little fellows, barely in long trousers, chattering blithely of their preference for the navy because of this, or the engineers because of that. Mr. Plung put an end to Tuffy's hopes by stating that he didn't like Canada much from camping trips he's spent there, and furthermore he didn't like camping. He thought he'd go ahead with his plans to study percussion, and if he had to, he'd play in the Army band at a summons from his country. "Oh, yes, percussion!" Vicky said, utterly mystified. It seemed a noble enough course to Tuffy, judging by her grave nods of agreement, but it did ruin her plans of annoying her sister. A more immediate means of effecting this end suggested itself, however, and she suddenly led Plung and two undersized, eczematic lads off to the "nursery" to listen to some Bix Biederbecke records with appropriate stampings. Vicky was drawn again into Mrs. Elroy's little circle, and urged to tell the amusing story about Amanda Keeler Evans running away from home that time, which showed what a really human side the girl had, you know, so different from her public impression.

"This is awful," Vicky thought desperately, squirming out of her task as gracefully as was possible. "I've got to tell them I am not Amanda's friend anymore and it's no good being nice to me on that score because I never can produce her here, never could have and certainly can't now."

The few guests Nancy had permitted Tuffy to ask from the very young set were now being herded out by the carefully instructed Tuffy to Hamburger Heaven. Tuffy was not required for the family supper this Sunday because Uncle Rockman was bringing an elderly gentleman friend, and naturally the talk would be on a lofty mature plane which would not brook juvenile interruption.

"I am really quite flattered that Rockman is favoring us by bringing a friend," Mrs. Elroy confided in Vicky, as the departure of guests gave her a moment for her own tea. "I've told him over and over again that I should—all of us should—be delighted to meet his friends here. I want him to feel that this place is still his home, and his friends are welcome. He knows I am perfectly willing to be his hostess at any time he cares to entertain, but he always takes his friends to his clubs or the Gotham and we practically never meet them. They must think, really, that we're to be ashamed of."

She fetched a wry smile at this and shook her beautifully built coiffure so that the lavender gleamed in its shining surface like amethyst. Vicky murmured her congratulations at family feeling finally overcoming Uncle Rockman's bachelor eccentricities, and almost at once the two gentlemen arrived, bringing a head scent of cigars and fresh newspapers and manly Scotch, welcome change from the spearmint and Coca-Cola atmosphere they were replacing. Mrs. Elroy resumed her sweet, genteel smile, tilting her fine head at a more queenly angle, and welcomed her brother-in-law's friend with arch reproaches for their tardiness, and for Rockman's naughtiness in not bringing his friends oftener to what was really his home. Nancy placed a daughterly right arm around her mother's blue lace back, leaving her engagement hand free for an informal but glittering handclasp.

"And here is Nancy's friend, Vicky Haven," Mrs. Elroy said in fluty tones, drawing Vicky to her side. "Perhaps Rockman mentioned her."

The stranger looked piercingly at Vicky.

"Oh, so this is the gal you spoke of, Rocky?" he asked, mysteriously enough.

"Vicky is a childhood friend of Amanda Keeler Evans, you know," Mrs. Elroy went on, while Vicky found her knees slowly melting beneath her. "Vicky is more or less Amanda's protégée, aren't you, my dear? You must tell Doctor Swick some of your amusing stories about Amanda."

"Fine," said Doctor Swick. "As a matter of fact I met the young lady at the Evanses home just a week or two ago."

The familiar black bullet-eyes once more shot through rimless lenses at Vicky, giving her once again the burning picture of that whole dreadful evening. she had a frantic impulse to shriek out, "All right, go ahead and tell what happened, you old monster. Tell how I was insulted and humiliated, and maybe that will stop Mrs. Elroy from making it all the worse right now."

But nothing would stop Mrs. Elroy, now, for if both her guests had met at the Evanses table, then she was all the more honored to have them her guests, and she urged the quailing Vicky to give Doctor Swick all her data on Amanda, her doting friend. Vicky escaped by getting Nancy to go to the bedroom with her, an exit gladly accepted by Nancy who was annoyed by her mother's elegant efforts to be coy. Smoking a cigarette and gulping down some martini left on the dressing table, Vicky decided to confide in Nancy a little of her problem.

"I can't go through with supper facing that awful man, Nancy," she blurted out. "You see—well—he was there when Amanda said some things to me, and—well, he just looks at me as if he knew all about me. You see—"

It was even harder to tell than she thought but Nancy unexpectedly helped her, by being almost ominously interested.

"You mean you've quarreled with Amanda?" Nancy broke in, after a brief silence. "You're not on good terms with her?"

"No, you see—it was about the apartment. You see—I guess I told you I lived in her—well, what she used for an outside workroom. So—"

"I didn't know that," Nancy said, in almost an offended tone. Vicky recalled that the reason she'd never mentioned it here was that the Elroys were sure to make conversational capital of such an arrangement, stressing the intimacy of the thing. But Nancy now saw another meaning.

"You mean she paid for the apartment?"

"Yes, but she never used it at night—"

By Nancy's cold intent eyes Vicky knew she was putting her foot in it, implicitly confessing that she had never been anything but a charity to Amanda and had boasted of equality in order to win the Elroy friendship. She stumbled on, trying to explain without telling really anything, but only succeeding in making herself sound like the most unscrupulous of impostors. Nancy fell silent, ominously, and only said, "Come on, we'd better be going out. Supper will be ready."

There was nothing to do but pray for strength to get through the meal, drinking as much as she could get of the martinis in case heavenly support was not enough. Uncle Rockman beamed rosily at her and won a wave of love from her by his dogged insistence that he'd never heard of any Amanda Keeler Evans since she was no connection of his great friend Doctor Keeler of Leland Stanford, and by discoursing weightily on the Dobler ef-

fect and various scientific phenomena; and just as Mrs. Elroy resolutely snatched the conversation to speak of a violet at the
Flower Show being named the Amanda Evans, Uncle Rockman
triumphantly snatched it back by declaring that the violet was
the shrillest color in the spectrum, an octave higher than any
other color as Doctor Swick himself could testify. Mrs. Elroy's
voice rose higher and higher in her efforts to keep the conversation within her own gracious bounds, but a word was enough to
set Doctor Swick off on war, and a fresh drink was enough to
make Uncle Rockman interrupt, with renewed radiance on his
own joyous world of the abstract. His eyes sparkled, he flushed,
he positively bubbled with joy in his own fountain of youth, the
atom, the electron, the measuring of the soul, the surveying of
infinity. Vicky alone was entranced by his words, for Doctor
Swick wanted to talk and Mrs. Elroy wanted to please. Nancy
was silent and as usual Harry Cosgrove Jones, IV merely agreed
or exclaimed and obliged everyone but pleased nobody by his tact.

"Rockman, dear," Mrs. Elroy finally interrupted, when a dish
of crab meat ravigote stopped the philosopher's tongue tem-
porarily, "won't you let Doctor Swick finish his sentence?"

"All right, call me a bore," chuckled Uncle Rockman, with a
wink at Vicky. "Victoria likes to hear me, don't you, girl? Victoria's
the only intelligent woman I ever met. I told you so, Swick."

"Yes, said Doctor Swick, staring at Vicky. "You told me."

"I don't think any of us have realized how very intelligent
Vicky *is*," said Nancy slowly.

Doctor Swick was her evil genius, Vicky thought. Wherever
he went he made trouble for her, just by being present. She
wanted to make him squirm, too, and so she said, courageously,
"Doctor Swick finds much to admire in Hitler, don't you, Doctor
Swick?"

"Oh, no, Doctor Swick!" Mrs. Elroy was definitely shocked, and
Vicky was pleased to see that the doctor grew red, and flustered.

"I may have made some remark in a satirical sense," he said stiffly. "Naturally I have no respect for the Nazi régime."

Mrs. Elroy looked reproachfully at Vicky.

"Of course not. How could anyone respect people who are willing to be led by such an upstart as Adolf Hilter? The Kaiser was at least a gentleman, an aristocrat, but imagine letting yourself be led by a common hoodlum."

As this special reason for discounting nazism was a fresh twist to the problem, everyone was silent, and Mrs. Elroy eagerly strove to persuade Doctor Swick of her political awareness.

"He used to sit around in cafés with other hoodlums in Munich, or Berlin or wherever it was," she said, daintily brushing crumbs away from her plate. "They sang songs and actually walked from one café to another in the middle of the streets, singing and playing instruments. Hoodlums."

The picture of Hitler as a musical hoodlum was the only appealing thing Vicky ever heard about him, but this vulgar unconventionality seemed to have aroused the Elroy political conscience as no other atrocities could, and Mrs. Elroy went on in this vein, repeating what a cousin of an attaché in Germany had told her personally about Hindenburg's dinner for his new Chancellor years ago, when all the ambassadors simply ignored the upstart, who did not know his way around among the noble glasses and cutlery, and who was snubbed by everyone naturally, since in those days no one ever dreamed the common people would consent to be led by a wrong-fork-user, a café-sitter.

So that's why people like the Elroys are against Hitler, Vicky thought, getting angry. They would stand for any barbarism but mean birth and bad manners, and it was a cruel trick for them to make a Cinderella of the monster just by their contempt for him. How dared people like the Elroys and Julian Evanses be on *our* side, besmirching it with their snide reasons? Making country club of a great cause, joining it only because its membership was above reproach, its parties and privileges the most superior, its officers all the best people? Why didn't they stay on the oppressor side where they belonged and where their tastes actually were? They did in the Spanish War, and for the same reasons that they switched over in this war. Vicky was aware of a wave of indignation bringing unexpected strength to her spirits.

"You don't object to cannibalism, then," she said. "It's the table manners they use, isn't it, Mrs. Elroy?"

Uncle Rockman was staring at his sister-in-law with a peculiar hostility.

"I actually believe you'd excuse the bastard if he was a Groton boy," he said in a choked voice. "Louise, you're talking like a damned fool. Isn't that so, Victoria? I've a good mind to get up and walk out of this house, by God."

"He's joking, of course," Harry Cosgrove Jones smilingly explained to Nancy, who was looking at her uncle in alarm, naturally enough, since she had never before seen him as anything but a benign, hoodwinked Santa.

"Come, now, Rocky," Doctor Swick said, showing a row of big white teeth and rubbing his hands as if he expected a fine cannibal treat himself. "Individuals are for or against nazis for a million reasons, most of them foolish, or personal."

"You know it's true, he's nobody," Nancy addressed her uncle defensively.

This made Uncle Rockman throw his napkin on the table.

"Of course he's nobody!" he exploded. "He's nobody because he's got neither brains nor humanity, not for your reasons! I won't listen to another word! Not another word!"

"Let her talk, Rocky, it's an angle," Doctor Swick urged, winking at Nancy. "I like all the angles. It's a hobby of mine."

"There's only one angle," said Uncle Rockman with such biting dignity that his family looked at him in complete bewilderment.

"Rockman, you're being a tiny bit rude, I believe," Mrs. Elroy said tremulously, her handkerchief springing to her fine blue nose in readiness for the eyes to well over.

"I think what your Uncle Rockman means—" pacifically interposed Harry Jones, apparently under the impression that handling an eccentric uncle was the duty of the groom-to-be.

This was the last straw to the thoroughly aroused gentleman.

"You don't have any idea of what I mean, young man, and you never could, I don't care if you marched out to war tomorrow! Swick, if you can stand listening to such gabble, the brains of a wasp, the—the—" Choking, Uncle Rockman backed his chair from the table and rose. "I said I'd leave. By God, I will!"

"Nancy, say something to your uncle!" wailed Mrs. Elroy. "Dr. Swick, I assure you there must be something the matter with him. I said nothing at all. I can't understand you, Rockman, really—when you know you're all I've got—all *we've* got—"

Uncle Rockman was in the hall picking up his stick and derby in ominous silence. They heard his grim, four-square footsteps marching toward the door as if he was leaving the house forever, an inconvenience frightening in its possibilities, so that Nancy and other exchanged looks of dawning horror. Doctor Swick scratched his head thoughtfully, and Harry Jones, IV murmured inadequately. "You just don't *do* those things, you know." Vicky felt that she was left in a den of wolves, and without a second's reflection was on her feet, dashing after Uncle Rockman, breathlessly.

"Wait!" she cried, as the front door started to close. "I understand what you mean, Mr. Elroy."

Silently he stepped back and brought her hat and gloves from the closet, and with a red, angry face whisked her to the elevator.

"Of course you do, Vicky, my girl," he said. "Naturally, Vicky, my girl."

In the dining room, confusion broke forth.

"How dare she run after Uncle Rocky?" Nancy cried out.

"But what did I say?" Mrs. Elroy begged of Doctor Swick. "Did I say anything?"

Doctor Swick beat on the table with his square-tipped, thick fingers, and his eyes roved from mother to daughter.

"Rocky's too intolerant for a scientist and philosopher," he observed. "He ought to be more interested in all the angles. So that's the girl he wants to marry, eh?"

Nancy and her mother gave a single cry of pain.

"Doctor Swick! Is that what Rockman told you? Good heavens!"

"I can't stand hearing another word! Mother, when I think how that girl has tricked us! So it was just to get Uncle Rockman! And turning him against us!"

"Oh, he wants her all right," Doctor Swick said, comfortably. "Fed up facing old age alone, you know. Usual bachelor type of thing, Pretty face, youth, sort of daughter business."

His words seemed to strike straight to the hearts, for both mother and daughter burst openly into tears, and Harry Jones patted Nancy helplessly on the back as if she'd swallowed a foreign object. Doctor Swick himself was puzzled by the effect Rockman's exit and his own words was having on the others and tried to distract them with a little gossip.

"Funny thing happened the other night at the Julian Evanses when that girl was there. Maybe she *is* some sort of adventuress, if that's what you think. It happened this way—"

11

AMANDA HAD NOT SLEPT for so long now that she wondered how she ever had. Allanol, veronal, luminol, and the whole battery of sedatives did no more than induce a half-dozing state in which her thoughts raced even faster. It was ridiculous that with all the money and influence at her command she couldn't buy or wangle a simple thing like sleep. Bemel slept. The servants slept. If you went down to the basement at night you could hear their triumphant snores. True, Julian was an insomniac, and when she complained to him he merely said, "People who deal in the affairs of nations seldom sleep, my dear. Very likely you won't rest well until the war is over." The war! The war was getting too big for Amanda, it was no longer her private property, it was beyond one person's signature. It was like a club that had finally been opened to the public, the original members lost in the scuffle. The time for the amateurs was over, the pretty prologue was over, the play proper was to begin. The

Amandas were almost at the end of their function, which was to entertain the audience until the professionals arrived. Never caring for any game in which she was not the leader, Amanda cast about in her mind for ways of easing out before she became *used* by the war instead of using it. There were other games where she could be the star. Without Julian Evans, too, God willing. It was hatred that was keeping her awake, Amanda thought, as if you couldn't hate somebody and forget it. But her feeling for Julian was like some flowering nightshade, a dark, growing thing that stood between her and every sensation. It was beyond all reason, now, so that she shuddered to pick up a newspaper he had just touched; she winced at his breakfast kiss so rudely that he stopped the little ceremony, and in her relief she did not care that he now seemed fully as hostile to her as she to him. The faintest possible suspicion that she might be pregnant occurred to her, but it was too soon to worry and moreover she was supposed to be sterile. The thought that she might have to sleep with Julian to cover up the slip was as odious as the galling knowledge that the lover in the case had left her like some village cavalier. No, this was too outrageous a trick for Fate to play, and Amanda would have none of it.

Sometimes she gave up even trying to sleep and paced restlessly around the study, reading a page or two of Malraux, Hemingway, or her favorite Callingham, for these were the only three writers she considered her peers. But underneath the surface level of her thoughts ran her furious desire for Ken Saunders, the absolute necessity for subjugating him and so restore her lost complacency. If she were in love with him, she kept wailing to herself, there would be some excuse for this obsession, but she could not possibly be in love with anyone so far beneath her in every way.

In the morning it was Bemel. Opening her eyes Amanda would think of Miss Bemel and clench her teeth. Bemel epitomized everything that was going wrong in her life, and worse, Bemel knew things were going wrong. Things wouldn't really be going wrong, perhaps, if it wasn't for Bemel *knowing* they were and making them come out that way. At nine Miss Bemel came into the bedroom with the mail, pouncing on the new day as if it were a runaway horse to be yanked into control. She would stand behind Mrs. Pons as she was serving Amanda's breakfast tray, impatiently watching this brief rite, tapping her teeth with her pencil in her anxiety to get going, or get her machine, namely Amanda, going.

"That coffee doesn't look hot, Mrs. Pons," she would say, frowning. "Take it out and heat it up. Can't expect Mrs. Evans to begin the day on cold coffee."

This sort of thing made Amanda immediately declare she liked cold coffee or quince preserve instead of marmalade or whatever it was Bemel was so sure she did not like. Once the tray was out of the way, Bemel's performance began. There was the appointment pad to be recited, the hours cut into the tiniest little wedges like a poorhouse pie with Miss Bemel presiding over the distribution. There was the mail to be summarized and the choice bits served to the mistress, the rest handled imperiously by Miss Bemel as she chose. It was only natural that such grave responsibilities should in time go to Miss Bemel's head, since they were the sole source of her importance. As the quantity of correspondence increased, Miss Bemel's arrogance mounted until she was permitting herself the same tantrums around the other servants with which Amanda favored her. Such busy, important creatures as Amanda and Miss Bemel had no time for curbing tempers or smoothing out other people's feelings. The old days when Miss Bemel had groveled in her devotion, and gloried in having her brains picked for Amanda's dear use, were well-nigh over, for Miss Bemel was being recognized now on her own. She had been interviewed for a great magazine as "The Woman Behind the Scenes" along with other famous secretaries in the

White House and Wall Street. She was invited to join a Discussion Group where she sounded forth with authority on matters Amanda had not yet put into print, both on literature and politics, and when the ladies brought to her their arguments on Amanda's magazine and newspaper pieces Miss Bemel patronizingly explained the whole matter, not hesitating to use the pronoun "I" instead of "we," or better, "she." It was only natural that the rising glory of her private life should reveal itself in added self-satisfaction which could not be disguised even for policy's sake with Amanda herself.

"Mrs. Evans will probably go to China again very soon," she told the Discussion Group, mysteriously. "I haven't said anything definite about it to her, but the situation there is changing so fast I'm going to talk to her about going very soon."

The more Miss Bemel revealed herself as the Brains and Conscience of her employer in public, the more was she treated as the Pest and Whipping Boy of her employer in private, and there was brewing in the loyal secretary's heart the first seed of sedition, though it might take years to really mature. It was aggravating to have her vanity advanced two feet by night and then penalized three feet by day, like some arithmetic problem with no answer. At present all she could do was persevere doggedly in her efforts to keep control of Amanda.

"You really must make up your mind about the trip to China," she said, waving a telegram under Amanda's nose this morning. "It means postponing your novel, but it will mean infinitely more than that in the long run. I wired the Recorder that you were delaying in order to discuss it further with Mr. Evans."

"I make my own decisions, please, Bemel," Amanda said. "Is the hairdresser coming here this morning?"

"I canceled him," Miss Bemel said. "In fact, you have so much more correspondence and people to see now that things are happening, I've spoken to Mr. Castor about an office away from the house for general details. War work, charity, and lectures. Keep the home free for your creative work."

Amanda handed Bemel the phone quietly.

"Call the hairdresser and tell him to be here as soon as possible," she said.

Miss Bemel looked affronted, then bit her lip, and took the phone reluctantly.

"Damn it, do as I say!" Amanda suddenly shouted, unable to bear more.

In the early days of their relationship Miss Bemel would have lowered her head and butted out of the room, lips trembling, prepared to scold every servant in the house by way of balancing her blood pressure. The Discussion Group, however, had given her poise.

"I should think with the war creeping in on us, you would have less time than ever for hair and massage and clothes," she said gravely. "The worse things get the more time you spend at fittings, and Arden's. I'm only saying this because it's been commented upon by the columnists."

Amanda controlled herself with difficulty.

"Thank you for reminding me," she said. "Call the hairdresser."

Miss Bemel's bushy brows met in a tangle of disapproval. God, she's an ugly female, thought Amanda, and even if she had a heart of valuable priorities her appearance in itself was a crime against mankind. As she swiveled around on her bovine rump to pick up the telephone, Amanda saw that she was getting bigger than ever, and it was not only in flesh but an increase in muscle and bone with a bosom as formidable and as sexless as a German general's. This rocky treasure taxed the capacity of whatever blouse she wore, especially the pockmarked yellow print now gracing her form, strained in a taut line across her back and then across her front so that bosoms popped out behind and before, above and below as if there were dozens of them, all crying for freedom. Certainly no man had ever touched her and no man ever would, reflected Amanda sourly. Frustration was what made the woman so detestable. But what about herself, then, Amanda thought, stunned. Wasn't she in the same boat as Bemel? She, too, was undesired. Ken Saunders had walked away from her open arms. Even Julian no longer approached her. She and Bemel, two frustrated women, and how do you like that? Instead of being softened by this link with her loyal slave Amanda found her temper mounting to murderous heights, doubled by her disgust with herself.

"Emerson ten to eleven," Miss Bemel said, consulting her pad. "He's up to page 176 of the novel and is waiting for your okay on the fencing scene he has outlined. He worked with Signor Florelle over the details last night. They were both very much pleased with it, but it seemed a little weak to me."

Oh, so it seemed weak to Miss Bemel's superbly informed mind, did it?

"Hereafter, it won't be necessary for you to go over the novel," Amanda said. "I will deal with Mr. Emerson directly on that."

"But you haven't talked over the revised structure, yet, and I have," Miss Bemel protested. "You'd better let me sit in on it when he comes today."

Amanda's eyes blazed.

"Keep out of that novel, do you hear? You're not hired to tinker with that end of things."

Miss Bemel was shaken but not to be swerved.

"Well, I can tell you you'll never get it done with Emerson alone," she started. "He's not the worker Thirer used to be."

"All right, I'll fire him and do it all myself," Amanda shouted.

She snatched at the letters Miss Bemel still held in her hand, seething at the annotations Miss Bemel had made for reply on each one. The presumption of her, thought Amanda! The cheek! And furthermore the cheek of her fine assistant, young Emerson, in planning Amanda Keeler Evans's novel with the lady's secretary! All Julian's fault, Amanda concluded, dividing her bitterness now. By day Miss Bemel and by night Julian, driving her in the road that they chose. It was as if they and their helpers had built her tower for her to rule the world and then locked her in. What had once seemed getting her own way now was *their* way, she had no choice anymore.

Miss Bemel tramped into the next room, her head lowered, her square back conveying wounded sensitivity.

"For God's sake, Bemel, go out and get yourself a girdle!" Amanda cried after her, unable to endure the sight of the creature.

"I wear a foundation garment, Mrs. Evans," Miss Bemel, now utterly at bay, turned to her tormentor with quivering lips.

"Garment! I hate calling things *garments*!" Amanda said savagely. "A lovely garment, a useful garment. God, how genteel!"

To this Miss Bemel proudly made no answer. She comforted her wounded pride with the note on her spindle from Mr. Castor stating that Mr. Evans would not be in for dinner as he was due at a conference upstate with his syndicate chief. Conference indeed! The first Mrs. Evans, of course! Small wonder with the present Mrs. Evans letting her hair down over the slightest thing. Not so clever, after all, was this Number Two who still hadn't caught on to what her husband was doing. Miss Bemel permitted herself a spiteful little smile as she sat down to the typewriter.

Amanda lay in bed for a moment considering the chances of running down Ken Saunders. She hadn't seen him since the day he walked out of the studio. His hotel said he'd given up his apartment there and left no address. One night in the middle of dinner he had telephoned her, very drunk, but she was entertaining a Free French official and a Facts and Figures man, so she could not talk. Five minutes later she had called frantically all the places he might be, but he was not to be found. The nerve of him, she thought passionately, the cheek of all these people, these Bemels, these Vickys, these Kens, who dared to clutter the smooth pattern of her life! If she went over to her studio, she thought, she might find a message from him there. It was absolute nonsense that this one little man's rejection of her should be ruining her life, making her brain a constant whirl of rage and futile storming. She got up and went into the study. Seeing the pile of papers beside Miss Bemel, it occurred to her that she might revenge herself on this officious creature by handling her own mail and reducing the other to merest office boy. She frowned through her glasses at a few of the letters and realized with vague bewilderment that her public life was so completely in Miss Bemel's hands that she herself knew scarcely anything about it. She could no more pick up the professional correspondence of this Amanda Evans than she could any stranger's.

"I'm a dummy. They've made a dummy of me," she thought. "They own me, Bemel and Julian."

There was a note acknowledging Mr. Evans' check in settling the broken lease for the Murray Hill studio. Amanda gave a little gasp. The note had been routed from Julian to Castor to Bemel. There was something ominous in Julian canceling that lease without a word to her. What had he found out? Had Vicky given him the address after the night here? Why hadn't Miss Bemel mentioned it, or did she too suspect something when she found out about the place which had been kept pointedly secret from her? What if Julian had found some clue there? She saw that Miss Bemel would not give any satisfaction on these queries, for she was far too hurt that the business had been conducted without her knowledge. Thoughtfully Amanda picked up the manuscript of her new novel, and began reading it from the very beginning. There were many passages she had never even glanced at, sections of her own rewritten by Mr. Emerson in a richly florid style quite different from the style she had used, with Mr. Thirer's help, in *Such Is the Legend*. She had given Emerson too much leeway, that was clear, and as she read her face darkened with new indignation.

"He's changed this all around, Bemel," she said slowly. "Where'd he get the idea of having Le Maz come to New York after he left Virginia?"

"Mr. Evans suggested that," said Miss Bemel. "He thought a chapter or two on the New York of that period would give a little variety, and then it would appeal more to the motion pictures."

"Mr. Evans might have spoken to me about it," said Amanda stiffly.

"He didn't want to disturb you until Emerson had worked it out a little more," said Miss Bemel. "He did talk it over with the publishers and some picture people and they agreed with him."

Amanda sat still waiting for her rage to permit her to speak.

"Settle with Emerson when he comes," she said, finally. "The book is off."

"Off?" Miss Bemel said blankly, jaw dropping. "Off?"

"That's right. Write my publishers. I have decided to abandon the Le Maz story. Whatever I do next will be entirely different."

As soon as she saw Miss Bemel's horrified expression, a feeling of triumphant exaltation came over Amanda. She saw herself deliberately destroying the figurehead Julian had created and avenging herself by making herself a new Amanda, an Amanda who was none of their doing, none of their business. She wasn't sure how she was going to do this, but a sense of limitless power surged through her, a high elation. Chains would be cast off, she would be free again as she was when she first conquered Julian; she would be free of Julian, Bemel, Ken, just as she had freed herself once of her family and Lakeville. What had been done, could be done again.

Miss Bemel was staring at her helplessly, as if she sensed the change in the woman she was so certain she knew completely.

"You can't mean it, Mrs. Evans," she said weakly. "You can't mean you're dropping the book. Do wait till Mr. Evans comes back."

"This is no one's concern but mine," said Amanda coldly, and then she picked up the newspaper with the picture of Andrew Callingham on the front page, just back from Lisbon. It was a sign from heaven. The one person she admired more than anyone else, the great man of the age, the one for whom she was really destined. Not a little Julian Evans, but a genius, a brave man, really worthy of being conquered by an Amanda. Fleetingly Amanda saw the two of them, the two greatest of their kind, sweeping through the world together, enriching each other, fulfilling each other, worthy of each other.

"Call Mr. Callingham at his hotel and tell him we are expecting him for dinner," said Amanda.

She was calm, again, the way she was when there was a challenge ahead she knew she could meet, and great rewards to be won. A man who could stir her physically as Ken had done, without the afterfeeling of being trapped by an inferior! A man whose very name could swing her to unheard-of glories, so that she would be fulfilled as woman and honored as queen! Amanda took a swift glance at herself in the mirror, examining herself as she always did, not with vanity in her beauty for itself but appraising it for what it could buy. Her blonde hair needed the hairdresser, certainly, for it hung about her shoulders, straight and careless as if she had walked through the woods in the rain. But that was right, thought Amanda, that was exactly right for the man who was supposed to hate civilized women!

"Cancel the hairdresser," she said briefly.

Miss Bemel looked at her without expression.

"Very well," she said. "But Mr. Evans won't be here for dinner, you know."

"You don't need to mention that to Mr. Callingham," said Amanda, realizing that only Julian could make these regal demands on his contributors. To get Callingham she still needed Julian. She ruffled through her papers, knowing Miss Bemel was looking at her strangely.

"What's this about Mrs. Elroy calling?" she asked.

"Mrs. Beaver Elroy. She's telephoned several times for an appointment, but would not tell me what it was about," Miss Bemel said. "It didn't seem important enough to call to your attention before."

"Perhaps it was personal," Amanda said softly. "Something you know nothing about."

"It was something about Miss Haven, she said," Miss Bemel said, wincing at the implication of secrets withheld from her.

Amanda frowned. She was glad to have Vicky and her last link with Lakeville off the records, though their last encounter still made her flush. But through this friend she might find something about Ken Saunders. Before she could wholeheartedly set out for Callingham she must clear it up once and for all with Saunders that it was she who was having the final word. She could not leave it that he had been the one to get out. She owed herself that satisfaction.

"Call her and make an appointment," she said coldly.

2

Mrs. Beaver Elroy had never in her whole fifty-one years been so distraught as she found herself on learning of her brother-in-law's sinister plans against her happiness. The Elroy home, never a model of contentment, now was a hornet's nest, with its members in such a dangerous state of hysterics that they might well have been quarantined as victims of the Vicky Haven Disease. It was Nancy's fault for ever bringing her to the house, it was Mother's fault for encouraging her, it was Tuffy's fault for not telling them what Uncle Rocky had confided in her regarding his admiration for Miss Haven. It was all their faults and they blamed each other without reserve, but most of all they blamed the designing, artful way in which the gold digger from Lakeville had wormed herself into their confidence and taken away their only means of support, their father-advisor, their bank, their moral guide, Uncle Rockman. It was a tribute to that gentleman's foxiness in never permitting them to possess him that they did not allow their indignation to touch him. He was the object of pity and regret for having his innocent affections preyed upon by the Lakeville vixen, he was a poor lost angel whose mind was being poisoned by this interloper so that he neither answered Mrs. Elroy's letters nor appeared inside their door since the fateful night the truth had been revealed.

Nancy indicated that Vicky's treachery hastened her resignation from *Peabody's* since, she informed Mr. Peabody, it was impossible for her to work for the organization that harbored Miss Haven. It was a wicked interruption to the prewedding festivities, casting as it did a veil of doubt on whether Uncle Rockman would try to use some of his money on his bride-to-be rather than on those worthy and deserving of it. Nancy's angry voice went on all night in the bedroom with her mother, and was stopped only when her mother, wishing to go to sleep, would tell her it was all her own fault for mixing with girls from offices, and indeed her fault for ever going into Business against her mother's wishes. Tuffy made things worse by cluttering up the house with her crowd so that free discussion of the family catastrophe was hampered. She did cry a great deal at the idea of being supplanted by a wife as Uncle's pet, but she was crying also over the stormy path of her own love life which was far from satisfactory. The real sufferer in the case was Mrs. Elroy, for, as she told them, she was first of all a mother and stricken by any danger to her babies' well-being. Secondly she had given up her entire life to making a home for her brother-in-law, as a sort of monument to Beaver. It was regrettable, but not a diminishing fact, that Rockman had seldom made use of her sacrifice. She had, as she looked back on it, given up very good marriages with reputable widowers, to give Rockman the entire wealth of her heart. Now these years of patient, selfless devotion were proved unappreciated. A Miss Nobody, pretending to be a friend of Amanda Evans instead of a charity, had bemused the innocent man with her youth and wiles. The long cherished hopes of Mrs. Elroy to finally put Rockman into Beaver's shoes was dashed to bits, and moreover no one, not even Nancy, had ever shared this secret. A mother is above all a mother, but there are times when she is just a woman, and Mrs. Elroy was in that anguished condition.

She consulted her astrologer, a marvelous woman who had actually brought about Nancy's engagement by her timely advice, but this time the lady failed her by promising a new man, a Taurus with a heart condition. Mrs. Elroy would have no part of a Taurus with a heart condition. She wanted Rockman or nothing. She worked at the planchette with a spiritualistic friend from Columbus, hoping to receive guidance from Beaver. The friend may have done a little pushing, but as Mrs. Elroy said to herself in all fairness, if somebody didn't push, the thing wouldn't move. The two ladies worked feverishly over the board all one evening and contacted some of the most exclusive dead, including Edward VII and President Polk, but none offered wisdom to Mrs. Elroy in the problem of saving her brother-in-law. It occurred to her later that Beaver might have deliberately held off out of jealousy. Mrs. Elroy and her friend sat at the ouija board, fingertips meeting, eyes closed, summoning Beaver's ghost from the Beyond, but Beaver was quite as undependable dead as he had been alive. Mrs. Elroy pictured him with lifelike vividness leaning over the golden

bar of heaven, while the telephone rang and rang, his wife's urgent messages unheeded by the celestial bartender. Mrs. Elroy
gave up the little séance with a resigned shrug.

"Beaver always let me down," she sighed bravely to her friend.
"Now Rockman lets us down. Something in the Elroy blood."

She had counted so completely on this graceful flowering of
her connection with Rockman that she now felt as betrayed as if
vows had been exchanged, and it was hard to remember that
Rockman had never encouraged any such hopes. It had begun almost at Beaver's funeral. After the children grew up and married, then she would turn to the waiting Rockman and say,
"Now, Rockman. Now is our reward." But no such thing. And
since she dared not mention this special blow to her pride, it
wounded her that the fitness of the thing had never occurred to
the children any more than to Rockman. They prattled on about
their own deprivation and their own selfish little lives with no regard for the private anguish of their mother.

In her trying hour Mrs. Elroy had the inspiration of using the
calamity as a wedge into Amanda Evans' home. Her engagements, like her perfumes, furs, and handkerchiefs, were so much
family property that it was an exciting adventure to lie about a
"fitting" to Nancy, and then make her dignified dash for the
Evans' home. According to Doctor Swick, Amanda had as good
as ordered Vicky out of her house, so that she was certain to meet
sympathy and support here. Otherwise, indeed, the appointment
would not have been granted, since goodness knows all the Elroy
previous invitations had been most coldly received.

Mrs. Elroy, gotten up for this tremendous occasion, was quite
a job. An hour Pick-Me-Up facial at Rubenstein's had erased the
troubled lines in her broad brow; a saucer of violets in a swirl of
blue veiling served as crown for her fine new permanent; blue
kid slippers tipped the still handsome slender legs, with "matching accessories" as *Peabody's* always said, including an enormous

fine bag with silver trimmings large enough to carry the complete file of all the Elroy enemies. Her gray coat was both proper and feminine, allowing a ruffle of chiffon scarf to soften the betraying throat sag. There was not a doubt in the world that here was a lady, one well equipped by birth and appearance to visit the Evans' mansion. Mrs. Elroy had none of Ethel Carey's misapprehensions as she entered the marble foyer that afternoon, for she was a Chivers from Columbus and her proud memory had marbleized the entire family tree. But her heart did beat fast, thinking of the years spent in trying to bring about this contact, and it was no less a triumph that tragedy had affected what her social strategy had failed to do. And Amanda's immediate appearance in the drawing room confused her to a point where she was actually gushing out something about "we have a little friend in common—Victoria—er—er" before she recollected that it was more an enemy in common.

Amanda, never one to waste time on the pretty little amenities, confused Mrs. Elroy even further by conducting the interview on a bald businesslike basis quite different from the suave interchange Mrs. Elroy had dreamed.

"You see we accepted her as your protégée," Mrs. Elroy said, with a pained sweet smile. "Naturally anyone would be proud to accept your recommendation, Mrs. Evans. But when she used our house to conduct a campaign on poor brother Rockman! Isn't there anything you can do, Mrs. Evans, to stop her? Isn't there someone in her family back home who could talk to her? I assure you, we are all heartbroken. She seemed so simple. And all the time setting out to marry poor Rockman, twice her age, and completely blind so far as women are concerned. There's no talking to him."

Amanda listened to her caller attentively, with a little frown.

"But you haven't said anything about Vicky accepting him," she interrupted. "How do you know she's going through with it?"

This question absolutely floored Mrs. Elroy. Her jaw drooped and she stared helplessly at Amanda.

"But of course she will!" she finally stammered. "That's the whole thing. She wouldn't have gotten him to that stage without intending to go through with it."

Amanda looked skeptical, and Mrs. Elroy began to feel foolish and a little angry. A woman of Mrs. Evans's brains should know that anyone would marry Rockman Elroy who had a chance. Amanda's next query ruffled her even more.

"What's your objection to her marrying him?"

For this Mrs. Elroy mustered all her resources, her voice rising to a mildly querulous pitch in spite of her efforts to keep it low and silvery.

"The difference in their ages. And their class. But it's more than that, Mrs. Evans." Here Mrs. Elroy looked around to make sure that the dark room concealed no eavesdroppers. "She has a young man on the side, Nancy tells me. Mr. Saunders, who used to be at *Peabody's.* Of course she thinks she will get Rockman's name and his money and then keep up with her lover. It's plain as the nose on your face. And Mrs. Evans, one can't sit back and see one's brother, a fine wonderful man like Rockman, made a monkey of that way! That's why I came here."

That's it, Amanda thought. Ken had dared to leave her for little Vicky. He had made her leave the studio because it reminded him of Amanda. It was Ken's doing, all of it. Vicky couldn't know about them, Amanda was certain of that. Girls like Vicky had no flair for sensing undercurrents. She felt color coming into her face, thinking of being left for a little mouse like Vicky. Ken had planned it deliberately to humiliate her, to revenge himself for the years she had teased him. Excitement began burning inside her, knowing that through Vicky she could get back at him, recapture him, and then throw him back, always the sportsman's privilege. Of course, Vicky had no intention of marrying this old bachelor of Mrs. Elroy's. It would be a good job if she did. A plan formed in Amanda's mind swiftly.

"I can't promise anything will come of my talking to Vicky," she said carefully, stabbing her cigarette out in the ashtray. "Maybe she has made up her mind. I'll talk to her, in any case."

The interview was over, but it took Mrs. Elroy, unused to harsh business manners, a moment or two to realize the fact. She had expected to have a little polite chat to cover up the crude purpose of her call, but Amanda would have none of it. She stood in the doorway, unsmiling, uncivil, really, Mrs. Elroy thought, until the latter had collected her gloves and bag. Amanda rang for someone to see the lady out, and waiting beside the elevator, looked sharply at her guest.

"It's your brother-in-law, not your brother, isn't it?" she asked.

Mrs. Elroy nodded.

"About your age, you said," Amanda pursued, reflectively. "Oh. Now, I see."

The implications of what she saw made Mrs. Elroy's susceptible nose assume a delicate heliotrope shade, and shattered for the moment her satisfaction in the interview. Mrs. Elroy shuddered as she felt the heavy doors of Twenty-nine swing shut behind her, thinking of Amanda's cryptic "Oh, *now* I see." She had not said a word to suggest such a thing, but after all her trouble Amanda had merely thought the lady was only anxious to get Rockman for herself. Walking gracefully down Fifth Avenue the liquid spring air revived Mrs. Elroy's confidence. It didn't really matter what Amanda Evans thought if she could restore Rockman to his rightful owners. Yes, she really had accomplished something.

12

*E*VERYWHERE PEOPLE WERE whispering to each other, "I've just got back from Washington," with mysterious, significant looks as if now they knew the secrets of all nations. Merely by buying a round trip ticket to the nation's capital they acquired special powers of divination into the country's future, which on no account would they reveal. At every gathering a murmur fraught with spy papers, secret missions, dangerous responsibilities, would sweep the room—"He's leaving for Washington tonight!" heads would turn, everyone would stare eagerly at whatever man had been so honorably mentioned, as if out of the whole world the President himself had decided here is the one most able to advise him. The mere name of the city, hitherto evoking only images of cherry blossoms and grisly state banquets, now invested whoever mentioned it with curious, enviable knowledge, and so trains and planes were packed with citizens rushing to Washington with their letters to someone high up, their queries, their suggestions, their data. Initials of various departments and organizations buzzed up and down train corridors, hotel lobbies, club rooms, bars—OCD, COI, OFF, and anyone confessing bewilderment at these alphabetical symbols was socially as undesirable as any college freshman unable to grasp the fundamental difference between a Deke and a Beta. Briefcases shot back and forth bulging with state secrets, plans for making ploughs out of bent paper clips, paper clips out of bent ploughs, bullets out of iambic pentameters and tea out of poison ivy. Artists knocked each other down in their stampede to the Mayflower with a Functional Canvas, columnists thought up five-word slogans for civilian morale and rushed to headquarters for the proper medals; civilians wore uniforms to denote they were civilians; men in action wore civilian clothes to denote they were in the service, possibly too important for the obscurity of full military trappings. It was a time to be just back, just going, or to know someone who was just back or just going to Washington. Like any other holy city, the mere pilgrimage was in itself enough to insure respect from one's fellows.

Mr. Julian Evans flew back and forth to Washington in a private plane with his business secretary, Harnett, Amos Cheever, four minor secretaries, a photographer and public relations man, in short, with a suitable staff for a leading public-opinion molder. He had a five-room suite at the proper hotel where he conferred in the greatest secrecy (except for the secretaries, dictaphone, and reporters) with dignitaries too high up to be even named here; reports of these conferences were then photostated, mimeographed, and mailed for further protection of their sacred contents, copies filed in a steel trunk which accompanied Julian on all his trips like a gagman's joke box. In the city of Washington itself the rest of the country faded away; Washington was America, the rest of the country was spoken of as "the field," as if its acres and population were the testing laboratory for the myriad experiments being discussed in the Capitol.

Amanda Keeler Evans, in this constant shuffling of events and public names, was less in the public eye on her own merits and more as the charming young wife of the great Julian, who, it was rumored was wanted by the President's closest chiefs for a post of unparalleled importance. In the magazines, the Washington hostesses took precedence over individual achievements by Amanda; women volunteers and their organizers were publicized, and Amanda had neglected to get into this game. Unknown female patriots were springing up, their greatest vale in their earnest anonymity. Amanda was confused by the masses of women too simple to be rivals, too numerous to be dismissed, and too mass-minded in their ambitions to be even faintly understood by her, let alone led.

"I'm afraid Amanda has missed the boat somewhere in these last crises," Julian confided candidly to Amos Cheever.

In the midst of all his new dignities and his new hostility toward her, Julian was in no mood to smooth out his wife's problems or to advise her career. Amanda, conscious of her own recent deficiencies and jealous of Julian's rising star, jeered at his new honors and ambitions, since they were tacit evidence of who was now top man. She and Julian shouted at each other, disagreeing over the smallest trifle, they banged doors and carried on their wrangling even before the servants and guests, rather than be left alone with each other.

"At the most important period in my entire career," Julian gravely complained to Cheever, "the person I've done the most for in the whole world, the woman I have actually created—"

"You have, you have!" Cheever agreed, shaking his head sympathetically. "No one would ever deny it."

"—the woman I have not only made the queen of her field but honored with my name, turns against me and mocks me! What would the public say if they could see the torment she causes me? Incredible, Cheever! Incredible! People would laugh at me. They would! Oh, yes, they would! I would be ruined so far as public respect goes. No, no, Cheever, she must be curbed before she ruins us. I don't see how just yet, but I'll work it out. Ah, these human problems! They're the ones that defeat a man!"

It was only natural that hints of such domestic turmoil should reach the gossips, and if Amanda had been in a more perceptive state she might have observed that faint change in the responses of trades people, servants, and opportunistic friends always visible when a separation is in the air and it is not yet known which side is buttered. The abject loyalty, the humble adulation, dwindles to merely respectful attention in preparation for a graceful retreat in case the rich husband is now grooming a new bride. At the same time no open rudeness must be betrayed, for there is always the chance that the retiring wife may have wangled the bulk of the fortune.

Amanda observed none of these changes of wind, absorbed in her own private confusion. She had manipulated her course so far by complete self-confidence, remaining cool and in constant control of her reactions. Now panic was upon her, and she could think of no way to solve it but by destroying everything around her. She fought with her committees, broke lecture engagements, wept all night because she could not sleep, neglected social duties recklessly, allowed Julian to entertain dinner guests alone while she had tea in bed and sulked or else wrote furiously in her new book, which was to be none of Julian's or Miss Bemel's business. She telephoned Andrew Callingham every night, just as she had once done Julian, and would not be dismissed or hurt by his suave apologies. If he had not yet married that Swedish dancer with whom he traveled, then there was a fair chance he never would, and Amanda was staking her claim in advance.

"I'm working on an entirely different line, now," she confided in him. "You're the one person in the world to understand what I'm attempting. It's—well, it's your kind of thing."

But Mr. Callingham, charmed as he was by her good looks and the power she had over Julian Evans, would not take her literary aspirations seriously. Julian had been too easy game for her, Amanda admitted to herself. His extreme morality had made him a born gull, with no defense against a wily woman. Other men, real men like Callingham with a thousand women after them every minute, wanted to be the pursuers and put up a valiant defense against ladies who took away their hunting licenses. This resistance did not discourage Amanda, but rather gave her added zest for the game. But other matters troubled her, and made her life a nightmare. What was Julian's talk of being governor or cabinet minister or ambassador, what was a new country dragged into war, what were the new problems of her refugee groups to her own unbelievable dilemma? She might as well have been some debutante virgin, for the complicated horror of her condition. In all her sophisticated life she had never faced such a problem, and since she had never regarded women friends as anything but a burden, she had no one to trust. Here was a situation no lunch with a steel millionaire could adjust, no flattery from a visiting king could settle, this was a problem for the woman friend. Amanda thought fleetingly of Ethel Carey, but Ethel was far away and not likely to be won back to intimacy after Amanda's recent snubs. Even knowing this, Amanda wired her an invitation to lunch next time she was in New York. It was insulting to be answered, not by wire, but by letter from Miss Carey's housekeeper in Lakeville, stating that Miss Carey was now in residence in Washington as an official in the a.w.v.o.

"They can't do this to me," Amanda thought, indignantly, just as she would have blamed "they" for cancer or old age. Catastrophes happened to people, certainly, because people were stupid, emotional foolish animals. But they did not happen to Amanda. They *shouldn't*. If they seemed to be happening to her now, it must be someone's fault; some dolt had left a door open, some fool had given the wrong address. God himself must have gotten the name wrong. You would have thought that God was accustomed by this time to breaking the backs of those with already broken backs; it wasn't His way to inconvenience His own special hothouse flowers. He usually shipped them efficiently through life with the warning to all FRAGILE. THIS SIDE UP. Yet here He was, bungling up His own special Amanda Evans' nice plans with the most reverent inefficiency. Possibly He had been too long with the firm and had delusions of grandeur. The Board of Directors would hear of this. Send a memo, Miss Bemel, that one more mistake like the last one and out He'd go, without his pension, too. Mr. and Mrs. Julian Evans would not tolerate impudence, even from their Maker.

2

IN FRONT of Vicky's apartment Amanda looked out of the cab curiously. A moving van was backed up to the curb and an entire home was being transferred from truck to sidewalk. A butterfly sofa with a worn Paisley covering went out first, its bottom spilling wire coils and stuffing; a small, old-fashioned pine cupboard with roses and violins painted on its broken doors; an uneven, teetering cherry chest; a needlepoint footstool on beetle legs, and a bushel basket of clay dishes. Why anyone should bother to transfer these treasures from one tenement to another, Amanda could not imagine. She stepped out gingerly among this collection and opened her purse.

"You're Amanda Keeler Evans," grinned the driver.

Amanda gave a start, not prepared for recognition in this section.

"Knew you by those News Reels," said the driver, making change for her. He was beaming over his cleverness in having recognized her from such a vague clue as her picture in constant circulation. Amanda acknowledged his remark with a nervous nod, for she had no desire to be seen making this particular visit. When the man called after her if she'd like him to wait, she hurried on with bent head, pretending she hadn't heard. As she followed the sofa up the stone steps to the pet shop entrance, she heard the voice of another cabby, "Hey, Mac, wasn't that Amanda Evans?" and her own driver's proud assent. It was not easy living in a glass house. There were no provisions for an occasional black out, and Amanda wanted a black out for a little while. She had gone to some trouble to pick up a cab far from her own neighborhood, changing to another one later on but she seemed to carry her notoriety around with her like a hump. This was Vicky's fault for not being in the *Peabody* office when Amanda needed her, and for not answering telegrams. It was small-minded of Vicky to stay wounded over that last dinner, small-minded and extremely inconvenient for Amanda.

The moving man, a large red lobster of a fellow with white bristles sprinkled over head, nostrils, wattles and ears, stood in the tiny vestibule pressing a bell while his gaunt gray assistant stared at Amanda and stroked his unshaven cheek reflectively. Likely enough, they knew her too, Amanda thought, disturbed. Propinquity to the masses she championed in public always annoyed her in private, and she let them go ahead with their freight before entering. Then she climbed the stairs slowly, and absently picked up a kitten scampering in the path of the moving men. She heard Vicky's voice from the hall above.

"Here, Amanda!"

A little surprised Amanda looked up and saw Vicky's face looking down over the banisters.

"I meant the cat," Vicky said, embarrassed. "Her name's Amanda, too. Come on up."

Amanda handed the cat to Vicky and followed her into the apartment, bracing herself for what she was going to say. The low-ceilinged little apartment was like nothing she knew, and the wonder of why Vicky had thrown over the luxury of the Murray Hill studio for this funny little place made her realize how far removed they were from each other's understanding. Vicky covered whatever feelings she may have had at this unexpected call, by directing the moving men in placing the furniture.

"I bought out an apartment from a woman on MacDougal Street," she said, talking rapidly as if a pause between words might allow a real thought to be revealed. "Her husband's left her for someone else and so she's going to Africa with the Free French to be a nurse. It's exactly the kind of stuff I need, and it was cheap."

"I could have sent you furniture," said Amanda, sitting down in a little slipper chair and lighting a cigarette. "You could have had all the stuff in the studio. Modern stuff."

Vicky was pushing the little sofa against the wall.

"This is the kind I like, thanks," she answered. "I like furniture and houses all warm and used and kind. Old wood. I like old chairs and I like old houses. It's—well, they're friendlier."

Vicky looked confident and blooming in her candy-striped red apron and housecleaning gloves. Sometimes shy, uneasy girls bloomed this way in their own homes or on their own subjects.

"You weren't at *Peabody's*," Amanda began. "I do think you might have called me."

Vicky bent her head over the kitten, her hands stroking its black, furry neck. Then she looked up at her visitor with a troubled face.

"What do you want of me, Amanda?" she blurted out. "You want something or you wouldn't have followed me here. What is it?"

Amanda pressed her hands together tightly, and drew a long breath.

"Vicky, I'm in a ghastly mess. You're actually the only person who can do anything. Maybe, even you—but you've got to. You see, I was told I was sterile and I've never given it a thought, but now—" Her voice took on a strange hoarseness, as if confidences were so rare coming from her that they had to pass a dozen censors in her vocal chords before they could come out, and then they came out in a rusty creak with all the hidden corrosion clinging to them. She didn't look at Vicky who sat on the edge of the couch, staring blankly at her.

"Can you imagine! Like that idiot girl on the other side of the Lakeville Cemetery that everybody made fun of! Like those factory girls at the Fallen Women's Home outside Cleveland! Here I am—all the money in the world—thirty-two years old—and as helpless as some farm girl in trouble. Not a soul to help me—no one I dare ask!" Once the dam burst, the bitter words poured out, heedless of the effect on Vicky, Amanda being conscious only of the unbearable pressure that was forcing them out. "Half a dozen of the best doctors on Julian's payroll, but how dare I trust them? They'll go straight and tell him. He's tops right now. You'd think I could ask some women, but I don't gossip with any women. When I try to bring up the subject, they freeze up as if I was accusing them of something. What is it they all do, for God's sake? How do they get away with it? I know everything going on in the world but that one little matter of where a woman in my position can go for this sort of thing without being blackmailed. Think of it!" She gave a hard little laugh. "All this talk about birth control enlightenment, and what an advantage over the old dark ages! Nonsense! The professionals always knew what to do and still do. But right in the twentieth century a woman in a jam is still a woman in a jam! It's something to write about, isn't it?"

She got up and began slowly walking up and down, her slender hands hugging her elbows, her olive face pale and sick-yellow, with dark blue shadows under the eyes, and the eyes looking straight ahead, not seeing Vicky's numb, stricken figure.

"It's a joke, oh sure, I know it is," Amanda went on harshly. "Something cooked up to show me the only thing that matters is what's happening to you personally that very minute. Something to show me that if I know so much why don't I know how to get out of a jam that a million dumb clucks get out of everyday without thinking. The admirable Crichton business! Knowing what the categorical imperative is, and five languages including Sanskrit, but no idea of how to open a can of beans. Certainly, it's a laugh! Oh, Vicky, don't sit there. Help me."

Suddenly tears began streaming down Amanda's face and she dropped on the bed, shoulders shaking, her arm across her face. Quite as suddenly the tears stopped though her face worked for self-control.

Vicky put her hand on her shoulder, unwillingly. The sight of Amanda in hysterics, strange and terrifying as it was, only left her numb. Some persons were suited only to triumph and they existed only in a blaze of glory; in descent they were not the same people, and must find new personalities for themselves. They needed their daily transfusions of victory for their blood and brain, and without this they had no corpuscles for defense, no philosophy for defeat. So Amanda, broken with her little misfortune, was not Amanda to Vicky but the curious awful spectacle of a statue in fragments. The events of the last two months had destroyed all her sentiment for her old idol; all she felt now was despair at the unhappiness Amanda continued to pour over her, mingled with the dreary conviction that once again she must throw herself on the tracks to save the fairy princess.

"I could telephone Corinne Barrows," she said.

"Dennis Orphen's girl. I remember. He wrote that satire on Andrew Callingham. I hate him!" cried Amanda. "Don't tell her I'm here."

"I'll ask her advice," Vicky said. "She's the only person I could ask. I won't say it's for you."

Fortunately Corinne was in, and being a warm, obliging little creature, was quite free with her information about a certain doctor in old Chelsea who could be obtained by mentioning her name. She would telephone him herself right away.

"You poor darling!" Corinne gasped. "Does Ken know?"

Vicky gulped.

"I haven't told him," she said, and hung up. "It's all right, Amanda. I'll make an appointment with the man. Or better still, we'll go right over."

This was all that Amanda needed to restore a little of her old self. It proved that she could still will things to come out smoothly, at no matter what cost to others. She began to make up her face.

"Why didn't you tell Julian?" Vicky asked, half-knowing the truth, but for some reason wanting it proved.

"My dear, I haven't slept with that toad in six months!" Amanda gave a short laugh, her hand on the doorknob. "No, my betrayer is another matter. That's the whole trouble."

It was Ken, then.

"Someone you're in love with—" Vicky heard her own words without wanting the answer.

Amanda did not answer at once, and Vicky could feel her withdrawing now that she had revealed herself so dangerously to another human being. The statue was endeavoring to assemble itself once again.

"Certainly not," said Amanda. "Someone in love with *me*."

Vicky looked at the lovely blonde head, the smooth shining waves gleaming under the tiny figment of ribbons Amanda wore as a hat, the darkly troubled blue eyes, the lips thin but prettily curved, the sleek gypsy brown skin. Nothing so beautiful as this could be so intentionally cruel, so brazen. There must be some excuse, or was it excuse enough that her beauty gave such pleasure to a million undeserving eyes? She must have something beyond that, some inner kindness maybe not for friends or for Ken, but for somebody. But the radiance she cast was deadly, no matter how you excused it, and Vicky felt her own new happiness withering under it like a leaf in the drought.

"I can't understand why you don't marry Rockman Elroy," Amanda said on their way downstairs. "After all there needn't be anything final about it. A year, and then Reno and a nice alimony. Really, Vicky, you haven't a grain of sense!"

"I know it," Vicky said. "I don't suppose I ever will have."

She dropped her keys in the mailbox for Ken, and the guilty clang seemed to reverberate up and down the streets like the crack of doom.

"You're not still in love with Tom Turner?" Amanda accused.

"No," said Vicky. "Someone else."

"Good," said Amanda.

What's good about it, Vicky thought? He's in love with you and you're in love with somebody who's in love with somebody else—oh, splendid. Perfectly ducky, in fact.

3

VICKY SAT in the dark musty parlor in the brownstone house in Chelsea, with Julian Evans' newspaper in her hand. She read up and down the columns, the words piling on top of each other like coaches in a train wreck—Hitler—Churchill—Gunther—Hess—Laval—Lindbergh—Knox—strike—plane crash—D.A.R.—Disney—Coughlin— all the matters of which Mr. Evans had complete knowledge—at the control of a button. For all the sense they made to Vicky they might have been a trail of "shrdlu etaoin's." She was thinking how strange it was for Julian to know everything in the world except what was going on in this insignificant little doctor's office in an obscure corner of Chelsea. There was Amanda's article, too, authoritatively explaining what would happen in industry, the home, the arts, when America was pulled into the war. Amanda knew everything, too, except how to handle an elementary human problem. Mr. and Mrs. Atlas, with the world lightly on their shoulders, but unequal to the burden of one straw.

"What will happen to me if Julian ever finds out?" Vicky wondered, although she knew for a certainty what would happen. Julian would blame Vicky for everything, and Amanda would manage to unload the whole misadventure on someone else.

Supposing the doctor, a grave, enormous young man, with huge white hands, should discover that his patient was Amanda Evans. He would certainly know that this was a blackmailing matter, for if it was aboveboard her husband would have arranged the operations, with his own physician, under the most decorous protection. On the other hand, supposing this silence from the inner office meant that Amanda had died on the operating table. Who would tell Julian but Vicky herself, and how would she explain it? Under these dark imaginings ran the sickening knowledge that it was Ken's child that was being denied birth, that although he had said he was free of Amanda's hold, he was bound to her by this, and that she, Vicky, loved him desperately and wanted above everything in the world to have a child, a dozen children by him. This was the way things always happened. Amanda could always have what Vicky wanted anytime she liked. With a sick ache Vicky thought of how Amanda would use her to the end of her days, stepping into her life whenever she chose, taking what she liked. They were like the two ends of an hourglass that wouldn't work, the sand always staying in one, depriving the other. Amanda was the finest flower in the garden because she took the nourishment from all the other flowers, it was as natural and blameless as that.

"I knew he'd been in love with her and I know that's why he quit *Peabody's* and that's why he drinks all the time now so he can forget. I know that, even if I daren't let him know I do. But why must there always be more to know, one more little torment made especially for you?" Then Vicky shook her head sternly, instructing her thoughts to stop their destructive work.

She fixed her eyes on the largest rose in the elaborately ugly carpet. It was a bloated saffron rose and it was shaded in green spots that made a face of it, a mouthless Oriental face against the bright blood red background. She would dream of that carpet face for a long time. Outside, through the still red rep window curtains, she could see a dark garden with a high board fence around it. Somewhere the afternoon June sun was shining, but over these dingy back courts a perpetual rain cloud spread like a circus top, veiling it in a strange antique twilight. There was an ailanthus tree quivering in some secret wind against the fence, and beyond that the stained blackened rear of a tenement on the next street with clotheslines stretched across its windows up to the fifth story like a musical score with a pair of ragged pink cotton bloomers as *do,* running up the scale of dishtowels, shirts, sheets, and slips to a faded blue apron for high *C.* The windows in this bleak memory of a house varied, some with white ruffled curtains, then a single piece of cretonne pinned up, then a crooked green shade. The grimy little yards were separated by rotting board fences into squares, and sharp-nosed, gaunt cats loped along the edges to vanish into garbage pails.

In the doctor's stone-paved yard with its single tree, a yellow cocker spaniel was chained to the fence. From the floor above where she sat Vicky could hear a woman's voice calling out, "Lie down, Penny! Down, I said. Down, Penny!" at which the pup would gaze alertly upward, lie down, jump up again, tail wagging, bark happily, thus prolonging the conversation to "Quiet, Penny! Stop that, Penny! . . . No, no, Penny. Stop, Penny. I said quiet, Penny. Good dog, Penny."

She would dream about that yellow dog, too, Vicky thought. She could shut her eyes and already see the nightmare, the carpet-rose blending into the dog-face. Somewhere, maybe from the window in the opposite tenement, the one with the ruffled curtains, she could hear another feminine voice, a voice with beer bubbles in it, a broad rich sound that must come from a full belly and fat throat. You could hear its laughter burbling behind the curtains of history, warm, sensual, satiated. Another voice swelled it with deep, baritone chuckles and under this bellow of laughter the small miseries of Vicky and the savage pain of Amanda were lost and buried.

Vicky watched the black onyx clock on the black marble mantelpiece. The clock's face was upheld by two golden fauns and its hands were fixed permanently at twelve-fifteen. Put that in the nightmare, too, Vicky told herself, put twelve-fifteen on the carpet-rose dog-face and give it the voice of the laughing woman. Put the whole dream in the unripe pickle green of these painted walls, and scent it with the combination of turpentine and disinfectant (either for bugs or anesthetic) that drifted through the air. This reminded Vicky to study once more the silent door behind which Amanda had vanished a half hour before. It occurred to her, with a shiver, that the inner room must be soundproof, since not a murmur had come out of it.

Around the walls hung pictures heavily framed in brown or black wood; steel engravings of the *The Operation* (sinister looking doctors gathered around a skeletonic patient), *The Sick Child* (weeping, praying mother at bedside of dying boy), and enormous hand-tinted photographs of two eager, busty little girls in ruffled confirmation dress, their mature, knowing faces incongruously framed in frizzling black hair that repellently resembled the doctor's. A small black walnut coffin on top of a too red mahogany-veneered console proved to be an old music box. Vicky experimentally turned something which aroused a croaking and coughing and eventually a faraway forlorn tinkle of the *Last Rose of Summer*. This wheezed croupily into *The Scarf Dance, Ben Bolt,* and finally cackling *Dance of the Demons* that seemed to shake the ancient entrails of the box. Vicky tried to turn it off, but it went on and on, rattling through its entire repertoire endlessly like a garrulous witch.

Two girls came in the hall door, a drab blonde in a cheap flowery hat and black silk dress that disguised no bulge or cranny, and an older one with a variety of henna shades in her hair, ten-cent store earhoops and a paper knitting bag over her arm, from which she now took some brown yarn and needles.

"For God's sake, don't start knitting!" sharply cried the blonde, looking for support toward Vicky. "You'll drive me nuts if you start knitting now."

The older one paid no heed but calmly set to work on her socks.

"Ah, you're just nervy. You shoulda had it done sooner like I told you. Me, I get done once a month regardless, just to be on the safe side."

"Where would I get that kinda money, kindly tell me?" muttered the other.

They both stared at Vicky with that combination of scorn and friendliness with which strange women are accustomed to regard each other when Fate throws them into the same situation. Sorority sisters, Vicky thought, Amanda's at that. But no, they were claiming her as their own, Amanda could always rise above them. Now she was thinking again, Vicky reproached herself, and there was no stopping the cruel process. She clenched her nails into her palms, trying to think of the woman laughing, the nightmare, anything to avoid her unhappy thoughts. If she only dared run away! . . . Then Amanda came out, white and angry. Indeed her indignation that such things could happen to her had anesthetized her to the pain of the operation. She kept her head high, refusing to look at the doctor whose pasty face was arranged in an expression of kindly professional concern. He motioned the other two women into the inner office, and followed Vicky and Amanda to the door.

"Walk a block or so before you take a cab," he instructed them in an undertone.

"Won't that be bad for her?" Vicky asked.

"It'll be bad for me if you don't" said the doctor, ironically.

On the street Amanda signaled at once for a cab.

"Let him protect his own dirty business," she said. "I paid him. I don't need to keep him out of jail."

Yes, he got her out of her trouble, and that was all he was put here for. Let other women whistle for help. None of Amanda's concern.

"You'll have to take me to your place for a couple of hours," Amanda said, lips set whitely. "I can't face Bemel, and I don't want to faint."

Vicky looked out the window, not knowing what to say. Ken might come in. He had said he would come in. He had told her he was happier with her than with anyone else. He had told her Amanda had been a poison in his life that had run its course. But already she had begun tainting it again.

"I should hate her," Vicky thought, puzzled. "But it's like hating a hurricane or the sea. It can't be helped."

"What will I do about the house?" Amanda murmured. "The best thing is for you to call Bemel and cancel everything I have arranged for tonight. Tell her you're sick and need me. Tell her anything."

When they got to Vicky's address, the taxicab which had followed theirs from the doctor's slowed up for a moment, then swung sharply onward and around the corner uptown.

"What's that guy looking for?" growled their own driver, looking after the other car. "What's the matter with these mugs?"

Vicky took her change and helped Amanda up the outer stone steps. In front of the pet shop window a man stood watching half a dozen infant Siamese kittens roll over each other.

"How funny for you to call your cat Amanda," said Amanda, remembering.

Vicky fumbled in the mailbox for the keys, hoping Ken had not come, for this meeting she could not face. But the keys were still there. She put her arms around Amanda and helped her slowly up the two flights. She could tell by Amanda's set lips that the effort was more than she had bargained for, and at the top step she sat down weakly, leaning her head against the railing. Her hat fell down and her hands clutched her fair hair.

"What if I die?" she whispered chokily. "Oh, God, what if I die! A fine mess! Oh, Vicky, do something! You're the only person . . . Vicky—" She buried her head in her hands and the words were hardly audible. "Get Ken Saunders, will you?"

Vicky drew a long breath.

"Come on inside," she said. "I'll see if I can find him."

She pulled off Amanda's shoes and laid her on the bed. This was the first time Amanda had ever needed anybody. It was the first time she had ever needed Ken in all the years he had needed her so badly. If he was here, that need of him might strike the bond once more, and someone would have to stand by him against the moment sure to come when Amanda would try to hurt him again. It would be she, Vicky, who would have to support him, sensing the pull of his old habit of love and help him not to be hurt again. It would be harder on Ken than on anybody,

Vicky told herself. He'd been in love with Amanda a long, long time, and you couldn't cut it off sharp and clean the way he had tried to do. Vicky knew that. Old love hung on to you like thistles. Whenever you brushed past, the thistles clung once more to your clothes, whether you would have them or not. It might have been that way for her, too, if Tom Turner had suddenly made a fresh claim on her. The person who hurt you most always had first claim.

"Did you call Ken?" Amanda murmured. "You know where he is. I don't. Please."

Vicky wished she could find some comforting thought, something to ease the dreadful pain in her heart. She went to the telephone and called Miss Bemel, first, as Amanda had instructed. Then she dialed Chez Jean, knowing he wasn't there, but to give herself time.

"What shall I tell him, if I find him?" she asked.

"Don't tell him anything," Amanda said quickly. "Just—just say I'm here and want to see him."

Ken wasn't at Chez Jean's or at Martin's, but he was at Dennis Orphen's. Corinne answered the phone.

"Vicky, I didn't tell him what you asked me," Corinne said, excitedly. "Was it you that wanted the address? You know."

"No," said Vicky, unable to think of a satisfactory answer to Corinne's curiosity. Ken was working with Dennis on some valuable new drink formula called Scotch Mist, Corinne explained with suitable reverence. But he wasn't tight, really—at least not yet. Usually Vicky did not mind when he was tight because it was then he was completely hers, the whole hard surface removed. But she was glad he was not in the soft stage yet, because he needed his toughness now. She did, too.

"Ken, can you come right over?" she asked urgently. "Amanda is here."

There was a pause.

"Let me know when she leaves," Ken said.

"But it's better for you to come now," Vicky protested, with an uneasy glance at Amanda. "Please hurry."

She couldn't tell by his silence whether he was disturbed over the imminence of Amanda or merely angry with herself for making any demand on him. Amanda's white, still face impelled her to say more.

"Amanda is sick, Ken," she said. "Do come. She—she wants you."

"I'll come," said Ken. "But, for God's sake, stay with me, will you?"

Vicky went into the kitchen and poured herself a little whiskey. If she could only get through this meeting of Ken and Amanda. With shaking hands she poured one for Amanda, and took it in to her.

"Drink this. You'll feel better."

"Is he coming?" Amanda asked. She sat up, so pale and woebegone that Vicky wondered again, with a constricted heart, what would happen if she should die there. She would have to call Julian, she thought. But then Miss Bemel had mentioned that Mr. Evans would not be back. The whole problem was for one person to handle, and that inadequate person was Vicky Haven, now so shaky that her only thought was how to keep from crying, and how to keep from begging Amanda to stop tormenting her with demands for pity.

"You called Bemel?" Amanda weakly asked. "What did she say?"

"That Mr. Evans wouldn't be home," Vicky answered. "She said Mr. Callingham had telephoned that he was calling at six-thirty, and when he came she would explain."

"Andrew?" Amanda exclaimed, new life in her voice. She sat up now, and finished the whiskey with a wry grimace. "Why didn't you tell me before? Call Bemel and tell her I'll be right there. What time is it now? Six-ten. Call her and say I'll be a few minutes late but be sure and tell him to wait."

She got to her feet.

"But, Amanda, you're too weak—" Vicky protested, amazed at this transformation. "Can't you tell him another time—"

Amanda laughed mirthlessly. She was struggling with her sandals.

"You don't tell a man like Callingham—'another time,'" she said. "Do I look queer? Get a cab for me, will you?"

With mingled relief and alarm Vicky saw the pale, wan creature of a moment before suddenly transformed into the brittle, competent woman she was supposed to be. No, Amanda would not tolerate being accompanied home by Vicky, especially since she had said Vicky was sick. No, she would permit only Vicky's help going down the stairs to the taxi with the added support of another liqueur glass of Scotch. Callingham had put her off for several days now and nothing could stop her from meeting him now, even if she had to use an ambulance to get to him. The challenge of this longed-for encounter gave flushed beauty to her cheeks and a soft sparkle to her eyes. It was incredible, Vicky thought, bewildered. The woman was indestructible. She was ungrateful, too, for she stepped into the taxi without a word for the grueling afternoon she had given her old friend, merely a gay wave of the handkerchief.

"I'll try to find time for lunch someday," she called out blithely, "as soon as I can pull out of some of my war work. I've been doing too much, really. Soon, then, dear!"

The car rolled away and Vicky thought this was the way she wanted Amanda to be—triumphant, indestructible, selfish, perhaps, but anything rather than the frightened, broken creature of a little while before. Then she thought of Ken and her heart sank. As soon as Amanda discovered she could pull Ken back, she was satisfied. Now she was in the position once again to humiliate him by commanding his presence, and then running away for bigger game the way she always had done. Poor Ken. Poor Vicky. Poor everybody in Amanda's path, for that matter. But then, it took as much human energy, blood and tears to produce an Amanda as it did to produce any other successful institution. She wondered how she could tell him to save his feelings. She didn't care what Amanda ever did to her, if she would only stop hurting Ken. She wished there was something she could do to make up to him for all the things Amanda had done to him, but no matter how desperately you tried there seemed no way of keeping Fate from striking out at the person you loved. All you asked was the simple pleasure of saying, "Here, darling, is the moon you were crying for. That makes up for everything else, doesn't it?" But instead of that you had to say, "Darling, more bad news!"

She was sitting at the telephone, wondering if she could catch him at Corinne's in time, for it would be easier to tell him over the telephone without the necessity of seeing the disappointment in his face. Before she could make up her mind what to say, the door burst open and Ken came in. Afterward she remembered this, at times when she wanted to reassure herself of his love: he came straight to her without looking around for Amanda at all!

"Amanda really did send for you," she babbled. "But something happened—somebody called her—she wanted to see you but—"

"I don't give a damn whether she wanted to see me or not," Ken interrupted impatiently. "I came because your voice sounded as if sixteen parachutists had crashed through the roof right on your head. What in God's name was she doing to you? Pulling a gun on you?"

"In a way," Vicky said, with a great sigh of relief. He'd come on her account, not because Amanda needed him. It was too much to believe. It must be that he was tighter than Corinne said he was. She mustn't kid herself that his kindness to her was anything but that, because it couldn't possibly be love. Not after he'd been in love with a woman like Amanda.

"What made her track you down again after she kicked you out?" Ken asked. "Nothing good, I know that."

He lit a cigarette and put it in Vicky's mouth.

"Honey, you're all shaky. Don't tell me if it upsets you."

"I—I can't ever tell you, Ken," Vicky said, and then began to cry. "I'd rather just try to forget it all by myself."

Ken stroked her hair, then bent over and kissed her.

"Not enough for her to mess up my life but she had to start messing up the girl I'm crazy about," he muttered. "I don't give a damn what she does to me, but by God, she's got to leave you alone."

Of course he must be tight to say such sweet things to her, Vicky reminded herself. She mustn't let herself think it was anything else, because it would just be all the worse for her. But she didn't care what made him this way, so long as it made her happy at least for this minute.

"Mind if I have a drink?" he asked.

"Mind?" Vicky said happily. "Drink the whole bottle, darling!"

13

THE TRAIN TRIP FROM Canada turned out
to be a frightful one for Julian. Soldiers and boys on their way to
camps crowded the train, making his usual reservations out of
the question, so he must squeeze his party into two compart-
ments, and then when something went wrong with the air-conditioning in his car, he was obliged to go into the crowded lounge
car, and conduct his conferences in the middle of chattering
mobs. His party was not one to blend well under any circumstances, for there was Harnett, his business secretary, and Amos
Cheever, who disliked Harnett; a gentleman on extremely private business for Julian named Dupper; and a young English
refugee named Nugent about to be officially adopted by Julian.
Photographs had already been taken of Julian leading the child
on the train with a benign smile, but fortunately for all concerned none had been taken later when the little fellow's precoc-
ity had worn Julian down.

"Do you think your wife will like me, sir?" inquired the boy, following Julian through the cars to the lounge.

He was four feet tall, seraphic as to countenance except for some missing front teeth, wistful as became a war refugee newly torn from his mother's arms, and he was the son of a baronet, certainly enough to please any foster mother. Julian drew out a cigar and lit it, not prepared to inform his charge that Mrs. Evans was due for a surprise and could not be relied upon for a hundred percent favorable reaction.

"None of that, sir," young Nugent's voice called out peremptorily. He pointed upward. "You can read, can't you, sir? It says 'Smoking Only in the Lounge.'"

Julian heard Cheever's chuckle from behind the boy and silently put his cigar back into his pocket.

"You've got no hair at all, have you, sir?" Nugent's voice piped up above the rumble of the train, so that passengers in the coaches looked up, smiling as they passed. "What sort of house have you got? How big?"

"Big enough," Julian tried to sound kindly, though he was always at a loss with children and mosquitoes, neither of whom could be lectured successfully for their habits. "However, you'll be packed off to school soon enough."

Young Nugent considered this the length of one coach and then poked his patron firmly in the back with a smile forefinger.

"No, I shan't go to any school," he stated resolutely, and once more to Julian's chagrin passengers leaned in the aisle, smiling to hear the clear little British accents. "I'm not going to be shuttled about anymore, thank you. London, the country, back to London, Liverpool, back to London, back to Liverpool, Canada, and now New York, and New York is where I'm going to stay! I shall go straight to your house and stay. No school, thank you, sir."

Julian decided to waive this matter till arrival, and if possible delegate the entire responsibility for the child to someone else.

Delegate was a word he often used, though in anything but an executive the expression would have been "passing the buck." Amos Cheever was more or less responsible for this step, so Cheever would have to figure out the answer, particularly since without looking around Julian could feel the mischievous smiles of his associate.

Arriving in the lounge, the only car in which air-conditioning was working at the moment, Julian squeezed behind a small table with Harnett and Cheever, leaving Nugent to wander about, and Mr. Dupper, the mysterious stranger, to stand at the bar.

"What should I do, sir?" Nugent politely asked, just as Mr. Harnett had taken out pad and pencil to record Julian's instructions to Cheever for an editorial on the food at Fort Dix.

"Play bear," Julian snapped wearily, and the suggestion succeeded well enough to give the gentlemen a ten minute respite. At the end of this period a porter brought him back to his elders, saying that the other passengers were not prepared to cope with the little one, who had been really playing bear, crouching on all fours under table and pouncing on people.

"You said to play bear, sir," Nugent stiffly answered Julian's admonition. "I don't see very well how a person can play bear without biting people. There's no fun to a game unless you play it properly, you know, sir."

Again, Julian felt Cheever's discreet smile behind his back. He had intended deliberately to confront Amanda with this living example of her written exhortations, calling her bluff, and if she objected to adopting the child, it would give him further excuse for certain plans he was making. But already he saw that the knife could cut both ways, and he had once again laid himself open to the secret infuriating amusement of his staff.

"Perhaps it would be wiser to take Nugent to Far Off Hills," Mr. Harnett thoughtfully suggested, and Julian would have promoted him at once, if he dared, for voicing his own thought. "I think the country might be better for him, and we can drop off at Hudson on our way down."

"Exactly," said Julian approvingly. "I'll leave it all to you, Harnett."

Nugent looked doubtfully from one face to the other.

"How am I going to spend my birthday money?" he asked. "If I'm on a farm it gives me no chance to buy my boat with my birthday money."

He took out his wallet and waved his twenty-five dollars in front of Cheever's beard.

"I'll get your boat and send it up to you," offered Cheever genially. "What sort of boat is it?"

Julian rapped his fingers nervously on the table during this interruption, nerves quivering with the effort to be patient, since his first wife had protected him from all this sort of thing when he was a father.

Young Nugent produced from his wallet a much-handled cutting from a catalogue showing a beautiful toy sailboat of most flawless design for the sum of two hundred and fifty dollars. This was a problem Julian felt able to deal with, so he gave a fatherly talk on the value of money, and the difference between two hundred and fifty dollars and twenty-five dollars, dwelling on the interesting fact that his present of twenty-five dollars was a very tidy sum for a ten-year-old lad, a sum that would keep a working man's family for a whole week."

"But I don't want to keep a working man's family, sir," young Nugent expostulated with some annoyance. "What sort of birthday present would that be for me, sir, I ask you?"

Julian, staring at Cheever in order to keep the man from laughing at him, explained that he was not commanding the little fellow to support anyone's family with his gift money, merely suggesting that he select a present for himself within that figure.

He reminded him that twenty-five dollars was a lot of money and that money did not grow on bushes.

"Twenty-five dollars won't buy my sailboat," Nugent replied coldly. "If I can't buy my sailboat then twenty-five dollars is no good to me. Keep it, sir. It may mean a lot to you, but it can't do anything for me."

With this haughty gesture, Nugent laid his wallet before Julian and stalked down to the end of the car where he stood staring steadily at Mr. Dupper, something that no one else ever cared to do since the man was of a remarkably unsavory appearance.

It was next to impossible for Julian to dictate an editorial on the general idea of the brotherhood of man, the Little Man in uniform and nothing being too good for him, with soldiers jostling him on every side and Little Men and their Little Women spilling highballs over him every time the train swung round a bend. Mr. Cheever was growing more dignified every minute, in a stern effort to keep half a dozen double Scotches from betraying themselves to his chief, but occasionally his command of himself was lost and he burst into extremely loud laughter, pointing at little Nugent standing with legs wide apart before Dupper. His enemy, Harnett, was perfectly aware of the double Scotches, and glanced warningly at him from time to time, but Julian was so absorbed in his own complicated worries that he wouldn't have known what ailed Cheever if he'd gone into delirium tremens.

"Tell the porter we must have that air-conditioning fixed by the next station," Julian shouted above the tumult at Harnett. "We took a train instead of flying so we could get this work done. It's perfectly outrageous. I'm a stockholder on this railroad. At least we might have more room."

"They have to cut down the cars, Mr. Evans," Harnett explained, and this was a mistake as Julian hated anyone *explaining* as if he was a child.

"What's this man Dupper doing for us?" Cheever inquired.

Julian frowned out the window.

"Certain private business," he said.

"Disagreeable looking chap," said Cheever.

"You don't have to look at him," peevishly said Julian. "I'll see him alone as soon as somebody gets this train in condition."

Rising majestically Julian strode out of the car, and Harnett and Cheever exchanged a look.

"He's probably going to call up the President," said Cheever, in a low voice. "He always thinks that accidents like this, or sunburn or seasickness can be fixed by getting through to the President. He gets worse very year."

"Mrs. Evans Number One gets the kid, all right," Harnett said. "I knew he didn't know what he was letting himself in for. In a way I'd like to see Number Two's face when she clapped eyes on what the mister was bringing home."

Cheever, with a cautious eye toward the door through which Julian had vanished, signaled the waiter quickly for further refreshment.

"Better make it cuba libra," advised Harnett. "I'll have one too. Looks like Coca-Cola so he can't tell."

"Who is that mug, Dupper?" pondered Cheever. "Is he pimping for the boss? Looks like the type."

Harnett shrugged.

"I can give a guess, but not out loud," he said.

It was true that Mr. Dupper, who had so strangely joined the party at a station en route, had the appearance of a man engaged in the worst of underworld activities. He was a short, thick man with boiled gray eyes and an empty moon face, moist-lipped, wide-nosed, and horribly disfigured by a skin disease of a venereal nature if one could judge by the shameless lasciviousness of eyes and mouth. Born both lecherous and ugly, his only relief from his obsession must have been the most depraved of prostitutes, since there could never have been any choice for him.

As soon as he sat down to a table people got up and left. "Is this seat taken?" he would ask, and people would nod dumbly, looking at the nightmare face, so he had to stand at the bar, drinking highballs very fast, his derby hat pushed back on his round head, his ape shoulders hunched over, his wet shapeless mouth grinning defiantly. Two gray-haired men had nowhere to go but stand beside him, so he began talking to them, forcing them to look at him, while he talked fast, told amazing things, jokes, obscenities, riddles, secrets, anything to distract the mind from his face. The train swept down the Hudson, and he talked on feverishly, buying them drinks they dared not refuse, drinking fast so as not to see the mirror of his own horror in their eyes. The men left, other men appeared, and he went on talking, joking, showing he had something in the way of humor and strange experience that unharmed men had not. His tongue must have become swollen, his throat dry and sore from his frantic defense of his ugliness, from his always smiling mask of good nature. Then the air-conditioning in the Pullmans was restored and the lounge emptied, people no longer had to stand near him, no one needed to listen, no one even needed to look if they could drag their fearing eyes away. In the late twilight they came upon him after a while in the dark of the platform, all alone, his boiled eyes shining with stark evil, his lips drawn in sinister revealed hate, silent, a living sore, enemy of all good and all beauty, a man to fear in dark alleys, murderous, unpitying. The man with the diseased face stood in the shadows, spreading fear, sorrow, panic, and even with no crime in his soul, is accused.

Julian Evans, returning to the lounge satisfied with the train mechanism finally obeying his will and operating again, passed Dupper without seeing him, until Dupper touched him on the shoulder.

"When do you want me?" asked Dupper.

Julian hesitated, and then jerked his head back toward his compartment. He had not been prepared for Dupper's looks, and it seemed to him that anyone looking at the man could read his mission. Never mind, it had to be.

"The kid's playing rummy with some gob in there," Dupper reassured him, as if that was the only cause for Julian's hesitation.

In the compartment Dupper took out a paper from his pocket.

"On the twentieth she had Callingham at the house to dinner while you were in Washington," said Dupper. "They left the house together at ten-thirty and drove to N.B.C. studios where he broadcast shortwave to London, and later they went into the Rainbow Room and sat in a corner talking for about an hour. She came back in a cab alone about one o'clock."

Julian felt his throat swelling as if his heart was about to pop out, and his head rang with Dupper's hoarse rasping voice, as if each word was scratched on sandpaper. He remembered his blood pressure as his temples began pounding, and he got up to get a glass of water. At the same time he turned off the light as if the evil in Dupper's words would be softened by shutting out the evil of his face. But the blue dusk coming through the window enhanced both words and face so that Julian switched the light on once again, and sat down, grasping his glass of water.

"She fired Emerson as you know on the twenty-first," pursued Dupper. "She was in the lobby of the Waldorf at four-thirty that afternoon. The Waldorf is Callingham's hotel. Asta Lundgren, the dancer that Callingham's been tied up with for the last few years, took a train for the West, presumably Milwaukee, late that night. She seemed to be crying. We lost track of both Callingham and Mrs. Evans after that, and don't know whether they were together or not. We haven't seen them together but we have reports on her movements."

"What?" Julian asked with dry lips, his palms sweating.

"She took a cab to Greenwich Village, stopped at the apartment of Victoria Haven, the same person who covered up her last apartment, then drove to a quack doctor in Chelsea. When they came out she went to the Thirteenth Street apartment and stayed one hour. Miss Bemel was told this was due to a serious sickness of Miss Haven's. Miss Haven was at work next day at *Peabody's*, with no signs of being sick. Mrs. Evans spent the next two days in bed, you remember. Mr. Callingham had an appointment for tea there. He sent flowers.

Julian struggled to open the window, gasping for breath. Dupper obligingly turned on the electric fan, and started to help him unfasten his collar, but his touch was too much for Julian who pushed him aside.

"You think it's certainly Callingham, then?" he whispered.

Dupper stared at him.

'That's the only guy you told us to watch," he said, defensively. "We could just as well have got the goods on somebody else, I reckon."

"What do you mean?"

Dupper laughed raucously.

"Probably a dozen more, too. That's the way we usually find it. Probably something about this man Emerson, too. That's why she fired him, maybe. A woman like that's got plenty of chances, you know, and she don't pass up anything. Too easy for her."

"How dare you say that?" Julian choked.

Dupper's eyes widened in astonishment.

"What's the matter? If she wasn't that way you wouldn't have set up trailing her, would you? Don't get touchy, there, governor. You started this deal, you know. You knew what time it was. You weren't being kidded, now, were you? Don't give me this innocent stuff. Not after what you gave us to start with."

"Get out of here," whispered Julian. "Get out. Don't say another word. You're saying—God knows what you're saying."

A gleam of fury shone in Dupper's eye, but after a moment's silence he got up, and put his papers back in his vest.

"After all, you asked for it, darling," he said, grinning. "You pay the bill. Nobody else cares who your wife's sleeping with."

He went out, whistling, letting the door close softly behind him. Julian sipped his water slowly, as if it would cool the boiling in his head. A Western Union blank suggested an outlet to him and he drew it toward him and wrote a wire to his staff lawyer, instructing him to buy off the paper's contract with Andrew Callingham, and to inform the syndicate heads that the name of Callingham was never under any circumstances to be mentioned, in book columns, theatre, society, or foreign news no matter what he might do. The yellow slip in his hand made him feel better, even though it could not be sent till the next stop. He would go into the lounge when he felt calmer and see Cheever next. Dupper would have to keep out of the way the rest of the journey. Little Nugent could be dropped off at Margaret's, and no one need know he had been intended as a test for Amanda. Poor Margaret. Dear Margaret. What in God's name had bewitched him into almost ruining his life for Amanda, when Margaret was his talisman, his refuge? Sex was a horrible thing for a man meant to lead people, Julian thought, especially if you couldn't get it anyway. His whole body tingled with the insult of being rejected by the woman he could swear he had created. At least he could break her, too. That was something she hadn't counted upon. Amandas were a dime a dozen this year. She'd find that out soon enough when she tried to get things on her own.

Julian sat in the dark, watching the lights of villages as the train flew along into a light summer rain. Inky puddles caught the headlights and glittered darkly in rhythmic swirls like the dark thoughts circling in Julian's pounding head. There was a sudden stop at some wayside, to signal. In the rain men on the little platform swung their lamps, their raincoats dripping, their hats pulled down. Looking out Julian could see no village behind the lonely station at all, but a great building that stretched interminably across the sky, lit up brilliantly for the night.

"State Insane Asylum," someone in the corridor murmured.

As the train screamed by figures appeared in every barred doorway, shadows were at every iron window, every aperture of the asylum was lined with the desolate prisoners. There they stood or crouched, hour after hour at doors or windows, like wild pets, knowing that this is the door and that the train whistle means escape, and someday the door will open to let them out as to let them in. In their torch-lit mad minds the train blazing and screaming past them in the night was no more real than the other images that shrieked through their minds, and when at bedtime the light would be dimmed for sleep, what did it matter, what peace was there in that silence for sleep? Darkness, four-footed, monstrous, blinked tiger-eyed in their minds, never sleeping, and at daylight the souls would wake to yesterday's torment, no pity or peace, no truce for them; the pursuit would continue, the demons yowling after their exhausted prey, tearing the shreds of poor brains to shake out one more wild cry of pain. This was the picture the passenger could see in the second's pause at the institution, this was the picture on his eyeballs, on the windowpanes, tattooed on the backs of people sitting ahead, so that the Catskills sleeping the soft June rain, the winding brooks, the arching trees, dozing village churches, silvery river, the whole quiet countryside for miles and miles around all cried of Murder.

Amos Cheever stood in the doorway of the compartment.

"State Insane Asylum," he said. "Signal stop. Awful thing, insanity. Mind if I turn on this light?"

"People let themselves go," said Julian testily. "People have no control, that's all. Unless, of course, it's genuinely pathological. As a rule, though, people give into it too easily. Remind me to get an article on that, will you, for the Sunday magazine."

"Sometimes circumstances are too much for one human being to handle," Cheever argued. "Things do pile up, you know, sometimes."

"A man can handle them if he's a real man," Julian said, already feeling the sweet relief of power at the thought of what he would do to both Callingham and Amanda. "No excuse for anyone losing their grip."

Afterward Cheever remembered this, because when they dropped off at Hudson to deliver little Nugent to Margaret Evans, the poor woman had just been taken to a sanitarium in a strait jacket, screaming hallelujahs and oaths you would have sworn she had never even heard. Julian would have driven off to see her, shocked as he was by this failure of Margaret's to support him in his own misfortunes, but the doctor warned him he must not go. Mrs. Evans, it seems was obsessed with the desire to kill Julian.

Harnett left little Nugent at the farm, nevertheless, for there were nurses and servants in charge of all the other refugees Margaret had befriended. Julian and Cheever drove into New York that night in the rain, and neither spoke. Dupper had vanished with the train, his well-documented misinformation in his breast pocket.

2

MR. CASTOR met Miss Bemel on the third floor landing. Each bore an open copy of *Peabody's* for August. Miss Bemel was frowning and her free hand appeared to be searching her skull for some worthy trophy. Mr. Castor, on the contrary, was in the throes of a semismile, if the faint twitching of his saffron face could be described as that.

"Now *this*," said Mr. Castor, pausing to tap the periodical significantly, "is the real thing. This is what she should have been doing right along. It fits in with Mr. Evans' *Little American* policy."

"I think it's a great mistake on her part. A very great mistake," said Miss Bemel, with controlled passion. "I can assure you if I had seen the article before it went to the magazine it would never have gone. Never! But she seems to feel she can do things like this over my head. Very well. She will see."

"Mr. Evans will like this very much," Mr. Castor said doggedly. "The snob appeal is no longer the approach. *She* didn't seem to realize that at first. But this—this is the stuff."

Miss Bemel, in the very act of stamping her foot, remembered where she was and brought the member down without a sound. This frustrated foot-stamping had the expected unfavorable reaction in that her rage found outlet in an indiscreet raising of the voice.

"What's good about telling the world she came of humble people? What's good about saying that her father ran a haberdashery that he didn't even own, and that sometimes as a child she never had enough to eat and lived over a stored in some wretched little village? Nobody needs to tell things like that in order to get their public sympathy! Especially when all her interviews before have told about her royal blood, and being lonely in the big house on the hill, and all that!"

Mr. Castor, by way of subtle rebuke, lowered his own voice to a pitch of exquisite softness.

"Permit me to disagree with you *in toto,* Miss Bemel! The public is revolution-minded these days. They are massing against the favored few, the rich, the titled, the aristocrats. Nothing could have been more politic than building up herself as a woman of the people, at this stage of the game." He placed a forefinger on his lower lip as if this time to produce an organ note, though it actually turned out to be merely a qualification. "Unless of course she *is* a woman of the people. She isn't is she?"

"How do I know?" bellowed Miss Bemel. "I thought at least I was working for a *lady*. I can tell you my family wouldn't have let me do the dirty work for some cloak-and-suit man's daughter. The Bemels are *somebody*! And now this—this"—she spanked the magazine sharply—"about having no pocket money at school, and wearing somebody else's clothes and being snubbed by the country clubs! What will my Discussion Group think of me, slaving away for that sort of person? I'll bet Mr. Evans won't like it! I'll bet he doesn't want people thinking he picked his wife out of some Woolworth counter!"

Mr. Castor permitted the echoes of Miss Bemel's blast to finish their last bounce before he assuaged the air with his gentle croon.

"Possibly she might have indicated that although her people were poor, they were land-poor only," he admitted graciously. "Or she might have hinted that her mother's family, say, was connected with the Biddles or Cabots or Whitneys. Something of that sort."

"Of course she should have!" boomed Miss Bemel, folding her arms across her chest and letting the offending magazine shiver down the stairs. "That's what other people do. No matter how poor they were in childhood, or what sort of tearoom or boardinghouse their folks ran, they manage to find a grandmother who was a countess or an ancestor who ran for President! They don't have to go *all out* for being low class, like *she* does here!"

Noise was beginning to win out over discretion, and Mr. Castor strummed his lower lip again judiciously, regarding once again the full-length picture of Amanda which illustrated her article "I CAME FROM ACROSS THE TRACKS." The picture showed Amanda, bare-shouldered and bare-backed in fluid silver brocade, dripping emeralds and orchids, facing the mirror of her living room with a proud proletarian smile.

"In a way the picture does something for her," Mr. Castor said. He weighed silently the chances of Miss Bemel being right in regard to Julian's reaction.

"No," he finally shook his head. "Mr. Evans is primarily a publishing genius. Even if he personally did not like the idea of his wife presenting herself as a vulgarian, he would recognize the timeliness of it. He might possibly be annoyed that he knew nothing of the piece till it came out."

"Nobody did!" Having won her point on noise, Miss Bemel now obliged Castor's ears with a windy whisper fraught, as whispers so frequently are, with memories of garlic. "She does these things at night! Ever since she fired Emerson she's been doing things like this. Right here it says this is the first of several autobiographical sketches from her. How does that make *me* look? Her private secretary!"

Mr. Castor picked up her magazine and restored it to her.

"There are a number of things going on around here of which you are unaware," he said smiling. "Your work with Mrs. Evans is after all the least of the activities in this domicile."

Miss Bemel glared at him, her bosom heaving at this unfair taunt.

"That," she said majestically, "is a matter of opinion."

She pursued her path upstairs, head high while Mr. Castor crept softly and triumphantly on downstairs, knowing that he had started an unendurable curiosity in Miss Bemel's avid brain. This was his little revenge for permitting her to persuade him about Julian's reaction to Amanda's article. He was glad that she was not on hand to see how right she proved to be when he laid the magazine before his master a few minutes later, for Julian turned livid as he looked at it.

"How dare she do this to me!" he sputtered, pounding the desk. "How dare she—get out of here, Castor! Get out! What do you mean bringing me this sort of thing! Who told her to do this? What sort of funny business is this? No wonder everyone laughs at me! I pick a wife from the much, do I? The wife of Julian Evans is from immigrant stock—illiterates—trash! God, why do people do these things to me? Get Peabody on the phone! Wait a minute. . . . This reads like Andrew Callingham! That traitor! He did this. Where's Mrs. Evans?"

Mr. Castor moistened his lips and looked around to see if he was safely near an exit in case the master attacked him.

"She's having tea with Mr. Callingham," he whispered bravely.

"Where?" thundered Julian.

Mr. Castor backed toward the door.

"At his hotel, I believe," he faintly intoned. "He's leaving for Libya tomorrow, you know. You remember we signed him for some articles."

Julian gripped the arms of his chair.

"That contract is canceled," he said hoarsely. "Callingham is not to be mentioned or printed in any of my publications. Neither is Amanda Keeler Evans from now on."

Mr. Castor gulped.

"Those are your orders!" Julian shouted, trembling. "Get to work on them! You heard me! No more Callingham! No more Amanda Keeler in any Julian Evans publication!"

"Yes, sir," Mr. Castor gasped and fled into his office where he sat mopping his forehead feebly for a few minutes till he composed himself sufficiently to telephone Harnett.

Julian sat still for a while, his whole body trembling. He could feel his blood thudding away in his arteries, his heart knocking away in his chest, and he thought this is all very bad for me, very bad for my health, must call a doctor, get self in shape to cope with situation, must keep upper hand, getting mad no good . . . He remembered his Yogi exercises suddenly, and the importance of changing the circulation in moments of anger or mental disturbance. When Castor peeked through the crack in the door two minutes later he shuddered to see the great man standing on his head. Then he remembered it was only Yogi and shrank back with a moan of relief.

3

AMANDA DID not like to think of Vicky Haven anymore. Vicky was like everything connected with Lakeville, a carrier of calamity. That day with her was a precipice in her life, down which she had almost fallen, and she shuddered to think of it, and was slowly correcting it in her memory. It could not possibly have been true that she had felt a weak overwhelming need for Ken; it could not have been true that for a fleeting second she had wanted to promise him anything, even a divorce from Julian, to win him back. She must have had a fever, she explained to herself, she would under no other conditions have slipped into such a disgusting role of ordinary helpless female. Thank God, the mere mention of Callingham had saved the day, reminding her that she was on her way up, not down.

The conquest of Callingham was no easy matter, either, and Amanda tackled the job with all the more zest. There was his love of the last five years, the Swedish dancer. There had been a little talk about her recently, and Amanda had even speculated on the chances of getting Julian to put the FBI onto her. It irked her that she needed Julian more than ever to get Callingham. She realized that her greatest danger was that her passionate loathing for Julian might lead her to break with him before she was through using him. She needed every resource of her own and Julian's to get Callingham. She was skipping her special war activities to take part in those which he favored, so that they could be together on radio programs, benefit dinners, and all possible occasions where they might leave together quite naturally. She knew he admired her, and the fact that she had no idea how much further she had gotten with him made her even more intrigued with the game. His extreme egotism and complete indifference to her own literary ambitions only piqued her, since he was the only writer she herself owned was her superior. He must eventually admit her talent, she promised herself, even if she had to model her style exactly on his, in order for him to approve it. They would do brave things together, sweeping through India and Africa, on just such intrepid adventures as had characterized his life before, nonetheless daring for their wire net precautions of money, prestige, and unlimited political protection.

So Amanda pursued Andrew Callingham as she had pursued Julian four years before, being aggressively feminine over the telephone with him since that was what he liked, and keeping her glamour side away and playing the direct, four-square type, since he seemed to prefer that. He saw a great deal of Free French officials, so she saw them, too. He liked to go bowling so she took up bowling, too. He liked to work or play all night, using the mornings for sleep, so Amanda upset her own schedule to take over his, which gave her excuse to telephone him all hours of the night or to meet him for daybreak breakfast at Childs', a hobby of his. He was a cagey man, accustomed to holding his own against women, and indicated only a jovial amusement in Amanda's siege, ignoring all her playful bids for intimacy. A worthy lover, Amanda thought! Not a misfit like Ken Saunders, not just a glorified merchant like Julian, but a genius and what was most important, a successful genius with all the charm of a normal male.

The fateful day on which her story in *Peabody's* had affected Julian so vitally, she had wangled tea with Callingham, and since his friend the dancer had gone west on a tour, and he himself was going to Libya the next day he was in a mood for celebration with whoever it might be. Dozens of reporters, photographers, soldiers, sailors, and ladies in uniform drifted in and out of his suite, drinking his champagne or Scotch, so that the affair was not the intimate matter that Amanda had wished. She stayed on, however, shrugging away her dinner engagement at home with a Western governor and the Chinese Consul. Let Julian handle the political side of things. She was concentrating on her artistic ambitions. Callingham broke all his own engagements recklessly, and despised anyone ridden by a clock and appointment book. So that was Amanda's way now, too.

"What would you say if I turned up in Libya one of these days?" she asked him with seeming lightness, though the plan was already forming in her mind.

He would not be trapped into any indication of feeling.

"I'd probably say how-do-you-do," he countered, easily. "I'd try not to ask you if you were following me."

"That's what I'd be doing," said Amanda, firmly.

"Great mistake, I assure you," he laughed. "I'm a hard man to find when I start going. Like as not I'll nip off from Libya for Siam, or India."

"Leave word where you're going and I'll get there," Amanda said.

Callingham only smiled.

"I will, too," Amanda told herself. "He knows I will."

She would see someone tomorrow about an assignment in Libya. Julian would have to pave the way for her to go there. It would be the last thing he would ever be allowed to do for her, if everything worked out. Amanda dawdled over the champagne, trying to disguise her annoyance with the callers who came and went, preventing any privacy. She remembered that she had had to spend the night with Julian in order to clinch her conquest of him, and she should have managed the same thing with Callingham. He ought not to leave without her having established some claim on him. She disliked drinking, but she had no other excuse to stay on, so she drank more than she ever had done, trying to outstay everyone else. But at twelve he decided to go to Twenty-One with the last half dozen soldiers, and Amanda was obliged to admit defeat. She offered her lips in a farewell kiss, but he brushed his lips lightly over her cheek instead.

All the way coming home she made plans, calculating exactly what steps must be taken to make her pursuit plausible, just what angle to give Julian in order to insure his backing up to the moment when she dare dismiss it. One thing was certain—that no matter how elusive a man might be here in New York, he was easy prey on foreign soil for the girl from home. Say, she managed to get over there in the next month or so, she was positive they would be lovers soon after. He proposed staying abroad at least a year, this time, or even till the end of the war, if end there ever would be. Very well, she would stay, too. Let Julian be the one to ask for the divorce. Settle herself in Callingham's bed, first, then let matters take their proper course. The future looked so satisfactory to Amanda that it almost made up for her dissatisfaction at the way the evening had been taken away from her. She came into the house in a glow of secret excitement, even humming to herself, as if the victory had already been won.

She went into her own suite at once and here was her first shock, for Julian sat in her bedroom looking like a thundercloud. He never before had taken such a liberty and surprise overcame her, surprise and a sense of guilt at the thoughts she felt must be printed clearly on her brow.

"Why, Julian! What is the matter?" she gasped.

He stood up and pointed his finger at her, his face distorted with such fury that for the first time she was terrified of him.

"Get out of this house, you tramp!" he choked. "I know all about you. I've had you watched these many months. I know the kind of slime you are, now! I've got the whole story—the whole record! Don't dare to deny it—I've got witnesses. You can't sleep with me—no, oh no. But everybody else! Callingham, that's the man. I'll break you both! I'll show you how puny you are. Both of you! I built him up. I made you. I can tear you both apart like a toy, do you hear, like some toy!"

Amanda thought, "Oh, my God, he means murder! . . . He's gone crazy! . . . This is the end of me!"

She backed toward the door but Julian followed her, shaking a trembling finger at her, his eyes wild and bloodshot, his voice strange and shaking with hatred.

"You took that apartment with your sidekick Victoria Haven, so you could have men there. You roped me in. You made me believe your lies, your trickery. All right, but you're going to pay. You'll find out there are men that can beat you at your own tricky game! You forced me to marry you, ruin my good home, give you the greatest chance a girl ever had! Then you cheat and lie to pay me back. 'I Came from the Wrong Side of the Tracks'! You bet you did, and by God, you're going back there. That's where you belong, you—you tramp, you slut, you—" Suddenly Julian shook his fists at the futility of expressing his rage and his voice rose to a shrill cry. "Damn you! I'll kill you! Making fun of me—trying to wreck my life, using me to pimp for you, even, to bring you bigger and better men to cheat! Driving my poor wife mad! Get out—"

"Julian—please—" Amanda tried to get away from his reach but he seized her arms and forced her back to the bed, his hands closing on her throat so that her necklace broke and the pearls rolled over the floor. Amanda started to scream but his hand closed over her mouth, and this at least gave her respite from strangling. His fury had made him weak so that she managed to struggle out of his reach and run toward the door, trampling her hat under foot and trying to clasp together her dress where he had torn it. He came after her, panting, veins standing out on his head so that even in her fright she thought he must be going to drop dead of heart failure any minute.

"Get out of this house, do you hear me?" he screamed, and there was a sound of servants stirring somewhere outside, a sound Amanda did not know whether to welcome or fear. She stumbled over a chair and he caught at her dress, again, but she freed herself with a mighty wrench and made the door just as Mrs. Pons and her husband, both in nightclothes and white with fear, got to the hall. Amanda ran past them, Julian close behind her, and she heard a lamp crash past her as she flew downstairs, and the frightened cries of the servants. She got to the floor below, falling down on the landing, a slipper dropping off, which she dared not stop to retrieve. A vase crashed on the step behind her, just missing her, and she found herself crying out a prayer for help, though there seemed no hope, the servants paralyzed into futility.

"Curse you—curse you—" Julian was sobbing somewhere behind her. "Get out of here—get out of this house—damn you, damn you—oh, damn you!"

She reached the front door and by some miracle the lock worked at once and she was able to get outside into the midnight street before he could get to her. She ran, gasping and limping on her one shoe, holding her torn dress together, down the street. Someone must have managed to hold Julian in time, for the door did not open and she began murmuring, "Oh, thank God, thank God!" her forehead dripping with perspiration, her throat throbbing with the pain of his choking. There was a taxi on the corner and she sank into it, sobbing.

"Where to?" the driver asked. "Where to, Mrs. Evans?"

She was glad he knew her. At least, with her torn gown and one shoe off he did not mistake her for someone to be taken to the police station. Mrs. Julian Evans was still a name to protect the most suspicious circumstances. She sat still for a moment rocking back and forth with little gasping sobs, unable to think. It was something that Julian's detectives had never spotted the Ken Saunders affair. They had gotten the crime right but the man wrong. Then she remembered something, and gave the driver the address. At Twenty-One she sent him in to get Callingham, and presently he came out.

"What in heaven's name—" exclaimed Callingham.

"Take me to your hotel please," she said.

He flung away his cigarette, and looked at her, frowning.

"I'll have to borrow some shoes for you first," he said. "What size?

"Six," said Amanda.

He went back into the restaurant and came out, smiling, with a pair of blue pumps.

"Hope you don't mind blue with your gray dress. I'm not a good shopper. I took the first thing I could get. The driver can take them back."

He didn't say anything when she gasped out her story. If she had been more sensitized to other's reactions or less upset, she might have felt his bracing himself against her. But all she could think at the time was that she was out of Julian's murderous reach, and by some miracle was safe with Callingham.

"Take me with you, Andrew," she implored him. "You must take me with you."

"It's not as easy as all that," he said, almost irritably.

They reached his hotel and she managed to compose herself enough to enter. Now she began to wonder what he would do with her. No man could walk out on a lady in her own present plight. He took her arm, out of the elevator and led her to his suite. His valet was clearing up the ravages of the recent party.

"One thing, you can't stay here," he said scowling. "Bad enough with Julian thinking all that rot, without giving him reason to believe it. He might even have his detectives here this minute."

"I don't care," said Amanda. "Nothing would convince him any differently anyway."

He looked away from her, still frowning.

"I can tell you it isn't going to help you or me," he said. "Julian says he's going to break us and he could almost do it. I doubt if he can ruin us but he can make a hell of a lot of trouble. Frankly, I don't like it at all."

"We'd be in it together," said Amanda. "We're already in it. It's too late to do anything about it."

He laughed, unwillingly.

"I'm in love with somebody else, you know, and I'm going to marry her someday."

"No, you're not," said Amanda. "You're going to marry me."

"How?" he fended. "You're still married, and I'm going to Africa tomorrow and may never set eyes on you again."

"I'm coming over on the next boat," said Amanda. "I'll fix everything, never fear."

Callingham looked at her reflectively.

"Has it occurred to you that you may find it harder 'fixing' everything once you break with Julian? I don't think you know yet what you're up against, my dear girl. Personally, I've gotten along damn well before without Julian Evans's backing, and I can do it again. But you've used the man up to the hilt. What makes you think you can do without him now?"

He was being difficult. It was going to be harder than she thought.

"You'll help me," Amanda said.

"Don't count on it!" He grinned at her. "I'm not risking my hide and reputation for anybody, even a lovely anybody like you. Another thing, I'd better get you out of here as quietly as possible before hell breaks loose again."

"I don't care if it does," said Amanda boldly. "I'm staying with you tonight."

He burst out laughing.

"Fine. I never pass up a pretty gift like that. It won't change my mind on anything, though."

"It might," Amanda said, tossing her head.

"The talk is that you're no good in the hay, my dear," Callingham chuckled. "But I like to be open to conviction."

It might still work, Amanda thought, just as it had with Julian. With this farewell memory she could count on winning him over completely when she reached him in Africa. This was the way she had planned it and this was the way it would have to be. Unless, for the first time, something went wrong for her. Unless he was a stronger man than she. Unless he, in his own egotistical way, had other plans. Unless Julian really could put a hex on her.

Even under Callingham's rough embrace there came, along with her usual annoyance at the damage to her permanent, Amanda's first doubts.

14

ROCKMAN ELROY HAD Vicky Haven on his mind to the point of inconvenience. He would be strolling through the park, swinging his cane, dodging kiddycars and admiring the amiable antics of the sea lions, when he would think of a nice fact about sea lions which he would like to impart to some willing ear, and Vicky's was the only willing ear he had ever found. He would turn into the Metropolitan Museum for distraction and there would be a Tibetan temple piece and some Egyptian funerary jewelry suggesting a dozen informative tidbits certain to enchant his niece's friend. In the back room of the Plaza as soon afterward as modern conveniences could whisk him there he would contemplate the cathedral architecture of the sacred room, doubtless its appeal for the group of young curates drinking beer in the corner, and he would think that perhaps he would change his drinking habits to gayer surroundings, places more suited to a young woman. He had never been the problem drinker that his brother Beaver had been, inasmuch as he had never been provoked to such excesses by a good wife. Still, he would begin either tomorrow or day after tomorrow to moderate his requirements so as not to alarm a gentle little thing like Victoria. He supported these vows with an extra highball, but this only made him long for company, someone who liked good conversation which he felt bubbling up in him like a whistling teakettle about to blow.

"Victoria is the only good talker I've ever met in a woman," he told himself flatteringly enough, the picture of her charming young face coming before him, eyes fascinated, lips parted not in speech but in breathless interest. Yes, he admitted it, he would like nothing better than to offer his hand in marriage to the girl! It was not that he was at the age where youth excited him, for even in the often treacherous fifties it alarmed rather than intrigued him. The musical shows then popular with their rousing teenage casts brought out the Scrooge rather than the lecher in him, and he would have preferred to send the kiddies packing off to bed while he listened to Fritzi Scheff, or better still, nobody. No, he reflected, little Miss Haven was the very woman he should have had twenty-five years ago, and the difference in their ages was Time's mistake not his own.

Being a trained philosopher, he was accustomed to make his choices in life first and justify them afterward. Why had the thought of marriage never before struck him with anything but revulsion? Why did it suddenly occur to him as if the institution was his own invention, so pleased was he with the impulse? Even philosophers are naïvely astonished to find themselves subject to the ordinary rules for human behavior, and Rockman, having had a most enjoyable, self-indulgent bachelor life, was genuinely amazed at the strange, unexpected loneliness of the bachelor fifties, the middle age for which marriage was made. His indulgences now seemed his privations. Engagements for lunch or dinner with their pleasant absence of permanent responsibility, their casual "good-bye" restoring his privacy once again to him, now seemed insulting compromises to his need for constant companionship; they were fraught with the fear that in another moment, after one more nightcap, one more for the road, he would be alone again, his prized barriers safely up once more; but now they offered prison instead of freedom, and through their bars the chilly fingers of Age, gaunt and lonely, clutched at him.

Once his mind was made up Rockman was only impatient with his delay in informing Vicky. He chuckled at the picture of what consternation his move would bring to his brother's family! What a stew Nancy and her mother would be in when they found him married to their discarded friend! Hastening to the address Miss Finkelstein had given him, he entertained himself with another pleasing picture—a honeymoon of travel which enabled him to lecture on the scenery to his enthralled bride. A florist's shop reminded him of a bridegroom's duties, and he stopped to purchase a great box of roses. With this under one arm, his cane under the other, he arrived at the Thirteenth Street apartment. Delaying his happiness a little longer, he paused to admire the puppies in the pet shop before ascending the steps to the entrance hall. Here he encountered a brisk young woman in a most imposing uniform.

"You're Mr. Elroy, I believe," she said. "I met you at Victoria Haven's other place. I'm Ethel Carey from her hometown."

"Of course," said Rockman, who remembered neither faces nor names. "Are you—er—calling on her now?"

Ethel looked at him in surprise.

"Oh, no, I'm just here making arrangements about storage and subleting and all that for her, while I'm in town. The wedding was so unexpected, you see, it didn't leave her time to do anything, so she left it all to me."

"The—ah—you said the wedding?" Rockman asked dumbly.

"If you can call such a helter-skelter business a wedding!" Ethel exclaimed, with a shrug. She opened the mailbox, extracted some letters, dropped them in her purse. "Naturally, with Ken going into the Army, Vicky was too rattled to do anything ceremonial, so—"

Rockman shifted his roses to his other arm.

"She—she married Saunders, then?" He tried not to show the desolation in his heart.

Ethel nodded.

"Thank heavens, she's got something she wanted at last," she sighed! "Goodness knows how it will work out, what with him at camp, somewhere in the South, but she says she's going to follow him wherever he goes. Poor lamb is so crazy about him! I'm not sure, myself. Do you think he's good enough for her?"

Rockman set the box of flowers down, and mopped his forehead.

"Saunders? Ideal man for her, I would say," he said bravely. "Perfectly splendid chap. Couldn't have done any better. Certain to be happy. Best thing in the world for her. Wish 'em every happiness. Perfectly mated, I would say. Fine thing. Wonderful thing."

Ethel blinked as his enthusiasm mounted.

"I wish I was as optimistic as you about it, Mr. Elroy," she said, shaking her head. "But of course marriages aren't awfully important nowadays anyway. War makes love and all that sort of thing seem sort of silly, doesn't it?"

"It does, indeed," agreed Rockman. "I take it you're leaving here now? So am I. Er—would you care to have a drink with me, say at the Brevoort Terrace? I'm rather at loose ends."

"So am I," said Ethel. "Everything seems so haywire, lately. Vicky getting married out of a blue sky, Amanda Keeler Evans shooting off to Africa so mysteriously, and Julian making a fool of himself with all those statements about her. There must be something funny about it somewhere or he wouldn't go to such trouble to say there wasn't. Besides, everybody knows he's started the divorce proceedings. You knew Amanda Keeler, of course?"

Rockman followed her down the steps to the street, and in her preoccupation she did not notice that the florist's box had been left in the vestibule of the apartment.

"Keeler—Keeler—Amanda Keeler," he repeated, frowning. "Don't think I ever heard of her. Unless she was kin to Doctor Vestry Keeler, of Leland Stanford. A very sound man, Vestry Keeler—a good scholar. I remember when I worked with him at the University of Chicago—"

2

"There isn't a thing in the papers about it," marveled Vicky, sitting up in bed with her sandy topknot barely visible above the mound of Sunday papers. "How strange!"

Ken was pecking at a typewriter by the window, his fine new honeymoon dressing gown belted with a rag of a necktie. He looked up in amazement.

"You're not looking for Cholly Knickerbocker's account of our wedding, are you, my love?" He came over and gave her a benign, pitying kiss on the forehead. "Haven't I explained to you, pet, that people like us don't make news? What were you expecting—front page headlines—'saunders takes hillbilly bride to shady hotel'? No, dear, people like us have to push each other out the window before we're news. Even then we're only good for two sticks."

"I'm looking for Amanda, silly," Vicky answered, pulling him down beside her. "You never see a thing about her anymore. Ethel Carey claims she followed Callingham to Africa, but here it says his fiancée, Asta Lundgren, has flown to Egypt to marry him."

"Never mind, Amanda will get along," Ken shrugged. "She may not get who or what she wants but she'll get something."

"But, darling, no dispatches from her in any paper, no more articles, no mention of her after that first flurry of Julian's!" Vicky argued. "Things must have gone wrong with her! Maybe she did have to have Julian, after all! Maybe he's got people to gang up against her."

Ken meditated on this, lighting two cigarettes, and putting one in Vicky's mouth.

"Well, one thing, if Julian's stacking the cards against her, Andrew Callingham isn't going to be anywhere around her, I can promise you that," he said. "Callingham made his name saving his own nose and blowing his own horn, not looking after beautiful ladies on skids."

They were both silent, Vicky thinking that she would have to do a lot of talking in their married life to cover up these silences when Ken might be remembering another love. She would begin right now.

"If we don't get pulled into the war, won't you be sorry you enlisted, Ken? Won't you be sorry you didn't stay on at *Peabody's* or else freelance a while? I should think you'd get awfully embarrassed running around in your soldier suitie with no war."

"We'll be in all right," Ken said. "And if I wasn't in, think how proud of me you'd be, all the other boys fighting and me up at *Peabody's* all rosy from golf and roast beef, telling the boys how to brighten up their tanks with a pretty piece of chintz?"

"I suppose I'll feel the same way," Vicky confessed. "Of course I wouldn't dare knit, except for the enemy. I could drive a truck, though. I might even fly. You'd look up when you'd hear a whiz and there I'd be ferrying a bomber! You wait!"

"I'll bet you would do it, at that," Ken said, admiringly. "You wouldn't talk about it, you'd just go do it. I can't understand how an up-and-coming girl like you managed to wait this long for a lout like me. How'd you know I was your man?"

"A gypsy told me," Vicky said. Then she sighed because she knew she was going to ask that question.

"Ken—" she began haltingly. "if Amanda should ever come back again—I mean—would you—I mean—"

Ken kissed her.

"You're the one for me, darling. There couldn't ever be any Amanda in my life, now that I know about you. Never, never, again."

Vicky stroked his hair.

"Thank you for that, darling," she said gratefully.

But she was not at all sure whether he was speaking the truth or what he hoped was the truth.

For that matter, neither was Ken.

A NOTE ON THE BOOK

The text for this book was composed by Steerforth Press using a digital version of Granjon, a typeface designed by George W. Jones and first issued by Linotype in 1928.

A READER'S GUIDE

A Time To Be Born

DAWN POWELL

ZOLAND BOOKS
an imprint of
STEERFORTH PRESS
HANOVER, NEW HAMPSHIRE

Questions for Discussion

1. Discuss Amanda's childhood and the fact that she alludes to trying to forget it altogether. Why do you think it was so painful? Do you think her reputation from Lakeville haunts her as an adult? Discuss how she manipulated her parents.

2. Early in the book, it is said of Amanda that "she was sure she neither loved nor admired" Ken Saunders, "but could not dismiss him." What then attracts her to a man like Ken as opposed to a man as powerful as Julian? Do you think Ken is still "wrapped around Amanda's finger" at the end of the story? What could Julian have done as a husband to make Amanda feel more special and satisfied with their relationship?

3. Miss Bemel and Mr. Castor play a somewhat significant role in the story. Do you find it ironic that Amanda and Julian chose assistants who are so different from one another, which causes them to disagree fairly often? In what ways is this fact a telling reflection of their relationship?

4. Amanda's relationship with both Callingham and Saunders poses a serious risk to her relationship with Julian. She is clearly afraid that with one false move she could loose both her reputation and her relationship with Julian. What does she see in these other men that she does not get from Julian? Can her love for Julian be described as at all "true," or is it just a ploy to gain power and notoriety?

5. Amanda does Vicky Haven a favor by bringing her to New York and getting her situated. What do you think are her motivations for doing this good turn?

6. Powell wrote in her famous diaries: "There is only one city for everyone just as there is one major love. New York is my city because I have an investment I can always draw on — a bottomless investment of twenty-one years (I count the day I was born) of building up an idea of New York — so no matter what happens here I have the rock of my dreams of it that nothing can destroy." Since the time she was a girl Powell believed that New York was the one place she'd be able to fully realize herself and pursue her dreams. Though fame and fortune as a writer eluded her during her lifetime, she did have a stunningly productive career and never regretted her decision. What were Amanda's and Vicky's reasons for coming to New York? How did their experiences match up to Powell's own?

7. Gender roles and politics play a significant part in Powell's story. In some ways the roles Powell's characters choose or are forced to play are products of the place and time — America in the early 1940s. In other ways Powell's depiction of relations be-

tween the sexes transcend place and time. Discuss those elements of her plot that depend on outdated gender roles and those that reflect the truth of the old adage "the more things change the more they stay the same."